TEETH, LIES & CONSEQUENCES

A Novel By

DAN GREEN

ISBN: 1537529676
ISBN 13: 9781537529677
Library of Congress Control Number: 2016914973
CreateSpace Independent Publishing Platform
North Charleston, South Carolina

This book is a work of fiction. The characters, incidents, and dialogue are drawn from the author's imagination and are not to be construed as real. Any resemblance to actual events or persons, living or dead, is entirely coincidental.

DEDICATION

To the Dental Class of 1969 at The University of Manitoba and to all the dedicated and caring dentists, hygienists, assistants and reception coordinators I have had the privilege to know throughout my career.

ACKNOWLEDGEMENTS

As an independent author, I wish to acknowledge the freelance editorial advice I received from Pearl Luke, Kit Schindell and Mike Foley. Their unique insights, feedback and encouragement were indispensible in bringing this project to a higher level.

To Doctor David Sweet, certified specialist in forensic dentistry (DABFO) from the University of British Columbia, Faculty of Dentistry for his input on the DNA profiling material in this story.

To Doctor Richard Vaughn Tucker (1922-2016) for his generosity and wisdom and for setting a pinnacle of excellence in cast gold restorative dentistry to which all dentists can aspire.

To the Semiahmoo Dental Outreach from White Rock, British Columbia and the East Meets West Foundation from Oakland, California for the wonderful work they do helping children in the Philippines, Vietnam, Cambodia and Peru.

Finally I want to thank my wife, Maureen, for her detailed copy-editing and thoughtful critiques throughout the development of this manuscript and to my daughter, Shannon Mujagic, for her conception and creation of the cover art.

About The Author

Dan Green graduated as a Doctor of Dental Medicine from the University of Manitoba in 1969. After retiring from private practice in 2003, he studied creative writing at the University of British Columbia. He is an active member of the Canadian Authors Association, The Federation of BC Writers and the Palm Springs Writers Guild.

His first novel, "Blue Saltwater", published in 2010, chronicled a Haida teenager's struggle through the Indian Residential School System in British Columbia during the 1970's.

This second novel, "Teeth, Lies & Consequences", published in 2016, is a story set against the backdrop of racism, revenge and war where a father takes an oath to never reveal a secret but goes against his word to save the life of his son.

SECTION I

Chapter 1

Vienna, November, 1943

Friedrich Mueller exhaled a draft of smoke toward the ceiling and handed the cigarette to his dental assistant, Eva Schmidt. Naked under the sheets, he looked across the pillow and broached what had been grating on him for the past month. "Colonel Bauer's coming in tomorrow. My stomach's already talking to me."

"Do you think he knows?" she asked. "He gets that look sometimes."

He wrapped his arm around her, savouring the warmth of her skin against his body. "I don't think so, but you're right. He's nerve-racking as hell. Always puts me on edge."

She shivered and cuddled into his chest. "I'm afraid when he's here. It's as if he's going to reach out and grab me."

"He'll only need one more appointment after tomorrow. Then we'll be finished with him." He kissed the side of her neck. "And the sooner this goddamn war is over, the sooner we can start living like normal people, again." He massaged her shoulder and wished he felt as confident as he let her believe.

"I'd almost forgotten the word, 'normal', existed," she said.

He took the cigarette from her fingers and inhaled until he brought a coal to its tip. Would life ever be normal again? An allied invasion from the west was rumored but if it didn't come soon, rape and slaughter by Russians lay in store for beautiful women like Eva.

He rubbed at the knots in his forehead and exhaled another cloud. "Last time he was here, he mentioned someone who committed suicide. I wasn't paying close enough attention to understand what he was getting at. All I know is that the bastard is giving me an ulcer. I just want to be rid of him."

⋏

SS Colonel Heinz Bauer wiped fog from the face of his wristwatch, and then raised his head and sniffed. He loathed this top secret assignment to Auschwitz, but as a patriot and a soldier, he'd fallen into line and had got on with it. Now smoke spiraled up into a filthy mist from the two chimneys of a crematorium. The smell reminded him of uncured hides. He clapped circulation into his hands and stamped the deck of the guard-tower to warm his toes. "It looks like you finally have the damn thing working, lieutenant."

Lieutenant Rudy Krause flicked his eyelashes and grinned, fawning for the colonel's approval. "Yes, Colonel. It's less than an hour since they went inside."

"Herr Himmler will be pleased. I'm seeing him in Vienna this evening."

"We gained experience building the units at Treblinka," Krause said. "The new Zyclon gas is much more effective than what we used before and we made the holding area larger. Our biggest bottleneck was incineration. That smell is caused by our new four-muffle furnace. It's incredibly hot and can process ten thousand a day."

"You'd better have it right this time, lieutenant."

Reichsfuhrer Heinrich Himmler had made his wishes clear to Bauer. *Streamline the elimination operation.* Bauer's name headed the top of every order addressing the accelerated quota system from the feeder camps in the eastern sector. Its success or failure was his responsibility.

Bauer wished he had died next to his brother in North Africa. Instead, he had spent eighteen months in a hospital and still carried the silent burden of a warrior, with all the psychological and physical scars to prove it. He was a former tank commander under Generalfeldmarschall Erwin Rommel. The determination and discipline that had elevated him up the chain of command within the Deutsches Afrikakorps ensured that his latest orders would be dispatched without hesitation. He would not allow himself to fail.

The shriek of grating steel summoned his attention. A train negotiated a curve in front of the loading platform, and ten cattle-cars loaded with Hungarian Jews leaned at a precarious angle. Hysteria from within the slatted walls drowned out the hiss of air brakes. Like a beast coming to rest, the train creaked to a halt and the guards slid open the doors. A crush of humanity stumbled onto the platform.

"All that chaos down there is another thing I want to get organized," Bauer said. "Look at them. They're all over the place."

"Our part of the system is as efficient as possible," Krause said. "I must say, I'm pleased how it's turned out. The initial step is a shower. Lice are endemic with Jews, so they're eager to strip off their clothes while their suitcases are piled into carts. We mark an X on anyone with gold dental work. It's become a significant source of revenue, Colonel."

"Jews adore gold," Bauer said. "They hoard it and then walk around in rags like they haven't got a shekel to their name."

Krause chuckled in agreement. "The gas is released from showerheads near the front of the room. Their stupidity astounds me, Colonel. Mothers fight with each other to get their children closer. It only takes fifteen minutes. Then we ventilate the room, remove the gold and stack the bodies for incineration." He snapped his fingers and smiled. "Done. Just like that."

Bauer's eyes bore down on him, unimpressed by the light-hearted enthusiasm. "Let there be no misunderstandings here, Krause. I will not tolerate any more breakdowns."

Krause flinched and his smile vanished as he turned toward the chimneys.

Bauer stepped over to the railing to watch Hungarian Jews being herded into rows twenty feet below. An updraft brought the stench of human waste.

"Disgusting," Krause said, pinching his nose. "Worse than a carload of swine."

Bauer ignored him to scan the faces below, all frozen by fear, disorientation and five sleepless nights without food or water. Floodlights reflected the sheen of boots worn by an SS officer who strutted along the platform. Close behind, two dogs strained at their leashes. Pointing a baton with a silver tip, the officer barked out a terse "Nach links!" prompting the guards to separate the women, children and elderly off to the left side.

The officer viewed the length of the platform and then clicked his heels into an about-turn and started back as if he were taking an afternoon stroll. Every few paces he stopped to stare into the eyes of men whose agony was etched onto their faces by cries from their families. With clipped commands, he culled two dozen of the weakest. An assistant wrote down the number remaining while a photographer snapped pictures to document the arrival.

A sharp barrage of orders stirred the dogs to display their teeth. Guards waved their weapons and directed the chosen ones on the left toward the building with two chimney stacks. A sign written in Hungarian read: Bath and Disinfecting Rooms.

As the crowd descended the steps toward the bathhouse, a child cried out, "Apa...!" Two other children joined in, all calling for their father until a resonating voice rose from within the column of men still on the platform. "Katalin! Margit! Andras! Stay with Anya." Bauer and the guards scoured the rows for the source. The colonel's cigarette glowed as his eyes settled upon the shoulders of a man who towered over those standing on either side of him. The man looked toward the bathhouse and shouted again. "Stay with Anya."

As if he sensed the intensity emanating down from Bauer's eyes, Gabor Erhmann twisted around and peered up at the deck of the tower. Their eyes locked and the Hungarian's jaw jutted forward in defiance. The photographer trained his lens on the statuesque colonel, who seemed gripped by the huge man's gaze. The flash exploded and its reflection sparkled off gold beneath the rim of Bauer's snarled upper lip.

"No more pictures!" Bauer yelled. "Get them to the barracks."

Like a pillar of granite, Erhmann stood his ground while the other men on the platform stumbled over each other to pass around him. Three guards lunged forward and drove their rifle muzzles up to his face. Erhmann remained still, his expression, a slab of stone. A deep-throated rumble from the back of his throat brought forth a gob of mucous. He tilted his head up toward Bauer and spat. A viscous mass smeared the platform and a murmur rippled through the ranks still waiting to descend the stairs. Rifle butts slammed into Erhmann's chest, knocking him backward off the ramp. The guards jumped down beside him. Their boots breached the slats of his ribcage while their truncheons tore scalp from bone. When he ceased moving, they looked up at Bauer.

He flicked his cigarette and watched it drop down and smolder next to Erhmann's bloodied face. He pointed to the guardhouse where rats roamed in cells that bore no heat. The guards grabbed both legs and dragged Erhmann away. "Goliath's tough days are over now," Bauer said.

"Industrial efficiency," Krause chirped, trying to redirect Bauer's attention back toward the crematorium. "That's what will win us this war, Colonel."

"I've heard enough." Bauer's voice did little to hide his contempt as he watched the last of the men leave the platform.

He considered Krause a coddled man, a mediocre architect who had spent the war designing palaces for the likes of Heinrich Himmler and Joseph Goebbels. Unlike Bauer, Krause had never shed blood on the field of battle. Bauer had lost most of the sight in one eye, had only partial use of his left hand and walked with the aid of an implanted steel shaft in his left femur. Krause could never imagine the horror of men with flesh dripping from their bones. He didn't deserve to wear the distinguished field gray of the Schutzstaffel while the cream of German youth was being bled dry on the tundra of the Russian steppe.

Bauer stared out over the camp. Sullied by air-borne scum from a synthetic rubber plant, nothing could be so different from the brilliant skies and pinnacles of his native Bavaria. When the whistle of a steam engine and an updraft of smoke announced the arrival of another Hungarian death train, he brushed the memory aside and crushed his cigarette underfoot.

"Ten thousand a day until we're finished," he said. The creases around his eyes deepened and his voice descended into a sombre undertone. "Do not disappoint me, Krause."

The young man's Adam's apple sank. "You can rely on me, Colonel." His response could scarcely be heard over the mayhem building below.

A sedan stopped at the bottom of the tower and Bauer started toward the stairs. "I have a plane waiting."

Krause flourished his right arm. "Heil Hitler."

"Heil Hitler." Bauer planted his rigid leg at the top of the stairway and grimaced as he side-stepped to the bottom. The chauffeur held the door open until he edged into the back seat where a legal briefcase lay.

"Your other luggage is in the trunk, sir."

"Good. Let's go before this weather closes in."

The car turned toward the main gate and drove alongside the spot where the Hungarians were being unloaded. Children's screams pierced the windows of the Mercedes. Dogs lashed out, saliva dripping from their fangs. Bauer covered his ears. "Get the hell out of here."

The chauffeur jerked the car behind the crematorium, where the shrieks of terror muted. As guards waved them through the main gate and onto a roadway that ran to the airstrip, Bauer ground at his temples. Children should have no part in this.

He pulled out a file and scribbled notes of his conversation with Krause. Several minutes passed. Then his pen became still and his gaze drifted off the page. As the commander and only survivor of his crew, he had dragged his brother, Dieter, from their exploding tank, but too late. In a recurring vision, Dieter's only daughter, Petra, ran toward him, pleading with him to save her father's life. Translucent flames licked at her body and Bauer flailed with his arms to reach out to her.

The colonel's body shook. He wheezed and his pupils dilated like black pools of madness.

"Petra," he shouted, and his hands slammed into the back of the seat, scattering his papers to the floor.

The chauffeur pulled the car off to the side and looked around.

"Are you alright, sir? Do you want me to go back?"

Bauer dug his knuckles into his eyes while the symptoms abated.

"Get me to the goddamned plane."

A few minutes later they reached the airfield. An aircraft waited at the end of the runway with both propellers spinning. The wind sock stretched horizontal.

"You're getting out just in time, sir."

Bauer unfolded himself from the backseat and started up the steps to the cabin. He heard his name over the roar of the engines.

"Colonel Bauer."

The driver held up the bulky legal briefcase he had left in the backseat. "Do you want this in the hold?"

"Nein. I need it inside. Be careful, it's fragile."

Chapter 2

Bauer swivelled both legs out of the car and then braced his arm against the door to stand. Ice crystals stung like darts as he hiked up the collar of his overcoat. The flight from Auschwitz to Vienna had left him nauseous and the slippery drive into the city had compounded the sensation, but he was on time. When the chauffeur reached into the back seat and handed him the bulky briefcase, Bauer's facial muscles twitched. He sucked in a deep breath of cold air and peered at the office across the street, steeling himself for what was to come.

"Be back in three hours," he ordered.

Leaning into the wind, he held the fingers of his left hand against the brim of his cap and limped across the cobblestones to the sidewalk. Above him, letters in gold leaf on the second floor window of the narrow building read: Doktor Friedrich Mueller, Dental Surgeon. Slivers of light escaped the perimeter of a blackout curtain.

The waiting room was empty except for Helga Hoffmann. The dour receptionist sat behind a desk, her iron-gray hair tied back in a bun.

"Good afternoon, Colonel Bauer. It's been a hectic day. Doktor Mueller is a little behind. A cup of coffee perhaps?"

"No thank you, Frau Hoffmann," Bauer said. "Not too long, I hope." He frowned and looked at the time.

"A last minute emergency, Colonel. He should be finished soon."

Bauer draped his overcoat on a hanger, adjusting the shoulders to ensure that the coat hung straight. He flicked beads of moisture off his cap and set it on a shelf. At the wall-mirror, he ran a comb through his hair, turning his head right, then left, to see that both sides were even. He straightened the knot in his tie, slicked back his eyebrows and sat in the chair next to his briefcase.

The document he'd been reviewing on the plane had Klassifiziert stamped in red across its cover. As he scanned through the pages he stopped to re-read one section. His eyes narrowed.

The shriek of a child calling, "Mama, Mama!" shattered the calm in the room. Bauer's eyes darted toward Frau Hoffmann. He dropped the file back into his briefcase.

"What the hell's going on in there?" He unfolded a handkerchief to wipe droplets from his brow.

Focused on a column of figures, Frau Hoffmann did little to hide her annoyance.

"What is it, Colonel?" she sighed. "I'm sorry. I was busy with these accounts."

He struggled to speak.

"Mein Gott!" Hoffmann stood up and rushed around from behind her desk.

"Nein, nein, mir helfin, Mama!"

The child's second scream seized the muscles of his back, igniting memories from childhood, when he had endured needles that drained cysts at the base of his spine. His phobia had been rekindled by battlefield trauma and by the countless injections he had received in the hospital. Over this weakness, his iron will had no control.

His breathing came in rapid bursts and he covered both ears.

"Please Colonel, try to be calm. Doktor Mueller is doing his best to help that poor little girl. It will be over very soon."

Bauer opened his mouth to speak, but when he did, his tongue stuck to roof of his mouth. Hoffmann took the handkerchief from his fingers and wiped away the foam that clung to his lips. "Headache," he mumbled and pressed his finger into the middle of his forehead.

"Maybe you should step out to the hallway, sir. I'll get you a chair."

"Anywhere but here," he said, gasping. He grabbed his briefcase and staggered toward the door. "No chair. I must walk."

CHAPTER 3

The outcry that triggered Bauer's panic attack also sent a spike of adrenalin surging through Friedrich Mueller's body. This was the exact scenario which he had done his utmost to avoid. He stared down at two root stumps from the molar that had just disintegrated within the grip of his extraction forceps. The girl jerked to get off the chair, legs splayed to either side, her spine rigid as a board.

As Bauer's shrill voice carried into the operatory, Friedrich rolled his eyes at Eva.

"Just what I need right now," he said. He stroked his hand along the side of the girl's cheek and nodded toward a glass container where anesthetic syringes fitted with two-inch needles hung within a sterilizing solution. "Fill another," he said. "The infection is interfering with the freezing."

The girl was the last of ten people who had appeared throughout the day for tooth extractions, the only procedure they could afford. Each case had presented Friedrich with challenges, but in an instant, this rotten lower molar had become the most complicated. He looked down into the child's eyes.

"Shh..., Fraulein, it will be okay," he whispered. His right hand dropped from view and he set the bloodied forceps on a tray behind her. "Take deep breaths. We'll be just a little longer."

He accepted the loaded syringe from Eva, and then said, in the same calm tone, "Inform Colonel Bauer that we'll be delayed. While you're out there, get what I'll need to take care of this."

As Eva hurried from the room, he brought the syringe into position.

The girl's eyes locked on the needle.

"Nein, nein, mir helfin, Mama!" Her scream rocked the operating room. Friedrich heard the slam of the waiting room door and blinked.

Like water from a fountain, solution bubbled from the tip of a large bore needle designed for veterinary procedures, the only size available due to military shortages. Stabilizing the girl's head with his left forearm, Friedrich pried apart her lips.

The dull needle tip distorted the mucosa as if puncturing an under-inflated balloon. When it broke through, Friedrich advanced the shaft and dribbled numbing solution ahead of the point until it contacted bone next to the nerve canal. He flooded the zone with novocaine and freed the girl from his grasp.

Eva came into the room and looked over at the mother. "Very brave girl."

She took the spent syringe from Friedrich's hand and then un-wrapped a bundle of surgical instruments.

Friedrich probed the right side of the girl's jaw until her eyes showed no reaction. "We're ready," he said, his voice betraying the tension in the room.

Eva laid the handle of a scalpel into his palm and he made two vertical sweeps of the blade before peeling away a flap of gum. Three sharp blows with a chisel and a mallet cleaved off the outer wall of bone.

The child squirmed and Eva drew her tiny hands back to the side.

Applying controlled force gained from years of experience, Friedrich raised both roots from their sockets. Within moments he had finished and the child's body deflated into the back of the chair. Friedrich released a long exhalation as Eva dabbed his brow.

"All done, Fraulein," he said. "You're a strong courageous girl."

Eva handed him a curved needle looped with thread and he sutured the wound closed.

⅄

It had been thirty minutes since Bauer fled the waiting room, and bands of smoke drifted along the length of the ceiling above him.

Frau Hoffmann looked down the hallway where he stood holding an ashtray. "Doktor Mueller apologizes for keeping you waiting, Colonel. Please come in, sir."

Bauer stepped aside to allow the girl's mother to pass at the doorway, her hollow eyes testament that she hadn't slept in days. She held one arm around her sobbing daughter who cradled her cheek.

Bauer wrinkled his nose as if he smelled something foul and then entered the operatory and set his briefcase in the corner. He removed his jacket and looked around for a hanger.

"Please, Colonel." Eva's tone was flat, her eyes uninviting, as she took the garment from his hands.

"Be careful with that," he snapped.

Eva draped the custom-fitted SS dress-jacket over a varnished hanger and held it up for his approval. She carried it to Friedrich's private office, safe from any danger of it becoming soiled during the work they were about to commence.

⅄

Friedrich, his shoulders hunched, nodded to the Colonel and checked the instruments on the operating tray. Strain from the day's events showed in his eyes, but the anticipation of a complex task fueled him with a resurgence of energy. Restorative dentistry still exhilarated him and gave purpose to his life. Officers of the Schutzstaffel were among the privileged few with the resources to avail themselves of his specialized services. Distasteful as these men were to him, refusing them treatment would only invite disaster for himself and his practice. Their work allowed him to maintain his skills until life became normal again.

He made a vigorous display of scrubbing his hands before he dried with a fresh towel and picked up a mouth-mirror with his left hand. In his right, he held a hook-shaped explorer with a sharp pick.

Bauer cleared his throat and with a guarded expression, he opened his mouth. The surgical light revealed a glittering display of gold fillings, which Friedrich had placed over the preceding months.

"I trust that everything has been comfortable, Colonel?" Friedrich guided his explorer tip across the junctions where the gold met the enamel. Each interface was honed to such perfection that had he closed his eyes, he could not have discerned when the instrument crossed from one surface to the other. He had achieved this standard of clinical excellence by an obsessive attention to detail; a trait that both he and Colonel Heinz Bauer shared, and the reason each man was regarded so highly within his profession.

Friedrich rotated his mirror to visualize two molars on the upper right side. Both contained cracked and corroded silver-mercury fillings. Each tooth had at least one fractured cusp.

"These are the final two, Colonel. Any sensitivity?"

"Just when I chew on that side. Pastries and ice cream. I'm pleased that we're almost done."

Friedrich withdrew his mirror and explorer and Bauer wiped a handkerchief across his lips. "Can we begin, Herr Doktor? No anesthetic, as usual."

Eva carried in the scrubbed syringes that had been used on the little girl. The lid clattered as she hung both in sterilizing solution.

Bauer squeezed his eyes shut and shivered.

"Are you chilled, Colonel?" Eva took her position at the side of the chair, her voice as cold as her query.

"You know how I feel about those things," Bauer said.

Friedrich was intolerant of fools, most particularly when it came to his work. His admonishments directed toward anyone who tried his patience were legendary and one of the reasons his wife Katrina had left him the year before. Reluctantly, he had agreed to the colonel's demands for no anesthesia but at their last appointment, the jerking of the colonel's head when the drill came close to the nerves exasperated him. The stress of making an error had pushed him to his limit. Now, after the session with the little girl, he was in no mood for more aggravation.

"I must be very clear, Colonel. These preparations are the most extensive we have done so far. I can't tolerate even the slightest movement. Otherwise, I won't perform to my standards. Do we understand each other?"

Bauer blinked, as if he had never been spoken to in such terms. He took a deep breath and replied, "Discipline is my forte, Herr Doktor. I come to you because I want only the best."

"Very well." He glanced at Eva. "Let us begin."

A low-pitched whine filled the room as Friedrich's foot pressure brought an electrical pulse to the motor. A cable spun along pulleys connecting it to the driveshaft of the drill. The steel bur ground into the alloy and Bauer's eyelids quivered.

Burrowing deeper into the heart of the tooth, Friedrich sensed the drill's position. His fingers cramped as they braced for a reaction from the threatened dental nerve. He had witnessed the consequences of rogue burs shredding through lips, cheeks and tongues. It wasn't an experience he wished to recreate.

Accelerating to a higher speed, the drill penetrated to within millimeters of the nerve. Twitches rippled like a spider's web across Bauer's forehead and his hands gripped the arms of the chair. His head remained stable as a block of ice.

After thirty minutes of excavation, Friedrich removed the last chunks of alloy. Then, with a series of chisel-shaped instruments, he created the sharp angles and smooth planes necessary for the placement of two gold fillings. When he had completed both preparations, Eva handed him a tray of gel, a formulation he had perfected as a graduate student in New York. After it set, he snapped the impression from Bauer's mouth and studied the two imprints. Finding them defect-free, he handed the tray to Eva who carried it off to the adjacent room.

"We're all done, Colonel. Eva will complete the laboratory procedure immediately to avoid any distortions. When she's finished, we'll place your temporary fillings. You did very well indeed."

"You're a man who strives for excellence," Bauer said. "I respect you for that, Herr Doktor."

"It's my passion, Colonel." Such coldness emanated from Bauer's eyes that Friedrich wondered if he had said something to offend him. He reached for his pen and recorded the details in Bauer's chart.

⚔

While Eva mixed the temporary filling material, Friedrich tracked her slim torso down into the curvature of her hips. He glanced at his watch. Soon they would finish, and he looked forward to the evening in her apartment. He glanced at Bauer's closed eyes, relieved that the colonel hadn't noticed him staring, and then reprimanded himself for not staying focused on his task. Eva turned toward him with the compound and his fingers touched the underside of her hand. He felt himself blush as he tamped the material into place, his thoughts helplessly fused to the image of her naked body, soon to be cuddled next to him.

When Eva reached across to clean the excess material from his instrument tip, the rustling of her starched uniform made Bauer open his eyes. Friedrich fumed as the colonel savored the magnitude of her breasts. When she turned back, Bauer winked at Friedrich and flicked out his lizard tongue.

"We're all done, Colonel," Friedrich said, ignoring the colonel's grin. "When will you be back to the city?"

"At the end of the month."

Eva removed the bib protecting Bauer's shirt and tie. She handed him a mirror and a damp towel. He picked traces of debris from around his mouth and looked up at her. "Why so serious, Fraulein?"

Eva's eyes dropped. Her face and neck flushed crimson. She gathered up the soiled instruments and hurried from the room.

Bauer slicked a comb through his hair. "A bit of a moody one," he said. "She should be friendlier to your patients, don't you think?"

"It's been a trying day, Colonel." Friedrich rubbed his eyes and set down his pen. "We're both tired." He looked to see that Eva was out of earshot and whispered. "She's shy around an officer of your rank, sir." He closed the chart and stood to leave the room. "You can make your next appointment at the front desk."

"Before I go, Herr Doktor, we must have a word in private."

Friedrich met Bauer's eyes with a puzzled expression.

"Something you wish to discuss about your treatment?"

Bauer shook his head. "Something else." He held up his briefcase.

"Can't this wait, Colonel? I'm exhausted."

"It cannot. Do you remember our short conversation the last time I was here?"

"Regarding?"

"A man who committed suicide?"

"Vaguely," Friedrich said.

"It's about that."

"Very well. Come into my private office. I trust this won't take long."

CHAPTER 4

Friedrich closed the door behind him and walked over to a cabinet for a bottle of cognac. The cork squeaked and scents of oak drifted about the room. He held up a snifter and looked at Bauer.

"Colonel?"

"Yes, thank you. Not too much."

"This was a gift from a patient," Friedrich said. In truth, he had bartered for it in a tax-free exchange for dental treatment. But the colonel needn't know.

Bauer lifted his briefcase to the chair beside him.

Friedrich struck a match, lit a cigarette and exhaled a draft toward the ceiling. After a day of abstinence, the soothing effect was gratifying and he looked across at Bauer with a sense of calm.

"How can I assist you, Colonel?"

"How long have you worked in Vienna, Herr Doktor?"

"Six years," he said.

Bauer opened the latch of the briefcase and pulled out a file.

Friedrich's facial muscles stiffened as he saw the word Klassifiziert stamped across the front cover. What the hell? He smothered his cough with a swig of liquor.

Bauer licked his index finger and flipped through the first pages.

"From where did you graduate?"

"Leipzig, 1931." A blossom of heat rose from under Friedrich's white tunic. He brought the snifter close to his nose and swirled it before taking another swallow. His eyes remained glued on Bauer as the colonel adjusted his glasses and focused on the page. A classified file could mean only one thing. Friedrich's mind swirled as he considered his options.

He propped his cigarette against the lip of the ashtray, took a breath and then cleared his throat.

"I served in an army dental division after graduation." His voice had an unnatural cadence that caused Bauer to look up and peer across the desk. "We were hit during a training exercise when a stray shell burst next to our field hospital. Two of us were wounded but I was the lucky one. My friend died a year later, just before I was discharged. That's when I accepted a residency to study in New York."

"Why America?"

"Doctor G.V. Black. He wrote the first scientific articles on operative dentistry. The professor under whom I studied had been a student of Black's, so it provided an opportunity to learn from the best and improve my English."

"This Doctor Black, he was not a negro, I presume?" Bauer snickered, and held out his glass for more.

Friedrich clenched his teeth at Bauer's tasteless remark. He popped the cork and replenished the drink. "Of course not. I wasn't aware that you understood English vernacular, Colonel."

"Some," Bauer said.

Friedrich drained his glass and glanced at the clock. "What is it you wish to discuss?"

"This." Bauer passed him a list of names. "The graduating class from Leipzig, 1931. I don't see your name, Herr Doktor."

Friedrich ran his eyes down the list and shook his head. "There must be a mistake. The make-up of the classes kept changing while we were doing our apprenticeships in different cities. A typographical error, I'm sure."

Bauer produced another page containing photographs of the class. He slid it across to Friedrich who perused each picture. Halfway down the page, his eyes stalled on a young man with a pencil moustache. Below was the name: Friedrich Mendelssohn.

"Everyone looks so young and eager," he said, with a grin. Acid gnawed at his stomach. He ran his finger down to the bottom of the page and slid it back to Bauer.

"Recognize anyone in particular?" Bauer exhaled funnels of smoke through his nostrils.

Friedrich shook his head. "No. I may have been in London on an exchange when they took those pictures."

"Come now, Herr Doktor. Do you think I came down with the last shower?" Bauer planted his finger on the picture of Mendelssohn and his voice spiked. "How long did you think you would get away with this?"

Bauer's index finger rapped louder on the image.

"You were never officially discharged from that hospital. Did you think that with our resources, we would never notice that a Jew had gone missing?"

"What the hell are you saying?" Friedrich's hand knocked his snifter, almost toppling it to the floor. He settled the stem and grabbed for his cigarettes. He needed to think of something fast.

"You're not a stupid man, Herr Doktor," Bauer said. "You're aware of the Nuremberg Laws and what classifies a person as a Jew." He held up a bundle of perforated punch cards. "These were passed on to me the other day," he said. "Ironically, they were invented by the German division of IBM. They allow us to keep track of citizen backgrounds. We know that your grandparents were Jews and that both grandfathers were bankers." He spat out the word, bankier, with distaste.

The match in Friedrich's fingers snapped in half as it struck the flint. Being a Jew had always been an inconvenient impediment to his ambitions. Insults from fellow students and professors had driven him to excel and prove them wrong. An explanation skirting the edges wouldn't be enough to satisfy the colonel. Telling the truth could mean a death sentence. And what about Eva? He looked at the letter opener on his desk and considered driving it through the colonel's chest. But then what?

"I'm waiting," Bauer said.

"My father came from a long line of musicians and composers. He taught at the conservatory for years. My mother had two brothers who were dentists. For generations we've been proud and honorable German citizens."

"Juden bankiers...!" Bauer hissed. "They forced my family into bankruptcy. A respected firm that provided hundreds of jobs was gone overnight. You have put me in a very difficult situation, Herr Doktor."

Friedrich poured himself a third glass. He set the bottle aside without offering more to Bauer. His only recourse was to appeal to Bauer's intellect.

"Both grandfathers you spoke of were killed serving the Kaiser in France and my parents died before I left for America. Friedrich Mueller was my injured colleague. He was paralyzed and I was ordered to care for him. We looked so much alike the nurses often called us brothers." He attempted a disarming smile.

Bauer only leaned back in the chair and drew on his cigarette.

"The Nuremberg Laws were an insult," Friedrich said. "They made it impossible for a European Jew to be accepted into an American post-graduate program. My colleague Mueller knew this. He convinced me to take his identity before he died."

Mueller's last wish had come as a godsend. It had allowed him to not only study in America but also to marry a Germanic beauty, a classical music icon that had made his charade even more believable. Now this.

Bauer blew a smoke ring into the air and watched it wilt.

"I would have stayed in New York, but for Katrina. She doesn't know about any of this."

"I am aware of that," Bauer said, snuffing his butt in the ashtray. "We make intelligence evaluations of musicians. It's amazing how so many turn out to be Jews. Our investigators came upon your information when they examined your wife's background. You deceived a sweet German girl into marrying you and then left her. How honorable, Herr Doktor."

The diameter of Friedrich's cigarette withered under the squeeze of his fingers. The bastard. He glared across the desk and cleared his throat to gain control.

"We were both too consumed with our work and we grew apart," he said. "Katrina demanded a divorce after she started seeing another musician. I was devastated."

"It appears to me that you haven't been wasting time though." Bauer's eyes lit up as he nodded toward the sterilization room. "You know what I'm talking about. Your moody assistant with the big..."

"That's none of your goddamned business." Friedrich's visceral response cast a mischievous grin over Bauer's face---the schweinhund. "Not another word," he said.

"My sincere apologies, Herr Doktor." Bauer raised his hands in mock submission and chuckled. "Just a little man-to-man joke, jah. Don't take it so serious."

Friedrich stared at him with unwavering contempt. Eva's appearance in his life had been a lucky stroke of fate.

After Katrina divorced him, he had been drinking alone in a bar until they kicked him out at closing time. Lowering his head into a north wind, he staggered around a corner and collided with a prostitute who shivered by the curbside. He had never imagined hiring one, but on this freezing night they were two lost souls craving the warmth of human touch, and she agreed to go back to his apartment.

The next morning, he woke with a splitting headache. When the bathroom door swung open, he rubbed his eyes, trying to jog a memory. She stood naked in the doorway with a blade in her hand. Bruises covered her legs and arms. Both wrists were raw and purple against her white skin. She walked to where her clothes were slung and dressed.

"Why the hurry, Fraulein? Are you afraid? The knife and the marks. What is that?

"Men become monsters when they drink."

A gust rattled the windows and he climbed out of the bed and put on his robe. "It's miserable out there. Stay and have some coffee with me."

She shook her head.

In the dim light of the room, he saw a beautiful young woman with deep shadows under her eyes. Somehow she looked familiar. As she turned and walked toward the door, he noticed a crimson birthmark on the side of her neck; like a crinkled leaf, fallen from a tree. He had only seen one like it before.

"You don't remember me, do you?"

She looked at him more closely.

"Why should I? I only met you last night. You were disgusting. Too drunk to do it."

"All I wanted was the comfort of your body next to me."

"The price is the same."

"You're from Leipzig, aren't you?"

"I don't know what you're talking about." She reached for the door.

"I know your older sister, Hester. I met you once very briefly years ago. When I visited your home."

At the sound of her sister's name, Eva's hand slid off the door handle. She stared at him, speechless, and dropped her coat to the floor. An hour passed before she could tell him how she had watched Hester and her parents being arrested at their Leipzig home the year before. She had been on the run ever since, working the streets to survive. Friedrich took her under his wing and fell in love.

He crushed his cigarette in the ashtray and looked back at Bauer.

"I do not find your comment funny in the least, Colonel."

The grin disappeared from Bauer's face and he turned away.

"Katrina and I still keep in contact. She's giving a benefit performance tonight for children of fallen soldiers. I sent a donation."

"I was invited to attend but I have another commitment," Bauer said. "She's the most accomplished violinist I've ever had the pleasure to hear."

"That's what shocks me, Colonel. That a man such as you, educated and cultured, has been taken in by all this nonsense. In the name of preserving racial purity! I've devoted my whole life to my work and to my country. That's what should be taken into account, not my hereditary background. What you people are doing is irrational. Worse. It's utter madness."

Bauer slammed his fist on the desk.

"Enough! I will ignore those derogatory comments, Herr Doktor, but I must caution you to watch your words. We would not be caught up in this war, if it were not for Jewish greed and arrogance."

With a jarring thud, Bauer set his briefcase on the desktop. He threw back the flap and withdrew a square metal box. He unlatched its lid and lifted out a charred human skull.

Friedrich stared dumbstruck.

On the right side of the cranium, a burnt perimeter circumscribed a bullet hole. On the left, he saw an exit wound ten times as large. He traced his finger around its jagged outline and then raised his eyes to Bauer for an explanation.

"The suicide I spoke of," Bauer said. "A man about my age. A wasteful shame." The coldness in the colonel's voice was not lost on Friedrich.

"It looks like he was badly burnt."

"He was mad," Bauer said. "He started a fire and shot himself."

Friedrich pressed down on the chin to open the lower jaw. The upper and lower back teeth were cratered with holes.

"What happened here?" He pointed to the gross cavitations.

"Routine procedure," Bauer replied. "If there's any value in the dental work, we remove the metal and melt it down, the individual's final contribution to the war effort."

"Why are you showing me this? It's repugnant."

"I have a request...and a proposition for you, Herr Doktor. Both of which I'm sure you'll find acceptable under the circumstances. I want you to restore these teeth identically to the fillings you have placed in my mouth."

"You want me to do...what?"

"Hear me out, Mendelssohn. I will die defending Berlin. I have volunteered to command the conscripts who will be slaughtered in the final assault. We will fight to the death and make our nation proud. When my remains are dug from the rubble, I want an accurate record for identification. So I can be buried with my family in Bavaria."

His eyes brightened as he held up the skull. "This man's generosity and your expertise will provide me with that identity insurance after the American and Bolshevik hordes overrun us."

"Why go to all that trouble? You already have a written record in your chart."

"Paper records aren't durable. With incendiary bombs being dropped on us, this skull will provide the most indestructible record. Without a doubt."

"It could also be used to forge your identity. It puts me in an unethical position."

Bauer looked to see that the door behind him was closed. "How dare you question my motives, Mendelssohn?" The fury in his voice was palpable. "You carry out this order in an expeditious and confidential manner or I will hand you and your girlfriend over to the Gestapo. I will also have your ex-wife Katrina removed from her position with the symphony and sent to a labor camp for collusion."

"You needn't threaten me, Colonel." Their eyes locked as each man took stock of the other. Friedrich was first to break the impasse. He took a final gulp of cognac and set down his empty glass. "If that is your request, what is your proposition?"

"Your safe passage out of the country. To Palestine, perhaps."

"Don't be ludicrous." He pointed up to the framed degrees and citations that hung on the walls. "Look at those," he said. "My qualifications and expertise are recognized all over Europe. Even in the United States. And you want to treat me like a common ghetto Jew? Trundle me off to some foreign land. No. I am a German. This is my home."

Bauer's gaze was glacial. "This is the home of the Aryan people. Not Jews..., who mingle among us as uninvited trespassers. Take my offer while it's available."

Friedrich read the meaning in Bauer's eyes and passed the skull back to him. His fingers left their damp imprint on the shell of the cranium.

"On one condition," he said.

"You're in no position to bargain, Mendelssohn." Bauer sneered and took another cigarette from his package.

"I want passage for Eva as well. She has no family. Without this job, who knows what will happen to her?"

"Ach! So she's a Jew too, is she? You people are so sly with your disguises. The blonde hair, the bleached eyebrows. Very clever. I would have never known. I suspect that the smelly woman and her screaming child were Jews as well. Quite a little operation you have going here, Herr Doktor."

"It's clear that you've never had children, Colonel. Or you wouldn't be so cynical. A child has no racial identity in my eyes or the eyes of God. They're all treated the same."

At the mention of children, Bauer's jaw set and he rubbed at his throat.

"You're making things very difficult. One visa alone is hard enough to obtain."

"Both of us...or no deal." Friedrich's stare held steady until Bauer's eyes wavered.

"I will find a way," he said, kneading his cheek muscles. "Have everything done when I return at the end of the month. And be ready to leave."

Friedrich pointed to a space where a tooth was missing on the skull's lower left. "What about that?"

"I noticed it too," Bauer said. He placed the skull back in the box and shut the lid. He slid it across to Friedrich. "You'll have to pull out one of mine, so it matches."

CHAPTER 5

When he had seen Bauer to the door and Frau Hoffmann had left for the day, he looked into the operatory where Eva was finishing her wipe-down of the room.

"We must talk before you leave," he said. "I'll be in my office."

"Almost done." Her eyes searched his face. "Are you okay? You look like you've just seen a ghost. I'll be right there."

He slumped into his armchair and reached for his cigarettes, and then he threw them aside. His chest thumped as if he'd been running a marathon. He took a deep breath to calm himself.

"It's about Colonel Bauer, isn't it?" Eva said, coming into his office. "I heard his smart remark. I'm sorry Friedrich. I just can't be polite around an ass like him."

"I wish it were about him," he said, with a sigh. "But it's more serious than that. He knows."

Eva's mouth dropped and she groped to gain her balance.

Friedrich pushed back from his desk and helped her to a chair.

As he related his conversation with Bauer, Eva strangled a towel with her hands. When he finished, she flung it across the room and burst into tears.

"I cannot believe this is happening," she sobbed. "I thought that we would be able to remain hidden until..." She stood up, her eyes wild, struck again by the terror she had suppressed since he had come into her life. She gasped to breathe.

"If they've found you, it won't be long before...." She buried her face into his chest.

"Shh, shh," he whispered. "I've made an agreement with him so we can both leave the country. When he confronted me, I thought I would have a heart attack. That they could discover this after all these years is unimaginable."

"What did you agree to?"

Friedrich set the metal box on the desk and explained how he would create an exact copy of Bauer's dental work in the skull. "It won't be easy but I can do it."

Eva's tears had dried. Her weepy voice now carried a tone that was loud and direct. "He's using you to provide him with a way to evade capture at the end of the war. Surely you can see this, Friedrich."

"It's possible, but we have no other choice." He looked into her eyes to see that she understood.

"Can you trust him, Friedrich?"

"He's more interested in saving his own skin than anything else. And what he needs is something only I can provide. But I'll have to see that he keeps his side of the bargain, so that if he breaks his word he'll be doomed. If ever there was a deal with the goddamned devil, this is it."

Chapter 6

The following day after work, Friedrich carried the box into his laboratory and set the skull on the counter. The lingering odor of soot clung to his fingers as he compared its dentition to Bauer's. Over the previous year, he had placed fourteen gold fillings in the colonel's back teeth and one in the front to restore the chipped corner of an incisor. He wrote the details required to transform each tooth in the skull and realized the complexity of what lay ahead. If he got any sleep, he'd be lucky.

Each night over the next three weeks, he returned to the laboratory in his office after dinner. Referring to his plaster models of Bauer's previous treatments, he measured the dimensions of each box-shaped tooth preparation before drilling a duplicate in the corresponding tooth of the skull. Satisfied that the preparations were identical in every respect, he made anatomical wax carvings of each filling and invested them in a hard-setting material.

Employing a lost-wax technique developed by bronze sculptors centuries before, he placed the invested carvings into the intense heat of a casting oven. When the wax evaporated, he used a propane torch and a centrifugal casting machine to spin molten alloy into the negative molds, creating precise gold fillings for each tooth.

λ

Twenty-one days later, long after midnight, on the day of Bauer's scheduled appointment, Friedrich placed the skull back into the box and switched off the overhead light.

Adding a splash of cognac to his cold coffee, he lit a cigarette and went out to the tidy reception desk. He opened the filing cabinet and flipped through many names he recognized, reminiscing about the unique challenges that each case had presented. Back in his private office he looked at the framed degrees and citations that hung on the walls. His eyes welled as he grabbed his coat. Everything he had ever worked for, stolen, by idiots. He looked around once more and then switched off the lights and slammed the door. How could he have been so goddamn stupid as to think they'd never find him?

⅄

Late the following afternoon, he walked into the operatory, scrubbed his hands and draped the towel over its rack.

"Well?" he said, turning to face Bauer, who sat upright in the chair with a bib covering his shirt and tie.

"Everything's been arranged," Bauer said, tucking the bib tighter into his collar. "What about you?"

"I'll show you when we're finished. Open your mouth."

Friedrich removed the temporary filling material and Eva flushed away the debris. Both gold fillings clicked into place. Satisfied with their snug fit, he placed a marking tape across the biting surfaces.

"Close and tap together."

Bauer clamped his teeth and ground from side-to-side."

Friedrich adjusted pressure spots on the gold until Bauer confirmed both were comfortable. He handed each filling to Eva so that she could not see what he had engraved into their undersides. It was information that could only hurt her if something went wrong and led to a Gestapo interrogation. She couldn't confess to what she didn't know.

Coating both with an adhesive, Eva passed the fillings back and he inserted them. As the adhesive set, he burnished down the gold edges until his explorer tip glided across without deflection.

"Perfect." He set his instruments on the tray and looked at Bauer.

"Only one thing left. You'll require anesthetic for this, Colonel. Believe me."

Bauer shook his head. "You know that I refuse needles under all circumstances. Besides I have meetings this evening."

"Very well." He looked over at Eva with worn-out eyes. "Elevator, please."

Eva laid the screwdriver-shaped instrument into the sole of his palm. As he directed his light to the lower left, the disintegration of the girl's tooth three weeks earlier was fresh in his mind. Clamminess rose along his back as Eva blotted his brow. Digging fractured roots from the colonel's jaw without anesthesia would be the most brutal form of torture, though it was what the bastard really deserved.

"Ready, Colonel?"

Bauer nodded and closed his eyes. His fingers sat relaxed on the hand-rests. Eva stood behind the chair, positioning her hands on either side of his head, careful not to mess his hair. Friedrich dug the elevator tip under the gums and levered it upward. The instrument's stab wiped the tranquillity from Bauer's face and his arms stiffened like rods. His blanched right hand twisted the arm-rest, making it creak and groan, while his paralytic left trembled to hold on. The arteries of his neck bulged like fire-hoses and his mouth began to close.

"Wider!" Friedrich snapped. The command jarred open Bauer's eyes and his jaw dropped, but only a little. Friedrich pried around the tooth's perimeter but the roots refused to budge. He needed to slow down and give it a chance. Wait for the release. His hand cramped and he slammed the instrument down on the tray. "You're fighting me, Colonel. Open wider or I must insist on anesthetic."

Bauer's unfocused eyes looked up. "I need a moment to compose myself," he said, panting. "I can do this." He dried both hands with his handkerchief and then wiped off the hand-rests. His chest heaved and a semblance of color returned to his face. "I'm ready. Proceed."

Friedrich engaged again, pressing harder and deeper, until his hand sensed the shift. He kept going now, pacing himself, measuring his force, until he saw the tooth begin to sway. A guttural crescendo rose from Bauer's throat as the roots tore away from the socket walls.

"Forceps."

Eva took the elevator and thrust a pair of extraction pliers into his hand.

He closed the forceps around the molar, employing a technique he had perfected as an exchange student at Royal London Hospital, a skill impossible to learn in a lecture hall. The best oral surgeons were gifted with patience and feel. The crack of fractured roots foreshadowed nothing but grief.

The intact molar surrendered itself into the room. Eva dropped it into a cup of water while Friedrich compressed a pack of gauze over the socket. "Bite down."

Eva winked at him and moved her lips. Well done!

Bauer opened his eyes and mumbled through his clenched teeth. "I'm proud of myself."

"Not many like you, Colonel," Friedrich said. "That will be tender for a few days so chew on the other side."

⅄

When the bleeding stopped, Eva escorted Bauer into Friedrich's private office.

"Thank you, Fraulein Schmidt. You are extremely proficient. Your soft hands were comforting."

His compliment did nothing to allay her flat expression. "It's Doktor Mueller you should thank, Colonel. That could easily have been a disaster." She turned and left.

Friedrich came in and shut the door, his expression stoic as he sat down and slid a copy of Bauer's chart across the desk. "For your records. I have back-dated the appointments so there's no correlation with our departure."

"You're skilled at covering your tracks, Herr Doktor."

"I'm concerned about my reputation."

"And a brilliant one it is. I appreciate your expertise."

Friedrich opened the box and placed the skull on the desk.

"Here it is."

Carefully opening the lower jaw to expose the fillings, Bauer surveyed their golden lustre and smiled. "A wonderful talent you possess, Mendelssohn. You're certain these are identical?"

"Once your socket heals, there'll be no difference."

Bauer reached into his breast pocket and withdrew two envelopes. "Exit visas and passports."

Friedrich examined each one and saw the word, Dentist, on the working visas. "When do we leave?"

Bauer grimaced and rubbed his lower jaw. "Pain's getting worse," he said. "How long can I expect this?"

"Several days but the less you disturb it, the faster it will resolve. No smoking until tomorrow. It will cause it to bleed."

"Very well," Bauer said. "You leave in thirty-six hours. 0200 Sunday morning. The forecast is good and the skies should be quiet. We have a short window. The net is closing."

"That's too soon. I must make arrangements for the practice. I have a responsibility to my patients."

"That's been taken care of. A member of the party will take over next week."

"A dentist? What's his name? I'll need to assist with the transition."

"Irrelevant and unnecessary," Bauer said, with a wave of his hand. "Bring only one small suitcase each. Your furniture and apartment will be turned over to the state. No compensation. Withdraw any funds you have because they'll be confiscating your bank accounts next week. You're fortunate that you haven't already been picked up. The Gestapo is active on both files. Sunday, 0200. After that no guarantee."

"Guarantee of what?"

"That you will get out of the country alive."

Friedrich's eyes twitched. He put the skull in the box and closed the latch. Bauer hadn't mentioned any possibility of not being able to uphold his end of the bargain. Was this where things would change? Eva's distrust had convinced him that he needed insurance. He met Bauer's eyes and said, "After I give you this, how do I know you won't turn us into the police?"

"You have my word, Herr Doktor."

"I need more than that." Friedrich matched the intensity in Bauer's eyes. "I've placed confidential documentation with a lawyer. If anything happens to either of us while we're under German jurisdiction, it will mean the end of your illustrious career."

Bauer shrugged. "I'm offended that you show so little trust." He pulled the chair closer and lowered his voice. "But let me remind you, Mendelssohn. If you ever divulge this matter to anyone, it will be over for you and your buxom girlfriend. Do you understand this...Herr Doktor?"

"Understood." Friedrich took a deep drag and coughed. "Where are you sending us?"

"First to Romania and then Turkey. From there, overland to Palestine."

"That's preposterous. We'll be like fish out of water. Why not Switzerland?"

"You are so arrogant, Mendelssohn," he hissed. "You're Jews, for God's sake. Nobody wants you. Palestine or some labor camp in Poland. Take your pick." He removed a folded sheet of paper from his pocket and reviewed the notes. "The car will arrive here at midnight Saturday. You'll be flown to an airstrip in Romania and then driven to the Port of Constanta. Show them your documents at the dock. A refugee ship, Salvatore, will take you to Istanbul. There are two spots reserved. My obligation is completed at that point and I cannot guarantee your safety once you board. When you reach Istanbul, contact the Red Crescent. They are transporting refugees from Turkey to Palestine. Any questions?"

"This visa identifies me as Friedrich Mueller. You couldn't have changed it to Mendelssohn?"

"That's what your passport reads. No time to change it."

"They'll think I'm a German spy."

"Your problem, Herr Doktor. Saturday midnight. We won't wait." He rubbed his jaw again. "Throbbing like hell now."

Friedrich stood up and handed him the box. "And that's your problem, Colonel. I'll see you to the door."

✦

Friedrich inserted Bauer's chart into its alphabetical location in the filing cabinet. Frau Hoffmann closed the cover of her journal and slipped on her coat.

"You look exhausted, Doktor. Good that it's the end of the week."

"I haven't been sleeping well. A few days off and I'll be fine. Have a pleasant weekend, Frau Hoffmann." Helga had been with him for six years and ran the business end of the practice as if it were her own. She had been the only one he could talk to after the shock of Katrina's infidelity. Her home baking and casseroles had sustained him for the first few months. He watched as she walked out the door, knowing he would never see her again.

He returned to his desk, poured a stiff cognac and kneaded his temples. Eva stepped into the doorway and he beckoned her to sit beside him.

"We leave for Palestine the day after tomorrow."

She put her hand to her mouth and looked at him with disbelief.

"If it wasn't for this dreadful arrangement..." His voice broke and he took a sip and swallowed. "I hate to think what could happen. I have a feeling there's more going on at those camps than we know."

With the mention of the concentration camps, Eva's eyes became glossy. She stared into the distance and voiced a muffled cry.

"I'm sorry, I didn't mean..."

Before he could finish, she turned back and met his eyes. "I'm sorry for being weak like that," she said, brushing back tears. She spoke with a firmness he'd never heard before. "It won't happen again. What you're doing is the right thing and I won't let my feelings get in the way. I'll be fine. I promise."

He stepped forward to hold her but she waved him away. "When do we go?"

"Sunday, 0200. A car will meet us here Saturday midnight."

"People must need our help in Palestine. Can we start a new clinic?"

"If they'll let us in." He smothered his anxiety with another drag.

Her voice raised a notch. "What if the Gestapo is waiting for us at the plane?"

He answered with all the reassurance he could muster. "If anything happens, I'm taking steps to see that this arrangement is brought to the attention of the Swiss police. It will become public knowledge and his reputation will be ruined. He could even be put on trial. I've warned him. I don't think he will be so stupid."

"Let's hope so," she said.

"Go home now and get some rest. Pack only what will fit into a small case. You never know who's watching, so bring everything in a laundry bag. We'll meet tomorrow at my apartment around noon. I've got an extra suitcase." He lowered his voice. "Don't say a word to anyone: landlord, friends... anyone."

"What do you want me to do with this?" She took Bauer's extracted molar from her pocket and handed it to him.

He rolled it across his palm admiring the precision of his gold-work. "I'll keep it for a teaching aid," he said. "It's one of the best I've ever done."

"It's good that I asked," she said. "I almost threw it away." She leaned over and kissed his cheek. "Thank you for being so strong. I'll see you tomorrow."

⅄

After she left the office, he retrieved Bauer's chart from the cabinet. He filled his pen with ink and took out two sheets of stationary with his letterhead at the top. On the first sheet, he wrote down the details of the arrangement and on the second, he listed his instructions. He signed and dated both pages and inserted them with the chart into a brown envelope that he slid into his briefcase. He grabbed his coat and walked down to the corner where he caught a streetcar to Maria-Theresien Platz.

Stepping off the tram, he lingered for a few moments at a newspaper stand until others exiting the coach had dispersed. He couldn't be too careful. The octagonal crown of the Kunsthistorisches Museum dominated the other side of the plaza. Halfway across, at a square where pigeons competed for scatterings of crumbs, he sat on a bench across from a younger couple. He noticed the knitted scarf wrapped about the woman's neck. Her face was pale and she twisted the ends of the scarf while the man looked into her eyes as if he wanted to console her. Friedrich took his time to smoke a cigarette and watched for anyone who looked suspicious. As he stood up to leave, he registered the anxiety gripping the young couple's faces. They could be Jews.

Passing the bronze statues fronting the museum he walked in through the main doors. A concierge directed him to a gallery where sunlight cast shadows across filigreed reliefs.

He saw the solicitor sitting in an armchair next to the far wall, a trim older man with sparse white hair, wearing a herringbone suit. Gunter Schreiber leaned on his cane to stand as Friedrich approached and they shook hands.

"We can talk in there," Schreiber said, pointing to a room with a table and two chairs.

"Thank you for meeting me, Herr Schreiber." He set the brown envelope on the table.

"What does this concern, Herr Doktor?"

"A Gestapo investigation involving matters from the past. I have distant relatives who were Jewish. This has put me in a compromised position with the Nuremberg Laws. I thought it better to meet here than at your office."

"Those laws have had many unforeseen consequences," Schreiber said. "They're far too broad. We've lost many prominent professional men to this. It's a terrible waste."

"I have no choice but to leave the country. It will be dangerous and in case of problems, these are my confidential instructions to you." Schreiber put on a pair of glasses and read through the two pages twice. He looked through Bauer's chart and placed everything back in the envelope. He shook his head.

"I'm disgusted it has come to this," he said. He stamped a dated notarized seal across the flap and put it in his briefcase.

Urgent voices echoed through the hallways, disturbing the tranquillity of the space. Friedrich glanced out from where they sat and recognized the scarf worn by the woman he had seen in the park. She and the man stood with their backs to him looking at a self-portrait of Rembrandt. With the sound of footsteps rushing into the gallery, the couple bolted toward a connecting doorway.

"Polizei zu stoppen." The command reverberated across the vaulted ceilings as three Gestapo officers ran to where the couple had fled.

"Best we talk outside," Schreiber said. "They're everywhere." He pressed one hand on the tabletop to stand and then put on his overcoat. Friedrich walked slowly alongside as Schreiber limped down to the entrance and out to the plaza. Emerging into the evening air, Schreiber struck a match and lit a Meerschaum pipe. With smoke billowing around them, he pulled the stem from his lips and spoke, his eyes directed out into the plaza.

"This will be kept in my security vault until it can be delivered to the Union Bank of Switzerland as per your instructions. If my colleagues or I become aware of anything untoward it will be handed over to the Swiss police. Otherwise, it will not see the light of day until you claim it under your signature. This is a very dangerous undertaking. I wish you both a safe passage. My wife and I will miss your gentle touch, Herr Doktor."

Schreiber turned and walked toward a row of waiting taxis. Friedrich reached into his pocket for his cigarettes. Strolling pedestrians and patrons lingering in cafes still busied the plaza. He would miss this so much. Cupping his hands to shelter the match, he stepped aside as the entrance doors swung open.

Three Gestapo officers shoved the handcuffed couple into the street. The man's face was puffed and red and the woman's scarf hung askew. The officers hustled the couple toward a black sedan and pushed them into the backseat. While the sedan merged with the traffic, Friedrich checked the taxi stand, relieved to see that Schreiber was gone. He took a drag on his cigarette and moved toward his bank where the lights remained on.

CHAPTER 7

The next morning, Friedrich slid back a loose floorboard under his bed and pulled out a leather pouch. He jingled the one-pennyweight wafers of dental casting gold that he had accumulated each month since opening his practice. With the journey they were about to undertake he knew bribes would be demanded. Gold would be the only thing people were certain to accept. He stacked them in piles and calculated their value to be around two thousand Reichsmarks. With another three thousand in notes that he had withdrawn from the bank, he hoped it would be enough.

He put the wafers and notes back in the bag and made up a plate of sandwiches with the food he had left. At noon, a soft knock sounded on the door. He looked through the peep-hole, unlatched the door and brought Eva inside. Checking the hall both ways, he closed the door and slid the deadbolt closed.

"Did you see anything suspicious out there?"

"I browsed in a few shops along the way," she said. "Nobody seemed to be following me."

He gave her a gentle hug and then took her coat and pulled out a chair at the table. He grabbed the coffee pot off the stove and brought over the sandwiches. "We'll eat first. Then we've got work to do."

When they had finished their lunch, he tore off strips of adhesive tape which he stuck to the edge of the table. He opened the bag and spread the wafers and banknotes in front of her.

"Mein Gott, Friedrich! I've never seen so much money. Where did you get all that?"

"From the bank. I left enough to cover Frau Hoffmann's salary and the rest of my bills. I hate to leave without saying goodbye but I can't get her involved. She's the most competent receptionist I ever worked with."

"Perhaps you could leave a note and tell her that," Eva said. "It would mean a lot."

"She always comes in early on Mondays. I'll put it in her journal with a bonus for all her years of service. At least she'll know what's going on before that Nazi arrives. Makes me ill to think she'll have to work with someone like that."

"Helga's a tough one," Eva said. "She won't put up with any nonsense, I'm sure." She pointed at the gold wafers. "Did you bring those from the office?"

"I buy what I can afford each month to use for my cases and for emergencies. But I never imagined it would be for something like this." He set two rows of wafers along one strip of tape and then covered them over with another. "I've got enough to make six of these." He handed her a pair of scissors. "Slit the lining of our suitcases and stitch three of these underneath. Sew the other two into the hems of our coats. I'll keep one handy in my sock."

She saw his black suit draped over a chair. "You're getting all dressed up?"

"Can't take much," he said. "I might as well look my best for the Brits when we arrive at the border. They're always impressed by a little spit and polish."

Eva pulled fifty Reichsmarks from her purse. "It's all I have. Take it."

"Keep it with you," he said. "Just in case." He smiled and kissed her on the cheek.

⚐

At eleven o'clock that night, they returned to the office with their suitcases. Friedrich tucked an envelope into Frau Hoffman's journal containing two-hundred Reichsmarks and a farewell letter signed by both of them. In the clinical area, he gathered together a bundle of the only other currency he possessed: One pair of extraction forceps, one straight elevator, a syringe with three needles, two vials of novocaine, suture needles with thread and two packages of gauze. Wrapping everything in a towel, he stuffed it into a leather satchel. "Just the basics," he said.

He reached into a cupboard for his last full bottle of cognac and poured a taste into two glasses. "This isn't the most romantic of settings, but I must ask you before we leave. Will you be my wife? I love you, Eva."

"Oh, Friedrich." She stood on her toes and kissed his lips. "To think that I almost didn't go with you the night we met on the street. You were a drunken mess. But I was so cold and tired, I took a chance." She smiled and kissed him again. "I was so relieved when you passed out. The only thing that kept me awake was your snoring."

"Yes, I'll have to work on that," he said.

She looked into his eyes and stroked the side of his face.

"I love you just as you are, and I accept your proposal."

In her eyes he sensed her vulnerability. It made him want her more. They embraced and kissed long and deep before he stepped back.

"The ceremony will come later but please wear this now." He took her left hand and placed a plain gold band on her finger. "It was my mother's."

They raised their glasses.

"To Dr. and Mrs. Friedrich Mendelssohn," she said.

"And to their safe uneventful honeymoon." He threw back the liquor and frowned.

Downstairs, they waited until an unmarked Mercedes-Benz sedan stopped by the curb. Bauer rolled down the front passenger window and tilted his head toward the back.

"Get in."

They drove in silence through blacked-out streets to an airstrip beyond the city limits. The car pulled up beside a floodlit tarmac where a twin-engine aircraft stood by, a Luftwaffe eagle painted on its side.

"Cloudier than forecast," Bauer said, as they stepped from the car.

A queue of businessmen wearing fedoras and carrying briefcases stood in line while two men in trench coats checked identification and exit visas. A third man behind a table inspected the contents of suitcases. Eva squeezed Friedrich's hand and pulled back. Bauer noticed her hesitation.

"A problem, Fraulein?"

"She's never flown before, Colonel." Friedrich led her toward the table and started to unbuckle the suitcase flaps. Bauer tapped him on the shoulder.

"I am a man who keeps my word, Herr Doktor. You may go to the plane. No need to stand in this line." He pulled Friedrich aside and whispered under his breath. "Do not underestimate me, Mendelssohn." He looked over at Eva and his lips parted in a tight smile. Gold sparkled off his right incisor. "Have a pleasant trip, Fraulein."

Friedrich slid the suitcases into the hold and followed Eva up the steps into the empty cabin. Down the aisle, they took two seats and held hands while eight businessmen, bantering in Romanian and German, filed in. Through the window Bauer gesticulated with his hands as he discussed something with the three men in trench coats. All four lit cigarettes and watched the pilot start the engines.

"Gestapo?" Eva mouthed the word.

Friedrich nodded and squeezed her hand.

The cabin door thumped closed. Two workers ducked under the propellers and removed the blocks under the wheels.

"We're safe now," he whispered.

The motors revved to a higher pitch and the plane lurched forward. Through the window, Friedrich watched Bauer return to his car. The cabin shook as the pilot depressed the throttle and the plane picked up speed. Friedrich's eyes narrowed as he noticed a brown envelope in Bauer's right hand, similar to the one he had given to Schreiber. It couldn't be. He cursed under his breath as possibilities flashed through his mind. Had Schreiber betrayed him? Had they followed him? He had known the solicitor since he first opened his practice and considered him a friend and a man of integrity. No! Impossible. Then the likelihood of Schreiber's arrest occurred to him.

A chill ramped through his body as he thought of the horrible consequences that would befall this good man and his family. What had he done?

"What's the matter?" Eva's voice was shrill above the engines. "You're hurting my fingers."

"Sorry," he said, releasing her hand. "I'm a little jumpy." He leaned over and kissed her cheek.

When he turned back to the window, two of the Gestapo officers were running toward the plane waving their hands. The pilot drew back on the throttle and slowed to a halt.

"They're coming for us," Eva said. Friedrich gripped her hand again, his eyes glued on the scene outside the window. Bauer's car sped up alongside the plane and skidded to a stop below the wing. The car door slammed. He heard loud voices, then the clunk of the cabin door as it released.

"Let me do the talking," he said, his voice cracking. Palpitations thumped wild through his chest. He inhaled, fighting to maintain a pretence of calm.

The Gestapo officers stepped into the cabin and squinted down the aisle. One caught Friedrich's eye near the back and strode toward him.

"Forget something, Herr Doktor?"

A flush crossed his face and he shook his head. "Nein."

The officer held up the satchel and grinned. "Colonel Bauer noticed it in his backseat." Friedrich reached out his sweaty hand.

"How careless of me. Please express my appreciation to the Colonel. I'd be useless without these instruments."

His stomach rolled as the pilot fought for altitude through thick clouds and turbulence. The plane dropped into an air-pocket and Eva screamed. The startled men in front turned to look back as Friedrich wrapped her closer with his arm. When the engines finally throttled back and the plane leveled off, the brightness of a full moon flooded through the window.

"Okay now," he said. She huddled tight to his chest and they stared out the window without saying more. He felt her tension ease and as her breathing slowed, snores and coughs floated about the cabin. Where the hell was this leading? Dread of what lay ahead burrowed into his thoughts until he too succumbed to the engine's din and closed his eyes.

⚊

They both jerked upright as the wheels slammed down on a gravel runway. Fog hugged barren slopes as the plane taxied to a shed where a lamp illuminated the entrance. When the businessmen had exited the cabin, Friedrich grabbed his satchel and led Eva down the steps. They retrieved their suitcases and followed the others to a shed where a driver punching tickets pointed the business crowd toward a waiting bus. An older man sitting on a chair stood and approached them. He smoked a pipe and Friedrich could see the nicotine hue in his moustache. "Doktor und Frau Mueller?"

Friedrich raised his hand to acknowledge the greeting. The man pointed to the rear door and led them outside to where a driver dozed in the front seat of a car. The old man knocked on the roof and shouted. "Andrei!"

Stubble shadowed the young driver's face as he stepped out and put their luggage into the trunk. The older man held out his grease-stained hand.

"The fare is three hundred Reichsmarks." As Friedrich peeled off the notes, the driver opened the back door and beckoned Eva inside.

"Andrei will take you to Constanta," the older man said. "It's a long way." He pointed to a basket on the seat. "Fruit and water."

⚊

They drove all day through mountain passes with vertical walls of snow on either side. The only sound from Andrei was his grumbling each time he pulled over for military convoys crawling the other way. As darkness fell, they stopped at a roadside tavern where the smell of mutton drifted off a spit. Andrei went inside and negotiated for gasoline, food and use of the toilets. An hour later they continued deeper into the mountains, winding up through switchbacks until the road straightened and descended. As Andrei geared down, a light flickered near the bottom of the grade.

"Checkpoint," Andrei mumbled. "Iron Guard."

Friedrich saw Andrei's hands tighten on the steering wheel and looked around to where Eva lay asleep.

"Wake up," he said, reaching back to rustle her. "Road-block ahead."

Eva bolted up and squinted through the windshield. She dug into her purse and opened a knife, slipping the blade up her sleeve with the handle in her palm.

"Don't stop," she said. "It's local militia. Who knows what they'll do?"

Andrei bit into his chapped lips.

From three hundred meters, Friedrich saw no sign of movement.

"Can we run it?" he asked.

"We try, they shoot," Andrei said. "They'll want some money, that's all."

"Maybe we should turn around while there's still time."

"I saw their men in the tavern. They'd stop us."

Friedrich turned to the back seat. "Lie down, Eva. Curl up like you've got stomach pain. We'll tell them you need to see a doctor."

As they pulled up, three men in ragged uniforms ducked out from under a shelter of flapping tarps. Flames reeking of diesel oil cast an orange halo along the road. The armed men walked around the car and peered into the backseat. Friedrich fingered the banknotes in his pocket as Andrei rolled down his window.

"Papers," shouted the tallest of the three, whose right sleeve flaunted a corporal's patch. Below it, a black and white triple cross. Friedrich had seen it before in newspapers promoting fascist propaganda. The Iron Guard ruled the Romanian countryside with thugs who would kill for a pittance.

The corporal leaned his head through Andrei's window and pointed a flashlight into the front and back seats. One cheek was bulbous with taut skin polished by the glow of the fire. His face looked ashen as the clouds overhead. Andrei spoke in a rapid Romanian dialect. Friedrich recognized one word: Deutsche. From where he sat, he smelled putrefaction on the man's breath.

"He wants to see your identification papers," Andrei said.

Friedrich handed over the passports and visas, astounded by the girth of the corporal's fingers. His jagged nails were black as if he had scraped tar from the bottom of a barrel.

The corporal examined the documents while the other guards opened the trunk and looked through both suitcases. Finding nothing other than clothes they slammed down the lid. The corporal barked out the word, Mita.

"Two hundred Reichsmarks...for each of you," Andrei said.

"Too much." Friedrich's rebuttal triggered a glare through the window.

Andrei shook his head, his eyes pleading for Friedrich to reconsider.

"Tell him," Friedrich said. "It's robbery."

With the toxic face leaning through his window, Andrei relayed Friedrich's message in a hushed voice. The corporal hammered his fist on the roof. He stuffed the documents into his pocket, wrenched open the back door and dragged Eva from the car. While the other two men held her arms, the corporal fondled her breasts and laughed.

"Tell him to stop," Friedrich said. "I'll pay. I'll pay what he wants." He flung open his door and ran around the front of the car. The corporal drew a Luger and aimed. Friedrich backed away and raised both hands.

Surviving for a year on the mean streets of Germany and Austria had hardened Eva. She drove both elbows into the midsections of the men holding her. It was enough to loosen their grip. Her knife whizzed through the air and slashed the corporal's cheek. Jerking his head away, he growled and twisted her wrist until her knees buckled and the knife dropped to the ground. Her screams echoed through the canyons alongside the road.

The corporal yanked her upright while his tongue licked at the blood trickling down on his upper lip. He spat in her face.

"Tough little cunt aren't you," he said, grinning into her burning eyes. "Just the kind I like."

Eva scratched and bit as the guards pulled her dress above her head. They tore off her undergarments and slammed her forward over the fender of the car. The impact made her eyes roll and brought drool to her lips. The corporal stuck his middle finger into his mouth and then drove a potion of pus and blood deep into her vagina. Eva's anguish reverberated into the night until her eyes closed and she went still. Andrei pulled on the corporal's arm and was swatted to the ground. Jamming the pistol into Eva's ear, the corporal barked out a barrage of obscenity toward Friedrich.

"He wants to know what you pay now," Andrei said. The subtext was clear. Do something or we all die.

"Tell him to let her go. I'll pay him four hundred each. And I'll pull out his bad teeth."

Andrei cried out the words, his voice strained to its highest pitch.

The corporal smirked at Friedrich. He slipped the pistol into his pocket and loosened his belt to straddle Eva from behind.

"Stop." Friedrich drove his knuckles into the ballooned cheek. Like a wounded bear, the corporal roared back and clutched at his face. Friedrich's glare froze the other two men as he lifted Eva off the hood and carried her to the backseat of the car. Tossing her clothes down beside her, he yelled at Andrei. "Get my instruments. I'll pay him and take out his goddamn teeth."

Andrei's translation elicited a nod from the corporal who slumped down on a stump of wood and moaned.

Friedrich grabbed his satchel then walked up to the corporal and fanned out eight-hundred Reichsmarks. As the visas and passports scattered at his feet, the grotesque fingers snatched the money from his hand. He bent down to pick up the documents and looked at Andrei.

"Wait in the car and start the engine."

He focused the beam of his flashlight into the corporal's mouth and saw an engorged mass surrounding three upper molars. He popped the cork on the cognac and its bite filled the air. He handed the bottle to the corporal who tilted his head back and guzzled down half.

Friedrich pressed his fingers against the abscessed teeth and felt them move. The corporal jerked away, but Friedrich breathed a sigh of relief. The infection had dissolved some of the bone around the teeth and would make them easier to extract. He gestured for the corporal to drink more and watched him empty the bottle. The backdoor of the car slammed and Eva walked toward them. The guards raised their muzzles as she bent down to pick up her knife. Her eyes dared them to shoot. She folded the blade and put it in her pocket. Crimson streaks ran down the inside of her legs and her dress hung like a rag.

"You're going to need some help with this maniac," she said. The corporal looked at her and grinned like a clown.

"No," Friedrich said. "Get back in the car."

Eva pressed her full weight down on the corporal's forearms and yelled at the guards to do the same. She looked at Friedrich. "Get on with it while that liquor's working."

Friedrich jacked open the corporal's jaw. This was no time to hesitate. He locked his forceps on the molar easiest to reach while the corporal struggled to pull his hand away. Eva screamed at the guards. "Bear down, you bastards. Harder!...Harder than that!"

Friedrich yarded right, then left and dragged the tooth free. The corporal bellowed and an eruption of blood burst from his mouth.

Friedrich flung the molar over his shoulder and dispatched the other two in the same lightening fashion. Eva stuffed a wad of gauze into the corporal's mouth. She drove her fist under his jaw and slammed it shut. Blinking and rubbing the side of his cheek, the corporal yelled something to Andrei who watched stunned from the car.

"What's he saying?" Friedrich asked.

"He said you're the best tooth puller he's ever had."

The corporal grunted and looked at Eva as she rinsed the forceps in a puddle at the side of the road. Pulling the blood-soaked gauze from his mouth, he rattled off a slur of words and raised his hand in a mock salute.

"And that?" Friedrich said.

"He apologises to your tough little nurse. He says don't be so cheap, next time. They need the money to feed their families. We're free to go."

"Fascist brute." Friedrich muttered and drew Eva toward the car. The corporal spat another bloodied gob on the ground and twirled the Luger on his finger like a matinee cowboy. As the pistol came to rest, he aimed it toward the car. He laughed and then raised the muzzle to wave them on their way.

"Get the hell out of here, Andrei, before he pulls that trigger," Friedrich said. "We need to find a place where my wife can take a bath and get some rest."

"Nothing between here and the dock," Andrei said. "Maybe on the ship."

Chapter 8

Andrei stopped next to the pier and pulled their suitcases from the trunk. He pointed toward the crowd.

"Many Jews trying to get on that boat," he said, getting back in the car. "Not enough room for them all."

Friedrich looked at the oily water sputtering from a pipe near the ship's stern. The hull revealed wide swaths of rust and corrosion.

"That's the Salvatore?" he said. "It looks like a leaky old scow."

"It's old but it still comes back from Istanbul every week," Andrei said. "And always too many people want to leave, like right now. There will be fighting after dark."

"But we have reservations," Friedrich said. He stuck a cigarette in his lips and cupped his hands around the match. "Surely we don't need to go back there." He jerked his head toward the end of the line where he heard the shouts of people fighting to protect their position. "Goddamn madness never ends," he muttered.

Andrei pointed toward the front. "You must speak to that man at the desk. Try to buy a spot that is closer. It will be expensive but better to get on earlier and find a place out of the wind. It leaves at midnight." He tipped his hat and drove away.

Along the pier, adults with howling children guarded belongings and shuffled toward the check-in table near the gangway. Friedrich pulled out the length of tape he had hidden in his sock. Separating the two strips, he stuffed the gold wafers into his pocket. He straightened his tie and buffed his shoes on the back of his trousers while Eva held a hand-mirror and rubbed makeup over the bruises on her face. As she folded the torn hem of her dress beneath her coat, Friedrich grabbed their suitcases.

"We don't stand a chance of getting on if we go back there," he said. "We need to find someone who's desperate. We'll walk the line and pretend we're looking for Helga."

Eva pressed her hand against his chest. "We can't bargain for someone else's freedom. It's not right."

"Quit being so goddamn naive." The words burst from his mouth and brought questioning looks from along the pier. He clutched her hands and whispered. "I'm sorry. My nerves have had it. Please, try to understand. The Nazis here are rabid. We must get on that boat tonight."

They walked toward the front of the line calling out Helga's name. Friedrich singled out a man and woman whose faces were furrowed with exhaustion. The wife sat on the ground massaging her daughter's stomach while the husband slapped the side of his son's head, for 'crying like a baby'. Friedrich reckoned the two children looked about twelve and were likely twins. He reached into his pocket and handed the man the last apple from the basket in the car. The man's eyes widened as he bit off half and handed the rest to his wife.

"The children are too sick to eat," he said.

"I'm a doctor," Friedrich said. He touched their foreheads and felt the heat penetrate his fingers. "Your children have dysentery. If they don't get medicine they will die."

"I know," said the father, "but I have no money." Friedrich opened his hand so that the man could see two wafers of gold.

"This will buy medicine and food. In exchange for your place."

The man looked back at the chaos along the pier.

"We've waited in this line for two days. If we give up our spot now, we'll never get on."

"There's another boat next week, but you cannot replace these children."

The boy stuck out his tongue and retched up a dribble of bile. The father muttered another curse about being weak and shoved him toward his wife. He stepped closer to Friedrich. "I won't be bought with your blood money."

"Don't be a fool. It's your only chance to save them."

The girl grimaced as another wave of stomach cramps took hold. She curled her knees to her chest without uttering a sound. A wave of self-loathing washed over Friedrich. How did he ever sink this low?

"We're getting out of here today," said the father. Between the knuckles of his raised fist Friedrich saw the serrations of rusted metal. "Another word and I'll carve your face to shreds."

The queue made a sudden shift forward. The man pulled his wife to her feet and they scrambled ahead before anyone could fill the gap. Friedrich picked up their tattered belongings and brought them forward. The man's eyes hardened as he set them down.

"I said we don't need your help."

Friedrich pressed the wafers into his hand. "I apologize...for putting that choice on your shoulders. Buy some medicine and food when you get on board."

⚓

They heard anger coming from the Romanian official who sat behind the table at the front of the line. An elderly man and woman pleaded as the official refused to stamp their visas. Shoving their documents back across the table, the official ordered his deputy to pull them away.

"There's our chance," Friedrich said, grabbing Eva's hand. "Work with me on this." They rushed forward to the table before the deputy could haul the couple aside.

"They're with us!" Friedrich said.

"Tante! Onkle!" Eva said. "Gott sei Dank we've found you."

The old couple's eyes swung from one to the other as they tried to understand what was happening. Eva hugged them and smiled. "Don't be afraid," she whispered. "We will help you."

"They wandered away from us last night," Friedrich said, to the official. "They cannot be on their own." He opened his hand so that the Romanian glimpsed a flash of gold.

A man standing behind grabbed Friedrich's shoulder and yanked him backward. "Wait your fucking turn."

Friedrich jerked free and leaned closer to the official where he caught a whiff of cheap brandy.

"They suffer with dementia," he said. "They'll never make it without us." He pressed his documents into the man's hand. "Please."

The official glanced at their passport photos and work visas before pausing a moment to compare their resemblance to the documents. He lifted a paperweight and rifled through a stack of papers. When he found what he was looking for, he adjusted his glasses and tracked the words with a stubby index finger. Friedrich recognized the Gestapo seal at the top of the page and his pulse quickened. What now?

"Dr. Friedrich Mueller and your wife?" He looked over at Eva.

"Correct," Friedrich said, coughing out the word. "These two are her aunt and uncle."

"There is no mention of anyone else travelling with you. Their visas have expired."

Friedrich leaned in again and whispered, "I told you...they have dementia. They forgot to renew them. Eight pieces of gold for the four of us."

The man standing behind wrenched his collar again. "He's butting in."

Friedrich cursed and pulled himself loose. The official scribbled his signature across the page and shouted at his deputy who threw the man to the ground. Raising his eyes to Friedrich, the official slipped his hand off the desk. Eight wafers of gold dropped into his palm.

"Get on board before I change my mind," he said, stamping the visas.

Friedrich grabbed all four suitcases and started toward the gangway. Streaks of rust blotted the letters on the side of the bow but as they reached the ramp, he was able to piece together the word: Salvatore.

↟

Reaching the top deck, they found a spot protected from the wind blowing off the bay. Friedrich stacked the suitcases up against the bulkhead while Eva helped the old couple to sit and catch their breath.

"Wait here while I look for cabins," he said. "Andrei said we'll be on-board for a week."

He lit a cigarette and started walking. The vessel had been built to carry freight and the cabins he found were locked. Signs indicated they were reserved for officers and crew. At the midway point of the ship he came upon a throng squeezing through a narrow passageway leading below. He elbowed his way to the front and followed the gangway down past two decks already full. On the lower deck forward of the engine room, several families guarded spots under ventilation portholes. He spotted an empty corner on the far side and stumbled over outstretched bodies to reach it, but two men with knives shoved him back. The clatter of pistons and fumes from the engines made him dizzy. Everywhere he looked, bodies were crammed against each other. The walls seemed to close in and trap him. His chest tightened so he could hardly breathe and he bulled his way back up the gangway through a crush of descending bodies. Bursting through the doorway, he gasped for air and staggered back to where Eva and the couple waited.

"No room below," he said. "The stairs are too steep anyway. We'd never get out in an emergency."

He led them toward the bow where four lifeboats hung from gables on the port and starboard sides, each draped and lashed with canvas tarps. Eva passed him her knife and he slit the cords on one to look underneath.

"We can stay under here," he said. "At least it'll be dry."

He dragged over a crate to use as a step and peeled away the tarp. Climbing inside, he removed the cross slats and laid them flat so they would have more room to stretch out. Lifejackets from the forward locker served as cushions. He helped the others inside and then found a vendor at the stern hawking provisions. Three hundred Reichsmarks bought him four loaves of bread, two rounds of sausage, four jugs of water and two packages of cigarettes. When he returned, Eva sat outside waiting for him.

"They're inside sleeping," she said. "They're from a Yiddish village near here. It's Frieda and Avrum. They're traumatized. They said something about a son."

"We'll look after them until we get to Istanbul," he said. "How are you feeling?"

"Cramping," she said, rubbing her lower abdomen. "There was some bleeding but it's stopped. I'll be okay."

"I've calculated how much food and water we can have each day. We have to make it last because there won't be any more. They've loaded this thing with as many as they could get on. It's going to be a cesspool."

"Dangerous too," Eva said, nodding toward four men leaning against the rail. "Over there."

"Gypsies. I saw them when I came back. One of us will have to stay here all the time...with the knife. We'll eat undercover and keep everything hidden in the bow."

She looked down the length of the ship. "I've never been on the ocean before. I hope I don't get seasick."

Wind off the coal-colored bay gusted across the deck. "It could be rough by the look of those clouds. It's best if you stand outside and keep your eyes on the horizon." The first time he'd been to sea, sailing from Hamburg to London, the enjoyable passage down the Elbe came to an end when the ship entered the North Sea. He'd spent the rest of the voyage heaving over the stern. His mouth filled with saliva at the memory and he changed the subject.

"Let's get them up," he said. "We should eat before dark."

Just after midnight the hull shuddered. With smoke and sparks belching from the stack, Salvatore slipped its lines and rolled into the turbulent waters of the Black Sea. As they plowed into rising swells, Friedrich tied the tarp over them and looped his shoelaces through the handles of their suitcases. He directed his flashlight down toward the bow and saw the old couple smiling at him.

"Tante und Onkle! Are you comfortable up there?" He spoke slower to be understood.

"We are fine," Avrum said. "We cannot thank you enough for helping us."

Frieda whispered into Avrum's ear. "She says you have the same eyes as our son. He was killed defending our village against the Iron Guard."

"I'm sorry to hear that," Friedrich said.

"His courage saved our lives. You remind us of him."

"Try to sleep now," Friedrich said. "We'll see what the morning brings." He rested his head on a lifejacket and closed his eyes, listening as the breathing within their cramped cocoon became even and slow. Seven days of this, he thought, and then what?

They fell into a routine as the ship yawed and wallowed through a series of weather fronts and battering seas. In the mornings, they stood in unruly lines and took turns helping the couple toward two water faucets where they could wash and brush their teeth. During the day they waited for hours to relieve themselves in sloshing barrels that served as latrines. While they didn't share much beyond a few kind words, they protected Tante und Oncle as family.

On the second afternoon at sea, Friedrich sat near the wheelhouse, where a physician assessed those in need of the limited medicaments he had available. When the twins appeared with their father, Friedrich slipped the doctor two-hundred Reichmarks and mumbled the words dysentery and sulfonamide. He stood up and greeted the father before touching the children's foreheads.

"They're still pretty hot," he said. "The doctor will give you the medicine you need."

As the doctor examined his children, the father grabbed Friedrich's arm. "God will bless you for this."

For the next four days, Friedrich and the physician took up their afternoon posts, triaging those most in need. Friedrich extracted aching teeth and sutured up facial slashes from night battles over food or space. With no means of sterilization, he scrubbed his instruments in seawater from firehoses that washed away the vomit, urine and feces pooling over the deck.

Since their first night offshore Eva mostly stayed close to the lifeboat, too sick to do much of anything but retch over the side. Tante und Onkle could do little more than provide her sips of water and keep an eye on their dwindling food supply.

⚑

On the seventh day, Friedrich stirred from a fretful sleep and slipped outside for a smoke. A mild breeze left only a light chop on the water, a welcome change from the steep swells that had dogged them since leaving Constanta. They had consumed the last of their provisions the evening before. Unable to eat much all week, Eva's cheeks had shrunk and her skin was as gray as the elements around them. Most worrying was her fever, which had worsened during the night. Her shivering had woken him more than once.

Inhaling deep pulls off his cigarette, he walked the deck looking east over the monotonous expanse of water. Not a hint of brightness anywhere. Then, out of the side of his eye, a slash of white off the port side. Skirting across the top of the waves it looked to be on a converging angle with the ship. Dolphins? It couldn't be.

No sooner had he cupped his eyes than he recognized the stem of a periscope. He went numb as he saw two shadows skimming toward the ship just beneath the surface. "Oh nein Code! Zwei Torpedos," he yelled, running along the rail with the hope that their trajectory was off course. But as they came nearer, they were right on target. He scrambled back toward the lifeboat screaming, "Torpedos! Torpedos!"

Two explosions rocked the hull and tripped him forward. As he stumbled to regain his balance, a fireball burst through the wheelhouse curling up the deck like the lid of a sardine can. The bow dug in as if it had struck a reef. The shock wave threw him through the air until he slammed down skidding forward on his hands and knees.

He staggered to his feet and looked back to see the rear of the ship engulfed in flame. Smoke billowed up from the passenger decks below. Faces caked with sulfur groped through the doorway like ghosts from the underworld. He ripped off the canopy of the lifeboat and saw Eva and the couple cowering near the bow.

"Torpedos," he cried. "We're going down. Put on your lifejackets."

As the ship listed to port, Friedrich blocked three men who clambered to get inside their boat.

"Women, children, elderly first," he hollered.

He glared down at Eva who was still huddled near the front. "Eva! No time to be sick now. Get up here and help load people on." He saw the strain in her eyes as she struggled to get up. "Move!" He jumped down and ran across the deck to help people into the other lifeboats.

Avrum touched Eva's shoulder as she braced her arms to stand. "You're too sick, Eva." he said. "Friedrich didn't mean to be that way. Frieda and I will load the boat and get on last. You stay here."

When all four boats were loaded, Friedrich helped a crewman with the winches. As they lowered the first three down on steel cables, water flooding through the stern caused the list to steepen. With the deck at forty-five degrees, the boat carrying Eva and the couple skidded sideways and dropped. The winch's spool whined like a fishing reel until the cable snagged. Frantic passengers dangled twenty feet above the water.

The crewman cried out to Friedrich. "Jump down and get on. I'll cut it loose."

The lifeboat swayed like a pendulum and looked miles away. As it swung in closer, he closed his eyes and jumped. Landing hard against the oarlocks, he clutched at his ribs and strained to breathe. Above him, he heard the thuds of an ax. The cable snapped and a sensation of weightlessness swept through him as the boat plunged down to the water.

A wall of green broached the gunwales and swamped the boat. The impact hammered his teeth together and salt spray burned into his shredded tongue like acid.

"Bailing buckets..., under the seats!" he hollered. Waves slammed them against the ship's hull until the wooden lifeboat groaned and creaked as if it would split. With all his strength, he pushed away from the ship with one oar and screamed at the two men holding the other.

"Heave!...Heave!...Heave!..."

His cadence brought a stout woman to his side and the four of them pulled together until the gap between their lifeboat and the ship widened. When they pulled free from the drag of the undertow, all four sat wheezing over the oars and watched the smoking hulk slip beneath the surface. Fifty meters away, the other three lifeboats bobbed parallel to them.

With his tongue swollen twice its size, Friedrich looked around for Eva and the couple. Foreboding swept through him when he couldn't see them near the bow where he'd left them. Then he spotted Eva, sitting alone several rows behind, bundled in a packing quilt. Her shoulders trembled under the soaked fabric and he called out. "Eva."

She turned with an unfocused gaze as if she didn't recognize him, her eyes jaundiced and her voice inaudible. He scrambled over the seats and crouched beside her.

"Where are they? Tante und Oncle."

She pointed toward the oily patch of debris and stared.

"What happened?" He shook her shoulders and searched her eyes looking for an answer. When she spoke, he leaned close to hear.

"They gave their seats to the twins who were on their way up to the latrines when the torpedoes hit. They barely escaped. Their parents never made it out."

The boy and girl huddled next to her and gazed at him with flat expressions of shock, their faces blistered raw.

"Tante und Oncle could have taken my place," he said. "I could have hung alongside."

"They didn't want you to die."

Friedrich's voice broke. "All they wanted was to kiss the soil of Israel."

"Or to join their son. They made a choice."

He had only enough time to process the thought before the submarine burst to the surface one hundred meters away. Foam gushed from its deck and the hatch flew open. Two sailors climbed out and aimed submachine guns toward the lifeboats.

"Oh Gott, no!" he shouted. He drove his weight into Eva's side and followed her into the water. The guns raked fire across the open boats until the screams of panic and horror were silenced. From where he clung behind the hull he couldn't see the position of the submarine but he heard it coming closer. Something touched his hand and he looked up at the twin girl who stood to jump into his arms. He pulled Eva's head down and cringed as another fusillade of bullets ripped the child to pieces and turned the water red.

With the deafening rumble of the engine coming closer, he peaked over the gunwale and saw the submarine circling towards them, both gunners spraying volleys into any body that still moved. Eva slipped from his grasp and went under. He pulled her up and slapped her face. Her eyes were blanks. Water sputtered from her nose and mouth. "Eva, stay with me! They're coming this way." Her head slumped and he sucked in deep breaths preparing to pull her under.

As the submarine's bow came into sight, its dive alarm sounded. The two sailors stopped shooting and scrambled for the hatch. Through plugged ears, Friedrich heard sirens and saw plumes from two gunboats speeding toward them. He watched the rotund belly of the submarine slither beneath the surface like a python satiated on prey.

"Hypothermia," he yelled, as Turkish sailors in a rescue craft pulled Eva's unconscious body from his arms.

Chapter 9

The gunboat docked in Istanbul with the sun setting over the city. The call to evening prayer echoed from loudspeakers at the top of minarets. A dose of morphine, dry clothes and warm blankets had kept Friedrich asleep all the way back. His eyelids flickered with the sound of voices, and he dreamt he was floating on air as sailors carried his gurney into a naval emergency ward.

"What happened out there?" A man wearing a suit pulled off his jacket and slipped on a white laboratory coat.

"Another U-boat attack," said a seaman. "They sunk the Salvatore out of Constanta. Nothing but a debris field left when we got there."

"Survivors?"

"We found six but only these two made it. The others had lost too much blood. The Salvatore carried around five hundred passengers and a small crew."

"No lifeboats?"

"Only four launched. We saw the u-boat surface through binoculars but she submerged again before we arrived. It was a massacre, sir. One hundred and sixty killed by machine gun fire. Somehow this man and woman survived...but it doesn't look like she'll make it."

The seaman's comment jolted Friedrich from his opiate slumber. He pried himself up and focused on the blurry outline of a sailor in blue serge talking to the man in white. As his vision cleared, he saw Eva lying still on a bed by the wall, her eyes closed. An oxygen mask covered her nose but the rise and fall of her chest was hardly perceptible. They were letting her go.

"My wife," he shouted. "She needs help." He threw his blanket aside and rolled off the gurney. His legs buckled and two nurses ran over and lifted him back on. "Stay where you are, sir. You're in no condition to get up. We'll take care of her."

The man in the white coat walked over and said, "I'm Doctor Ahmet Mustafa. What can you tell me?"

Friedrich rubbed the fogginess from his eyes and saw a moustachioed man with the knotted hair of a Turk. A goddamn Ottoman! He respected German, American and British physicians but Turks were another matter. "Is there a European physician I can discuss this with?" he asked.

"You have a problem?" said Mustafa. "Am I not good enough for your Jewish princess? We're well aware of who the Salvatore transports and so are the Germans. Do you think you were attacked for any other reason?"

Friedrich deferred by raising his trembling hand. "I apologize for my arrogance, Doctor. But I'm terrified that I'll lose her. She's..."

Before he could continue, a nurse holding a thermometer called from across the room.

"She's burning up. Almost forty degrees." She lifted the blanket and pointed to the discharge on the gurney. "And she's bleeding!"

"Was she shot?" asked Mustafa, as he hurried across the room.

"Not that I'm aware of," Friedrich said. He ignored the nurse's plea and swivelled his feet to the floor.

Cutting Eva's dress away, another nurse pointed to the stains on her underwear. "It's coming from her vagina."

Mustafa looked at Friedrich. "A miscarriage?"

"She would have told me," Friedrich said, shaking his head. "It's an infection."

Mustafa dipped a cotton swab into the discharge and brought it to his nose. "Right," he said, moving to the sink to wash his hands.

"She was raped a week ago," Friedrich said. "She's been vomiting ever since but we thought it was sea sickness. She started having trouble urinating. The fever spiked last night."

Mustafa placed his hands on her bloated belly and probed her organs with his fingers. Eva winced as the pain opened her eyes. Friedrich cradled her hand and watched Mustafa's expression turn grave.

"How bad is it?" he said.

"Not good. It's spread into her abdomen."

"Do you have penicillin?"

"Only sulfa. We'll start her now and see how she's doing over the next few hours. If it doesn't break we'll operate."

The word, operate, and the risk posed by surgery within a zone of infection, sent a shock wave through Friedrich's frazzled system. "I'll stay with her tonight," he said. "Get me a tub of cold water and some towels. I'll try to cool her down." He rubbed Eva's hand as he looked into the dull slits of her eyes. He bent to kiss her cheek and whispered, "You're very ill, leibling. We're in the hospital and the doctor is giving you medicine to get better. Try to sleep now. I'll be right here beside you."

Her eyes drifted closed as his lips pressed against her cheek.

⅄

Throughout the night, he refilled the tub with cold water and draped towels along her legs and body. Mustafa entered the room at five the next morning.

"You must operate, doctor," Friedrich said. "They just took her temperature. There's been no change. She's failing. The sulfa's no match for what that sonovabitch pushed inside her."

"You're aware of the danger?" Mustafa said, as he rested a stethoscope on her chest and held his finger on her wrist. "She's very weak."

Friedrich breathed a slow in and out to gather himself. Even the slightest accident within an infected mass would provide a bacterial sluiceway into the bloodstream. It would kill her. He nodded his assent. "It will only get worse if we wait."

Mustafa looked at the nurse. "Prepare for surgery."

"I'm a dental surgeon," Friedrich said. "Could I be of assistance?"

Mustafa paused a moment before he spoke. "Under normal circumstances, I would say no. But this could become complicated and I've had a long night. Another pair of hands won't hurt. Come. I'll show you where to scrub."

⋏

After three hours at the operating table, Mustafa flushed a final bowl of sterile water into the abdominal cavity where Eva's uterus, ovaries and fallopian tubes had been. Friedrich suctioned the water into a separate glass container and saw that it was clear.

"We've done the best we can," Mustafa said. "Her belly was full of pus. The next twenty-four hours are in the hands of God." The nurse handed him suture forceps and a threaded needle to close the twelve-inch incision. His hands trembled.

"Allow me, doctor," Friedrich said.

"Have you ever closed anything like this before?"

"Traumatic jaw fractures in the military. Not as long but harder to reach."

Mustafa exhaled a sigh that puffed out his mask and fogged his eyeglasses. He passed Friedrich the instruments. "Thank you. I'm dead on my feet."

"Your hands are as sure as any I've ever seen," Friedrich said. "I'm eternally grateful and I apologize again for my foolish remark last night."

He sutured the abdominal musculature and then the overlying skin while Mustufa dabbed away droplets of blood and snipped the silk thread at the completion of each knot. Friedrich tied forty-seven sutures, before he finished.

"Very well done," Mustafa said. "You must have repaired a lot of jaws."

"I also spent time at Harlem General when I studied in New York. All we did was close stab wounds."

⋏

Twelve hours later, Eva still had not regained consciousness, but she had a strong pulse and her temperature had dropped. Friedrich had provided three pints of his own blood to help. As he sat next to the bed, sipping broth, he held her hand and monitored the rhythm of her heartbeat. He mumbled Psalms he had memorized as a child, and though they hadn't crossed his lips for years, the words rang clear in his mind.

Around midnight, a gentle hand woke him in his chair.

"Somebody wants to talk to you." The nurse spoke with an English accent.

When he saw Eva gazing at him, his eyes welled and he murmured a prayer of gratitude. He pressed his lips to her forehead and relished the coolness of her skin. "You've had surgery, liebling. You had a very serious infection but it's all taken care of now."

With pinned pupils, she looked into his eyes and blinked, affirming his words, and then another dose of morphine swept over her.

"I gave her more so she can sleep," the nurse said.

"You're English?"

"Married a Turkish doctor of all things," she said, grinning. "No offense Doctor Mueller, but you look like death warmed over. Doctor Mustafa said you could use the surgeon's room. Go take a hot bath and we'll bring you some food. I'll stay with her until you get back."

⅄

Over the next three months, Friedrich rarely left Eva's side as her wounds healed and she rebuilt her strength. As March 1944 approached, she had progressed from taking a few steps in her room to walking circuits around the hospital. Although she had regained most of her weight and her feisty personality had re-emerged, her biggest challenge still lay ahead.

She would never bear a child.

Eva repressed the reality as she had done when her parents and sister were arrested by the Gestapo. But it was only a matter of time. Every night Friedrich lay awake wondering how best to support her when the moment arrived.

That day came on a warm, sunny morning after they had walked their first mile and stopped to rest. They sat on a bench sipping sweet tea and watched a ferry crossing the Golden Horn to the European side.

"When I look over there, all I can think of is the death and destruction that's still going on," he said. "An invasion from the west can't come too soon."

"Will we ever go back?"

"There will be very little to go back to." he said. 'We'll be travelling to Palestine in the next few weeks. They won't let us stay here much longer."

Eva stared across the water with an expression that said her thoughts were adrift. He put his arm around her and pulled her to his side. "I know what you're feeling," he said. "You've been so strong these last few months."

She began to tremble and then she broke, sobbing and burying her head into his chest.

"Let it go, liebling, let it go," he whispered.

"I'll never be a mother. We'll never have our own family."

He held her closer and wiped away the tears streaming down her cheeks. "Remember what you said about all the people who need our help?"

"It's not the same thing, Friedrich. I never imagined this would happen to me." Her eyes were devoid of hope, the sadness in her voice as deep and unyielding as he'd ever heard.

"I love you now more than ever," he said. "Let's find a rabbi who can marry us before we go any further. Enough of this pretending."

⅄

The Ashkenazi Synagogue founded by Austrian Jews in the Galata district of Istanbul provided the perfect place to hold their wedding the following week. With the medieval Galata Tower dominating the skyline, the ceremony was held on a beautiful afternoon with sunshine sparkling off the waters of the Golden Horn. The bride, slim and toned, shimmered in a dress trimmed with fine embroidery while the groom, looked strapping beside her in a new suit and tie. Doctor Ahmet Mustafa and his wife stood as witnesses while Eva and Friedrich made their vows official.

After the two couples enjoyed a leisurely lunch of the most delicious seafood Friedrich had tasted in years, Mustafa raised his glass of juice in a toast.

"May your journey be a swift and safe one," he said. "And God willing, our paths will cross again. Soon I hope. Iyi sanslar, my friends."

"Thank you, Ahmet," Friedrich said, in response. "Eva and I are both so grateful for all you've done for us. If it were not for your skill, your patience and your compassion, we wouldn't be here to celebrate this wonderful day. We can never thank you enough and we'll never forget you. Peace upon you and your family."

Chapter 10

After spending four days travelling across the Syrian plain in the back of a date truck, Friedrich and Eva stepped into a bus reeking of tobacco and bodies that hadn't seen a bar of soap in weeks. While a tribe of Bedouins squeezed onto the hard bench seats, their movements permeated the air with the stench of camel dung. Children playing tag scampered along the aisle.

Their shrieks brought a squint to Friedrich's eyes.

"Why would they let them run wild like that?" he mumbled. "Damned annoying. No discipline at all."

A soldier with a botched repair to his cleft lip snorted through his nose and crammed more people into the seats. "Move closer, you filthy bastards. Three to a row." He looked at Friedrich and pointed to an empty spot near the back.

Walking down the aisle Eva tripped on a leg jutting out from under a seat. Friedrich lurched forward to break her fall and both suitcases and the satchel hit the floor.

"Are you okay?" he said. He glared down at a boy whose bucked teeth were coated with slime that had never seen the bristles of a toothbrush. The boy rubbed his knee and his eyes began to well. Eva grimaced and held her stomach. She grasped the back edge of the bench and folded herself on to the unpadded seat. "I'll be alright," she said.

"Control these goddamn brats," the soldier yelled. He cuffed one of the robed men, casting a flurry of dust particles through sunbeams filtering through the windows. The boy buried his head in his mother's skirt and howled. Friedrich felt the animosity seething from eyes behind burqas.

As they rolled along the road a bleak landscape stretched on forever. Off to the side, a man with his face hidden behind a bandana used a switch to coax donkeys up a trail. As they passed, he disappeared into a cloud of dust thrown up by the wheels. Thirty minutes later, amid squeals and the smell of soiled new-borns, the driver broached the crest of a hill. The sight of a walled fortress in the distance triggered a rumble of anticipation through the bus.

A frayed *Union Jack* snapped at the top of a flagpole. They drove through the gate past the bored faces of two conscripts who waved the bus over to the edge of a parade square.

Friedrich squeezed Eva's hands.

"Are you feeling okay?"

"I'm scared."

He grabbed their luggage and helped Eva to her feet. "They're going to question us. Don't...mention...Bauer."

Outside, the Bedouins milled in front of a processing desk. A sergeant, his scarlet beret slanted down over one eye, shouted at them.

"You two...over here."

"We're Jews from Vienna," Friedrich said. His chest heaved as he pulled their papers from his breast pocket.

"I'm not blind," said the sergeant. "Why the hell you're here, is the question." With his tongue wetting chapped lips, he glanced at their documents.

"Escort," he hollered, and a military policeman with a white armband hurried over. "Interrogation." The sergeant scribbled on his clipboard and nodded toward Eva and Friedrich.

The MP, whose cheeks bore nests of acne, pointed toward a four-seated vehicle parked behind the bus. "This way."

Friedrich looked at the sergeant. "Where are we going?"

The sergeant ignored him, yelling at the troops standing around the Bedouin crowd. "We haven't got all goddamn day, gentlemen. Get them into line, for Christ's sake."

"Throw your gear in the back," said the MP. He flipped opened the door and pulled a pair of handcuffs from his belt. "In you go, missus."

"Is this really necessary?" Friedrich said, sliding on to the seat beside her. "We're not criminals, for God's sake."

The MP shook his head and shackled their wrists together. "Not my call, mate. I'd rather be sipping pints and playing darts too. You won't be going anywhere for awhile, so might as well catch a wink. Got to deal with that lot first." He indicated the Bedouins with jute sacks slung over their shoulders, identification papers clutched in their hands, the guards cursing those slow to move. "Pick it up you raghead, bastards!"

Friedrich's pulse raced under the squeeze of the cuff.

He fumbled with one hand to light a cigarette, but after the first drag, he gagged and threw it to the ground. Eva's face was a mask of exhaustion. He stroked his fingers through her hair and then cupped her shackled wrist to massage circulation into her hand.

"They're being extra cautious," he said. "There's a war on, after all. We'll sort everything out once we speak to the interrogators." She nodded and rested her head on his shoulder.

"I've been thinking about the attack," he said. "I didn't bring it up before but...I'll bet Bauer meant to have us killed."

Eva's eyes popped open and she cocked her head to the side. "What makes you think that?"

"That official on the pier matched our names to a Gestapo document before he let us on."

"I remember that," she said, "but didn't we hear about other ships that were torpedoed?"

"They occurred farther out at sea where there was less chance of encountering patrols. Resurfacing close to the coast was risky, so they must have had a reason. I can't help but think that bastard had something to do with it."

The sun disappeared behind the mountains and a breeze swept across the square. Eva shivered and looked over to where the line of Bedouins had dwindled. "They're almost done," she said. "What will we do if they think we're spies?"

"We'll have to convince them they're wrong because bribes won't work anymore." He shook his head and looked into her eyes. "I wish I had a better answer."

⋏

The MP jumped into the driver's seat, started the motor and flicked on the headlights. "Hang on back there," he said.

Gravel and dust kicked up as he pulled away and followed a road to the far side of the compound. He pulled up to the entrance of a building where reflections gleamed off bars covering the windows. He unlocked the cuffs so Friedrich could carry their luggage and led them up a flight of steps where a duty officer with a red face limped around from behind his desk. "Been waiting all afternoon for these two," he said, frowning. "What took so damn long?"

"Sorry sir. Big load of camel jockeys today."

The officer grunted and pointed along the hallway. "Fingerprints and photographs down there."

An older private, snoring with his mouth agape, snapped his head forward as they entered the room. With pursed lips, he clamped his teeth to position a floating lower denture.

"Thought you two got lost," he said. "Let's get on with it, shall we? Missing me time with the lads."

A bed-sheet served as a backdrop while a flashbulb flooded the room to record their mug shots. The private set the camera aside and took them to a table where he pressed their thumbs and fingers onto an inkpad. With a shaky hand, he transferred the imprints to sheets of paper, which he labeled with their name, the date and a number. Friedrich worried that the name, Mueller, was now a part of the permanent record. How the hell would he change that?

"Everything looks good," the private said. He called down to the duty officer. "All done here, sir." He looked at Friedrich and Eva and smiled. "Cheerio."

The duty officer set the phone back into its cradle and looked up at Friedrich. "You'll be in separate cells tonight," he said. "Someone's on the way to collect your missus."

"What!" Before he could protest further, the door swung open and a guard walked in and saluted. Her graying hair and businesslike demeanor reminded Friedrich of Helga.

"Just the one, sir?" she said, looking at Eva.

The duty officer nodded and kept writing.

"She's not well," Friedrich said, looking at the woman. "She's recovering from surgery. A bath and some decent food would be very much appreciated."

"I must say, you do look a little worse for wear, dearie." The officer took the suitcase from her hand. "Come along and I'll see what I can do."

Eva clutched Friedrich's hand as he kissed her cheek. The sheen of fatigue dampened her brow but her temperature felt normal. "I'll see you in the morning, liebling."

"Don't worry," she whispered. "I'll be fine."

The duty officer rattled a ring of keys and pointed to the stairwell.

"Down this way, mate. Bring your gear."

The door closed and Friedrich was left alone in a cell lit by a dangling bulb. A plate of biscuits and a jug of water sat next to a cot. Was this the end of the road? He lit his last cigarette and paced the room, scouring his mind for some way to prove their real identities. He crushed the butt into the concrete and dropped down on the cot. Pulling the blanket over himself, he turned his back to the light and stared at the bricks while he waited for sleep.

Shivering through the night, he bolted awake to voices and footsteps in the hallway. Only darkness through the barred window.

The door swung open. A captain with a waxed moustache walked into the room. A waft of shaving cologne followed behind.

"How was your rest, jerry?"

"Where's my wife?"

"You'll see her after we find out who you are."

"But I must..."

"I said...later."

Friedrich glared and stepped forward. "Nein," he shouted. "I want to see her now."

The captain's hand dropped to his holster. "Back away."

Friedrich retreated next to the cot. "It was freezing in here last night and those biscuits aren't fit for dogs." He pointed at the untouched plate and tossed the thin blanket to the floor. "That's nothing but a goddamn rag."

The captain's nostrils flared. He stepped across the room and his eyes bore into Friedrich's.

"It's a hell of lot better than where you'll be going if things don't pan out here, jerry. To make you feel better, I'll tell you that your wife received a superior standard of accommodation last night. She's fine and you'll see her after we've spoken to you both. Verstanden? Any funny stuff and I'll throw away the key and let you stew in here until you're ready."

Friedrich wiped away a tear running down his cheek.

"What do you need from me?"

⅄

Blindfolded, he was led from the room and up a flight of stairs. The clang of a door brought a wash of fresh air and the sun warmed the back of his neck. Pressed down into the backseat of a vehicle, its frame bounced with the weight of two men who climbed in and slammed the doors. The captain's cologne sweetened the air beside him.

The crunch of tires echoed off the walls of the fortress so he reckoned they were heading back toward the main gate. The driver came to a stop and he heard the words, prisoner interrogation, and the thump of a stamp. The vehicle accelerated through the gate and the smell of burning tobacco stirred his craving. His head jerked back as the unlit end of a cigarette touched his lips. "All yours," said the captain. His cheeks puckered as he sucked in the first nicotine of the day and exhaled through the open window.

"So tell me your story, Mueller. We've got lots of time."

"To begin with captain, my name is Friedrich Mendelssohn." He waited for a response but there was none. He heard the rustle of paper.

"Go on," said the captain. "You're saying that you and your wife are Jews. Is that correct?"

"Yes, and I'm a dental surgeon. I assumed the name Mueller after the Nazis enacted the Nuremberg Laws in 1933. It was the only way I could continue to work. I was born and raised in Leipzig where my family resided for centuries. Maybe you've heard of my great uncle, the composer?"

"Can't say that I have. I'm more of a Glenn Miller man, if you know what I mean."

In Friedrich's opinion, Miller's sanitized swing didn't come close to the pulsing rhythms of Count Basie. In the Roseland Ballroom in New York, he and Katrina had danced to both bands, but now was not the time to discuss trivial matters.

"About six months ago, the Gestapo uncovered my identity. Fortunately, my wife and I were able to obtain work visas to Romania." He took another drag and felt the nicotine sharpen his thoughts. He could afford no slips of the tongue. Speaking deliberately, he revisited their flight from Vienna, the assault in the mountains, the submarine attack and the surgery in Istanbul. When he finished, he heard the scratching of a pen.

"Quite a story, I'd say," the captain said.

Yes, but had it been enough? Another cigarette touched his lips and he heard the snap of a match. He sucked hard and held the smoke deep in his lungs before finally expelling it.

"Either you're a hell of a lucky man, Mendelssohn, or you have one vivid imagination," said the captain. "We'll have to see how it jibes with your wife's version, won't we?"

Friedrich nodded his head and continued to smoke, hoping that Eva's story had been consistent. Any mention of Bauer would be disastrous.

Chapter 11

The vehicle ground to a stop and someone tugged him from the backseat. They entered a building pungent with eugenol, a medicament used to treat painful teeth. The blindfold came off and he blinked to adjust to the brightness of a dental operatory. A surly man with a chevron on his sleeve sat in a dental chair cradling his lower jaw, his face swollen. Over his right eye, a two-inch gash needed stitches.

"What in your esteemed judgement is ailing this lad, Herr Doktor?"

The sarcastic London twang was not lost on Friedrich. Nor were they alone. A portly man in a white laboratory coat stood in the doorway.

"One of your professional colleagues...here to observe," the captain said.

Friedrich acknowledged the military dentist, whose neck bulged above a pinched shirt collar one size too small. He had the florid complexion of an obese choirboy. As Friedrich turned toward the patient, he wondered how the man could breathe.

"He's taken a blow to the face." Friedrich's English carried a thick German accent.

"If that's your best diagnosis, jerry, there's really no point in wasting our time...is there, now?"

The pontificating tone reminded Friedrich of his worst professors at dental school; verbose men with woeful skills who took refuge in teaching. Pompous ass.

Friedrich moved toward the sink and looked at the captain. "If I may sir, before I examine the patient."

"Be my guest."

"Then you can illuminate us, Herr Doktor."

Friedrich ignored the remark from the doorway and scrubbed his hands. Splashing his face with water, he dried with a towel and looked at the sullen man in the chair.

"I'll need you to move your hand, sir."

With fretful eyes the man drew his hand away and placed it on the armrest. Friedrich saw that his lower jaw was skewed to the left.

"How wide can you open your mouth, Corporal?"

The corporal strained to open and his jaw shifted further left. He winced and shook his head.

"Can't do it, mate," he mumbled.

Friedrich pressed his hand gently against the side of the jaw.

The corporal knocked it away and cursed. "I said it fuckin' 'urts, jerry."

Friedrich looked at the captain. "He has a fractured jaw, sir."

"Located where?"

The snap question from the door made Friedrich's eyes narrow.

"Below the left condyle," he said.

"Too technical for me." The captain looked at the dentist for guidance.

"I must concur, captain. The fracture is indeed on the left side, below the jaw joint."

"Jolly good, then," the captain said. "Let's move on to the next fellow, shall we."

Friedrich followed the men down the hall into another room where he heard moans coming from a soldier who held a compress to his face.

"Have a look at this bloke," the captain said.

On the counter, Friedrich spotted his instrument satchel, now empty. He scrubbed his hands once more and turned toward the chair.

The square-jawed sergeant looked to be in his forties. He opened his mouth and pointed to a rotted lower molar on the right side. His teeth were coated with tobacco tar, the front ones notched from the stem of a pipe. His lower lip was cracked with an open sore and he had swelling on his neck below the right side of his jaw. A red scar marked a recent incision. Friedrich looked at the dentist for an explanation.

"Your call, Herr Doktor."

Friedrich ran his finger over the scar. "It appears there's been an attempt to drain an abscess."

"It wasn't too successful now, was it? What's your next thought?"

"Extraction," Friedrich said.

"He's all yours, then. Have a go."

Friedrich loaded a syringe with anesthetic. When it was full, he turned around with the needle at his side. "Open please."

Before the sergeant was aware of its entry, the needle had advanced to its destination and the syringe was emptied. He refilled it and pumped in another dose for good measure. Within moments, the moaning ceased. The sergeant's jaw would be numb for hours.

"You're sure as hell good at that." The sergeant looked at him with a lop-sided grin.

An orderly walked into the room holding a tray covered with a white towel. "Your instruments" he said. "They're still a bit hot."

Friedrich uncovered the sterilized instruments and placed them in the order he planned to use them. Pressing his fingers alongside the molar, he confirmed his suspicion of thick bone around the tooth; it was an anatomical feature not unusual for a man of the sergeant's physique.

"Is there an X-ray?"

"The machine's on the fritz," the dentist said. "You'll have to fly by the seat of your pants." He chuckled and grinned at the captain.

Friedrich braced his left arm about the sergeant's head and then levered the screwdriver blade of his straight elevator between the molar and the bone. After ten minutes the tooth remained solid and unrepentant, as if locked in concrete. He engaged the forceps and applied side-to-side pressure until the molar loosened. Feeling beads of sweat on his forehead, he wiped, and then teased the tooth upwards until it snagged. An x-ray is what he needed. He saw the dentist looking at his watch and he reminded himself to stay calm. The idiot was timing him. The impatience he felt made his hand tighten so he backed off, admonishing himself to stop and think.

Moving the tooth upward again brought the same result. One or both of the roots were curved. Without an x-ray it was impossible to tell. He set down the forceps and turned to the dentist.

"I'll need a surgical drill to split the roots."

"That could take awhile. The motor's almost shot. Hardly any torque."

Friedrich inserted a bone drill into the hand-piece and started boring a vertical channel in the middle of the tooth. Because of the decay, he progressed faster than expected. When he felt that he'd gone far enough, he placed the blade of the elevator into the slot and twisted. The crack resounded into the hallway and the two roots separated. Blood rose from the socket and he met the sergeant's wild eyes. "It's not a problem, sergeant," he said, stuffing in the last pack of gauze. "Close for a moment."

"Not as easy as it looks, eh."

Friedrich was his own harshest critic but the cheeky tone from the doorway raised the hairs on his back.

He locked eyes with the moon-faced dentist and shouted. "Make yourself useful, goddamnit. I need more gauze. I can't see what the hell I'm doing here." His retort left the dentist flatfooted and speechless. The orderly rushed in and set more gauze on the tray. Friedrich sopped up the blood and looked at the captain whose face had turned chalky white. "I can do without the witty comments from the professor over there."

With sweat stinging his eyes, he probed his elevator through the blood until it grabbed and then, with a velvet touch, he pried upward until the curved root surrendered into his hand. He put the forceps on the other and delivered it a moment later.

"You can relax now, sergeant. We're done."

He rinsed and inspected both roots to insure he'd left nothing behind. As he suspected, one was straight and the other was bent to an angle of almost a forty-five degrees. The dentist peered over his shoulder.

"Are you satisfied now?" Friedrich turned off the tap and grabbed a towel.

"Will you look at the curve on that bugger," said the dentist. After all his flippant commentary, his voice carried a sense of awe as if he'd witnessed something extraordinary. "Wherever did you learn to use an elevator like that?"

"George Beesley at the Royal London Hospital," Friedrich said. 'One tooth in the air at all times', George used to say. He was a real character and one hell of a dentist."

His inside joke broke the ice. They both laughed at the idea of an oral surgeon pulling teeth with abandon and flinging them through the air. "George told me he learned his craft on the Eskimos in northern Canada." Friedrich said.

"Do you mean, the Boomer?" The dentist's eyes brightened. He turned to the captain who stood by the open window taking deep breaths and sipping from a cup of water.

"The Boomer?" Friedrich said. "I've never heard that before."

"It's a nickname. You can hear him a mile away. He's a bull of a man with a booming voice."

"George was a loud fellow alright but he had hands like silk. That was one of many techniques he showed me."

"He's a Canadian," said the dentist. "Major Beesley. He got posted here after we ran Rommel out of Egypt." He looked at the captain. "The major had some hospital cases in Jerusalem yesterday but he should be back by now."

Friedrich looked at the captain and broke into a smile. "If it's the same George Beesley I know, sir, then it's my lucky day."

"Send the orderly to get him then." The captain inhaled a deep breath.

Friedrich watched a semblance of color returning to his face, thankful that the captain hadn't passed out on him.

With the socket in the sergeant's mouth still oozing, he placed another pack of gauze and took a closer look at the sore on the lip he had noticed earlier. He ran his fingertip over the spot and felt its hard rolled edge. "Does this ever bother you?"

"Not at all, mate," the sergeant mumbled.

"Just a few more minutes then," he said. He looked over at the captain and the dentist and gestured them out to the hallway.

"I don't like the look of that thing on his lip," he whispered. "Or that swelling on his neck."

"What are you thinking?" said the dentist. "It's obviously associated with that molar."

"It could be cancer," Friedrich said. "You said you didn't get much drainage yesterday. The only way to rule it out is with a biopsy."

"You think it's a squamous cell carcinoma?"

The defensive posturing left little doubt in Friedrich's mind that the dentist viewed the lesion as nothing more than a cold sore. The lack of pus in the swelling should have indicated that it was something other than an infection. But at the same time, Friedrich was not about to pass judgement. Criticism, brought after the fact, when circumstances may have been different from how they now appeared, could ruin a colleague's reputation. Friedrich chose the diplomatic route. He hoped they weren't too late for the sergeant's sake.

"I've seen it before with pipe smokers," he said. "A simple biopsy will tell us. We can't be too careful with that."

⅄

"Well, I'll be a goddamned sonovabitch!" The boisterous assertion echoed down the hallway and the three men turned to look. A stocky man, over six feet tall, with a crew cut and a cigar stomped toward them. He came up to Friedrich and stuck out his right hand. "Freddie Mendelssohn! My Christ, lad, it's been a long time."

Beesley's hand pumping went on far too long as he chewed the cigar and grinned. Friedrich was grateful when he finally let go.

"Last I heard you'd gone to New York. What the hell brings you to this godforsaken part of the world?"

"It's a long story," Friedrich said. "Not many choices left for Jews these days."

Beesley scowled. "The sooner we finish off those bastards, the better." He took the cigar from his mouth and looked at the captain. "This man's not a spy, sir. He's one the finest dental operators I've ever known. I'll vouch for him one hundred percent." He clapped Friedrich on the back and laughed.

"We've got lots of catching up to do, Freddie. Still like a nip of cognac?"

"Sure do, but first I must see my wife." He looked at the captain.

"This puts the lid on it then. I'm sorry for the bother, Doctor Mendelssohn. I'll take you to her right now."

"Where are you heading after this?" Beesley asked.

"Jerusalem. I need to find work and look for a place to live."

"You're coming home with me then. We've got an empty bedroom at our place and we'll help you get settled. I'll call the wife. Damnit, Freddie! I'm sure glad to see you again, boy."

CHAPTER 12

The dining room rang with laughter while Friedrich and Eva finished the best meal they'd tasted since their wedding. As Friedrich savoured the Bordeaux left in his glass, George Beesley's wife, Hilary, gathered the empty dessert plates and looked across at Eva.

"You look exhausted, dear. Let's leave these two to their cigars and cognac. We'll get these dishes in the morning."

As the two women went to bed, Beesley stirred the fire and threw on another log. He poured a rich brown cognac into two snifters and offered Friedrich a cigar to go with it. He glanced to the top of the stairs. "It's been a helluva long haul for poor Eva, hasn't it?"

"I thought I'd lost her," Friedrich said. His eyes glazed as he sucked the cigar to life. "She's been so sick that she hasn't had time to deal with everything. The next few months will be rough when it all begins to sink in. I'll have to keep her busy."

"What are your plans?" The big man settled into his chair and seasoned the cigar with his lips.

"I want to find an apartment near the old city," Friedrich said. "I've still got a bit of money and I'm hoping to open a clinic in that area."

"Quite a hodgepodge down there," Beesley said. "There's still a lot of bad feelings between the locals and the Zionists about what happened ten years ago."

"What was that about?"

"The Arabs figured that the Jews were taking over the land and they attacked. There was butchery on both sides. Everything's been on a slow simmer ever since but it's heating up again. There've been some nasty incidents in the past few months."

"They should send delegations to Europe to see what can happen when things get out of control."

"I know, but it's like talking to a goddamn brick wall. You might want to think about the expat part of town, around here. It's more civilized and you'll get to do some of that fancy gold-work you love so much."

"I'm going to put all that aside for awhile," Friedrich said. "We just got kicked out of a so-called civilized country. I know how far that goes, when it comes to Jews. We felt that tension with the Arabs on our way here." He took a pull on his cigar and sighed. "With what's happened in Europe, people must learn to get along. There's got to be something I can do to help them see that."

"Do you really think that's your job, Freddie? We're just guys who fix goddamn teeth." Beesley chuckled and swirled the cognac in his snifter.

"It's tragic what's happened to our country, George. Until you've been on the receiving end, you can't understand how racial hatred brings out the worst in people. It turns them into something they never could have imagined. Providing a little pain relief might go a long way around here. It's all I can do."

"You were always a hard nut to crack Freddie, but I admire your gumption."

He poked a log and watched it flare. "You never know until you try, I guess. I'll make some phone calls in the morning and see what I can come up with."

ᛉ

With help from Beesley's friends, Friedrich and Eva found an apartment in a rooming house near the Old City. They began each day visiting the holy sites they had heard about as children. Afternoons were spent strolling through the narrow streets and lingering at outdoor cafes where they sipped Turkish coffee and discovered exotic flavors they'd never tasted.

On a warm evening, they came upon a chaotic market they had passed several days before. A crescent moon announced the end of the second week of Ramadan. The stalls were alive with families buying food to end the day of fasting. Grizzled men tugged at donkeys with backbreaking loads. Camels craned their necks at the sound of bleating goats penned for slaughter.

"This is unbelievable," Eva said, as they walked into the square. "It's like going back in time."

Friedrich rubbed his nose as he caught a whiff of the meat that hung from hooks in the stall next to them. "I wonder how long that's been up there." he said. "Remember what George said about the cleanliness of these places."

"Oh come on, Friedrich. You worry too much."

She pulled him along in front of stalls where they became enveloped by the cries of bartering and the aromas of spice, dried fish and animals on the hoof.

"Over here," she said. "Everything looks so fresh." They entered a shop where multicolored fabrics were draped over bins of vegetables. As she filled sacks with lettuce and beans, Friedrich felt the spurious glances from stall keepers and shoppers around them. A group of Arab men pressed closer. He winced as sharp elbows dug into his ribs and jostled him from both sides.

"Let's get the hell out of here," he said. He threw a hand-full of coins on the counter and pushed their way out to the square. "I don't have a good feeling here," he said, clutching his side. "We'll ask Hilary where it's safe to go."

Back at their apartment, he poured two glasses of wine. He handed one to Eva and stood by the open window, sucking deep on a cigarette. From the shops below, he heard the chatter of Jewish neighbours; most of it directed toward primitive Arabs and incompetent British overlords. Gloom settled in the pit of his stomach. What he'd hoped to escape had not been left far behind. This was not the normal life he wanted.

"I'm not sure about this," he said. "Maybe George was right. I don't feel welcome around here."

"No more running," Eva said. "We're going to help build a country where Jews can be safe."

"It's a foolish dream," he said. "It's not worth the trouble."

"What. To have a home where we can walk the streets without being threatened? What are we supposed to do? Stay caged up in some expatriate zone for the rest of our lives? We must make it into more than a dream, Friedrich. You and I will play our part."

"How do you expect to do that?" His voice was flat. He threw back his wine and poured more.

"The same as we did in Vienna. We'll take care of people and show them we're worthy of their trust." She wrapped her arms around his neck and kissed him. "What else can we do, Herr Doktor?"

⅄

The following week, Friedrich walked the streets until he came upon a vacated corner store with a For Rent sign in the window. The busy thoroughfare marked the boundary between the Arab and Jewish Quarters. The space looked neglected but through the dusty windows he could see a water spout and a light socket on the ceiling. With the grime cleaned off, the windows would provide a bright open feeling. He wrote down the address of the owner and followed a maze of alleys until he located a dry goods shop. A Palestinian man sweeping the floor looked up as he walked in. Friedrich spoke no Arabic so took a chance on English.

"Office for rent?" he said, holding up the slip of paper.

The man frowned as he stepped forward to look at the address. "What is your business?"

"Dentistry. I want to open a clinic. You speak English?"

"I learned as a boy. My family exported oranges to England for many years, until a Zionist kibbutz forced us out. If you're one of them do not expect favors from me."

"My wife and I have no ties to anyone," Friedrich said. "We're new here and we need to earn a living. I believe many people in this neighbourhood could use our help."

The man set down his broom and gestured toward a table next to the wall. "Take a seat and we'll have some tea." He shouted toward the back of the shop and offered his hand. "My name is Mohammed Abbas."

"Friedrich Mendelssohn. I'm pleased to meet you."

A teenager hurried out with two cups of tea and a bowl of sugar. His lack of eye contact or acknowledgement left Friedrich uneasy. Abbas stirred sugar into each cup and pulled out a package of Woodbine cigarettes. He offered one to Friedrich.

"Tell me about yourself," he said, snapping his lighter shut. "You speak with a different accent."

"I'm from Germany," Friedrich said. "My wife and I escaped to Istanbul and arrived here a month ago. Your space looks about the right size and it's in a good location."

"I see," Abbas said. "The store is in a mixed neighbourhood. Is that what you want?"

"Yes, it's near where I live."

"I have not rented this space since it was ransacked by Jews five years ago. They killed the butcher because he didn't follow kosher rules. He was my grandfather." Abbas's gaze drifted out to the street before he flicked his ash and looked back at Friedrich.

"I'm sorry," Friedrich said. "I'm hoping to help mend some of those wounds. They've been festering between our communities for too long."

Abbas exhaled through his nostrils and stubbed out his cigarette. "Do you plan to treat everyone who comes to your shop?"

"Yes," Friedrich said. "Anyone who comes through our door."

"And your employees? Will they all be Jews?"

"That wouldn't make sense," Friedrich said. "Not with so many Palestinians in the neighborhood. I'll need workers who speak both Arabic and Hebrew. My wife and I speak English but our German won't be of much use here."

"There will be resistance," Abbas said. "From both sides. People in the area deal with their own. With the pressures from Europe right now, this may not be a good idea. The western district might be a better choice for you." He stood up and called his boy to serve a customer who had just walked in. He lit another cigarette and said: "But the community needs someone like you, Mendelssohn. Let's go have a look and see if it will suit your purpose."

Friedrich measured the space and confirmed that nine hundred square feet was adequate. The back door opened to a courtyard with a dilapidated shed.

"That used to be the chicken coop," Abbas said.

"It will be good for storage." He looked around the shaded yard. "And this will be a nice quiet spot to have a smoke between patients."

They walked back to the shop and Abbas scribbled his terms on a sheet of paper.

"I'm doing you a favor," Abbas said. "Many will not be happy to see a Jew setting up business here. What can you do for me?"

"I'm almost broke," Friedrich said. "I can't afford to pay more. What do you want?"

Abbas pointed to the gap at the front of his mouth. "For me, my wife and my boys."

"Free dental work for you and your family?" Abbas nodded as he stuck another Woodbine between his lips. He offered one to Friedrich and flicked his lighter. Friedrich exhaled and met his eyes.

"I can't do that for nothing, Mohammed. How about two months free rent to get me on my feet?"

"Very well, but I must caution you again. Opening in this area is a risk. Your success will be good for me but I cannot provide compensation if you have to leave."

"My wife won't let me do that," Friedrich said. Both men chuckled and shook hands. Friedrich felt the acidity in his stomach. It could mean disaster. But if he located in the safer part of the city, he would always wonder. Could he help bridge the gap between the two cultures? He had to take the risk.

"I will spread a good word in my community," Abbas said, as he handed Friedrich the key.

"Thank you. I'll need all the help I can get."

⅄

When they had cleaned the floor and walls, Friedrich and Eva used chalk and a measuring tape to trace the dimensions of each room from a design he had drafted. They outlined the reception area with space for a wide counter, filing cabinets and a typewriter. A grin crossed his face.

"What?" she said.

"Helga used to grumble about being so cramped. She'd be happy with this."

"Yes, it's much better. I wonder how she is?"

"I hope she found another job and left those thieving bastards. She never said anything about Nazis but I know she had no use for them."

They outlined the dimensions of two operating rooms and positioned them against the windows to take advantage of the light. Between the rooms, they measured off space for sterilization and laboratory work. A hallway led to a private office that looked into the courtyard.

Outside in the shade they sipped tea while Friedrich reviewed five pages of specifications for the electrical and plumbing work. When he finished, he rolled them up and lit a cigarette.

"Can't think of anything else," he said. "We'll put it out for tenders next week."

"What about that?" Eva said, pointing at the chicken coop.

"No money to fix it right now. A good dose of bleach will get rid of that smell. We'll do something with it later."

He placed announcements in Jewish and Arabic newspapers and awarded all contracts to the lowest bidder. If he detected reluctance from either an Arab or a Jew to work alongside someone from the other community, he voided the contract. Word spread that the dentist, Mendelssohn, based his decisions upon merit.

Bartering services when possible to preserve his dwindling supply of cash, he demanded the highest quality of workmanship, holding back payment until everything was completed to his satisfaction. A man of his word, he expected nothing less in return.

George Beesley scoured surplus dental equipment from military warehouses while Eva canvassed schools for prospective employees. She settled upon a convent and interviewed each graduating student before she hired two bright girls best suited for the job. Friedrich had made his qualifications clear. One would be Jewish with fluency in both Yiddish and Hebrew. The other would be Arabic. Both candidates were to be proficient in English so they could communicate with each other and with Friedrich and Eva.

After thirty days, they had transformed the interior into a sparkling dental office, and on a rainy Monday morning they opened for business. Daniella Weinstein and Adlyia Habibi stood at the doorway in starched uniforms and looked down the street at a line of people stretching around the block. As the crowd pressed toward the entrance, their pushing and shoving, reminded Friedrich too much of the pier in Constanta.

"We can't let this get out of hand," he said, to the girls. "Cut slips of paper and number each one. Hand them out according to position in line." With both girls translating, he promised to see the first fifty people that day. The remainder could make appointments with Eva.

Their first patient was a pregnant sixteen-year-old Palestinian girl who looked as if she might give birth any minute. She had never seen a dentist in her life and every tooth in her mouth was decayed beyond repair. She needed them all extracted. Her tears reflected the agony caused by her rotted upper incisors.

Adlyia translated his instructions and the girl pulled her hands away from her mouth. He delivered two injections below each eye where the nerves ran down to the upper front teeth. Within moments her pain vanished and she looked up at him as if he were a god.

While her anaesthesia became profound, he walked into the second operatory, where an Orthodox Jew in a black hat and ringlets clutched the shoulders of a young boy. He hissed, "What kind of Jew keeps us waiting while my son suffers here in silence? It's disgusting that you're seeing one of them. I'm not sure I want you touching him."

Friedrich scrubbed and turned to face the man.

"The last time I heard a stupid remark like that was from an SS Colonel. He was referring to a Jewish girl with a toothache, about the same age as your boy here. I thought I left that kind of ignorance back in Europe. Unfortunately I was wrong."

"This is different. This land was promised to us by God. Arabs have no right to be here. They're trespassers. You encourage them to stay by treating them. Why don't they have their own dentists? Because they're too incompetent and lazy."

"Another word and I will ask you to take your son elsewhere."

"Water and oil never mix, Herr Doktor." He grabbed the boy's hand. "Come, Jacob. This place is not for us."

Daniella and Adlyia jumped out of the way as the man dragged his crying son from the room.

Friedrich spoke to the girls.

"That's the attitude I won't allow. No exceptions. We treat everyone, no matter who they are, what they look like or how much money they have. Is that understood?"

Adlyia was the first to speak. "But what he said is true, Doctor. Arabs and Jews don't associate here. It's not allowed. We keep to ourselves."

"We met at the convent," Daniella said. "I was sent there because the nuns give the best education. If not for that, my parents would never allow me to be around Arab girls. I have never told them that Adlyia is my best friend. They wouldn't allow it."

"When people see how we can work together in this office, it will change their minds," Friedrich said. He scribbled a note in the boys chart and tossed it to the side. "Now let's get back to that young woman before she has her baby in our chair."

For the next seven months, they worked ten hours a day, six days a week, closing only on the Sabbath. Friedrich's reputation of treating everyone regardless of ethnicity or social standing became widespread. Those who attended knew better than to test his patience. The animosity that prevailed on the streets was not tolerated within the walls of his office.

λ

Near the end of December 1944, after the last patient of the day had been dismissed, he latched the door, poured two glasses of wine and sat down at the reception desk beside Eva.

"A toast to our success," he said. "It's been about a year now."

With weary eyes she looked at him and sighed. "I was so optimistic when we started but now I'm not so sure. I still wake up in the middle of the night, thinking someone is going to knock down the door."

"That will take a long time to go away. Regardless of all the problems, we're more secure here. Nobody's going to arrest us or ship us off to a camp."

"But for how long? You can see how they look at us on the streets. It's getting worse. You never know if someone is going to walk up and knife you in the back. I'm always nervous, Friedrich." She brought the glass to her lips and didn't put it down until it was half empty.

"Try not to worry so much, liebling. The allies have crossed the German border. The Japanese are crumbling in the east. The war will be over this coming year. The British want to wash their hands of this place and go home. They'll come up with something fair to both sides."

"I wish I felt the same way. Both the Jews and the Arabs hate the British. Nobody trusts anyone around here." She finished her wine and held the glass out for more.

"We've survived and that's what counts." They intertwined arms but he saw the strain of the past twelve months in her eyes. Was it too soon to celebrate?

He raised his glass. "To life."

"L'Chaim," she said, pressing her lips to his.

CHAPTER 13

On the same day, in a colder and grimmer part of the world, SS Colonel Heinz Bauer stood on the platform from where he had inspected the high-efficiency crematorium the year before. Inside his pocket were orders to evacuate all able-bodied prisoners from the Auschwitz concentration camp. He looked over a crowd of fifty-six thousand men who were to be marched west into the German heartland. Standing at his side was Master Sergeant Werner Armbruster.

"Do you remember that Hungarian Jew who spat at me last year?" Bauer said. "The one who was calling to his children? Your men had to beat him unconscious before they could haul him away."

"How could I forget," Armbruster said. "We had problems with him after that but he was strong as hell so we kept him working. I lost track of him. He probably got shot or gassed."

⅄

Both men would have been unable to recognize the twenty-seven-year-old Gabor Erhmann had they been asked to pick him out from the crowd. In the past year, he had lost over forty pounds. With hunched shoulders and skin that clung like crepe paper, he looked beyond sixty. Ongoing insubordination had left him with a broken nose and a fractured jaw. His front teeth had been cleaved off by rifle butts, leaving infected roots that dripped pus into the back of his throat. Most of one ear had been chewed off in a fight. His frame shuddered as he coughed up phlegm from his latest bout with pneumonia.

Erhmann had been the eldest of three brothers, all weakened by months of deprivation in the Lodz ghetto before they arrived at Auschwitz. For the first two weeks, he had given his siblings all his daily rations but it proved not enough. Both died in his arms. He had not seen his wife or his children since he had called out to them on the ramp the year before. Their voices still rang in his ears and brought tears as he thought of them now. He had survived in Auschwitz long enough to know that they had been gassed in Bauer's industrialized slaughterhouse with thousands of others.

He vowed to avenge their deaths and had passed his nights lying on a plank visualizing how he would slice off the fingers, limbs and tongues of those responsible. His nostrils twitched, anticipating the scent of their roasting flesh while his victims hung over slow-burning fires begging to die. It was a scene he played each night until sleep rescued him a few hours before dawn.

Anonymous within the crowd, he peered up at the SS Colonel whose name was first on his list of retribution.

⅄

Master Sergeant Armbruster shouted into a microphone that amplified his voice to all corners of the camp.

"You men are being evacuated west to become part of a vital new mission. Our march will be long and hard but we have no time for delay. Anyone who slows down or tries to escape will be shot. Do not be the first to test us because our orders are clear." He looked over to the entrance and raised his arm. "Open the gates."

The men moved forward ten abreast, wearing ragged overcoats, light trousers and boots with little sole. Erhmann wrapped his arms around the two skeletal torsos walking on either side of him. "Stay close and maintain the pace," he whispered. "I won't let you fall."

As the column walked through the gate and lowered their shoulders into the headwinds of a blizzard, Bauer's eyes narrowed. "Goddamn incompetence," he said. "There should have never been this many left to evacuate." He returned the sergeant's salute and raised his voice. "Do your job, Armbruster. Kill off the weakest. We don't have the resources to feed them."

During the afternoon the two men Erhmann supported succumbed to the cold. Their legs stopped moving. To avoid attention from the guards, he held the collars of their coats and let the bodies slip down where they became trampled by the thousands walking behind. He bundled himself with one coat and passed the other forward.

Ten days later, he and twenty thousand others reached a rail-yard and were herded into cattle cars like the one that had brought him to Auschwitz. For another week, as the train moved west into howling winds, guards threw dead and dying bodies along the tracks until Erhmann and the remaining survivors trudged through the gates of the Dora-Mittelbau work camp. They had come to assemble V2 rockets in a final effort to save the Reich.

Deemed valuable as an engineer, he received better accommodation and a more nutritious diet than most. He increased his exercise regimen to one thousand push-ups and leg squats each night. He fell exhausted into bed, but sleep still did not come easy, as his mind planned. With duties that took him outside the camp, he studied routines and familiarized himself with the lay of the land.

On an overcast night in April 1945, after the snow had melted, he slipped out of his hut and crawled into the back of a truck delivering rockets to a rail-yard. He hid behind the driver and Master Sergeant Armbruster, until the truck pulled over on a deserted part of the highway. Armbruster and the driver stepped out of the cab and walked over to urinate in the ditch.

Nimble and strong, Erhmann jumped down and crept up behind them.

As they chuckled and turned back toward the headlights, their eyes bulged at his towering silhouette.

With two blows, he knocked them both to the ground. He snapped the driver's neck and then pulled Armbruster to his feet. With the Master Sergeant grappling to free himself, Erhmann's fingers encircled his throat and squeezed until the crunch of Armbruster's cartilage and bone rippled through the night.

He dragged both bodies to the truck, aware that he would reach the first security roadblock thirty minutes onward. He drove about half the distance and pulled alongside the rim of a canyon. As the truck rolled over the edge, he stood back to watch the explosion of munitions that engulfed the gorge.

Under the cover of darkness, he fled west, moving along creek-beds and coulees to escape the dog units who scoured the countryside for him. Raving like a madman, he stumbled upon a platoon of American soldiers who took him back to a hospital where he was treated for pneumonia, malnutrition and the acute psychosis that had almost got him killed.

A year later, standing on the front steps of the hospital, he looked east and then west. He yearned to return to his village, to bury the past and re-build his community that had been so ruthlessly extinguished. But a more primitive element within thirsted for revenge. His jaw thrust forward and a snarl curled his upper lip. A shadow clouded his eyes and a guttural sound rose from his throat. He descended the steps and walked toward the train that would take him west to Paris.

$$\lambda$$

In early January 1946, Friedrich sat at his kitchen table enjoying a moment with a copy of The London Times. Sipping from his cup, he turned to the front page and then suddenly bolted back in his chair. With spilt coffee drib-bling off the tabletop, he stared at the headline and an archival photograph of SS Colonel Heinz Bauer.

Architects of Death Camps Discovered in Munich. The article re-ported that the remains of SS Lieutenant Rudy Krause and members of his engineering team had been discovered in a basement. All the deceased except one had died of cyanide poisoning preceding an explosion and fire that de-stroyed the villa in which they hid. Friedrich turned the page.

A Luger pistol found next to one of the charred skeletons was identified as belonging to SS Colonel Heinz Bauer. Bauer was responsible for expedit-ing the accelerated death quotas in the camps during the last year of the war.

Investigators say he appears to have shot himself in the right temple after setting the timer which detonated the explosion. Dental records confirm that the skull found near the pistol was that of Bauer.

Friedrich fired up another cigarette and handed the paper to Eva.

"Now we know the truth," he said. "He wasn't planning to die like a hero defending Berlin. He was thinking of only one thing."

"Are you surprised? He was a psychopathic maniac and he used you."

"We're the only ones who know," he said. "You realize that I had no other choice." He paused and looked into her eyes. "We'd both be dead otherwise."

"We should contact the authorities," she said. "Right now. Before his trail gets cold."

"He knew we were coming here. If we let it be known that those may not be his remains, he could be captured or he might feel compromised. Either way he'll send someone to kill us."

"He could do that anyway."

"Yes, but if I'm right in my suspicions about the torpedo attack, he might already think we're dead. Even if he discovers we survived, he's likely to leave us alone to not bring attention to himself." He shook his head and looked at the picture. "We don't want to get involved with this in any way."

"I've heard rumors of Nazis fleeing to Argentina," Eva said.

"And if so we'll never hear of him again. He wants to disappear." He drummed his fingers on the table. "I'm certain that's behind us. Our trouble now is with the goddamn Arabs. Won't we ever be left alone?" He lit another cigarette.

"The Zionists have more political influence with Truman than the Arabs," he said. "He'll push the United Nations to vote in favour of an Israeli State. The Arabs won't stand for it...unless some kind of fair agreement is reached." He took another drag and exhaled. "I'm not holding my breath on that."

He went back to his paper but his mind buzzed. His reputation would be ruined if it were ever discovered that he provided a mass murderer with a means to escape justice, even if it had saved their lives. But maybe Eva was right and now was the time to come forward. Do the right thing. Orchestrate

Bauer's capture and see him hang for his crimes. He reread the piece. Nothing to gain and everything to lose. With the newspaper folded under his arm, he grabbed his jacket.

"It's still early," she said. "Where're you going?"

"I'm throwing this paper in the garbage and then I've got some things to do at the office. The walk will clear my head."

Chapter 14

Work was Friedrich's only refuge. Massacres and reprisals between Jews and Arabs had become commonplace. He found it easier to ignore newscasts with their grizzly details than to dwell on a situation beyond anyone's control. He no longer allowed Eva to shop or walk the streets by herself and they always returned home before dark. Nevertheless, they were still determined to provide dental care to the multitudes who needed their help.

The office was a brisk, half-hour walk away each morning. As he passed by stacks of copper pipe, he waved to Firouz, the plumber who had installed water lines in his office. Farther down the street he called out to Isadore, a carpenter from Poland, who had built his instrument cabinets. Both had been reluctant to work together until he threatened to terminate their contracts. They established a truce, and then found that they had much in common and began referring work to each other, exactly as Friedrich had hoped they would. It always brought a smile to his face when he greeted them.

He arrived at the office an hour before his first appointment. Oddly, the curtains were already drawn. Adlyia sat behind the front desk with circles under her eyes. She had obviously been crying.

"I'm surprised you're here so early," he said.

She blinked and dabbed away her tears. "Good morning, Doctor. I came in to catch up on a few things."

"Why the sad eyes?" He came around to her side of the desk. "Not feeling well? Is it the baby?"

"I'm feeling fine. It's my husband, Jamal." She sniffed and wiped her nose. "They took his job away."

"What do you mean?" Her tears started again and he waited while she composed herself, thinking how much he admired Jamal's murals that decorated the entrances of mosques in the area.

"There's no money to pay him. It's all going to the militias. I'll be having the baby in a few weeks. I don't know what we'll do, Doctor."

"Tell Jamal to come and see me this afternoon," he said.

⅄

Around five o'clock, Friedrich looked out into the empty waiting room and saw Jamal sitting in a chair staring at the floor.

"Jamal. Come out to the courtyard." They sat down and Friedrich poured coffee and lit cigarettes. "Adlyia told me what happened," he said, breaking the silence. "I want to help."

Jamal pulled the cigarette from his lips and crushed it into the dirt.

"How? By having Adlyia come back to work? She's must stay home with our child. It's not a man's place."

"That's not what I mean," Friedrich said. "I'm offering you a job...to train as a dental technician. I've seen the fine work that you do with glass. I'll pay you what you're earning now and teach you everything you need to know about this business."

Jamal stared across at Friedrich.

"Why are you helping me?"

"Just promise me you'll do the same when you have a chance. It's the only way our peoples will survive together in this land. We must become partners."

Jamal grabbed Friedrich's hands and dropped to his knees.

"No need for that," Friedrich said, helping him to his feet. "Thank me with your work. A master technician is a priceless asset for a dentist. I'll see you at 6:30 tomorrow morning and we'll get started."

⅄

The next morning Friedrich unrolled drawings of the shed with a renovated interior that included specifications for the electrical, plumbing and propane systems required to transform it into a dental laboratory.

"I've been planning this for some time," he told Jamal. "Come and take a look." He opened the door. "This used to be for chickens." Light flooded the floor and mice scurried for cover. "Whew! We'll need to leave this open for awhile." He fanned away the foul air. "You can start by getting it cleaned up. I'll put out tenders for the work."

"I just helped a friend build a bathroom inside his home," Jamal said. "We did it all ourselves."

"That's good," Friedrich said, "but I want to support the local tradesmen." He handed Jamal the drawings. "You can begin reinforcing those walls and replacing tiles on the roof. After that you'll supervise. I want you to have enough energy left in the evenings to master the material in this book."

He held up a manual with the sketch of a molar on its cover. The title read: Dental Anatomy. Inside, three-dimensional renderings illustrated each permanent tooth in the human dentition. He un-wrapped a pouch that held carving instruments and a pair of calipers graduated in millimeters. On the table was a box containing blocks of carving wax. He held one up.

"I want you to carve replicas of each tooth to their exact dimensions. They're listed at the side of each drawing. Don't be afraid of making mistakes and starting over. I've got lots of wax and this will take time. It's not easy and everything must be...precise. Don't bring me anything until it's the best you can do. You can start with the central incisor."

Over the next two weeks, Jamal reinforced the walls with new studs, replaced cracked roof tiles and framed in two large windows. When Friedrich had awarded the bids, Jamal coordinated the workers. Using Beesley's contacts again Friedrich purchased used laboratory equipment languishing in army warehouses. Two days after the construction was completed, Adlyia gave birth to their son, Fadi. A month later, Jamal walked into Friedrich's office smiling and set his first wax carving on the desk.

"What do you think?"

Friedrich rolled it in his fingers and sighed.

"It looks like a cribbage peg." He blurted out the words in the high-pitched German accent that escaped whenever he became upset or impatient. The pride in Jamal's eyes vanished and the corners of his lips turned down.

"What do you mean, 'cribbage peg'?" Jamal said. "I've never heard of that."

"Like a minaret, then. No shape, no flow, too many sharp edges." He snapped the carving in half and threw the chunks in the wastebasket. "You're a talented fellow, Jamal. I know because I've seen your mosaic work. But this is different." He saw that his words had bruised Jamal's confidence. He paused and took a breath.

"I'm sorry to be blunt," he said. "It's a commendable first effort but not nearly good enough. Come back this evening and I'll show you how to make it better."

"When can I start doing some real work?" Jamal said. "I want to earn what you're paying me. I don't feel right accepting money for this."

"Only when I say you're ready. Not a day before." He caught himself again. "I look upon this as an investment. You still have a long way to go and there are no shortcuts. This will be the hardest thing you've ever done." He slapped a new box of wax into Jamal's hand. "Now, I must get back to work. I'll see you tonight."

⅄

The long evenings spent redoing carvings paid off. After only three months, Friedrich made practical use of Jamal's improving skills by teaching him how to process wax molds into acrylic dentures. In a neighbourhood where most teenagers needed their teeth removed before they reached twenty, Jamal developed a reputation. The false teeth he fabricated were so white and straight that brides-to-be demanded their fathers pay to have their decayed and crooked ones extracted. A new set of Jamal's plates guaranteed a beautiful smile on their wedding day.

For the few with a viable dentition and the financial resources to afford his time, Friedrich rekindled his passion for the gold-work that had been his forte in Vienna. Jamal persevered and Friedrich's instincts proved correct. After a year, Jamal could fabricate gold fillings of shameless quality, on par with the finest European technicians with whom Friedrich had ever worked.

It had been almost three years since Friedrich and Eva had arrived in Jerusalem and opened the practice. Although Friedrich missed the culture and romance of Europe, he accepted that Palestine had become their home.

Eva's happiest moments came when she cared for Fadi. Adlyia had been raised by nuns and Jamal was estranged from his Sunni parents, who disapproved of his marriage to a Shia orphan. When the couple asked Friedrich and Eva to be honorary grandparents, they accepted with gratitude. Friedrich hoped Fadi would soon be joined by brothers and sisters who might fill Eva's void with more of the joy she deserved.

CHAPTER 15

Two nights after an eighteen-man platoon of Irgun militia had been found dead, their throats slit as they slept, Friedrich passed the shops owned by Firouz and Isadore and felt unsettled by the silence. No rattling of pipes or whines of a saw. When he reached the usually busy street connecting the Jewish and Arab quarters it sat empty. The store where he bought his coffee remained shuttered. He checked his watch to see if he hadn't mistaken the time and then noticed two Jordanian soldiers blocking traffic from entering or leaving the Jewish quarter. An officer stepped out of from behind a sandbagged barrier as Friedrich walked up.

"Stay back."

"I work here," Friedrich said. "That's my office across the street. What the hell's this all about?" He pointed toward the barbwire stretched across the road. "Many of my patients live around here. They need to pass."

"Nobody will be crossing."

"That's ridiculous," Friedrich said. "All their food comes in by truck. They'll starve without access."

"That's the point." The sneering officer folded his arms.

"Who's your commander?"

"General Abd al-Hasayni."

"I want to speak to him." Tensions in the neighbourhood were high. Revenge was on everyone's mind. This blockade was another escalation, a slow twisting of the blade.

"He has no time. Go about your business or I'll have you arrested."

Friedrich stormed across the street and burst into his office.

⋏

Baseema, the Palestinian receptionist who had replaced Adlyia ran around from behind the counter.

"I'm so thankful you're here, Doctor." She pointed at the soldiers through the window. "They're turning away our patients. They won't let anyone across."

"It's pure Ara...stupidity." Friedrich bit off the word, Arab. He had been doing a lot of this lately. Was the situation getting to him? Was he becoming a racist? "The British will order humanitarian convoys," he said. "But it could take days to put something in place."

"I'm afraid for what might happen," she said. "Omar won't listen to me. He wants to join the fight."

Friedrich rubbed the creases on his forehead. Since he'd opened the practice, he'd been treating Baseema's family in exchange for office cleaning. Baseema, the eldest, now worked fulltime in the clinic. Omar was the youngest. Friedrich had held a special fondness for the lad since he had first treated him as a courageous boy with a mouthful of abscessed teeth.

Now a bright outgoing teenager, Omar had expressed interest in becoming a dentist. When Friedrich invited him to spend time observing him work, his attentiveness and thoughtful questions had so impressed Friedrich that he borrowed textbooks from the British Army Dental Clinic for Omar to read. Only a week before, he had written a letter in support of Omar's university application. The ungrateful little sod. He pushed his disappointment aside.

"You're safe here, Baseema. Reschedule everyone who can't come in today. When you're done, go home and talk some sense into that brother of yours." He started toward his office and then stopped and looked back at her. "And tell him if he wants my help he must attend school and stay off the streets. Not act like a damn fool and get himself shot."

⋏

With no patients to treat, Friedrich cleaned up the paper work on his desk. Today was Fadi's first birthday, and with their larger apartment, he and Eva had invited Jamal and Adlyia over for a birthday party with Opa Friedrich and Oma Eva. By mid-afternoon he had finished.

He went to the desk where his assistant, Daniella, waited by the phone.

"We're all done for today," he said. "Take the back door and go straight home. No lingering at the market. Call me before you come in tomorrow morning."

He found Jamal hunched over his bench in the laboratory.

"Eva wants you to stay with us overnight," he said. "Adlyia and Fadi are already there. I'm walking home now."

"Just a few more things to do," Jamal said. "I brought my motorcycle. You can hop on and we'll drive over together."

"Before it gets dark," Friedrich said. "Too many guns out there right now."

⅄

They shared a meal accompanied by sombre conversation about the fighting, and then put their concerns aside and fussed over the birthday boy. When they had sung and blown out the single candle on the cake, Eva and Adlyia took Fadi upstairs for his bath. Friedrich spiked his coffee with cognac and sat down with Jamal.

"I'm proud of what you've accomplished this past year, Jamal."

"Thank you, Doctor. Adlyia and I can't thank you enough. I love this work."

"I can see that. You're damn near as obsessed as I am." He chuckled and they touched cups in a toast. "Eva and I have been talking. We want to offer you another opportunity. To help you build a future for your family."

"How do you mean?" Jamal tapped the ash off his cigarette.

"I want to sell you the laboratory business. At my cost."

Jamal coughed and set down his cup. "Me! Buy the business?"

"I'll provide you with an interest free loan. You'll attract other dentists as clients and pay me back over the next few years."

Jamal held up his cup and looked over at the bottle of cognac. "Can I have a little of that?"

Friedrich grinned as he popped the cork and poured.

"I've never dreamed of ever having my own business," Jamal said. "It has never happened in my family. They would be proud...if they knew." He stood up and clasped Friedrich's hand. "I won't let you down, Doctor. I promise."

"Maybe, you can let them know in a year or so," Friedrich said. "Break the ice and introduce them to their grandson."

Jamal looked up with a smile as the two women started down the stairs.

"You tell her." Friedrich said.

"What are you two up to?" Adlyia trotted down the steps. A quizzical smile lit up her face.

Friedrich looked at Eva and winked.

"Opa has offered to sell me the laboratory," Jamal said.

Adyia shrieked then covered her mouth and looked up. "It's good that he's a sound sleeper." She ran over and wrapped her arms around Friedrich and Jamal.

Then a muffled explosion made the windows shudder and wiped the smiles from their faces. They listened for Fadi, but no sounds came from the bedroom.

"That was close," Friedrich said. "Good that you're staying here tonight."

"I'll make more coffee to have with the cake," Eva said. She filled the kettle and set it on the stove. Before she could return to the table, a loud thumping jarred the hinges of the front door.

Friedrich brought his index finger across his lips. "Shh..."

Eva tiptoed to the bottom of the stairs and held Adlyia's hand. "He's still sleeping," she whispered. "Leave him for now."

Three harder bangs cracked the wooden molding around the deadbolt. Friedrich moved to get the door.

"Wait." Jamal grabbed the poker from the fireplace and raised it like a bat. Outside, a truck screeched to a stop.

"Who is it?" Friedrich yelled.

"Irgun militia. Open up or we'll knock it down." Friedrich looked at Jamal and then over at the two women who cringed at the bottom of the stairs.

"Okay, open it...slowly," Jamal said.

As Friedrich turned the latch, the door flew inwards and caught him square on the chin.

An armed commando tumbled through the doorway and trained his gun on Jamal. "Drop it," he yelled, "or you're dead."

Two other commandos bolted into the room followed by an officer who looked over at the women and pointed to the sofa. "You two...sit down over there."

The commandos wrenched the poker from Jamal's hand and frisked him for weapons. Screams from the street came through the doorway as Friedrich staggered to his feet. Through the cloud of diesel exhaust drifting into the room, he saw his Arab neighbours being shoved into the back of a military transport.

"Identification!" The officer glared at Adlyia, then Jamal.

"You have no right to barge in here," Friedrich said, slamming the door. His Yiddish bore a thick German accent.

The officer grabbed his throat and shoved him against the wall. He drew a dagger from its scabbard and pressed it against Friedrich's jugular vein. "Don't tell me what's right, you German prick or I'll slit your fucking throat." He glanced at Jamal and Adlyia's identification cards. "You two don't belong here." He threw Friedrich aside and ordered his men. "Get'em outta here."

Adlyia started for the stairs but Eva grabbed her arm and yelled at the commando who stepped in her way. "Don't touch her." She locked eyes with the commando and pulled Adlyia's coat off the banister. "She'll need this." She draped the coat over Adlyia's shoulders and whispered. "Shhh...we'll bring him when it's safe."

"Let's go." The officer flung open the door and the commandos prodded Jamal and Adlyia out to the street.

"No, wait." Friedrich held up a business card with his name, address and phone number.

"I'm Doctor Friedrich Mendelssohn. These people work for me. Jamal is my technician and Adlyia is my assistant. Jamal and I worked together every evening this week. I can guarantee that he had nothing to do with those murders. I'll take full responsibility for both of them."

"They're Arab scum," the officer said. "If he's from around here, he knows who did it. The fucking cowards killed them in their sleep. One was my brother."

The word 'brother' sounded like braada to Friedrich, spoken with an inflection that he'd first heard in New York.

"You're from New York?"

"Na, Brooklyn."

"I'm truly sorry about your brother, sir." While the officer glared, his eyes red, Friedrich stepped forward and handed him his card. "You're making a terrible mistake here, officer. I can vouch for these two. They're not terrorists."

"You can't tell who is or who isn't. My orders are to ship them all across the Jordanian border. They'll be interrogated. If they're cleared, you can pick them up there."

Friedrich raised his arms to block the open doorway. "You're an American Jew for God's sake. Surely you can see this is wrong. It's the rule of the jungle."

"After what happened in Europe, I talked my braada into coming over here to help. We've been in the country two fucking weeks and he's dead." The officer's voice cracked and he wiped away the smudges on his cheek. "It's gonna' kill my maada when she finds out. Now get the fuck out of my way."

The truck pulled away. Eva ran upstairs and came back down with Fadi in her arms. The glazed expression that Friedrich hadn't seen since the mountains of Romania gripped her face again. She wavered from side to side and her chest heaved. He took her arm and helped her sit down with the baby.

"Did I do the right thing?" she said, bursting into tears. "Who knows where they're taking them?"

"You made the only decision you could," he whispered. He stroked his fingers through the boy's hair and kissed his forehead. "I'll get hold of George. Maybe he knows somebody who can help." He brought the phone to his ear and then dropped it back down. "They've cut the goddamn lines. I'll try and get over to Army Headquarters."

"He's going to be hungry soon," she said. "Try and find some fresh goat's milk before you go over there."

⚔

Flames reeking of gasoline stung his nose as he stepped out into the street. Down the block, the fence around Firouz's plumbing yard had been torn down. Shelves of pipe had been looted. Up the block more detonations sounded as the transport truck inched its way along the road. Jogging to catch up, he tried to look through a narrow gap in the awning for Adlyia and Jamal. Rifle butts broke his stride and knocked him windless to the curb. The raging fires, broken glass and most of all, the wailing of women and children, took him back to Vienna on the night the Nazi's came to power. What had they become?

He hurried to a night market where he found the last bottle of goat's milk floating in a bowl of melted ice. He snapped off the lid and sniffed before paying and stepped back outside. Light from a hotel on the other side of the street caught his eye and he ran into the lobby with money in his hand.

"Telephone, telephone," he said.

The clerk held up the receiver and shook his head. "Kaput."

By the time he rounded the corner of his block, the transport truck and militia were gone. The glow of lamps coloured the window shades of his Jewish neighbours while the smouldering homes and barking dogs of Arab families filled the void. Shattered glass glistened in the moonlight and his hands struggled to fit the key in the lock. The sense of déjà vu was over-whelming. Kristallnacht.

⚔

Adlyia and Jamal huddled together in the back of the transport with their knees scrunched to their chests.

As the truck drove along the empty streets, Adlyia nodded to other Arab families who were patients of the office. Children still wearing night clothes screamed at having been pulled from their beds by strange men, while mothers and fathers coaxed them to be quiet, assuring them they were safe.

After about an hour, the transport pulled to the side and as the dust cleared, Jamal saw that they had stopped at a cross-road. The lights of East Jerusalem flickered below and a convoy of six trucks and three escort vehicles drew up beside them. With his limited Hebrew, Jamal listened to the Jewish chatter filtering through the canopy.

"They're running two supply convoys to a kibbutz near the border," he whispered to Adlyia. "They're putting us with the first one and taking us to a camp inside Jordan."

"That's so far away," she said. The panic in her voice brought threatening glares from the two guards standing at the rear of the truck. She covered her mouth with her shawl. "I want to be with my baby, Jamal. I'm afraid we'll never see him again."

He wrapped his arm around her and drew her closer. "Stay calm. We'll figure out a way to jump off but it's too light right now." He nodded toward the two guards who drew on cigarettes. "They'd shoot us if we tried." He tugged at the ligatures holding the canvas to the frame. "I'll untie these knots. We'll slip out as soon as it's dark enough. Don't do anything to attract their attention."

In the escort vehicle behind them, he could see the American officer and the commandos who had pulled them from the house. The four men stood in the flatbed with their guns trained at the hills.

"They're expecting trouble," he whispered. "We might get lucky if there's a diversion."

The trucks jerked forward and the guards flicked their cigarettes and climbed back inside. As night fell and the convoy rolled east, Jamal worked the two knots behind his back until he felt them release. Leaning back, he pushed out the canvas from the frame until he could slip his arm through. He gathered the flap in his hands and nudged Adlyia.

"I've got them loose. There's enough room to slip out. I'll tell you when."

The convoy made good time along a straight road bordered by foothills until the drivers shifted gears and slowed for the descent toward the Jordan

River. The moon disappeared behind steep ridges and it got darker. Random flashes of headlights glanced along canyon walls.

"Now." Adlyia whispered. "We should jump now."

"We're still going too fast," Jamal said. "I'll tell you when and you go first. Don't wait for me. Run and hide behind the rocks and shrubs. Anywhere you can't be seen. Stay there and I'll find you, even if it takes 'till sunrise. Do you understand, Adlyia? Run as fast as you can."

She squeezed his hand. "I'm so afraid we won't see Fadi again. What's going to happen to him?"

"Don't worry about that now. He's safe with Oma and Opa. I promise you we'll be back with him soon. Just do what I say and we'll be fine."

⚘

When the last truck cleared the entrance to the pass, several furtive shadows leapt out from the roadside and rolled boulders into the middle. Moments later, an anti-tank shell exploded under the lead vehicle and spewed shrapnel through the driver's groin. The crackle of small arms fire reverberated through the corridor and bullets tore through the canopy. Jamal pulled Adlyia to the floor. "Stay down."

"Back this fucking thing up," the American officer screamed at the driver behind him. A shell whistled through the blackness and turned the truck into a fireball. Its blistering heat drove the American officer and his men behind the boulders.

Jamal kicked out the canvas with his legs. "Now, Adlyia, go! Hide and I'll find you." He pushed her through the opening and then started climbing out behind her. She pulled on his jacket and he rolled out hitting the ground and grabbing his shoulder. Another man pushed his children out behind them.

"I'm hit," Jamal said. His left arm dangled and Adlyia strained to pull him to his feet. They locked hands. "Run, run."

The American officer glanced toward the truck and pointed at the moving shadows.

"They're getting away," he yelled. "Let'em have it."

The commandos raked the canopy with gunfire and the officer lobbed two grenades under the truck's fuel tank. The explosion lit the canyon walls, incinerating everything within a ten-foot radius.

CHAPTER 16

Alerted by the sounds of battle from ahead, the soldiers in the second convoy climbed the ridges and counterattacked from the rear. The Arab attackers dissolved into the mountains and by sunrise all that remained was a tangle of smoking metal and a mass of charred bodies.

The American officer devoured one Camel cigarette after another as his men dragged the dead Palestinian civilians from the back of the destroyed transport. The bodies of the two he'd seen escaping lay splayed against the rocks. He kicked over their burnt torsos and recognized both faces. "These are the two innocents who were trying to escape. They got what they fucking deserved."

He and his second-in-command walked alongside the wreckage until beyond the ridges the road opened to a plain. The outlines of two village minarets stood like pencils in the distant hills.

"The bastards came from up there," he said. "Cordon off the road and comb the hillsides. Finish off any of those fuckers that're still twitchin'. We'll flatten those villages later."

He pointed to a level stretch of road near the bottom of the hill. "Bring up that tractor with the shovel. We'll dig a hole down there and bury them. Nobody needs to know about this."

人

Friedrich parked Jamal's motorcycle in front of British Army Headquarters. He rapped hard on the front door and paced back and forth until a bleary-eyed private released the latch and looked out.

"I need to speak to the officer-in-charge," he said. "Now. It's important."

"Pretty early for a Saturday morning, mate," said the private. "You'll have to wait." Friedrich sat and fidgeted for another half hour until the private ushered him in front of the duty officer.

"Sorry to barge in like this," Friedrich said. The officer, who looked about half his age, poured boiling water into a teapot.

"Care for a cup?"

Friedrich shook his head and spilled out the words. "An Irgun militia raided our street last night. They detained two of my Arab employees. Do you have any idea where they might be?"

"Slow down for Christ sake," said the officer. "My tea needs to steep." He opened a can of Sweet Caporal tobacco.

It had been Friedrich's favourite brand during his sojourn in London. The good old days. The officer rolled a pinch into a cigarette paper and licked the glue to seal it. He brought the tip to life before finally pouring the tea and sitting behind his desk. He looked across at Friedrich.

"We're goddamn near finished with this place. It can't come soon enough for me, mate. We should just let them have a go at each other until they come to their senses."

"But have you heard anything about this, sir?" The impatience in his voice raised the officer's eyebrows.

"There were rumblings last night about an ambush on the way to the river but we can't be sure. Getting to be one almost every night, isn't there?"

"Do you know about any camp inside the Jordanian border?"

"That's a UN thing," the officer said. "You'd have to check with them."

Friedrich swore and stormed out of the office. Goddamn useless bastard. He roared through empty streets until he reached a building used as a temporary UN headquarters. Inside the front door, he recognized a Swedish official he'd seen for an emergency toothache the week before. The heavyset man with blond hair neatly parted to the side, smiled at Friedrich as he walked up to the counter.

"Good morning, Herr Doctor. This is a surprise. I must thank you again for seeing me the other day." He rubbed his jaw. "Everything feels good. How can I help you?"

"My two Palestinian employees were arrested last night by what I'm sure was a rogue Irgun militia. They said they were taking them to a camp inside Jordan. Do you know anything about that?"

"There was a skirmish on the way to the river last night. We're trying to get some men in there right now but they've blocked the road. Have a seat. I'll make a few calls."

Friedrich watched the man's frown become more severe as he pressed the receiver to his ear. He could hear an agitated voice shouting on the other end of the line until the official hung up the phone. He dialed another number and spoke rapidly in Swedish before beckoning Friedrich into a room behind the counter.

"That first call was to the Irgun head of command. He's livid about the number of men he lost out there last night. A supply convoy was attacked. If he has any information about detained Palestinians, he isn't letting on. I also called the camp. They didn't receive a transport of Palestinians last night. I'm sorry I can't help you more but it's such a mess right now. I'll contact you if I hear anything."

Friedrich thanked the official for his assistance and turned toward the door. Sidestepping the people crowding behind him, he noticed a photo-graph tacked to an UNWRA bulletin board. A headline proclaimed the significance of the aid work being done by the United Nations agency for refugees displaced by the hostilities. What caught Friedrich's eye was a European looking man with an un-groomed beard who stood in the back-ground behind two Palestinian militants. Although the man did not look at all like Heinz Bauer, his fair skin filled Friedrich with of sense of unease. It couldn't be. He clambered out through the door his chest squeezed so tight he had a hard time breathing. Straddling the bike, he kick started the motor and roared away.

ᴧ

Friedrich arrived home to check on Eva and reassure her. She rocked Fadi in her arms and sat next to the radio which droned in the background.

"Did you find anything out?" she asked.

"Nobody knows a goddamned thing." He looked at the radio. "Turn it up, in case they announce something. I'm going to the office to see what's happening down there."

Be careful," she said. "There've been mobs on the streets."

He stuck to back lanes, avoiding the gangs of Arabs bent on killing Jews until he pulled up to the front of his office, where the curtains billowed through smashed glass. The front door hung ajar, torn off its hinges. Slashed wires from overhead lights dangled from the ceiling and patient charts littered the floor. He heard the sound of running water and saw it pooling into the hallway. Sloshing back to the operatories, he found geysers shooting up from where his dental equipment had been ripped from its moorings. He kicked open the door to the toilet and gagged at the foulness. Pinching his nose, he bent under the sink and turned off the main water valve. Smeared in feces across the wall: Massacre the Jews. Nausea flooded his body as he thought of the harm that might have come to his interracial team, Daniella, Baseema, Adlyia and Jamal. They had done so much good working together. Why had it come to this?

At the sound of a knock, he snapped his head around to see Baseema's fifteen-year-old brother, Omar, taller and more muscular than when he'd seen him last.

"What the hell are you doing here? Coming to look at your handiwork?"

Omar's face blanched at the harshness in Friedrich's voice.

"I saw the motorcycle outside. I'm sorry this had to happen, Doctor Mendelssohn."

"It's a goddamned disgrace, Omar. After all we did for your people."

"We had no choice. The Irgun attacked our neighbourhood, so we came back and destroyed everything owned by Jews. Two of my brothers got shot and killed. Baseema and my mother and father were taken to one of the camps in Jordan. I still can't find them."

Friedrich hadn't heard from Baseema since he'd sent her home the morning the barricade went up. Now he feared the worst. "What about Daniella?"

"I don't know." Omar went to the ransacked reception desk. "After the mob passed I came in and hid some instruments. Maybe you can still use them."

He pulled a burlap sack from under the rubble and handed it to Friedrich. "These were all over the floor," he said, opening the sack to the glint of stainless steel.

"I'm sad to hear about your brothers. They were so gentle with you when we extracted your baby teeth. What happened to them?"

"They were protecting our house when the Irgun cleared the neighbourhood. A grenade killed them both. Baseema and I are the only ones left to look after my mother. My father's blind and has arthritis. He can't walk."

Friedrich righted a chair and sat down. "So many bad things going on," he said. "It's terrible for both sides." He dug in his wallet and handed Omar one of his last gold wafers. "Until you can find work," he said.

"This is very kind of you," Omar said. "I hear what my people say about Jews, but with you, I know it's not true."

"What do they say?"

"That Jews are stealing our land. That they all must be slaughtered."

"I hear the same things about Arabs," Friedrich said. "That you have no right to be here."

"This is our home," Omar said. "And I must take revenge on those who killed my brothers. You're a good man, Doctor, but most Jews are not. They hate us and they want to drive us into Jordan."

Omar's anger echoed through the empty rooms and he turned toward the door. Without looking back, he said, "Take your family away while you can, Doctor Mendelssohn. This is only the beginning. We'll never rest until the Jews are gone from this place. It's ours."

Friedrich followed him outside and shouted as Omar waded into the crowds filling the street. "Be careful, Omar. Shalom, my friend."

He went back to look for anything else of value. He found a plaster model on the floor that had not shattered when a cupboard was torn from the wall. When he read the patient's name, he pictured a Palestinian woman, the principal of the school around the corner, now closed. He remembered how snug her gold fillings had fit, true clinical works of art that represented the only part of his life over which he had any control.

His eyes misted and he tossed the model into the corner amidst other chunks of broken plaster. At the door, he took one last look around and walked out. What a goddamn shame.

Across the road three Jordanian soldiers stood guard.

"Anyone here speak English?" he asked, approaching them.

The guard holding rank stepped forward and spoke with a boarding school accent.

"What is it?"

"Who destroyed my office?"

"The people who live here are taking back their neighbourhood. It looks like you've been warned. Move your business."

"You should have stopped them."

"Can't you see? You're not wanted here." The officer shouted an order and the other two soldiers raised their weapons. "Get out of here before something worse happens."

⋏

Friedrich drove toward the outskirts of the city until the blinking lights of a roadblock suggested trouble. He pulled onto a trail that led into the hills, bypassed the checkpoint and drove east toward the Jordanian border. A cloud of dust enveloped him as he stopped near a summit. Below him, smoke rose from the carcasses of the destroyed transports. He heard a shot and laid the bike on its side and crawled forward on his hands and knees. Irgun militia cheered as they dragged bodies from a cave. On the valley floor, a shovel-fitted tractor burrowed a wide trench next to the road. He inched forward for a better look and cursed himself for not bringing binoculars.

An officer's command rousted two militiamen dozing in the shade. Beside them was the twisted skeleton of a transport like the one Adlyia and Jamal had been on.

That's it," he thought.

The militia men climbed into the back of two pickup trucks parked next to the trench and flung corpses into the hole.

Counting fifty-three stiff and distorted bodies Friedrich spat out the bitterness in his throat. He stared in disbelief while the tractor backfilled the excavation until it became indistinguishable from the ground surrounding it.

As if in a spell, he stumbled back to the motorcycle and dug through Jamal's saddlebag until he found a pencil. From his vantage point he noted the minarets of two villages that looked about a mile away. On a scrap of paper, he drew triangulated lines toward each spire and a third bisecting line from his position to the grave below. He marked it with an X and wrote down the estimated distance of five hundred yards.

⅄

Eva's eyes were frantic when he returned to the apartment. He took Fadi from her arms and removed the bottle from a pan of heated water before he sat down beside her. He put the nipple to the boy's mouth.

"Where were you?" she said. "They were hammering on the door. I thought someone was going to break in. They set some cars on fire."

Her voice had the same hollowness as when he'd rescued her on the street in Vienna. For weeks afterwards she hardly spoke or ate and he knew she still carried visions that she couldn't reveal. He feared another descent into that empty zone. Telling her the truth now would spiral her over the edge.

"All the roads are blocked," he said. "A mob completely destroyed our office. The Jordanians are preventing supplies from coming into the city. It's not safe for us here now. We need to get to the Notre Dame Hospice on the west side. I know people there who can help us."

"What should I bring?"

"Just what you need for tonight. They're warning everyone to stay in their homes but after last night, what good is that? There could be more reprisals."

"What about Jamal and Adlyia?"

"There's no information," he lied. "Hurry, we must go. We're going to have to find someone to take care of him."

Eva froze halfway up the stairs and looked down.

"Are you crazy?" Her voice cracked through the room like a whip and Fadi started to cry. She came down and took him from Friedrich's arms. "Adlyia and Jamal have no family, Friedrich. If we give him up, he'll be another unwanted orphan in a refugee camp. We will look after him until they return. Never speak of this again. Never."

"He's not one of us, damn it." The prejudice in his voice made her clutch Fadi to her breast and step back. He closed his eyes and reprimanded himself for yelling. "He's different," he said, as if he didn't want to be overheard. "That's all I'm saying. It's best that he's amongst his own."

Her eyes bore into him so hard that he turned his head away. "What aren't you telling me?" she asked.

He wrung his hands and stared out the window to find words. "They won't be coming back. They were both killed."

"No, this can't be." Her body deflated and her eyes pleaded that what he'd said, could not be true. "No, don't tell me this please. No, no, no."

He moved to embrace her but she pulled away.

"I saw them burying the bodies."

Eva stared at him as if she had been struck dumb. Tears flooded her eyes.

"I stopped Adlyia from going up the stairs and it saved his life. He's our responsibility now, Friedrich. We're his only chance."

She searched his eyes for affirmation and he nodded. The debate was over.

⅄

He said nothing more as she took Fadi and went upstairs to pack a suitcase. He lit a cigarette and paced the room, anxiously blowing smoke through the open window. Since their arrival in Palestine, he had witnessed stark differences between the behavior of European Jews and the local Arabs. He had noticed it in his practice when Palestinian families missed appointments or came late without any hint of apology.

He had assumed at first that their behavior was accidental, but he soon realized that most had no conception of being on time. As an obsessive personality, who checked his watch every few minutes, this drove him to distraction. With families where missed or late appointments became the norm, he made them wait, sometimes for a whole day, before he would fit them in. This challenged his philosophy of treating everyone equally, whatever their station or ethnicity, and he struggled to come to terms with his feelings.

In the short time Jews had been settling in Palestine they had transformed their barren lands with crops, orchards and modern settlements while the Arabs lived in squalid villages without running water or sewers, as they had for centuries. Was this all the will of God? Inshallah.

Or was this the reality of racial prejudice? Was he a bigoted Jew, no better than a German? Night after night he twisted in the sheets while the possibility gnawed inside him. His restlessness had become so incessant that Eva had taken to a separate bed.

Of course there were exceptions like Jamal and Adlyia, but who knew what tendencies lay dormant within this baby boy? He exhaled another waft of smoke before snuffing the butt and lighting another. If they adopted Fadi, the role of instilling a sense of discipline and purpose would fall on his shoulders. There would have to be conditions to this adoption. He looked up as she came down with a suitcase in her hand.

"We'll raise him as a Jew then...to set a higher standard," he said. "He can never know the truth. It's for his own good."

"Someday we'll have to tell him," she said. "When he's old enough to understand."

"That day will never come," he shouted. "Now, let's get the hell out of here."

Chapter 17

He strapped the suitcase to the motorcycle and positioned Eva and Fadi, on the forward part of the seat. Wrapping both arms around them, he reached for the handlebars and pulled into snarled traffic. With belongings lashed to cars, trucks and buses, drivers leaned on their horns and cursed each other as they tried to extricate their families from the city.

Arab militias blocking the road between Tel Aviv and Jerusalem had isolated the Jewish population in the Old City. The Arab Legion led by former British Lieutenant-General John Glubb was massing troops and equipment to mount a final attack.

Following a less direct route into the western section of town, Friedrich used side-streets and lanes to avoid congestion. Darkness had almost fallen when he saw the turrets of Notre Dame Hospice. Built by French nuns in 1882, the granite edifice resembled a fortress. The Haganah militia had taken up defensive positions within its walls.

He drove the motorcycle through an archway that led to an interior square where he turned off the key and steadied the bike. Eva got off and sat down with Fadi next to a statue of the Virgin. Buffered from the confusion on the streets, trickling water and the fragrance of blossoms brought relief. He kissed Fadi and gave Eva a gentle squeeze.

"Rest here while I look for my friend, Moshe. He'll help us."

Haganuh commander, Moshe Herzog, closed the door of his office. He motioned Friedrich to a chair and poured tea.

"What the hell are you doing here, Friedrich? It's dangerous out there right now."

"We're not safe in our home, Moshe. We need a place to stay. We're caring for the baby of two Palestinian employees who were abducted by the Irgun."

"One of our convoys was ambushed last night," Herzog said. "Some of the wounded were brought here but nobody's saying a damn thing."

"I was out there, Moshe. I saw them burying the bodies. I've never witnessed anything more sickening. I went to my office and found it trashed. Everything's destroyed. Bands of men roamed the streets this morning. My wife feared for our child. I've brought them with me."

The mention of, our child, was a slip of the tongue. He opened his mouth to correct himself but realized it was now a fact. The sight of earth and rocks tumbling into the trench riveted his mind and he broke into a clammy sweat. He couldn't deny it. He was a father now and the head of his family. He would do whatever was necessary to protect them.

"They want to massacre us, Moshe," he said. "They smeared that message in shit across the walls in my office. They're fanatics. I'll do whatever I can to help."

Moshe set down his cup. "We're all feeling the same way." he said. "There's an empty set of rooms you can use. What we've got here is a group of nineteen and twenty year old kids. They're Gadna; Haganuh youth. They have no fear but they need leadership."

"I spent a couple of years in the army," Friedrich said. "I had some explosives training but it's been a long time. I'm probably best for helping the wounded."

Herzog picked up the phone and several moments later there was a knock on the door. A girl who spoke Yiddish entered the office.

"What is it, sir?"

"There's a woman with her baby in the square. Take her to that empty suite and get whatever she needs. This is her husband, Doctor Mendelssohn. They'll be staying with us." Herzog poured more tea as the girl left the room.

"Have you seen this morning's paper?" he asked. "They're tightening the noose."

Friedrich read the headline on the front page. **Jerusalem Blockade.** Below that, a photograph of three men. Arab commander, Abd-al Kadir Husseini, wore a headscarf and crossed bandoliers. Standing next to him were, King Abdullah of Jordan and British Lieutenant-General Glubb. The picture had been taken at a conference in Amman six months before.

"Who's this fellow with the moustache?" Friedrich said.

"Retired British army," Herzog said. "They call him Glubb Pasha. He's been training the Arab Legion for King Abdullah. They're planning to attack the hospice to gain access to West Jerusalem. Our only chance is to surprise them. We're bringing in weapons and supplies right now. It could come anytime. After what happened at Deir Yassin, they want revenge."

"What was that?"

"The Irgun attacked the village a week ago to clear out Arab fighters. They were ordered not to harm civilians but things got out of hand. Grenades and house-to-house fighting. Women and children killed. It was a fucking mess."

"Too many of those guys are loose cannons," Friedrich said. "They're the ones who kidnapped my employees and got them killed. This is not what we stand for, Moshe. It's not who we are."

"Agreed," Herzog said, "but right now we do whatever it takes to survive. Or be annihilated." He stood up. "I want to introduce you to someone. She can use your help."

They walked into a room where a girl in her early twenties glanced up with a blank expression. She was wiring a detonator. Beside her, sticks of dynamite were tied in bundles of three.

"Netiva, this is Friedrich Mendelssohn. He's had experience with explosives. I've asked him to give you a hand." She tossed a lock of her hair to one side, her eyes filled with skepticism.

"I don't need help," she said. "He'll just complicate things." Herzog picked up a Sten gun leaning against the wall and handed it to Friedrich.

"You'll need someone to watch your back, Netiva. Take him with you."

"What about my wife and child?" Friedrich said. "Shouldn't I stay with them? I could organize a triage room for the wounded."

"We're okay with that and I'll see that your family's protected. The best thing you can do is help us stop those bastards from getting up here."

Friedrich's heart raced at the thought of shooting someone and his hands felt slippery against the cold metal. He hadn't held a gun since he'd been in basic training and then it had only been for target practice, but he heard the urgency in Herzog's voice. He couldn't refuse. "Whatever you want," he said.

"Netiva's a sabra." Herzog patted her shoulder. "We're lucky to have her on our side. She's going to arrange a surprise for Glubb Pasha. But his men are well trained. We'll need to catch them flat-footed if we're to have any chance."

Friedrich couldn't help but notice the definition of Nativa's biceps as she stuck the bundles of dynamite into her rucksack. She threw it over her shoulder and started toward the door. "Let's go." She left Friedrich to follow and ran down steps into an underground passageway, where she swung open an iron door and exited into a lane behind the hospice. Dim street lamps lit their way in the dark.

"Stay close and do what I say. I don't need any fuck-ups."

He wheezed to match her pace through a warren of streets where women and children leaned out from windows and looked down. They emerged onto a wide, deserted road that led straight up the hill. The turret lights of the hospice glowed at the top.

"The locals know something's up," she said. "It's too quiet for this time of night."

A pack of dogs barked and started running toward them. She flung a rock at the leader, a mean looking pit-bull cross, who whined and pulled up as it nicked his brow. Grabbing another chunk and raising her arm, the pack retreated around the corner.

He followed her across rough-hewn cobblestones to an intersection where she crouched down and opened her rucksack. "They'll turn here before they go up the hill." She unravelled the connected bundles of dynamite and spaced them at six foot intervals along a drainage culvert strewn with trash. "Cover them up."

She unwound a spool of detonator wire and pulled it across the road toward a stone wall where they could wait for the approach of the legion. When the wire ran ten feet short, she pulled an extra length from her sack and spliced the ends together to make the final connection to the detonator. She looked at the Sten gun slung over his shoulder.

"Ever used one of those?"

"Something like it."

"It won't do you much good like that." She flipped off the safety and pointed to the rooftops on the other side of the road. "Look up there."

He squinted up at the rooflines but couldn't see anything in the dark. She pointed a flashlight and switched it on and off. He saw flickers in return.

"They know we're ready," she said. "Stay behind this wall. They'll be shooting this way once I blow the charge." She glanced over her shoulder at a path between two buildings. "We'll go back through there."

Friedrich leaned against the wall, his chest heaving. Calm down, he told himself.

Netiva pulled up the plunger on the detonator and sat beside him.

"You were born here?" he asked.

"In Haifa. I grew up in Ma'abarot."

"A kibbutz. I've never been to one."

She looked out to the street where everything remained quiet, then she turned back and said: "Why didn't you Ashkenazi's stand up and fight when you realized what the German's were doing?"

A bed sheet hung drying on an apartment balcony behind them. He watched it waver in the breeze as he formulated an answer. What would she say if he told her that he'd spent the war hiding behind a false identity? So he could lead a normal life. "We weren't really aware of what was happening," he lied. Bauer's skull had confirmed that. "Jews were being deported but we thought it was to work camps. We expected things would change when the Nazis were deposed. People were afraid of losing their homes and jobs so they cooperated. Now we know it was the wrong thing to do...but at the time."

"We've fought for every inch of land since the start of our return. If we'd acted like that, we wouldn't be here now."

"That's uncalled for." His retort echoed along the street.

She looked around the corner then glared at him.

"Keep it down," she hissed. "We don't need to warn them."

"I won't accept being labeled a coward," Friedrich said. "You have no idea what we were up against."

"That's what you all say," she said, rolling her eyes.

"It's true."

"We need to sleep," she said. "Two on, two off. I'll take the first shift. You'll need every ounce of courage when the sun rises tomorrow."

⅄

The rumble of an engine triggered his nightmare of the u-boat and his eyes snapped wide open. The glimmer of dawn gave shape to the buildings across the road. He crawled beside Netiva and saw a military truck carrying an armed platoon turning into the intersection.

"When it starts up the grade," she said. The truck reached the corner and the engine roared. Gears shifted and it started climbing toward the hospice. Netiva pressed on the plunger but nothing happened. "Fuck." She pulled up the handle and tried again but still no explosion.

"The main connector's come loose," she said. She pulled the cable off the plunger box and stripped back the insulation with her knife. As she twisted two copper wires back together, shots came down from the roof-tops on the opposite side. The truck driver's brains splattered against the inside glass of the cab.

Friedrich's knuckles blanched white on the stock of his gun. Legionnaires jumped down from the truck and scrambled toward the wall where he and Netiva hid.

"The idiots should have waited," she said. "They're driving them this way."

Friedrich's eyes froze on the first petrified soldier that reached them. "Shoot him, shoot him," she screamed. With his fingers paralyzed on the trigger, Netiva slashed the soldier's jugular vein before he could open fire. She pulled the gun from Friedrich's hands and sprayed volleys. Three more legionnaires dropped dead in front of them before others following behind scrambled back for cover.

Chunks of mortar and rock flew up into Friedrich's face. Cringing against the sting, he looked back to see the muzzle flash from a second shot that rang out from behind the sheet on the balcony. Netiva grunted and fell to the side clutching her thigh. Arterial blood gushed from the wound, flooding the gaps between the road-stones. The shooter on the balcony ripped the sheet aside and ejected the cartridge from his rifle. Friedrich locked eyes as the man took dead aim.

The shell casing clattered down in front of him and his adrenalin spiked. He grabbed the Sten gun and spun over on his back to squeeze the trigger. The volley drove his shoulder into the pavement and riddled the man with holes. A woman rushed to the man's side and screamed slurs, slashing her index finger across her throat. A boy of about thirteen took the rifle and pointed down. Friedrich emptied his clip and watched both mother and son collapse behind the railing.

He dropped the gun and dragged Netiva behind the wall. Her eyes were an empty void, her face the color of parchment. Seeing her drifting in and out of consciousness, he tore off his belt and cinched it around the top of her thigh. Over the rattle of gunfire, he read her lips. "Press the plunger."

The wires she'd tried to reconnect were still free. He twisted both ends again and squeezed the copper tips together with his molars. He shouted into her ear.

"Netiva, Netiva."

Her eyelids fluttered.

"Listen."

The detonation numbed his eardrums. Two troop transports buckled into the air and tumbled on their sides. Exploding gasoline and ammunition rocked the neighbourhood, blasting out windows along both sides of the street.

He hiked her over his shoulder and groaned to stand. "Stay with me, Netiva. I'm taking you back." She dangled off him like a rag-doll.

⅄

He laid her on the floor of the hospice and pressed his finger to the side of her neck.

"Still a pulse," he said to the doctor who crouched down beside him. "The bullet tore an artery. She lost a lot of blood before I got this on."

Helpless to quell his shaking, he sat dazed as they wheeled her to an operating room. A polished wall in front of him radiated images of the family he had killed. The convulsions of their bodies wouldn't leave him, each slug ripping apart their flesh, chunk-by-chunk. A cry of full throated anguish erupted from the deepest part of his soul and brought the nurses running from their stations. He howled into an abyss, unaware of a needle's entry and the flood of barbiturates into his vein.

⅄

"Where's Netiva?" Herzog said, as two men lifted Friedrich onto a bed.

"In surgery. She might lose her leg."

"They took out two platoons at the bottom of the hill," Herzog said. "Glubb had to pull back."

The nurse looked down at Friedrich. "His tourniquet saved her life."

⅄

After two days under an umbrella of Phenobarbital, Friedrich woke to a nurse who offered him tea and honey. He stared around the room struggling to make sense of where he was. The tea sat untouched on the tray. Then Fadi's gurgling brought a smile to his face. Eva stood by the bed and kissed him. He looked up at her until his eyes welled and his body trembled. Drawing his knees to his chest, he clutched the sheet and wept.

"Shh, shh, Friedrich," she said, stroking his hair."You must rest now. You've been through a lot."

"So scared," he said, his voice a parched whisper. "I thought I'd never see you again."

"You're safe now."

"Evil has filled my heart." He scrubbed his fist on the left side of his chest and shivered. "It's devouring me."

"What do you mean, love? You saved a young woman's life."

"I murdered a family." His knuckles dug into the sides of his head to banish the images. "But it gave me satisfaction. Why?" His frenzied eyes looked at her for an explanation.

"You did what you had to do. If it wasn't for you and Netiva, the legion would have overrun the hospice. You forced them to withdraw." She picked up Fadi and brought him closer. "You saved our lives, Friedrich."

"I can't live like this." His voice was flat as he sat up and stared at her. "I was a fool. The Arabs are as bad as the Germans. They'll never accept us."

The space between them fell silent while a starling's melody drifted through the window. Eva kissed Fadi on the cheek and said, "This is our home. We must take a stand."

"I won't raise him in this hellhole that has already claimed the life of his parents."

"What else can we do?"

"I don't know yet." He gulped the tea and set down the cup. "We'll get adoption papers and find someone to sponsor us to another country. Anywhere but here." He threw the covers off the bed.

"You shouldn't be getting up yet," the nurse said.

"Who the hell are you to be telling me what to do?" His feet touched the floor and he clutched the bed-frame to stop the spinning.

"Be careful," Eva said. "Do as she says."

"Nonsense. Get my clothes."

"Please, Friedrich. You're still too weak."

"Listen to me," he said. "You and Fadi are all I live for now. Nothing else matters. Including this ridiculous notion of a Jewish homeland."

CHAPTER 18

General John Glubb saved face the following night by destroying the south wing of the hospice. The assault left thirty-six dead and a section of the building uninhabitable. Within the ruins, the Jewish Haganah built a guard post manned by machine guns and anti-tank cannons to defend against further attacks. Pilgrims now crowded into the north wing and the rooms surrounding the square.

While the nuns carried on with their mission, Friedrich drew on the experience he had gained in the Royal London Hospital years before. He found a room in the basement where he wired fractured jaws and sutured facial wounds destined to leave terrifying disfigurations. As he was finishing up at the end of the day, his assistant ducked her head into his office.

"A person I've never seen before just walked in. He says he needs to speak to you."

"I'm exhausted," Friedrich said. "If he's not injured, tell him to come back tomorrow."

"He said it's regarding a man named, Bauer."

Friedrich felt his forearms bristle and he made a stab for his cigarettes.

"I don't know anyone by that name."

"He's awful looking. His nose is all squashed in. I told him you were busy. He insisted on waiting."

As she left the room, he slumped in his chair and dragged on his cigarette. He'd deny everything. There was nothing anyone could prove.

The man, who looked at least sixty, waited on a bench in the hall. He was clean-shaven and wore a starched white shirt, but the lapels of his suit were tattered and his trousers bore no evidence of a crease. Friedrich guessed him for an ex-boxer. Shadows rimmed both eyes and his cheeks sagged into gaps left by missing teeth. His gaze, when he looked at Friedrich, was hard to read.

"What is it?" Friedrich crushed his butt into a bucket filled with sand.

When the man rose from the bench, he stood almost a foot taller than Friedrich.

"My name is Gabor Erhmann," he said, without extending his hand. Friedrich recognized the east European accent. "I want to speak to you about Colonel Heinz Bauer".

"Bauer's a common name," Friedrich said. "I knew many in Vienna."

"There's only one that I'm interested in. This won't take long."

"I hope not," Friedrich said. "Come in and sit down."

Erhmann folded his frame into a chair and Friedrich reached for a bottle of brandy. "One of these at the end of the day helps me relax," he said. In truth, it took two or three brandies a day, and now, with Erhmann's eyes burrowing into him, the latter was more likely.

"None for me."

Friedrich poured himself three fingers and offered Erhmann a cigarette which he refused. He struck a match, exhaled into the room and looked across the desk. Erhmann could do the talking.

"Do you speak Hebrew?" Erhmann asked.

"Very little."

"The word, Nakam, means nothing to you then?"

"I've heard of it." He felt beads of sweat dotting his brow. "It has something to do with revenge against Nazis, I think."

"The word means, vengeance. On those responsible for what happened. Our organization seeks a more comprehensive form of punishment. An eye for an eye." His gaze became darker and Friedrich avoided it by raising the glass to his lips.

Erhmann reached into an attaché case, inadvertently displaying the numbers tattooed across his forearm. He withdrew a crinkled photograph that had been torn and repaired with tape. It showed two SS officers standing on the platform of a guard-tower. The roof behind them looked burdened by ice. Breath fog rose about their faces. The taller of the two snarled down at the camera as if he was shouting an order. A flashbulb's sparkle lit the corner of his upper right front tooth.

"Recognize him?" Erhmann pointed to the image.

Friedrich brought the photograph closer and swallowed another slug. As the liquor burned down his esophagus, his mind raced to consider a response.

"It's blurry. I can't really say."

Erhmann handed him a second image that was magnified.

"Does this help?"

Friedrich's eyelid twitched as he squinted at the second photograph.

"Not really."

Erhmann pulled out a document on which Friedrich recognized the disciplined script of his own handwriting. His heart skipped a beat.

"What do you have there?" It was a stupid question he wished he hadn't asked.

Erhmann's expression remained blank as he handed over the document. "Read it for yourself. It might help your memory."

"It looks like my handwriting." Friedrich recognized the stiff paper of a dental chart while the name, Heinz Bauer, leapt out from the right hand corner and gave him reflux. "Ah, ha," he said, swallowing back the bitterness. "I remember him now. Yes, yes, that Bauer. He took no anesthetic. Very few people like that."

He scanned down through the entries, which described the configuration and weight of each gold filling. The last notation described the extraction of the lower left first molar.

He flicked the ash and cleared his throat.

"He came to see me when he worked at SS headquarters in Vienna. He'd served with Rommel before that and I believe he was being reassigned to Holland." He glanced down at the bottom of the page. "Yes, it's noted right here. We made this copy of the chart to take with him."

Erhmann scribbled as Friedrich spoke and turned to a fresh page in his journal. "Bauer served under Rommel but after he was wounded he never went back to tank command," he said. "He was given other responsibilities. Do you know what they were?"

"I remember that he had a limp and a bad eye. He only came to see me when he was in Vienna for meetings. I was under the impression that..."

Erhmann raised his hand to interrupt. "Bauer reported to Himmler. He was responsible for the construction and operation of the crematoriums at Auschwitz that killed at least a million Jews. Six members of my family were among them."

Friedrich held the close-up photograph under the light again. "This could possibly be the same man. This reflection below his lip is what catches my eye." He grabbed the chart again and scanned the entries. "Yes. Here it is. The upper right central incisor. Fractured inside corner edge. I restored it with a gold inlay."

"There's no doubt that it is him. I obtained the negative in Auschwitz by bribing the photographer who took it. Two packs of cigarettes. After I escaped and reached the American lines, I worked as an interpreter for a while. Then I helped found Nakam. We made a list that's getting shorter each year. But Heinz Bauer's still at the top."

"I'm sorry about your family," Friedrich said

"Then help me find him. His death was reported after the end of the war in late '45. It was in the newspapers."

"I wasn't aware." The lie made his eyelid twitch again and he stilled it with another gulp of courage. The headline **Architect of Death Camps** passed through his mind. Not a word, he cautioned himself. "If he's dead, why are you asking all this?"

"Certain things don't add up," Erhmann said. "Bauer's remains and those of some other SS officers were found in a burned-out basement in Munich." Erhmann winced to stretch his back. "It was a safe-house they used before escaping to Argentina. Our team was closing in and they knew it. They chose a quick exit rather than face what we had in store for them."

"I see," Friedrich said. "But that still doesn't explain..."

"It was an incendiary explosion. The bodies were blown apart and burned to almost nothing. SS officers were reimbursed through a benefit program and that's how we discovered this copy of his dental chart. We found re-imbursement receipts for five or six more of your patients. It appears they all took cyanide. Everyone, except Bauer. He set a timer with an explosive charge and shot himself before it went off."

"How did you identify his remains?

"An American forensic dentist compared the chart descriptions to the gold fillings in the skull with the bullet hole. It matched for Bauer. But his dentist's name was Friedrich Mueller." Erhmann turned a page and looked at his notes again. "I interviewed a woman named...Helga, who worked in the practice. She said that Mueller and his assistant, Eva Schmidt, disappeared in December of 1943."

"I can explain that." Friedrich stubbed out his cigarette and fumbled for another, willing himself to slow down. He left it unlit in the ashtray and folded his hands. "It's a long story."

"So tell me," Erhmann said.

"After graduating, I was drafted into the army. I got wounded when a shell hit our hospital. Recuperation took a year and during that time, I helped care for my colleague, Friedrich Mueller, who was mortally wounded in the same accident. Because the Nazis were stripping Jews of their licence to prac-tice, he insisted that I take his identity and I did...after he died." Friedrich rubbed his forehead and took a breath.

"Get to the point."

"I told you it was a long story," Friedrich said, raising his voice. "Do you want to hear it or not?"

Erhmann slapped down his hand and rattled the desk. "How did you get out of the country?"

Friedrich took another swig of brandy. "The Gestapo started reviewing university records. I knew it was just a matter of time and I paid a pilot to get myself and Eva into Romania. We eventually made it here. We're now married with a child." He refilled his glass and dabbed his eyes with a handkerchief. "Talking about it makes me emotional."

Erhmann remained unmoved as he looked at his notes.

"We have access to all immigration records here in Israel. We know that you and your wife were processed at the border in February '44. Your papers identified you as Friedrich Mueller, so your story fits. The record says an army dentist vouched for you. What happened there?"

"That was George Beesley. I worked with him in London before the war. He knew me as Mendelssohn. When we got to the border, the British suspected we were spies. They found my instruments and took me to a dental clinic to perform several procedures. It was a test. By coincidence, Beesley was posted to the same clinic and he identified us. He saved our skin, as they say. Those were dangerous days."

"You were lucky."

"We could have been shot."

Friedrich grabbed the unlit cigarette from the ashtray and threw the empty package into the wastebasket. As he flicked the lighter, it slipped from his hand and bounced off the floor. Erhmann looked up with raised eyebrows and bent over to pick it up.

"A little anxious, Herr Doktor? Your forehead's soaked."

"It's the brandy," Friedrich said. "I hope you're just about finished." He lit the cigarette and wiped his brow.

"One of our investigators discovered files that were removed from your office before it was destroyed by bombing. They had been taken to a small town outside Vienna. We've been able to match all the SS benefit claims with the original patient charts, but for some reason we couldn't find a chart for Bauer. Why would this be?"

"I have no goddamned idea," Friedrich said. "And how the hell should I know? Maybe it got lost when the records were transferred."

The pitch of his voice made Erhmann blink. "No need to get so upset, Mendelssohn. We're almost done."

Friedrich scolded himself for overreacting. He cleared his throat and continued in a slower, more deliberate tone. "For all I know, others could have been lost as well. You wouldn't be aware that a chart was missing unless you had access to a corresponding benefit claim. There could be many." He pressed his fingers against his eyelids to quell the drumming. Although he craved another stiff one, he knew he couldn't drink anymore. Shaking off the urge, he leaned back in his chair and sighed. "Many unexplained things happen during wartime, Mister Erhmann."

"There was no original yet you had made a handwritten copy. That's odd. You're sure you don't have it stuffed away somewhere?"

"Bauer was a fastidious man. Obsessed with every detail. He was like a robot during the most difficult procedures. He insisted on us making this copy when he learned that he was going to Holland. He didn't want to take a chance that the original could be lost or destroyed. It was rare to have a request like that. Like I said, we never saw him after that last appointment. I have no idea what happened to it."

Erhmann wrote on the page before lifting his eyes. "One last thing. A Luger was found next to the skull with the bullet hole and exit wound. The gun was registered to Bauer and there was one bullet missing from the chamber. Remnants of that bullet were recovered in the wall but investigators could find no sign of bone fragments that would have exploded outward. The room was gutted by the fire but there should have been some evidence of that."

Friedrich coughed out an exasperated burst of smoke.

"What the hell do you want from me, Erhmann? I wasn't in the room... you weren't in the room. An explosion occurred. It's amazing that you found anything, for Christ's sake."

Erhrman moved close enough so that the foulness percolating from beneath his gums made Friedrich flinch. Erhmann enunciated each word with the tone of an accuser.

"You're not telling me everything, Mendelssohn. You're hiding something. With the Gestapo on your trail, I don't believe that you and your assistant could have slipped out of Austria without some help."

"I've told you everything I know, goddamnit." Friedrich stood up and opened the door. "Goodbye, Mister Erhmann."

"Too many loose ends," Erhmann said. "I know that murderer is still alive." He slapped his journal closed. "If you remember anything more, reach me here." He threw down a card with an address and phone number.

"There's nothing more I can tell you."

Erhmann walked to the door and then turned.

"Sometimes our minds play tricks on us, Mendelssohn. Good people forget bad things that happen. They want to get on with their lives. Even the British have stopped prosecuting war criminals. They want to dispose of the past. We're going to see that doesn't happen."

Friedrich felt the menace in Erhmann's voice.

"Don't get caught on the wrong side of this, Herr Doktor. If you're hiding something...I will find out."

"Get out," Friedrich yelled. "You sound like the goddamned Gestapo."

Erhmann turned and left the room. Friedrich slammed the door behind him and retreated back to his desk where he emptied the last drop from the bottle. He tore open a new pack of cigarettes and watched the flame tremble as he brought it to the tip. He dropped the lighter and extended both hands to see how long he could keep his fingers steady. Within moments they began to vibrate against his will. He winced on the last of what remained in his glass and stared into the veil of smoke filling the room. The time had come to leave. Erhmann would hound him until he died. He opened the directory on his desk and scribbled down the last address he had for George Beesley.

CHAPTER 19

Sleep wasn't possible after Erhmann's visit. Friedrich tried to read when Eva went to bed but his thoughts were too scattered to concentrate. Well after midnight, he slipped out and left the hospice by the rear gate. Walking alone through the streets, he mulled over everything that had been said and what it all meant. He discounted Erhmann's suspicion about the missing chart and felt that his challenge had been sufficient. After hostilities ended in 1945, he had contacted Schreiber who gave him the number of the box where Bauer's chart and the letter concerning the arrangement were hidden away. No loose ends there. The question was Bauer. Was he dead or alive? Friedrich was the only one who could determine that by examining the fillings in the skull. But that would put him and his family at risk. It wasn't going to happen. No, the best thing was to get the hell out of Israel and start a new life. A normal life. He thought of Fadi and struck a match to light another cigarette. He'd never need to know.

The first rays of sunrise sharpened the texture of the hills. He thought of all those who had witnessed the same landscapes over the millennia and whose lives had also been torn apart by hatred and war. As shop owners emerged to sweep the sidewalks in front of their stores, he returned to the cottage and slipped back into bed.

Eyes closed, he listened to the rhythm of Eva's breathing beside him. Fadi rustled and released a contented sigh. What future could there be for the boy if his options were forever clouded by whether he was European or

Arabic? As a proud German with Jewish roots, he knew how easily those roots could be ripped from the soil. Israel was a land sown with the same seed, and destined to fail, a hopeless dream that never stood a chance of bearing fruit. Eva woke and rolled over to face him.

"I never heard you come to bed," she said, rubbing the sleep from her eyes. Friedrich stared up at a spider harvesting its web of overnight intruders. Just like Israel; a country of entanglements. Jews had no future here.

"A man named Gabor Erhmann came to see me yesterday," he said. "He lost his family in Auschwitz. He leads a group of Nazi hunters who thirst for revenge. They don't believe in courts of law or anything like that. He's not convinced that Bauer's dead and he suspects that I know something about it."

Eva sat up in the bed.

"If he ever discovers that you assisted Bauer, think what he'd do to you. Why doesn't he believe that he's dead? What evidence does he have?" The alarm in her voice caused Fadi to stir.

"Shh, you'll wake him." He rolled out of bed and pulled the blanket over Fadi's shoulders. "They found a skull with fillings that matched the entries in Bauer's chart. But he suspects there was a setup."

"Why?"

"Because they couldn't find fragments from the bullet's exit wound. The place where they found the bodies was burnt to a crisp, but he won't listen to reason. He's like a dog with a bone. He's never going to leave us in peace. I'm going to contact Beesley. Maybe he can sponsor us into Canada."

Fadi let out a cry and Eva went to the crib. "I never thought I'd say this but with everything that's been going on, it's the right thing to do." She picked up Fadi and held him close. "Especially for him. I want to get as far away from here as we can."

ᛉ

Since the battle with the Legion, any loud or unexpected noise threw Friedrich right back into the moment. Contorted images of the family he'd killed ignited migraine headaches and drove him into a room without windows where he cowered in the dark until the demons released their grip.

He needed at least a half bottle of brandy before he could even think of bed. The hangovers left him in a foul mood until lunchtime when he downed a shot or two of vodka to take off the edge and get through the afternoon.

He tried working shorter days but the energy required to steady a needle or hold a drill fatigued him. He couldn't continue without putting his patients at risk. Feeling useless and depressed, he forced himself out of bed each morning to hike into the hills and clear his mind. In the afternoons, he made himself useful by helping to make impressions for prosthetic limbs.

With his moods impossible to fathom, Eva took Fadi to a volunteer center each morning, where she watched over the children of parents staffing barricades and checkpoints around the city. When she returned home late in the afternoon, Friedrich sat at the kitchen table in front of a bottle of brandy.

"What's the matter?" she asked. "I thought you were working with the amputees this afternoon."

"I never left. As soon as I touched the door handle I started to hyperventilate. I thought I was having a heart attack. Like something terrible would happen. I couldn't shake it."

"That's not going to help," she said, pointing to the bottle as she yanked up the blind. "Stop feeling sorry for yourself. Do you think you're the only one who has been hurt by this war?"

Friedrich squinted at the brightness. "What the hell would you know? You weren't there. You didn't see their faces."

His voice rose to a crescendo before he threw back another mouthful and slammed the bottle on the table. Then as if a light switched off, his defiance dissolved into submission and pain. Dropping his head, he reached out for her hand and sobbed.

She pulled up a chair and wrapped him in her arms.

"Where is the old Friedrich I knew?" she whispered. "The man who mended my heart when it was torn and bleeding?"

"I wish I knew," he said, cupping his face. "God help me, I wish I knew."

She cradled him to her bosom and he felt the strength of her love, a sensation he'd never had with Katrina, however hard he'd tried to pretend. He wiped away his tears and picked Fadi up from the floor. He held him on his lap and looked into the clarity of the boy's eyes. He didn't deserve this drunken old fool for a father. He took Fadi's tiny hand in his palm, the fingers long and delicate, just as he remembered Jamal's.

"He has the hands of an artist," he said. "I'm going to raise him to become the man his father and mother would have wanted. I'll see to it that he makes them proud." He sat Fadi on the floor with his toys and took his brandy bottle to the trash, where he let it fall from his hand. "I'm finished with it," he said. "Let's take him out for a walk and make plans."

The next afternoon he rode the motorcycle through a Jewish market where the air smelled of moldy fruit and vegetables. Women jostled against one another, picking through dwindling bins to feed their families. He drove deeper into the Old City until he stopped in front a shop with boarded windows. The clatter of a printing press and fumes of hot lead filled the room as he walked through the door.

"Hello Avi," he shouted. A man with a sparse beard looked over through wire-rimmed glasses. Avi Kleinberg rolled the handle of his printing machine to the top of its arc and his ink-stained face cracked into a smile.

"Doctor Mendelssohn. I can't believe what I am seeing with my eyes. Someone said you were not well."

"Just a few problems like we all have these days," Friedrich said. "I'm glad to see you're back in your shop. Did you suffer much damage?"

"Nobody knows how to repair this old machinery anymore." He laughed and his eyes twinkled. "It was useless to them. They broke a few windows but that's all."

"Good. You look a hell of a lot better than the last time I saw you."

"Oh, those abscessed teeth," Kleinberg said. "I feel so much better now. I can't thank you enough."

"I need your help, Avi."

"After all you did for me. Anything. What do you need?" He struck a match and lit his pipe.

"I remember you telling me about documents that you forged in the camps," Friedrich said. He held out a picture of Fadi. "I need a birth certificate for my boy as well as new passports for my wife Eva and myself. Can you do that?"

Kleinberg's cheeks caved inward as he sucked the tobacco to life. He took the picture in his hand and grinned.

"Handsome boy," he said. "I wasn't aware you had a child this age."

"He's an orphan," Friedrich said. "His mother and father were my employees. More like family, actually. They were killed in an ambush. We adopted him."

"What happened to his birth certificate?" Friedrich heard the concern in Kleinberg's voice.

"All their belongings were destroyed."

Kleinberg puffed and studied the photograph. "He's dark. What's his name?"

"Fadi al-Massri."

"Egyptian," Kleinberg said. "This could be a problem."

"That's why I brought this to you, Avi," he said. "His father came from Gaza but he was estranged from his family. We want to change his name to Franklin Ben Mendelssohn. We'll call him Frankie. It's a popular name in the States."

"Like the singer?"

"That's right."

Kleinberg wrote down the name on the back of Fadi's picture.

"When was he born?"

"October 16, 1946. The same day as Ben-Gurion." Friedrich reached into his pocket and pulled out photos of himself and Eva. "Our information's on the back. How long will this take?"

Kleinberg set the pictures aside and struck another match.

"You're changing both his name and his ancestry. Are you sure?"

"It's the only way we'll get him out. It's either this or a refugee camp."

Kleinberg nodded and looked at the picture again.

"I'll have to access the materials. Come back in a couple of months."

"That long?"

"This won't be easy, Doctor Mendelssohn. Getting an orphan out of the country is difficult in the best of circumstances. We must be very discreet."

CHAPTER 20

He drove back through the market where the crowds had thinned with many stalls closed or empty. Merchants sat in the shade and smoked.

Pathetic, he thought. There was no hope for this place.

He took a short-cut through another ransacked neighbourhood to the check-point guarding British Army headquarters. "Emigration department," he said.

"Park the bike over there and see the corporal inside."

After an hour in a queue that stretched the length of the lobby, the corporal slammed down the phone and glared at him.

"And what the hell do you want?"

"Emigration applications. For me and my family."

"To where?"

"Canada."

"Do you have a sponsor?"

"I know one but I don't have his address. I thought you could help."

"And how would I go about that?" The corporal's eyes rolled as he looked at the line stretching behind Friedrich.

"Major George Beesley. A Canadian dentist who was posted here. I hoped you might have some information on his whereabouts. A forwarding address, perhaps."

"The name rings a bell. Big bloke, right?"

"Yes."

"Take a seat over there."

While he waited, Friedrich flipped through a dog-eared issue of Time Magazine until a headline caught his attention. **Nazi Hide-Out Discovered.** An abandoned safe house had been located near Hitler's summer retreat in Berchtesgaden, Bavaria. Allied forces had overlooked it when they took control in May, 1945. Was he dead or alive?

Below, he read another article entitled, **Butchers on the Lam**, describing The Organization of Former SS-Members (Odessa), a network spiriting war criminals to Argentina. His fingers trembled as he tore out the page and folded it into his pocket. How many were still out there?

The corporal came back and looked over at Friedrich. "Are you okay there, mate? You're white as a sheet."

"Feeling a bit queasy," he said, rubbing his stomach. "Something I ate."

"I found this and it might help. Major Beesley was posted back to Canada but for some reason we later received a request from a university in Los Angeles, California. We sent them a copy of his service records. Here's their address."

"Are you sure this is the right man?" Friedrich said. "What would he be doing down there?"

"Can't say for sure, but that's all I have." He handed Friedrich an envelope. "These are the emigration forms and you'll need a sponsorship letter from Beesley." He looked over Friedrich's shoulder and waved the next person forward. "Next." Friedrich looked around and saw that the queue was now outside the lobby.

"You're not the only one who wants out of here," the corporal said.

⋏

In the apartment, he grabbed the newspaper and scanned for more news about escaping Nazis. As he did, his heart pounded and he thirsted for a shot of brandy. One would settle his nerves but one was never enough.

If the skull found in Munich was indeed the one he had restored, it meant that Bauer did not die defending his beloved Berlin but was likely somewhere in South America. A free man. That he was responsible made him want a drink even more.

Sipping sweet tea and smoking more than he knew he should, he read through the magazine clipping once more. Eva set her knitting aside. "What's bothering you?" she said.

"This." He handed her the clipping. "It's about Nazis escaping to Argentina. He could be one of them."

"So what are you thinking? Telling the truth to that Hungarian man who spoke to you? It would be the right thing to do."

"But think of the risks," he said. "To us...and Frankie. Whether he's captured or not, if we exposed him, they'd come after us. We'd never be safe, no matter where we lived." He lit a cigarette from his third pack of the day and brought the match to the clipping. "That settles it." As it caught flame, he dropped it in the ashtray. "Bauer's dead and that's the way it will be."

⅄

He returned to the printing shop two months later and paid Avi Kleinberg for the birth certificate of Franklin Ben Mendelssohn and passports for himself and Eva. The next week, a letter arrived stamped with an American postmark. On a bench in the square he opened the letter.

Dear Freddie:

Good to hear from you, lad. Sorry that I didn't get a chance to say goodbye when I left Jerusalem. My reassignment was unexpected and I was discharged soon after we returned to Canada. I was looking to start a practice in Toronto when I was offered an opportunity to teach here at the University of Southern California. I've been appointed to head up the Department of Oral Surgery.

With the huge number of vets taking advantage of the GI Bill, there's an opening in the Restorative Department. Right up your alley, Freddie boy. I mentioned your name to the Dean and he remembers a lecture you gave on 'Gold Restorations' before the war. The position is for a part-time clinical instructor but you could work your way up. Wire me if you're interested. I'll be more than happy to sponsor you.

Best to you and Eva,

George.

PS: Los Angeles is hectic but the weather beats the hell out of Toronto.

Friedrich read the letter over twice before he folded it back into the envelope. He blew a plume of smoke into the air and laughed. Three nuns looked up from their prayer books to see what was so funny.

"I'm the luckiest man in the world," he shouted. He danced a jig and hurried to tell Eva the news.

λ

At noon on October 16, 1949, under a blue sky with billowing cloud, Friedrich carried Frankie in one arm and held Eva close with the other. They stood on the upper deck of a passenger liner departing for England and looked out at the fleet of small boats below them.

Festooned in blue and white flags emblazoned with the Star of David, the fleet chimed their horns in unison with the ship saluting the sixtieth birthday of David Ben Gurion. Friedrich held Frankie high in his arms so he could see the jets of water shooting up from the fireboats abreast of the liner.

Passengers lining the rail three rows deep applauded the announcement of the birthday and sang Hatikvah, the national anthem of hope that had been proclaimed the year before. As he sang, *To be a free people in our land, the land of Zion and Jerusalem,* Friedrich's tears blurred the sights of celebration around him. He looked out into the hills that stretched toward Jordan and thought of Jamal and Adlyia. He hugged Frankie and kissed his rosy cheeks.

"Happy birthday to you too, Frankie." he said. "I hope I can explain this to you one day." He put his arm around Eva and drew the three of them together. "We'll never forget this moment," he said. "Celebrating Frankie's second birthday while sailing off to our new life in America."

Eva stood on her toes to kiss him and looked into his eyes. "You're a very wise man, Doctor Mendelssohn."

As they steamed out of the harbour, he looked back at the tended fields, a testament to the work and perseverance of the Jewish people. The lush panorama filled him with a mix of pride and unease. Inside, he still harbored a feeling of responsibility to stay and build the future. Why then was he was running away and leaving it to others? He had struggled with this question since making his decision. But as he held his son and his wife, the answer was clear. He would not stake their future on an irrational quest to build a country amid a hostile Muslim population governed by fatalistic apathy. For that he felt not a shred of guilt or doubt.

As a chilling breeze blew across the deck, more joy and love filled his heart than he'd ever thought possible. He hugged his adopted son and realized what a fool he'd been to ever doubt Eva's decision. He was a wise and... very lucky man.

SECTION II

Chapter 21

Los Angeles, California 1992

Friedrich stepped out of the side entrance of Parkside Grove Retirement Lodge and walked along a path that led to a nature preserve. The close proximity of the park had attracted him to the upscale assisted-living facility after Eva's stroke. Today marked the tenth anniversary of that horrible day. She had given him courage when he was weak and had taught him to be considerate when he was difficult. Most importantly, she convinced him to take himself less seriously. Her vitality and sense of humor had always brought a smile to his face but there were few of those to be found these days. Her loss was a wound that wouldn't mend.

Entering a canopy of trees, he welcomed the comfort offered by songbirds and the gurgling stream. Under one arm he carried a wooden chest which he set on the handrail of a footbridge. The first time he'd come upon the structure, he'd named it Eva's Bridge, its sturdy granite a monument to her strength and resilience. Each day on his morning walk, he paused here to think of her and remember all the wonderful years they had together.

She had been taken so suddenly, like a feather whisked away by a rogue gust of wind, and only a week after she had been honored in New York for her volunteer work with Hadassah, the Women's Zionist Organization of America. Friedrich had also received good news; a neurologist's diagnosis confirmed that the tremors he had been experiencing were not that of Parkinson's disease but of a benign condition known as Essential Tremor.

After months of denial and worry, the news uplifted them. They were discussing taking a vacation to celebrate.

Eva went outside to tend her flowers while he retreated to his study. As he paged through a dental journal, an advertisement for a Cruise and Learn Seminar in the Hawaiian Islands caught his attention---the perfect solution: a vacation that also made good use of his time. When he hurried out to share his enthusiasm with Eva, he found her face down and unresponsive in the garden.

Since then, not a day had passed when he wasn't consumed by an emptiness that couldn't be filled, and today, as he had done on the nine previous anniversaries, he opened the chest and let the aroma of its cedar lining fill his senses. He removed an urn containing some of her ashes and sprinkled a handful into the water. He watched the flakes drift and dissolve, and then he capped the urn and picked out the photograph of himself, Eva and Frankie taken on the day they had sailed from Tel Aviv in 1949. A flood of emotion turned his eyes glassy. What a turning point that had been.

He set the photo aside and retrieved the last item in the box, a glass cylinder that held the tooth he had extracted from Colonel Heinz Bauer in 1943. During his long tenure as a professor of Restorative Dentistry at USC, he had used the gold filling in the molar as a clinical teaching aid. When magnified tenfold in the Kodak slides he showed during his lectures, the perfection he had achieved represented a remarkable triumph of art, function and durability. It was the standard of excellence to which all his students were expected to measure themselves. For over forty years, he hadn't heard of either Bauer or Erhmann, but their names still filled him with a lingering sense of dread. He hoped they were both dead and gone.

His reflection in the water caused him to think of Frankie who hadn't visited or spoken with him for over three months. He blamed himself for always having been so strict and unbending with Frankie although he still believed it had been for Frankie's own good. But what a price he had paid for his dogmatism.

Busyness was the new normal of the nineties. Friedrich and his friends in the lodge understood and accepted this, so they would never put pressure on their children to visit, lest their offspring fall behind in their quest for the good life. But like so many others in the residence, he wished he had spent more time with his child when he'd had the opportunity.

Under his tutelage, Frankie had graduated with the gold medal from the USC Faculty of Dentistry fifteen years before. He had worked alongside Friedrich in the office until Friedrich's tremors became troublesome. Then, after almost thirty-six years of private practice and teaching at USC, Friedrich had transitioned the practice to Frankie and had retired from the faculty. Honored with the title of professor emeritus on one of the most bittersweet days of his life, he bid farewell to his beloved profession.

⋏

At the same moment that Friedrich stood on Eva's Bridge feeling sorry for himself, Frankie Mendelssohn, dishevelled and unshaven, stood up to shake his lawyer's hand. A judge had just brought down his gavel and agreed to release Frankie from police custody on ten thousand dollars bail.

"I can't thank you enough for this Mal," Frankie said.

"You can start with a twenty thousand dollar retainer when we get back to the office. Your first hearing is the middle of next week. I need to get the details about what happened. I'll start working up a defense over the weekend."

Back in Mal Schneider's office, a secretary brought coffee and sandwiches into the boardroom and closed the door. Schneider grabbed a pen and a yellow legal pad. "Okay," he said to Frankie, "start from the beginning."

"Is this going to mean jail? Jesus, some of the guys I saw in there last night were so wired. I couldn't imagine..."

"Relax, you're getting way ahead of yourself. Tell me how this all went down."

Frankie rubbed his wrists. "Fucking cops left the cuffs on for about three hours." He raised his hands. "Look. They're raw. I'm going to sue the bastards."

Schneider exhaled smoke from a cigar and gazed across his desk. "When you're finished, we'll get started."

"How far back do you want me to go?"

Schneider sucked on his stogie and waited.

"It all started after the divorce. I was hanging out with some guys from the gym. You know the shtick. Work hard all week and blow it off on the weekends. Ladies, booze, weed, coke, all that shit. The problem was that after awhile it started happening during the week too. A physician buddy turned me on to Ritalin, a little pick-me-up for those mornings after the night before. But with that stuff I couldn't sleep, so I mellowed it out with Percodan."

"That's what they caught you with last night, right? Vitamin R and Percs."

"Yeah, what a bummer."

"They've charged you with trafficking. What happened there?"

"I cannot believe this." Frankie threw back the last of his coffee and slammed the cup down. "I swear. It was the last time I was going to do it. I knew it was getting too fucking risky."

"So?"

"There're lots of people who love prescription meds. Especially the guys from the gym. They see them as clean. You never know what's in that shit cocaine these days."

Schneider added to his notes and looked up again.

"We were working non-stop at the office but my finances got tighter. Loan payments, alimony and all this other stuff, like I said. I was tapped out at the bank and a real estate deal I got involved with in Santa Barbara went into the dumpster. The developers started squeezing me for cash. Russian motherfuckers. They said they'd mangle my fingers if I didn't pay."

"They physically threatened you?"

"Sure as hell did. They scared the hell out of me. A friend, Lenny Goldstein, who owns a clothing shop and barters with me for his dentistry, said the market was hot for pills. He would buy all I could get. I started writing prescriptions all over Orange County for Ritalin and Percodan. I sold to him for about ten times what I paid so I made a piss pot of cash. Enough to keep the Russians happy. But then I started seeing articles in the paper about the DEA getting wind of this kind of thing. I decided to get out while I could. I'd already told Lenny this was my last deal."

"How much do you think you've made?"

"Over the last couple of years, about a hundred and fifty K."

Schneider whistled and circled the figure one hundred and fifty thousand on his pad. He relit his cigar and tapped the ash in the tray.

"This could mean jail time plus a big fine. And you'll probably lose your license."

"No fucking way."

"You bet pal. I'll do the best I can but you'd better make some arrangements for your practice. You could be behind bars for a year."

⊁

Later that afternoon as Friedrich plucked deadheads in the memorial garden, the sound of Frankie's voice broke into his thoughts. Thank God. He'd remembered.

"There you are," Frankie said. "I thought you'd be in your room."

"It's ten years today."

"I know, Dad. That's why I came over. Sorry I haven't been around. I've been so damn busy with work."

"You look like you've been up all night," Friedrich said. The bags under Frankie's eyes made it look like he'd been doing something other than working. He'd been spending time with a fast crowd since he divorced Kandi. Now, the piper was taking his toll.

"I thought you worked on Saturdays."

"I blocked today out because I wanted to come over and spend some time with you. It's been awhile."

"I know you're busy. How are things going?"

"The practice is humming along as usual. Lots of people getting their teeth capped. White, whiter and whitest," he said. "Almost psychedelic."

"How about the investments?"

"Things are slowing down a bit. Job layoffs. People are nervous. Joey Kazlov is the developer and he's done a lot of these projects. He's confident it'll pick up soon."

"I hope so for your sake."

Frankie pulled a package of Marlboros from his pocket and lit one.

"I thought you'd given that up." Friedrich waved the smoke away from his face.

"Lots of pressure these days, Dad. It helps take off the edge. I should have listened to you and stepped back from that deal."

"Some projects take awhile to work themselves out," Friedrich said. "Fortunately, the practice is solid. Things will turn around eventually."

Frankie took another drag and snuffed the butt into the ground. "I can't believe it's been ten years," he said. "It's like it was yesterday."

Friedrich remembered the eulogy Frankie had given as if it were yesterday as well. His final words had been, "Mom, I'll always love you and you'll always have a special place in my heart." Feelings of regret filled Friedrich once again but he pushed them away. Frankie and Eva had been closer than he could ever hope to be. Too late now.

"I brought something to clean up the marker," Frankie said. As he had done each year, he dropped to his knees and dug away tufts of grass around Eva's memorial headstone. He washed it clean, and then used a rag with polish and buffed the surface. He stood and admired the engraved marble. "That looks better."

"Yes, thank you," Friedrich said. "What're you doing for the rest of the day? I was hoping we could go somewhere for supper."

"I'd love to, Dad but I've got a meeting with Kazlov." He looked at his watch and frowned. "Shit, I better get going. He hates it when I'm late."

"It's good to see you," Friedrich said. "Come anytime you get a moment. By the way, I'd like to take some of Eva's ashes back to Israel before I get too old. She was so fond of the country. I'd like you to come with me. I'll pay for the trip."

Frankie wrapped Friedrich in his arms and embraced him longer than usual. When he stepped back, his eyes were watering and he wiped them with his sleeve.

"Are you okay?"

"Yeah, I'm fine, Dad. It's a sad day, that's all." He cleared his throat and smiled. "I'd love to go with you. Once this business deal is all wrapped up, we'll plan for it."

⋏

Frankie left Parkside Grove with tears in his eyes. He drove back to his apartment building and pulled into his spot next to the elevator, grateful he had not renewed his lease on his Mercedes convertible. He had paid cash for a smaller used model instead. At least that wouldn't be hanging over his head.

A week's worth of dirty dishes and gym clothes lay strewn over the unmade bed, causing the studio to reek like a dumpster on a hot day. He swore and slid open the window to let in the breeze and then he loaded the dishwasher and made quick work of the bed. He threw the rest of the stuff into the washing machine. That would be good enough for now.

He grabbed a beer from the fridge. When he looked around the room, he didn't see much that he would miss. The furniture, tired and worn, was junk handed down from the remodeled beach house of Kandi's parents. It was all she had agreed to give him after they split. She'd been a real piece of work.

He stuffed a suitcase with clothes and toiletries and then scanned the room one more time. His favorite guitar caught his eye, a Stratocaster, and also two framed pictures on a side table. One showed him laughing among a beaming group of Vietnamese school children in Da Nang, when he'd worked with The East Meets West Foundation. He had organized six trips and was planning a seventh that would take his team of dentists, hygienists and assistants into the highlands to care for the tribes. That and the music were what really turned him on. He took the photo out of the frame and tucked it in with his clothes. The other picture showed him with Lenny Goldstein on the beach in Puerto Vallarta. Lenny had scribbled underneath *Buds forever, 1991.* Those were the days. All over now. He stuffed it in the trash with all the food left in the fridge.

At five o'clock he cracked another beer and dialed a cab. For the last time, he went onto the balcony to smoke a joint and watch the sun go down.

⋏

The following Wednesday, as Friedrich worked on a new clay sculpture in the courtyard, the director of the lodge, Rosalia Gonzales, came up from behind and tapped him on the shoulder. A man and a woman in uniform stood behind her at the entrance.

"Good afternoon, Doctor Mendelssohn. Those two police officers want to see you. I think you should speak to them in the boardroom."

"What is it, Rosalia? What do they want?"

She spoke quietly. "They said it was confidential. I'll seat them and bring some coffee."

Friedrich set down his spatula. What the hell was this all about? "Tell them I'll be there in a few minutes."

He took the elevator up to his room. The police could only mean one thing. Frankie was in some kind of trouble. If he'd missed any alimony payments, Kandi and her father would have been quick to react. He could help him with that. Or maybe it had something to do with that pie-in-the-sky investment scheme he'd been talking about. He grabbed a pen and paper and returned to the main floor.

Rosalia met him at the door to the boardroom and introduced him.

"Officers Robinson and Werner," she said, smiling. "There's a carafe of coffee on the bureau. Call me if you need anything more." She closed the door and the two officers stepped forward to shake Friedrich's hand.

"Good afternoon, Doctor."

When the three of them sat, the female officer opened a notepad and spoke first. "We understand that you're the father of Dr. Frank Mendelssohn who operates a dental practice on Wiltshire Boulevard."

"Yes," Friedrich said. "Why are you here? Is there a problem?"

"When did you see him last?"

Friedrich's mouth parted and he removed his glasses.

"A few days ago, on Saturday. For the anniversary of his mother's passing."

"We're sorry to hear about that." The male officer folded his sunglasses on the table and met Friedrich's eyes. "Do you have any knowledge of your son's financial affairs?"

"How do you mean? His dental practice or...?"

"Any money that he may owe. That kind of thing."

"He has bank loans and overhead like anyone else. And a hefty alimony payment that he always complains about. Is that why you're here?"

The woman scribbled notes then looked up. "Are you aware of a current investigation into fraudulent insurance billings?"

"Oh God no. Tell me that's not true. Sacrificing his integrity. That would be unconscionable."

"There are other liabilities as well," she said. "Unfortunately they're owed to people known to be more intimidating than an insurance company or an ex-wife."

"Who are you talking about?"

"The Russian mafia."

His forehead creased like an accordion and his tremor doubled in tempo.

"I knew he was dealing with some pretty smooth real estate developers and I had concerns that he'd borrowed too much money. He did mention a man named, Kazlov, the other day. But I had no idea..."

"You're talking about the Santa Barbara project?"

"I think that's where he said it was. A no-lose real estate situation."

"Until sales ground to a halt and loans were called," said the woman. "The whole thing went bust."

"Frankie was convinced that he'd triple his investment. He made it sound like things were just taking a little longer."

"He's committed around two hundred thousand and he still owes over half of that to them. These people can be brutal if they don't get paid. We think they shook him down and coerced him into writing fake prescriptions for Percodan and Ritalin. He was selling the pills to a guy named Lenny Goldstein and using the profits to pay off the Russians. When we arrested Goldstein, he named your son as his supplier. We caught him in the act of making a drug deal. He's been charged with trafficking."

"My son is not a drug dealer." Friedrich's voice rang shrill. He gripped his thighs and glared across at the two officers whose eyes never wavered.

"We arrested him last Friday night and he got out on bail Saturday morning."

Friedrich's eyes widened. "He came here Saturday afternoon, to talk about his mother. I thought he looked worn out."

"He'd been in custody all night. On Monday morning, his office had a message saying he was sick. But he didn't return their calls. After three days, they went to his apartment but he didn't answer the door. So, they called us. We found no sign of a forced entry and most of his things are still there. Do you have any idea where he might be?"

Friedrich shook his head. He pulled his handkerchief from his pocket and coughed into it. "I could never have imagined this," he said. "Frankie has made his share of mistakes, but this is not who he is, I assure you. These men must have threatened him in some way. He would never stoop so low."

"We're checking all the flights out of LAX over the weekend and should have some idea soon. We're sorry to have to bring this to you, Doctor."

"What if they've kidnapped him? I've heard stories about this." He blinked back tears.

"It's too soon to jump to conclusions," said the man. "We'll let you know when we have anything."

"Should I be calling a lawyer?" Friedrich asked. "I must do all I can to help him. And, oh my God, what about the office? I've surrendered my license so I can't help him there." He slammed his fist on the table. "Damn it all. I cannot believe he's got himself into this kind of trouble."

⟑

Friedrich sat alone in the boardroom unsure where to start. If Frankie had been abducted by Russian thugs, then it was only a matter of time until he was contacted for a ransom. The thought of Frankie being tortured made him sick to his stomach. He got up and walked outside for a breath of air. If Frankie had skipped bail to avoid going to jail, the question was where would he go? Israel? Never.

With the perpetual state of unrest between Palestinians and Israelis, Friedrich had remained reluctant to tell Frankie about his Arabic ancestry, certain it would cause nothing but confusion and tension within the family. But Eva had insisted, and now Friedrich was thankful that she told Frankie when he was a teenager. He had never shown any interest in pursuing his roots or finding out more about his relatives in Gaza, so Friedrich felt sure he wouldn't have gone over there. He paced the sidewalk outside the residence and debated whether he should have mentioned Frankie's heritage to the police. Finally he turned back toward the entrance and said to himself, "Miriam will know what to do."

Miriam was one of the first people he had met at the residence. They had become good friends and formidable bridge partners. He took the elevator to the second floor and knocked on her door.

"How ya doin' love?" she said. "You're looking a little pale. Are you feeling alright?"

Friedrich stepped into the room and Miriam closed the door behind him. "I was just making a cup of tea. Do you want some?"

"Frankie's disappeared," he said. "I'm sick with worry."

The smile disappeared from Miriam's face. She sat beside him and stilled his hand. "Okay," she said. "Tell me what's going on."

"I don't know what's going on," Friedrich said. "That's the problem."

"How do you know that he's disappeared?"

Friedrich told her about the police visit and about Frankie's arrest and his involvement with the Russian mafia. Friedrich had known something was wrong but he didn't push it, hoping to avoid the inevitable fight. "Before he left, he gave me a long hug, almost as if he was saying goodbye."

CHAPTER 22

Relieved to have snagged a seat on standby, Frankie settled in by the window. The engines roared and he felt pressed back in the seat. The ground whizzed by until the wheels lifted and the jet lumbered into the air. He tried to doze while they climbed to forty thousand feet but his mind refused, replaying it all for the millionth time. Everything that had ever happened to bring him to this point...of no return.

The good fortune of being adopted by two loving parents was like winning the lottery when he considered the alternative---life as an orphan in a refugee camp. Sure, things had been firm and regimented but they always acted in fairness and good faith. If problems arose, and there had been many, he shared full responsibility. Friedrich and Eva were gifts from heaven. But oh how he'd let them down. He caught the flight attendant's eye and ordered a double Jack Daniels.

Marrying Kandi turned out to be his biggest mistake but that was all behind him now. What happened after was the problem.

Friedrich had tried to warn him but it was no use. He had to have it all. The over-the-top office, fast cars, women, the rock-star lifestyle. Frankie Mendelssohn, Superstar. What a fucking joke. Superjerk on a treadmill to hell was more like it. Right before his cocaine eyes. Duh. How could he have missed it?

With production quotas, he pressured his staff to recommend unnecessary treatment and cook the books. Stupid investments put him into hock with Russian thieves and left him no choice but to run drugs like some ghetto schmuck. There it was, pure and simple. Fifteen wasted years summed up in a few short paragraphs. He raised his hand for another double, promising himself it'd be his last.

⋏

The soles of his Italian shoes were no match for the heat radiating into the bottom of his feet off the Cairo tarmac. Inside, the hot passenger terminal felt cool by comparison. Amongst incoherent announcements and the suffocating odors of humanity and spice, he looked around for anything familiar to get his bearings.

He recognized a woman who had sat across the aisle from him on the flight. She wore American-style clothing and tugged at the arm of her daughter. He waited for them to pass and followed them to the baggage carousel, where the conveyor belt spilled luggage from below. As the crowd surged forward to collect their belongings he stood back and waited. After four circuits of the belt, his suitcase had still not appeared. Either his bag was lost or security was already on to him.

With only a half dozen items left on the belt, a terminal employee pulled up with a cart. As he hurried over to inquire, his case tumbled through the chute, one of its buckles undone and a strap hanging loose. He grabbed it off the conveyor and carried it over to a bench to inspect the contents. His folded clothes were ruffled and creased. Somebody had gone through it.

The employee in the cart stared at him.

He glanced around, half expecting someone to tap him on the shoulder. When no one did, he zipped the bag closed and headed for the exits.

With his shirt clinging like a rag and a thirty-six hour shadow covering his face, he resembled one of the locals as he lined up at the customs counter. But his passport said otherwise. The customs officer examined it and then checked a list on a clipboard. He lifted his gaze and met Frankie's eyes.

"American," the agent said. "Why are you here?"

His grip tightened on the handle of the suitcase. "Family matters."

The officer waited for an explanation. "Your name is Jew."

"Relatives in Gaza. I'm here to visit." He hoped that would be good enough because he had no address or other contact information. He knew only what Friedrich and Eva had told him years before---that his father's name was Jamal al-Massri and that the family had lived somewhere in Gaza.

The officer stamped his passport and waved him through.

In the arrival section a woman wearing a niqab behind a currency counter surprised him by speaking perfect English as he exchanged American cash for a bundle of Egyptian pounds. How weird is that? He walked back into the heat and hailed a taxi to take him downtown.

"Tahrir Square," he said. Pictures and a description on the front of the in-flight magazine referred to it as the historic heart of Cairo. It would be a good place to start.

The taxi drove deeper into the city along Qasr al-Ayni Street where traffic and pedestrians competed for every inch, creating a crushing density from all sides. Peering down side streets choked with shoppers, pack-animals and street vendors, he felt a strange affinity with all those who had the same olive skin and black hair as he did. At a traffic light, scents of cumin and coriander wafted through the open window and stirred his appetite.

The driver turned around and pointed. "Tahrir, Tahrir." Frankie looked through the windshield at a circular road with four lanes of stalled traffic.

He elicited a smile from the driver when he handed him a fifty-pound note and got out of the car. Up the first side street, he approached a line of people waiting to be served at a vending cart, the word *Koshari* printed red on its side. Behind the counter, a man blended a concoction of rice, lentils and macaroni. Frankie handed him a one pound note for a pita roll stuffed to the brim. The first mouthful tasted of cloves and reminded him of a medicament he'd often used to treat sensitive teeth. He nearly choked thinking of what he'd left behind and threw back a swig of sweet tea to wash the food down. Where was this all going?

An overhead sign down the street marked the first words he'd seen printed in English: Pyramid Hotel. A ceiling fan in the lobby worked double duty with little effect and as he wiped a sleeve across his brow, a clerk wearing a rumpled suit glanced up from behind the desk. The badge on his chest read: Amir.

"One night room," Frankie said, holding up a single finger.

"How will you pay for that, sir?"

"You speak English, Amir. That's a relief. How much?"

"Twenty pounds. I had a good teacher at school. I will need to see your passport, sir."

"Is there a bus station around here?" Frankie tapped his fingers on the desk and kept one eye on the door.

Amir filled in a registration card and returned his passport.

"You look like you're in a hurry, sir. Where do you want to go?"

"Gaza."

Amir frowned and set down his pen. "Things are very tense there right now," he said. "Intifada. The Israelis have been shutting down the border and there have been disturbances. Kids throwing rocks at the soldiers, tear gas, things like that. Some people have been killed. Are you staying with anyone?"

"Not yet. I'm a dentist and I've come to volunteer. My father was from there and I want to locate my relatives. The family name is al-Massri."

"al-Massri is an old Egyptian name. Very common in Gaza. Like Smith or Jones."

"There must be a registry. Someplace where I can get information?"

"Not in Gaza. It's a different world there, sir. And, I must caution you. You will not be welcome. Either at the border or inside. It's a very dangerous place right now."

"Not good to be an American, huh?"

"Even worse. A Jew."

"I'm not a Jew, damn it. Mendelssohn's my adopted name. I was born al-Massri." His voice echoed through the room and he glanced out to the street fearing he'd been overheard. "Sorry," he said. "I'm overtired."

"I believe you, sir. But here everyone lies. People are suspicious. You must be careful."

Frankie climbed a flight of stairs and opened the door to a dingy room that overlooked the street. He dropped his suitcase on the floor and collapsed on the bed. If any of his clothes or belongings had been stolen, he'd find out tomorrow. He tucked his wallet and passport under the mattress and with the din of horns and shouts coming through the window he closed his eyes and drifted off.

⚔

The next morning he devoured a breakfast of bread, yoghurt, tomatoes, cucumbers and the best coffee he'd ever tasted. He guessed that getting into Gaza wouldn't be easy. Being stopped at the border could mean being sent back to serve time in the States. But the sooner he tried, the better his chances of getting through. Surely the Israelis wouldn't be refusing entry to humanitarian volunteers. In the lobby, he spoke to another desk clerk who hailed him a taxi and gave the driver instructions in Arabic.

"He will take you to the bus depot, sir."

"I'll need him to bring me back too," Frankie said.

"Yes sir. He will wait for you."

The taxi drove through congested streets and alleys until it pulled into a plaza where a fleet of dust-laden buses had parked diagonally in front of the depot. Frankie inched his way toward a counter with the word, Gaza, printed above the grate. He purchased a one-way ticket to the border town of Rafah.

When he arrived back at the hotel, Amir waved him over from across the street.

"What's going on?" Frankie said.

"Have you changed you mind, sir? About Gaza."

"No, why?"

"Some men asked for you this morning after you checked out. They might have been Egyptian Military Police. Very nasty people."

"Did you tell them anything?"

"No. We don't trust the police. The clerk on duty told them you stayed for one night and left. Which is the truth, is it not?"

"I'm taking the bus to Rafah at eight-thirty tonight," Frankie said. "I appreciate your concern, Amir, but I've come all this way. I've got to give it a shot."

"Just like John Wayne," Amir said, with a grin.

Frankie chuckled. "You like cowboy movies?"

"Oh yes, very much. They help with my English. 'True Grit' is my favorite one. You're like John Wayne, sir...riding off into the Indian Country."

"That bad, is it?" He dug into his pocket and handed Amir a five pound note. "Will this get you into a movie?"

"More than one," Amir said, smiling.

"Be my guest. Can you do me a favor?"

"Yes sir, anything."

"I need to locate a dental supply company. I want to buy some equipment."

"Not to worry, sir. Give me a few minutes. I'll bring your belongings."

As Amir dodged through traffic and crossed to the hotel, Frankie looked up and down sidewalks that already bustled with commerce. A bearded man wearing dark sunglasses sat by the entrance to the hotel and stared at him. Frankie felt a chill and paced back and forth smoking a cigarette until Amir ran back across the street with his suitcase.

"I called a dentist I know from my mosque. It's not far." He waved and a taxi pulled up in front of them. "I will speak to your driver. It is best you do not return here. The police may come back. Good luck my friend."

"You bet, pilgrim." They shared a laugh as Frankie got in and Amir closed the door.

⅄

A sales clerk who spoke English led Frankie into the back of a warehouse. As he followed, he heard the voice of another customer from one of the side aisles who looked similar to the man he'd seen in front of the hotel. His creepy feeling returned. The man pointed to boxes on shelves, while a clerk with a ladder pulled them down and loaded a cart.

"I'm looking for oral surgery instruments," Frankie said, to his clerk. "I'll need forceps, elevators, scalpels, the works."

"Right this way, sir. I'm sure we have everything you'll need. Top quality. Where will you need it delivered?"

"I'll take it with me," Frankie said. "I'm on my way to Rafah tonight. I'm going to volunteer in the refugee camps up there."

The salesman glanced at him with a frown. "Lots of problems, right now," he said.

"So I hear," Frankie said.

"When you get across the border ask someone to direct you to the orphanage. They need volunteers. But be careful. It's a dangerous place."

"Right," Frankie said.

He spent the next hour choosing from an array of English manufactured instruments. He paid the bill and then crossed through traffic to a bazaar where he bought two duffle-bags to carry it all. He tapped the driver on the shoulder. "Bus depot."

The driver got him back to the depot with two hours to spare. He got rid of his suitcase by dumping his stuff into one of the bags and then dragged them to a shady spot near the bus with, Rafah 2030, on its front window. Resting his head on one, he looped his arm through the straps of the other and closed his eyes. He grimaced, thinking about the mess he'd left behind for Friedrich and his staff to sort out. How the fuck had he ever let this happen?

Chapter 23

Half asleep and confused, he jerked awake when a man in a tattered robe bumped into his foot. As the man raised a hand to apologize, Frankie noticed the crowd milling about the front door of his bus. He looked at his watch. Almost eight-thirty. He'd damn near missed it.

By pushing aside a cage with two goats, he made enough room to squeeze his bags into the storage bin underneath. The driver punched his ticket and he looked for an empty seat. The evening air was oppressive and the interior of the bus felt like a sauna. He walked back about halfway, to where a man about his own age, with a beard, lifted his briefcase off the seat beside him.

"Empty?" Frankie asked, unsure whether it was the same man he'd seen earlier or not.

The man gestured for him to sit. He wore a wrinkled suit and an open-necked shirt.

Frankie nodded and sat down.

"No speak, Arabic," he said.

"Where are you from?"

Frankie took a double-take.

"California."

"Did I see you earlier today?" the man said. "At the dental warehouse?"

"Okay, that's where it was," Frankie said. "I've just arrived and everybody around here looks the same to me. It's the dark hair and beards. You speak with an English accent."

"I was educated in London. At a boarding school. You're a long way from home."

"Sure am," Frankie said. "Are you from Cairo?"

"Rafah."

"The border crossing."

"It's a town, of about ten thousand. Mostly refugees. It straddles the border between Egypt and the Gaza Strip. What brings you here?"

"I'm not sure yet," Frankie said. "My parents were killed in 1947 when I was a year old. A Jewish couple from Jerusalem adopted me and we moved to the States when I was two."

"Why are you going to Gaza?"

"I think my father was from there. I've come back to see if I can find anyone who may have known him. Maybe I can learn more about what happened to my family."

"It will be very difficult. Most of the old people are descendants of the refugees from the '48 war. Some aren't even sure when they were born. The younger ones have little connection that far back."

"Well at least I can be of some use," Frankie said. "I'm a dentist."

"I thought you might be. That's why I saved a seat when I saw you outside. I overheard you speaking to the clerk in the warehouse. I was buying supplies for one of our orphanages."

"And you need volunteers?"

"Desperately. With all the unrest, volunteers are scarce. My name is Hassan Mashurr."

"Frankie Mendelssohn. It's a pleasure."

From his wallet, Frankie pulled the faded photograph that Friedrich had given him years before and passed it to Hassan. "This was taken just after I was born. It's the only picture I have of my parents. Adlyia and Jamal al-Massri. My name was Fadi...before they changed it to Frankie."

"Do you know how your father got to Gaza?"

"No idea. I don't know anything about them. That's why I've come back."

"The border will be a problem," Hassan said. "The Israeli guards will do whatever they can to make it difficult. They might even detain you."

"Why?"

"It's always about security. They'll contact the American Embassy to do a background check on your passport and get authorization. And they'll do whatever they can to prevent you from assisting us. They don't like outsiders seeing what it's like in those camps."

As night fell, Hassan closed his eyes and dozed.

Frankie stared out into the darkness where lights from villages appeared like apparitions through the blowing sand. His pulse raced and he took deep breaths to quell the angst. Hassan's comment about the reception that lay in store for him marked his third warning. Maybe this was a bad idea.

⋏

As light from the streets filtered through the windows, and horns from on-coming buses and trucks blared, Hassan woke up and took a folded sheet of paper from his pocket. The Arabic printing on the page meant nothing to Frankie but at the top in a bold letters he could read: al-Ikhwan al Muslimin.

"I'm a member of the Muslim Brotherhood," Hassan said. He pointed to the words at the top of the page. If they let you across, call me. I can put you to work." He scribbled down a number and handed the sheet to Frankie. "I won't be able to help you here. Too many complications." He looked over his shoulder. "I see a couple of free seats back there. Move to one of them. When the guard comes in, act like you've never met me."

Frankie had only just moved when floodlights illuminated the entry and departure lanes of the border station that enclosed both sides of the highway. As traffic slowed, he leaned out his window to see a procession of buses, trucks and vans crawling forward toward the crossing. Flashers pulsed from two camouflaged vehicles with machine guns mounted on their rooftops. The bus stopped and his heart leapt as a guard stepped inside and peered down the aisle. The street food he'd eaten the night before rippled through his gut.

"Papers!" The guard, pale and thin, wore a lieutenant's stripes on his shoulder. He walked along the aisle examining identity documents until he came to the seat where Hassan was sitting. About twenty, if that, he had the freckled face of a redhead and feigned an air of superiority, no doubt to disguise his fear. Frankie had fought guys like that in high school. God's chosen people. Frankie's darker hair and complexion had always set him apart.

Hassan handed his documents to the lieutenant who barked a question in Arabic. Hassan answered in a calm voice and nodded. The officer handed him back his papers and looked over at Frankie.

"Passport," he said. Frankie rubbed the cover against his pants and handed it over.

"What are you doing here?" the guard said. "Looking to get killed?"

"Humanitarian work...dentistry."

"Where?" Frankie glanced at Hassan who looked away.

"Wherever I can help."

"You with him?" The lieutenant nodded toward to Hassan.

"No," Hassan said.

"I wasn't talking to you, Mashurr." The officer glared at Hassan and tossed Frankie's passport back into his lap.

"You should help your own people," he said, looking at Frankie. "Not these animals."

Hassan's eyes narrowed. The officer turned and shifted his attention toward the Arabs in last row.

Frankie followed Hassan's lead and looked straight ahead while the guard checked the last two passengers then turned back toward the front. Coming abreast of Frankie's seat, he stopped.

"Let me see that passport again." Snatching it from Frankie's hand, the lieutenant held it up and scratched at the finish of the photograph with his fingernail. He glanced back down at Frankie to compare the image with who he saw in front of him.

Frankie dropped his eyes as he'd seen Hassan and other Arabs doing. Staring down at his shoes, he felt like a fool. His face flushed and he bolted to his feet. "I'm an American citizen. What's your goddamn problem?" He stood toe-to-toe with the lieutenant.

The officer drew his Glock from its holster. "Don't make stupid," he said, and stuffed the passport into the pocket of his battle tunic. He waved the pistol toward the front. "Move...outside." He shouted an order in Hebrew and Frankie heard a sharp reply from another guard standing on the ground.

"What the hell's this about?" Frankie said.

The lieutenant racked the slide of his pistol. "Walk to the front and get off."

Frankie stepped down from the bus and winced as a rifle butt dug into his back and shoved him toward an armored vehicle. Static crackled from a short-wave radio and a leashed dog bared its teeth and growled. The lieutenant spoke into a handset and relayed the passport information in Hebrew. Mendelssohn and Los Angeles were the only words Frankie could pick out. The second guard held an automatic rifle and stared at him with a Marlboro stuck between his lips. The lieutenant hung up and turned around. Frankie stiffened.

"Do you have a sponsor?"

"No, I've come alone. I brought my own equipment and supplies."

"You need authorization from the American Embassy. Collect your luggage and wait across the road. There's a bus going back to Cairo."

Frankie heard shouting and turned to see another guard pulling a driver down from his truck. The man hit the ground hard with his right arm twisted back. Writhing beside the truck with a separated shoulder, other drivers jumped from their trucks and ran forward shouting. Electric motors whizzed. Two machine gunners perched atop the personnel carriers spun around and trained their sights on the drivers. The lieutenant handed him back his passport and shouted into his ear.

"Grab your gear and get over to the other side. Now."

"This isn't right," Frankie said.

"Go, before I lock you up with the rest of them."

Frankie watched several drivers herded at gunpoint into a holding pen. On the other side of the checkpoint a hand-painted sign read: *Welcome to Rafah Land*. An Israeli sergeant waved his arms and ordered the trucks off the road. Crowds of Palestinian boys pressed up against the fence and jeered. Frankie ducked as rocks bounced off the military vehicle beside him.

"Over here." Frankie saw Hassan standing next to the bus driver who opened the baggage compartment. "Which are yours?"

"Those two," Frankie said. "But they won't let me through. I need to get authorization."

Frankie cringed down at the sound of an explosion. "Whoa. That was close."

"Tear gas," Hassan said. "No matter what you do they'll find another excuse. They don't want you to help us." He picked up one of the bags. "Follow me."

"That lieutenant told me to take that bus on the other side."

"Do you want to get in or not? They're clamping down because of the demonstrations. They're going to block the crossing until we starve. It could take weeks."

On the other side the bus had begun to load. But going back to the embassy in Cairo meant nothing but a trip home to the slammer. With nothing to lose, he grabbed the other bag and followed Hassan.

Guards harassed a group of Palestinian women carrying burlap sacks over their shoulders. Yelling Hebrew obscenities that Frankie had heard in high school, the guards wrenched sacks from the women's hands and dumped their stale fruit and vegetables on the ground. As the women bent down to pick up what hadn't been squashed by the soldiers' boots, Palestinian men in checked headscarves watched from the side of the road.

He could have been in a scene from 'Lawrence of Arabia'. Seething expressions of hatred caused him to quicken his pace to catch up with Hassan. Before he reached him, he stumbled into a girl, dressed in black. With tears streaming down her face and a howling infant in her arms, she spat at the guards and crossed the road to join the queue boarding the bus back to Cairo.

He couldn't fathom what he was seeing. As a child, he'd been told about Israeli heroes who had fought against Arab hordes to win back their homeland. He'd been dragged to fundraisers where old men and women spoke about the horrors of the Holocaust. How it must never happen again. He'd served on the campaigns of politicians who promised to do the right thing for Israel. Any party who even dared to suggest that the Arabs had valid grievances deserved to be defeated.

Everything he'd heard or seen had painted the Israeli military as a courageous citizen army fighting for the rights of Jews to survive. Now all he saw was arrogance, humiliation and deceit. How could he have believed all that shit?

"They're turning everyone back," yelled Hassan. "We need to get out of here before the Egyptian Police come."

The flash of headlights startled Frankie. A pickup truck parked in the darkness to his left started its engine and pulled forward. Hassan threw the duffle bags and two cartons into the flatbed and pulled Frankie up beside him. "Crouch down and hold on."

"Where are we going?" Frankie coughed and covered his face to block the dust.

"They treat us like animals," Hassan said. "Believe me, their time is coming."

Hassan was invisible to Frankie in the dark but the revulsion in his voice rang clear, unique and unmistakable, intended solely for enemies of a different race. This was what his father had always talked about.

Chapter 24

The truck rolled to a stop and the driver doused the lights. Hassan dropped the bags and cartons to the ground and leapt over the side."Stay right behind me." Under a full moon, they crept down an alley that stunk of raw sewage until Hassan stopped to fumble with a ring of keys. He opened a chained padlock and they entered a yard encompassed by stony limits six feet high.

In the moonlight, Frankie saw the roofline of a house.

An armed man wearing a baklava appeared from the shadows. "This way."

They followed him down an outside stairwell where a sliver of light seeped from under a door. Three knocks and it creaked open. Two men in mud-caked overalls sipped coffee and smoked around a coal-oil lamp. They stood and welcomed Hassan with presses to his cheeks, and then Hassan nodded toward Frankie and said, "American."

They scowled and yelled their concerns at Hassan until he slammed his fist on the table and the room became quiet. He opened the zippers of the bags to show them the contents. All three spoke at once.

"They think you're a spy," he said. "They want you blind-folded."

Frankie looked at the cold expressions blocking the doorway.

"Who are these guys?" His voice cracked and he coughed to rid his throat of the dust sticking to it.

"They're from the Rafah Camp on the other side. They dig the tunnels. That's how they support their families. They can take no chances of being discovered."

"What if I don't go?"

Hassan brought a glow to the tip of a cigarette and met Frankie's eyes. "You already know too much, Mendelssohn. This is the only way now."

⚓

Frankie read his meaning and took stock. What if no one had heard of Jamal and Adlyia? Friedrich had said there were no relatives. Only that one was ˙hia, the other Sunni, whatever that meant. On top of that he had no proof that he was Fadi al-Massri, only a passport identifying him as Franklin Ben Mendelssohn, an American Jew, born in Jerusalem. What the hell had he been thinking?

Hassan raised his voice and gave an order. One of the men stepped forward with a twisted length of cloth. Frankie recognized the checked pattern of the headscarves worn by the drivers at the border. The man cinched it tight across his eyes. The door creaked again and a breeze touched his face. He was pushed up the steps and across the yard until he heard the clink of chain and the squeak of the gate. For what seemed like fifteen or twenty minutes, callused hands pushed him along a path until they stopped. The screech of a sliding door rattled him and someone lifted his foot to the threshold of a vehicle. As his fingers sought something to grasp, other hands shoved him inside. The door ground back along its runner and slammed shut.

His chest heaved and his bladder felt ready to burst. He stretched out both arms and touched the walls and the roof. Wooden-slats on the floor made him think of packing crates. As his panting subsided, he listened to the silence, unsure whether he could sense the breathing of others or not. In the distance he heard sirens.

He huddled in the stifling interior until he heard voices outside. The front doors opened and the sliding door beside him grated back across its runner. A wash of air flooded his face and the vehicle jostled under the weight of men clambering inside. Now the smell of tobacco breath dominated the space. With two meaty shoulders pressing against his, the vehicle pulled away and the blindfold tugged loose.

He was inside the back of a van with the driver's section blocked off. The two men he'd seen in the room sat on either side of him.

Hassan leaned over toward him and said, "If we're stopped by an Egyptian patrol, don't say a word."

The van's nose tipped and the driver pumped his brakes to control their descent down a grade. The front wheels skidded to the right when they reached the bottom. The carriage twisted and the vehicle shook and bounced along a trail of rocks and potholes. Frankie's tailbone had gone numb by the time they stopped. One of the men cinched the blindfold back over his eyes. The door rasped and he was walked into another building where he smelled gasoline fumes and a door thudded behind him.

"We'll be going down in a few minutes," Hassan said.

Enclosed spaces had haunted Frankie's dreams for years and bitterness filled the back of his throat. His heart pounded with renewed vengeance and urine dribbled down the inside of his legs. Rocking back and forth to contain himself, he heard Hassan shout in Arabic. The blindfold dropped from his eyes and he was led outside to where a flashlight revealed a hole in the ground. Pinching his nose against the stench, he started to urinate but the impatient pacing behind him and the thought of what might come next, made his bladder seize. Before he could finish, the man grabbed his shoulder and pulled him back to the room. It didn't matter, he was soaked anyway.

A four-foot opening in the floor exposed a shaft leading down to the tunnel. The rumble of a gasoline motor had the sound of a lawnmower back home. If only.

A pulley raised a wooden cradle from below and when it reached floor level, a switch kicked the engine into neutral. One of the men grunted and loaded on three reinforced cartons. Two were stamped, *Medical Supplies* and the third read: *High Explosive*.

When the cartons dropped, he almost puked.

More shouts from below and the empty cradle shot back up.

"I'll go first," Hassan said. "Your bags are down there." He stepped on the cradle and his head descended into the darkness.

Frankie glanced back toward the doorway where two sets of hard eyes made it plain there was only one way to go---down.

The inside of both cheeks bled where he had bitten through with his molars. His tongue felt glued to his palate. The hiss of air leaking from a hose snaking down through the floor reminded him of the compressors in his dental office, where he should've been, if he had any brains at all.

The cradle reappeared and he stepped on. As it dropped down, he counted about thirty ladder slats along the shaft wall until he touched ground. The dank smell caused him to spit vomit on his shoes. A single bulb threw shadows across a dirt chamber as the trapdoor above him closed.

"They broke through a month ago," Hassan said. He pointed his light at the tunnel opening which looked about the same size as the shaft they'd just come down. A track made of planks extended into the chamber where three carts sat tethered one behind the other. A steel cable hooked to the lead cart ran into the tunnel's entrance.

Frankie saw the explosives, medical supplies and his bags lashed to the last cart. "There's hardly room to fit," he said. "What if we need to turn around?"

"There will be no need for that." Hassan pushed the two empty carts forward with the loaded one trailing behind. "See how smooth they roll." He grinned and took a last drag off his cigarette. "Ball-bearing wheels from grocery carts in Tel Aviv. The Israelis would be shocked if they knew how helpful they've been. You lie flat on the first one and drag yourself forward. I'll make sure this loaded cart behind us stays on the track. They're pulling us from the other end but with three carts, it's heavy. The sides aren't reinforced yet, so don't rub against them. If you feel anything falling just keep moving."

Frankie clutched one hand to his larynx and wheezed. "I don't know if I can do this."

"Don't worry. It's safe. We've been using it for three weeks with no problems. I'll be right behind you. Take this flashlight."

Frankie bent down and crawled forward into a prone position. He pulled himself into the entrance and looked back. Hassan lay stretched out on the cart behind him. He had no way out now.

"How far is it?"

Hassan aimed his flashlight up the tunnel and flicked it off and on. Three dim flashes came back from the other end. "See, it's not that far. Here we go." The cable tugged and the carts started to move. "Watch that your front wheels don't wander off the track."

Grains of sand dusted his shoulders as they moved into the darkness. The temperature rose and the air thinned as they moved farther from the entrance. After creeping along for about fifteen minutes, to what Frankie hoped was at least halfway, his right front wheel veered into the clay. Hassan bumped into his feet from behind.

"What's going on?"

"One wheel off the track."

"It's happened before," Hassan said. "Get off and lift it back on. Check to see that the castor isn't broken." Frankie rolled to the side and pressed himself against the wall of the tunnel. He turned the cart over and aimed his light on the wheel. Rapid gunfire echoed down the shaft behind them.

"Switch off your light!" Hassan said.

It was darker than his worst nightmares. He reached back to feel Hassan's arm. A convergence of shouts and flashlight beams probed the entrance.

"Egyptian military. Hurry. Get back on and pull the cable.

An explosion sent a shockwave up through the tunnel making Frankie's eardrums burn as if they were being pierced by hot nails. Rocks and clay flew through its wake like asteroids and the domed ceiling collapsed down on them. Hassan screamed. Frankie sensed the crush coming from behind and pulled his legs up into a fetal position. When the shuddering stopped, he felt like he was trapped inside a bubble. The siren of tinnitus rang from the center of his brain. He poked into the blackness and felt the cart wedged above him. Spitting and coughing into the triangular air space, he clawed at the loose debris in front of him. A rush of air came through from the other end.

"Cave-in," he yelled. "Help."

A shaft of light found his eyes.

"Hassan," he yelled. "Hassan?" There was nothing. He pushed his legs back and felt the packed rubble that buried Hassan. Twisting around to dig with his hands, the ground began to crumble and he stopped. Arabic shouts that he couldn't understand sounded like far away echoes. Shovels and picks brought a tumble of earth around his face and he felt a hand reach through. With two men opening a hole to drag him out, he pointed behind and shouted: "Hassan, back there, Hassan, dig, dig."

He crawled toward the light and climbed up a ladder to emerge on a floodlit patch of ground on the Gaza side. A man with a gray beard handed him a jug of water. He drank and spat out mouthfuls until the color changed from brown to clear. He pressed each nostril with his finger and blew out mucous and dirt until he could breathe. Men clambered from the tunnel and he heard the anguish of voices still below. Through dazed eyes, he watched. What the fuck had happened?

⚴

Calls from the shaft snapped him back to reality as Hassan was dragged out and laid beside him. He felt for a pulse but found none. He pried open Hassan's lower jaw and clawed out the debris until he could see to the back of his throat. Sealing his lips over Hassan's, he blew eight times and watched the chest expand. He followed with sixteen compressions over the sternum. Moving to repeat the sequence, he shouted at the men gathered around him. "Ambulance, ambulance." In the distance he heard a siren. "Stick with me, Hassan," he said. "You're all I've got, man."

A delivery truck pulled up beside them. Hassan coughed and the crowd murmured. Two men in white uniforms crouched down beside Frankie. As one inserted a needle into Hassan's vein, the other placed an oxygen mask over his nose.

Hassan's legs were skewed.

The medic slit open Hassan's pants, where the yellow bone of both femurs pierced the skin of his thighs. They lifted him into the makeshift ambulance; a moment later, a hand-held siren wailed and they drove away. The grizzled man who had given him the water came up and spoke.

"My name is Issa Mashurr, Hassan's brother. Thank you for saving his life."

"I hope he makes it," Frankie said.

"Hassan called me before you went down. I know who you are. You will stay with me tonight."

"We were just about through when..."

"Egyptian soldiers discovered the tunnel and blew it up. Someone informed."

Through a veil of cloud they heard the thumping of helicopters. "We must go," Issa said, looking up. "Israelis coming."

They got into a car idling with its headlights off and dissolved into the nameless streets of the refugee camp. The man beside the driver pressed a radiophone to his ear while observers on rooftops relayed the positions of personnel carriers converging on the tunnel. Frankie braced himself each time the driver made a sudden turn to avoid the dragnet closing in on them.

Flares boomed in the sky, illuminating roadsides littered with blasted concrete and rebar. The chatter on the phone became more frantic and the tension inside the car escalated. They skidded into a blind alley and stopped. Helicopter spotlights probed and missed. The driver said something and they all looked at a dim light blinking in front. Two men stepped out of the shadows and directed them into a garage off to the side. Issa opened the car door and spoke to them before he looked back at Frankie.

"We'll be safe here tonight," he said. "Tomorrow we'll find out how this happened."

"Hassan?" Frankie said.

"They just told me he's in surgery. God willing, he will survive."

CHAPTER 25

A rooster's crow awakened Frankie the next morning. He picked at the grime lodged in the corners of his eyes and looked out through the garage door. Issa and the two men who had been in the car stood under a tin roof brewing coffee over a burner. Groaning and rubbing his back, he got up from the concrete floor and stepped outside. Issa handed him a cup and he felt its warmth bring the blood into his fingers. In the chill air, the men's breath mingled with exhalations of smoke.

"Any word about Hassan?"

"He made it through the night. He will never walk again but he should survive, God willing."

A transistor radio playing Arabic music crackled with the voice of an announcer. Issa turned up the volume and grim expressions returned to the men's faces. As the music resumed, their voices rose in a rapid exchange until Issa threw the rest of his coffee on the ground and turned to Frankie.

"There's a demonstration. Not far from here. The Israelis are using tear-gas and rubber bullets. We're going to help. You will come with us."

They drove along a road behind a mob of young men carrying rocks and bottles. On either side lay mounds of shattered concrete and collapsed buildings, worse than any demolition site Frankie had ever seen. This was hardball at the limit.

Black smoke and tear gas billowed above the buildings surrounding an open square. An explosion made him cover his ears. Issa ran toward a stairwell and Frankie followed him and the others up between two buildings. Climbing three at a time they reached a rooftop overlooking the riot.

"Stay low," Issa said. "They have snipers everywhere."

Frankie crawled to the ledge and looked down on the square, where Israeli troops launched tear gas toward flaming barricades. Stones of all sizes smashed off their personnel carriers and cracks of gunfire echoed in return. Screams pierced the air as soldiers clubbed anyone not quick enough to retreat behind stacks of burning tires.

"We're going down," Issa said.

Frankie's fatigue and stiffness had vanished. On the street, he watched wounded Palestinian youth being hustled away in beat up cars and pick-up trucks.

"Look, over there," Issa said. Four boys, no more than fifteen or sixteen, staggered toward them with Israeli soldiers in pursuit. Issa and his men pulled three behind the safety of the barricade. The one lagging behind stumbled and fell. Three soldiers swarmed with batons flashing. Frankie grabbed the private closest to him and pulled him off.

"Enough," he yelled. "You're going to kill him."

The private tore himself away while two other soldiers wrestled Frankie's arms. A sergeant running toward them lifted his face shield and shouted an order in Hebrew. As the privates stepped back, Frankie dropped to his knees. The teenager clutched his throat and gasped. His eyes rolled back and he lost consciousness. The sergeant shouted Arabic at Frankie and motioned for him to move away.

"They struck him in the neck," he said. "He's choking to death." Frankie wrapped his fingers around his own throat and stuck out his tongue.

"Too fucking bad," said the sergeant.

Frankie saw the boy's face turning blue. "For Christ's sake, man. The kid's suffocating. Give me a knife or he'll die."

"For what?"

"An airway."

The sergeant shouted into a radiophone attached to his tunic and a medic carrying a white box ran toward them. As Frankie ran his index finger across the boy's thyroid cartilage, the medic ripped the sterile packaging from a scalpel and sliced through the skin. Frankie grabbed a tongue blade from the kit and stuck it into the hole. "I've got it open. Insert the fucking thing."

The boy's chest heaved with an inflation of air. A siren sounded and the sergeant standing over them barked an order. He looked down at Frankie.

"Where you from, asshole?"

"LA."

"That figures. Get him off the street before I change my mind."

The sergeant turned and ran to catch up to his men climbing into the back of the personnel carriers. Tire smoke and tear gas blackened the air. Frankie helped Issa and his men lift the boy on to a slab of plywood.

"That was brave," Issa said. "He could have arrested you."

"He might have been American. Maybe that helped."

"Americans and Israelis. They're one and the same. That's why you're going to have to prove yourself."

The intensity from Issa's eyes felt like lasers. "What do you mean?"

"We'll talk later. There're things we need to know about you."

⚔

The next morning, the driver stopped in front of a two-story building where off to the side, a group of boys ran around kicking a football. "This is the school and orphanage that Hassan told you about," Issa said. "We brought your bags and they're inside. There's a room where you can sleep and the staff will give you food. I'll be back in a few weeks."

A woman about Frankie's age stood at the entrance wearing a black dress and headscarf that made her look like a nun.

"I am Basheer Almasi, the principal of the school," she said, smiling. "Issa told me he was bringing you. We're grateful for your help."

"You're welcome," Frankie said. "How many kids have you got here?"

"Around one hundred, depending on the day. Most have never seen a dentist."

"That's why I'm here," Frankie said. "Let's see what we've got."

He followed her down a corridor. Through open classroom doors children of about six or seven repeated phrases by memory. Like kids everywhere, they returned his smile as he passed.

Almasi stopped in front of a door painted with white enamel and pulled a key from her pocket.

"The Muslim Brotherhood accepts donations from a businessman in Cairo. He provided us with this dental equipment from Germany. It was delivered before the blockade, so we were able to have it shipped across the border. It's never been used because we haven't found any dentists willing to come and work. Everybody's afraid. We can't afford supplies for fillings and things like that, so you'll just be removing bad teeth."

"I'll do what I can," Frankie said. He pointed at his two duffel bags. "I brought some stuff with me."

"The fact that you're even here...is a surprise," she said. "Most Americans won't come near this place. Your government brands us all as terrorists."

"It's been an eye-opener for me," Frankie said. "Lots of misinformation out there."

She opened the door and switched on the lights.

"Not bad," Frankie said, as he surveyed two dental chairs with a curtain hanging between them. Next to each chair were high and low speed dental drills, air-water syringes and vacuum hoses. He saw the word, Seimans, a recognizable German brand.

"I've never used this type of equipment myself but I have colleagues back home who swear by it. I'm impressed." Farther back in the room he saw, a sterilizer, a sink and a row of plastic rinsing tubs.

"This will work just fine. I'll spend today checking things out and getting organized. I'll need some people to assist and translate."

"I want you to start right now," Almasi said. "We have two dormitories. In each one there are children who cry all night with toothaches. I have people here to help you." She clapped her hands and a man and a woman came through the door. "This is Ibrihim and Eta. They both speak English but you will have to train them."

"Then that's what we'll do," Frankie said. "Bring the kids and we'll get going. Once we get the emergencies taken care of, I'll examine the rest and set priorities. You said you have about a hundred? That shouldn't take too long."

"That's just in this one orphanage. But there are two others about the same size. Don't worry. We'll keep you busy, Doctor Mendelssohn."

"Just call me, Fadi."

"That's Arabic."

"It's my birth name. I'd be honored if you used it."

Almasi smiled. "Okay, Doctor Fadi, it will be."

"I love it," Frankie said, zipping open the duffel bags. "Let's get down to work."

By the end of the afternoon, Frankie had treated eleven children with abscessed teeth and examined thirty more. After he was done, he got down on his knees to fix a leaky waterline. When he looked up from the floor, a teenager with a peach-fuzz moustache stood in the doorway. With slender fingers, the boy brushed the hair off his face.

"Hey. What's up, man?" Frankie grunted to tighten a nut.

"I'm Asaf Mashuur. My father sent me here. To help you."

"Your Issa's son?" The boy nodded and dropped his eyes.

Frankie gave the wrench a final tug and stood up smiling. The boy was rail thin, with a face-full of pimples and hair down to his shoulders. "Coulda' fooled me," Frankie said. A flush rose on Asaf's face.

"Hey, I didn't mean anything by it." He grinned and rubbed the kid's shoulder. "Your Dad looks like a linebacker. You're built for speed, like a wide receiver."

The boy only shuffled and fidgeted with his hands so Frankie asked, "Have you worked in a place like this before?"

"No," Asaf said. "My father wants me to learn something more useful than playing the guitar."

"You some kind of rock and roll guy?"

"I try to play like John Fogerty."

"Fathers aren't always so keen about their sons doing something they consider frivolous," Frankie said. "Mine was the same way. Come on in. Help me clean this up and then I'll show you how to sterilize the instruments. Something a bit more useful." His chuckle brought a smile to the boy's face. "Then maybe we can talk some music, Asaf. You like Creedence Clearwater Revival?"

Asaf smiled and sang the opening line to Green River. "Take me back down where cool water flows, yeah."

"All right," Frankie said, giving him a high-five. "Great riff on that one. If you've got an extra guitar we should jam sometime."

They mopped the floor and then Frankie took Asaf to the sterilization room and introduced him to Ibrihim and Eta, busy sorting the instruments they had used that afternoon. When he explained the infection control protocol again, Asaf listened to every word and was quick to ask a question when he didn't understand. A damn good kid, he thought.

He put all three to work scrubbing instruments in soapy water. After they were rinsed and inspected for traces of blood or debris they ran them through a sterilizer. According to the label, it had been donated by the Sonnenberg Foundation.

When Frankie was satisfied that the sequence was understood, he wrote the English word, Sterile, with a green felt pen above its Arabic equivalent, *Agir*. With a red marker, he wrote the word, Infected, above the word, *Qadir*. He had each of them pronounce the English translations and show him which containers contained soiled instruments and which contained sterile ones, ready for use.

"Okay," he said. "Sounds like you've got it. Never take short cuts and never miss a step. Contamination causes infection. Very bad."

The next day, he examined the rest of the children, overwhelmed by the damage to their teeth, worse than he'd seen in Vietnam or in the poorest neighborhoods of Los Angeles. Permanent molars that erupted around the age of six were decaying within months, destined for the extraction pail in less than a year.

⋏

For three weeks, he did nothing but treat those with a high priority X on their examination sheets. It left him both exhausted and exhilarated. With the immense backlog, he could work months before he even came close to putting out the fire. But children who had already experienced so much violence and pain understood the meaning of courage. They seldom shed a tear even through the toughest procedures. In their dark eyes he saw a reflection of himself and it made him proud.

Late one afternoon, after a group from one the other orphanages had left by bus, Issa came for him. He looked worn down and grim. "Hassan has left the hospital and he wants to see you. We have a car outside."

"I'm surprised he's out," Frankie said. "He didn't look that good when I saw him last."

"We can take better care of him at home. The hospital is overcrowded because of the riots. We've hired nurses."

At the house, three men huddled outside the front door smoking, animosity in their stares as he followed Issa inside. Hassan lay on a couch propped up by pillows, his legs covered by a blanket. He wore a jacket bundled at the neck and still shivered. The window shades were drawn and a fan moved stale air about the room. A dormant hookah pipe sat in the corner.

Hassan looked thinner and paler than when Frankie had visited him the previous week.

"Hello, my friend," Hassan said, his voice hardly audible. His handshake felt clammy and limp to Frankie's touch. Frankie pressed his cheek against Hassan's forehead and looked over at Issa.

"He's got a high fever. Are you sure this is the best place for him?"

"His legs have become infected. They're going to amputate if it doesn't improve. He wanted to see you before this happens."

"Mind if I take look?" Frankie said.

Hassan reached to pull off the blanket but his fingers slipped off as he tried.

"I'll get it, Hassan," Frankie whispered. The smell of necrotic tissue made him cough and take a step back. He looked down at the blistered domes of flesh and pressed the skin surrounding them. The crackling sound of gas bubbles. He waved his finger in front of Hassan's gaze but his eyes didn't track the movement.

"It's gangrene," he said. "He's going into shock."

"I saw he was getting worse," Issa said. "That's why I came for you. What do you think we should do?"

"Get him back to the hospital. They should operate right now."

The three men from outside entered the room. They kissed Hassan with gentle touches to both cheeks and slumped to cushions on the floor. Issa closed the door and nodded for Frankie to sit.

"First we need to talk about what happened the night of the explosion," Issa said. "Hassan told us that he saw you earlier in the day and that you met again on the bus on the way to the Rafah crossing. Quite a coincidence! He said that the Israeli guard ordered you off the bus and took you up to the gate. What happened there?"

"They told me I needed to get authorization from the American embassy. Hassan offered to help me cross the border. If I'd known we had to go through a tunnel, I wouldn't have gone. I was completely freaked out."

Issa turned toward the men on the floor and spoke to them in Arabic. The men sneered at Frankie and shouted what sounded like accusations.

"What are they saying?"

"They lost family in the attack. They think you had something to do with it."

"That's crazy. I had no idea where Hassan was taking me." He looked over at Hassan whose head had drooped forward, eyes closed. Saliva dribbled from his lips. Frankie touched his neck for a pulse and placed his other hand on Hassan's forehead.

"This isn't good, Issa. He needs surgery now or he won't make it."

Issa searched his eyes for a moment and then turned to the others and spoke. The men shook their heads and pointed at Frankie. Issa shouted a scathing torrent that brought all three to their feet. Frankie watched as they lifted Hassan and carried him outside to the car.

"They will take him to the hospital now. You and I will go to the Israeli compound and talk with them. They imprisoned our best surgeon last week. He is Hassan's only hope. God willing they will listen. We will discuss this matter--later."

"He needs intravenous antibiotics and they have to cool him down," Frankie said. "Tell them to hurry."

Issa spoke to the driver who snorted at Frankie and spat at him through the open window. Issa twisted the man's forearm until his face blanched and he cried out. "Get out of here," Issa shouted. "Go, go." As the car roared away he wiped a tear from his eye. "This is not America where antibiotics are always available when you need them."

"We need to talk to someone in charge," Frankie said. "I'll make something happen."

⅄

Converging concrete barriers narrowed the road down to a single lane as they approached the military checkpoint. Three soldiers aimed their weapons through gaps in the sandbags. A red light flashed and Issa stopped the vehicle. "Move slow when you get out," he said. "And keep your hands up where they can see them."

Hands in the air, they both stepped out and stood still under the lights until the soldiers directed them away from the car. A guard appeared from behind the blast barrier with a leashed dog and circled the vehicle twice before he nodded toward the others to pat them down for weapons. Finding nothing, the guards opened the trunk and the engine hood to let the dog sniff inside.

A soldier spoke to Issa in Arabic and Issa replied in a submissive tone completely unlike him. The soldier chuckled at his request and shouted at him to get back in the car. In his oversized helmet, he looked like a kid playing GI Joe.

"He's not letting us through," Issa said.

"American, American," Frankie shouted. "Does anyone around here speak English?"

An older officer stepped outside the shack and flicked a cigarette to the ground. Frankie recognized his captain's rank from time he'd spent in the army reserve at university.

"What business has an American got around here?"

"I'm a volunteer dentist in Rafah." He nodded toward Issa who stood on the other side of the car. "His brother suffered compound fractures to both legs. They're infected and need to be amputated. Apparently you're holding an orthopedic surgeon who can do this. We've come to ask for his temporary release."

"Are you fucking dreaming?" The captain turned to walk away.

"Wait," Frankie said. "This is a humanitarian request. His brother will die otherwise."

"You think this concerns me? It's one less against us."

"How is he going to fight with no legs, for fuck sake?"

"The surgeon's got connections with Hamas. He's not going anywhere. Turn around before I impound the car."

"This goes against everything we stand for," Frankie said.

The captain's eyes narrowed and he shook his head. Issa looked surprised too, as if unsure what Frankie had meant by "we."

"You're an American...and you're helping them?" said the captain. "You're telling me what 'we' should stand for? I should charge you right now for aiding the enemy. Get the hell out of here before I do." He glared at Issa and shouted his threat in Arabic.

Issa got behind the wheel and called to Frankie. "Come on. Before he arrests us both."

"Just a minute," Frankie said. "There's gotta be something we can do here. What's your name, Captain?" The captain ignored him and walked back inside the checkpoint. The guards raised their weapons. Issa ground the gears and jerked the clutch.

"Get in now or I'm leaving without you."

⋏

Issa's face was set like concrete when they arrived back at the hospital. He turned off the engine and looked over at Frankie, his eyes etched with pain. "Now you see how this occupation humiliates us. We'll fight and die until we're rid of them. There's no other choice."

Frankie followed him into the hospital. Dodging gurneys carrying bandaged teenagers, he struggled to understand. Why did it have to be this way? Both sides had so much to lose.

At fundraisers back in the States, Friedrich had often said, "More money pissed down the drain. Too many extremists on both sides who believe they're God's favorite. If it weren't so tragic Frankie, it'd be a goddamn joke. That's why we moved away from there. The place is a toxic graveyard."

The words rang in his ears, but as he took in the chaos around them, he felt that he'd come to the right place. That maybe...this was where he was meant to be. With roots in both communities, he could act as a bridge to bring the two sides together.

A mother's cry reverberated through the halls, and as they rounded the corner, she stood sobbing over a body draped with a sheet. It shook him from his pipe dream. He was no messiah. He needed to stick to what he knew.

A man approached Issa and whispered in his ear. Issa's body crumpled and the man grabbed his arm and helped him to a chair. Other men lined up to offer sympathy and show respect. As Frankie moved back to allow them to come closer, a little boy's agony pierced the room and went unnoticed. Frankie's eyes welled. It was too late.

⋏

Eight men lowered Hassan, wrapped in white linen like a mummy, into a grave. As an Imam read from the Koran, the men passed a shovel between them and threw dirt over the body. Frankie stepped forward to take his turn but two of the men pushed him back and pulled the shovel from his hands. Issa, his eyes red and swollen, drew him off to the side.

"Let them finish alone," he said. "Go stand over there."

Frankie returned to the car where two women in black clutched each other's hands and wept. At the grave, he watched Issa hugging the men and accepting their words of consolation. When Issa had finished, he raised his voice to leave no doubt about his intentions. Frankie picked out the words, Israeli murderers. The men raised their fists and roared. Frankie's chest tightened as Issa walked toward him.

"The others are taking my wife and daughter back home. There's a meeting now and you will come with me."

"I've got a bunch of kids at the clinic who need to see me."

"They can wait. They're used to it."

Chapter 26

The streets echoed with the call to prayer. At the mosque, a procession of men removed their shoes and washed their hands before entering.

"There will be many words for Hassan today," Issa said. "He was respected by everyone."

"He would still be here if he'd received the proper care," Frankie said. "I had no idea how bad this is. We never hear about any of it back home."

"The Israeli propaganda machine does not want the world to know."

"How long has it been like this?"

"In 1948 when I was a boy, I saw many people killed. Most were never identified...like your parents. In 1967 the Israelis attacked again."

Frankie knew that in 1967 Arab armies from Jordan, Syria and Egypt had massed along the borders to drive the Jews into the sea. Issa had skewed the narrative in his favor. He opened his mouth to interrupt, but the sorrow he saw on Issa's face changed his mind.

"It was another catastrophe for us," Issa said. "In six days their army took over our territory on the West Bank and here in Gaza. We've lived under their occupation ever since. Our Arab brothers, allies in whom we placed our faith, ran like whining dogs. When the Americans promised arms and money for Sadat and his generals, the Egyptians even signed a peace treaty.

They've all forgotten us. We're on our own. We'll never rest until we reclaim what's ours."

"But you're fighting a modern army with sticks and stones. All that's going to do is bring more death. Just like what happened to Hassan."

"We are not afraid to become martyrs like my brother. His death has brought honor to my family."

⋏

In a windowless room containing a table and eight chairs, Issa and Frankie sat at either end with six others in between.

"These men are members of Hamas," Issa said. "They want to hear again how you came to meet Hassan. I will translate."

Frankie tried to read their faces as Issa related the chance encounter between Hassan and himself, first at the warehouse and then on the bus. Whenever he used the words, Israeli or American, Frankie saw their expressions stiffen. When Issa finished, one of the men closest to him hissed the word, jasus. He pointed at Frankie and then stroked his index finger across his throat.

"What's he saying?" Frankie asked.

The man stood and glared at Frankie, gagging and sticking out his tongue. Issa's command brought him back down to his chair.

"He wants to slit your throat. He's saying you're an American spy."

"That's ridiculous," Frankie said. "I told you, I'd never set eyes on Hassan before the warehouse. I got on that bus and there he was again. It was a fluke. After the guard ordered me back to Cairo, Hassan convinced me to go with him, to work on the kids at the orphanage. That's what happened."

"If you're telling the truth, the mistake cost him his life. The Israelis tipped off the Egyptian police. But how did they know? What did you say to them at the guard station?"

"Nothing. Like I said before, they took my passport and I heard an officer talking on a radio. He told me I needed to get authorization from the American embassy in Cairo. That's it."

"There's something you're not telling us. Why did you come here?"

"To find out who my parents were." He reached into his wallet and pulled out the old photograph that Friedrich had given him. "Here, look at this. It was taken when they were married."

Issa glanced at the photo and handed it back. "Why would you trust someone you didn't know rather than go back to your own embassy? What were you afraid of?"

Frankie's heart felt as if it were about to burst from his chest. The legs of his chair scraped against the cement floor and he groped for words.

"Hassan said the Israelis would find another excuse to keep me out. But you're right, there was something else."

All eyes around the table focused on him now, as if they understood every word. "I got busted dealing drugs in Los Angeles. It's a long story. If I'd gone back to the embassy, I would have been arrested and sent back to serve time. When Hassan said he would help me get across the border, I jumped at the offer. But, believe me. I had no fucking idea what I was getting myself into."

Issa lit a cigarette and blew a funnel into the room. He spoke to the men and waited while each one expressed his opinion. After all six had their say, he delivered what sounded like a summation. The men nodded their affirmation as if a verdict had been handed down.

"Have you ever heard the expression, Inshallah?" Issa asked.

"I've heard it a few times since I've been here. It means, God's will, or something like that. Not really sure."

"It means that nothing in this world happens unless Allah deems it to be so. Muslim's are obliged to say it if they intend to do something in the future. Since that something can only occur, 'If God wills.'"

"Really." Frankie grinned.

"You're not convinced because you've been brainwashed by your Judeo-Christian culture with its arrogant idea of free will. It's a lie and an abomination. Has it ever occurred to you that you may have been sent here to do great things?"

"You're kidding, right. You're saying that I was sent here! By Allah?"

"Yes. He is offering you a chance to return to the faith of your ancestors."

"I don't believe that."

Issa's expression hardened and the tip of his cigarette grew hotter. He flicked the ash and met Frankie's eyes.

"The men still have doubts. They insist that you prove yourself."

"How?"

"The work you're doing with the children is helpful but we need you to do something more important."

"Sure," Frankie said. "Anything."

"Our men are being held illegally in Israeli prisons, many in solitary confinement. We are not allowed to visit and have no way of communicating. Some have died. We suspect they were tortured." He took another drag.

"We're preparing to raid an Israeli outpost five kilometers from our border. Khader's in charge." Issa nodded toward a man about Frankie's age who wore glasses with round metal frames. He looked more like an academic than a commando. "The plan is to take the four Israeli soldiers hostage and barter them for an exchange. Hassan was to be part of this and we want you to take his place. To show your loyalty."

Frankie scrambled for a way out.

"You can't be serious. I've never been involved with anything like this. I'm of much better use doing the work I'm trained to do."

"We need to know whose side you're on, Mendelssohn. There's no option here. These men are ready to cut you up and dump you on the street. Unless you convince them otherwise. It's up to you."

"I've never even held a gun, for Christ's sake."

"You won't have to shoot anyone. The others will carry the weapons and overrun the outpost. You will help bring the hostages back after they're captured."

"When is this supposed to happen?"

"After dark."

Frankie stared at Issa with his mouth half open. "Tonight?"

Issa nodded.

"This is crazy."

"You don't agree?" Issa raised his eyebrows. "Then I'll leave you here with them." He pushed back his chair and stood up to leave.

"No, no, no," Frankie said. "I'll do it."

ᴧ

At a house that Frankie had never seen before, Issa climbed a flight of steps and unlocked a door to a room containing a cot, an empty pail and a jug of water.

"We'll bring food later. My men are downstairs so don't try to leave. Get some rest. You'll be up all night."

Issa shut the door and Frankie dropped onto the cot. He closed his eyes but a moment later they snapped open and tracked the course of cracks in the ceiling toward the periphery. He recalled the stories he'd been told about the 1948 War when the Arabs attacked the newly proclaimed State of Israel. And how Israeli militias had driven them back and secured the borders.

In the spring of 1967, he and his friends had gathered around television sets while Arab armies massed on the borders of the Jewish state. They felt such jubilation and pride when Israel, outnumbered in troops, tanks and aircraft, surprised the invaders and struck first. Six days later, Israel had expanded its borders by almost one hundred percent. Israeli Defense Forces stood victorious over the ancient capital of Jerusalem and the biblical lands of Samaria and Judea on the West Bank of the Jordan River. Having now seen the poverty and destruction in Gaza, he understood why the Arabs used the word, nakba---catastrophe, to describe these wars. Was he to believe this was the will of God too?

He bolted up and made it to the pail before he vomited. He rinsed the sour from his mouth and splashed water on his face, certain he would never see Friedrich again. What had he done?

ᴧ

After midnight he heard sounds outside the door. Earlier, they had brought bread, cold meat and cheese. It still sat untouched.

He followed a man downstairs to a room where Issa had set a rucksack on the table.

"Did you eat?" Issa asked.

"Didn't feel like it."

"You better have something."

"I'm not hungry."

Issa said nothing more as he opened the flap and pulled out a pair of black pants and a black long-sleeved sweater. He reached into the bag again and brought out a roll of duct tape, strands of nylon cord and a flashlight. He tossed the clothes over to Frankie.

"Put these on. We'll be driving to the border soon. Once you cross, it's an hour's walk to the outpost."

Frankie swallowed back more bitterness and pulled the sweater over his head. "Are you coming?"

"No. I have bad knees. This job is for young men like you." He gave Frankie a mirror and a tin of ash. "Rub this on your face."

The door swung open and four men dressed like him entered. Frankie recognized Khader, who now wore thick-framed glasses secured with a neck-strap. They carried AK-47s that smelled of gun-grease. By the sheen of the barrels, Frankie assumed they were new. Khader switched on a radiophone and waited until he heard a voice on the other end. He answered and clicked it off.

"The signal's good," he said, smiling at Issa. "We just received them from the German. We'll use them to coordinate our attack and call in the escape truck."

Issa's face tightened at the mention of the word, German. He slammed his fist on the table and glared at Khader whose smile disappeared. He mumbled an apology and looked to the floor. A fifth man carrying the other radio came in from outside and gave a thumbs up. He had a slighter build than the others and like Frankie he carried no weapon.

Frankie recognized Asaf behind the ash-caked disguise and he winked.

Issa barked at Khader. "Get on with it."

Khader unfolded a map on the table while Issa strangled the shaft of another cigarette, the tension in his body evident. Arrows on the map marked the distances in kilometers.

A red circle drew Frankie's eyes to the middle.

"The border is here." Khader pointed to the bottom. He ran his finger up and stopped at the red circle. "This is the Israeli position, manned by four soldiers. When we get there, two will be sleeping and two will be on watch." He moved his finger down a short distance to where a bold green line ran from left to right. "This is an elevated road that runs in front of their sandbagged perimeter. When we're fifty meters out, we'll crawl in until we reach it. It will still be dark but it's in the open. We'll have to move slow."

"And with no noise," growled Issa.

"Of course," Khader said. "Absolute silence." He adjusted his glasses where beads of sweat ran down the bridge of his nose.

"When we reach the road, we'll split into two groups and take positions to either side. The radios will be muted. One blink from me will be the signal to attack. We'll be on top of them before they even know we're there."

He nodded at Frankie. "You'll stay with me. Asaf will go to the other side. You'll both keep down behind the bank until we've taken the target. We'll call you up for the tape and the cords and that." He pointed to bundles of dynamite on the floor and looked at Frankie. "You'll carry it all in that rucksack. We're going to set a trap for the rescuers before we leave. Killing Jews is a good thing, no?"

He pointed to an X at the very bottom of the page. "Our truck picks us up here. God willing, we'll be back inside our border with four hostages before their helicopters arrive."

"If you catch them by surprise," Frankie said.

"We've been watching them every night for two weeks."

"It's fifty meters. That's a long way on your belly with no cover. If they see anything, it's over. What if they hear your radio signal?" Crawling through open desert with explosives on his back wasn't what he had in mind.

"It's a silent off-on switch," Khader said. He clicked a button on his radio and they saw a red light blink on the unit clipped to Asaf's belt. "It will still be dark. The guards are bored and will be half asleep anyway. They take turns snoozing. Even if we have to kill them both, we'll bring back the other two."

As they stood to leave, Issa shook each man's hand and mumbled, "Allah Akbar." When he reached Asaf, he embraced him and said to Frankie. "Take care of my son."

"Sure will," Frankie said. He had a headache that a Percodan wouldn't touch. Keeping his shit together would be enough of a problem without looking after Issa's goddamn kid.

Khader opened the door and made eye contact with each man as he walked out. "Silence unless I talk to you."

⋏

Clouds blotted out any hint of moonlight, and as the truck pulled away with Issa, they waited in the shrubs until their eyes adjusted to the darkness. Khader gave the hand signal to move and they walked in single file, with two men in front of Frankie and three behind. After about thirty minutes, Khader stopped and pulled out his binoculars. He trained them north and whispered in Arabic. Each man took a look and then Khader handed the glasses to Frankie who sharpened the focus until he saw the silhouette of a helmet behind the sandbagged perimeter.

"Only one keeping watch," Khader said. "Stay right behind me. No sound." They followed Khader who darted like a phantom behind clumps of brush until light coming from the compound illuminated the webbing on the soldier's helmet. Khader raised his hand and they gathered around.

"We crawl in from here," he whispered. "Stay close to the man in front of you. When we get to the road, we'll join up and then split four meters to either side."

He peered at Asaf who knelt next to Frankie and fumbled with the radio on his belt. Khader hissed and squeezed his arm. "Don't be so fucking nervous, Asaf. Make your father proud. Be a man."

Frankie dug his elbows into the sand and dragged himself forward, staying right on Khader's heels until they reached the embankment. As they huddled up and caught their breath, Khader used hand signals to direct Asaf to the left flank. Asaf's lips trembled as he crawled away with two armed men close behind.

Khader pointed right. The safety switches on both guns released. Khader led the way with Frankie in the middle, stifling sneezes from the dust rising off Khader's soles.

When they reached their position on the right flank, Kadher motioned for them to huddle against the embankment beside him. He checked their rifles one more time and then raised his thumb and pressed the button on his radio. A loud squelch came from the other side.

Frankie froze.

"The idiot switched on the volume," Khader said, under his breath.

In an instant, a searchlight flooded the embankment. Khader brought the mouthpiece to his lips. "Allah Akbar."

The rattle of automatic gunfire fractured the night. Frankie curled into a fetal position with his hands wrapped about his head and his eyes squeezed shut. A fusillade of bullets chewed up the road and sprayed rocks and sand down on top of him. He heard the guttural screams of men being struck at close range. The noise ceased as suddenly as it had started. With his chest pounding like a drum, he hugged tight to the bank. Echoes of warfare dissipated into the desert.

The moans of dying combatants broke the stillness; the universal voice spanning the ages. Static crackled through the air and he heard a shrill voice speak into a radio. The words were not Arabic. The light swung past and he lifted his head to peer over the rim. Bullets chewed into the sand around him. Staying low, he tossed the backpack over the rim and raised both hands into the light. Amplified shouts called out toward him. "Qum Ben Zona."

"American." His voice cracked and trailed off as he pronounced the word. He coughed moisture to his tongue and tried again. "American."

"Throw out your gun."

"I'm unarmed."

"What's in the bag?" Frankie struggled to formulate a response. More than just tape, cords and a flashlight.

"What's in the goddamn bag?"

"Explosives. But they're not fused." With his hands high, he stood up and watched the light track down to the backpack.

"Come up...slowly...and keep your hands where I can see. Any quick moves, I blow your fucking head off." The Russian accent reminded him of Joey Kazlov.

"Don't shoot." Frankie climbed the embankment to the road and squinted. The light trained on his eyes, blinding him to everything in front.

"Take off your clothes." Frankie pulled off the sweater and let his pants drop around his ankles.

"Get down on your knees and empty the bag." The Russian voice boomed through a loudspeaker. Frankie crawled forward until he saw the domes of two helmets behind the blast barrier. He reached the bag and took a deep breath as he stuck his hand inside. Issa had assured him the charges weren't armed but what if he pulled on the wrong thing? He groped among a rats-nest of wire and then turned the rucksack upside down until the dynamite and connectors slipped out. He drew the bag upward as if pulling off a veil. An alarm clock with two unattached wires followed and then the tape, the cords and the flashlight. He held up the empty bag. "That's all," he said. "Nothing's connected."

"Throw it behind you."

As he flung the bag over his shoulder, the light blinded him again and he heard the crush of boots. A knee found the small of his back and drove him face down into the sand. Spitting out grit and coughing to breathe, his arms were wrenched back and cold steel clamped hard around his wrists. Both shoulders cracked like they'd been dislocated. He cried out as the soldier hauled him to his feet.

With a helmet dangling from his neck, one dead soldier was sprawled across the sandbagged barrier. The disjointed bodies of Khader and the three other fighters lay scattered in front of him, blood pooling around them. But where was Asaf?

The soldier manning the machine gun trained the barrel on him. "Your turn now, Yankee traitor." A cry came from behind. "Stop! Stop!" The gunner swung his barrel to the other side and sent a burst of tracer fire over Asaf's position.

"There's another one...over there," the gunner yelled. The searchlight whipped across to light the blackened face of Asaf who stood motionless, hands at his side.

"He's unarmed," Frankie yelled.

As the gunner leveled his barrel, Asaf panicked and ran. The cone of light swept across the sand and locked on to his zigzagging figure.

"He's got no gun," Frankie yelled. "Stop, Asaf stop."

Tracers threw up a trail of sand and stones until Asaf stumbled and clutched his left side. Squinting into the brightness, he held the radio in his right hand to block the glare.

"He's got a grenade." A sustained burst of heavy caliber bullets tossed Asaf around like a puppet. His knees crumbled and his face turned crimson mush. The soldier screamed Arabic slurs and poured more bullets into his corpse until the Russian sergeant pried his fingers off the trigger. The young soldier burst into tears and draped himself over the dead body lying next to him on the sandbags. Howling like an abandoned child, he pleaded up to a canopy of stars.

Frankie looked at the Russian and said: "You've killed everyone, except me."

A burst of static caused both men to look down at the distorted corpse of Khader. The Russian rolled the body over with the toe of his boot. When he bent to take the radio from Kader's blood-drenched pocket, Frankie recognized the rasp of Issa's voice. "Khader, Khader, come in."

The Russian brought the receiver to his mouth and said: "Fuck you, Arab dog."

Through a blur of tears, Frankie watched as they dragged Asaf's body ₋o the road like a sack of flour. The Russian held up his smashed radio and mumbled to the others in Hebrew. "German."

On his knees next to the five bodies, Frankie heard the thumps of helicopter rotors flying in from the south. It's game over now, you fucking putz.

⅄

Ducking beneath the spinning blades, he watched them lift the dead soldier into the helicopter. With sand whipping about his face, the five Palestinian bodies were thrown in behind, one on top of the other.

"You picked the wrong side, Yankee." The Russian sergeant yelled over the roar of the engine. He pointed to the machine gunner with robotic eyes who knelt next to the stretcher. "You killed his brother. He would have shredded you too, if I'd let him."

Frankie cringed as they pushed him against the sticky pile of corpses. Asaf's crumpled body haunted his soul. An intelligent kid, who wanted nothing more than to have a job, play some music and hang out with his friends and family. All the good things in life. But no! Instead he'd been born into a community mandated by a code of violence and hate. It wasn't any different for the Israeli soldier who had murdered him in a fit of revenge. He looked over at the traumatized young man, his life scarred forever. They'd both been hurtling toward this moment from day one.

The chopper lifted off and heightened the chill of the dead bodies against his skin. He viewed the desert below through clouds of swirling sand. With the helicopter banking in a circle to gain altitude, the outpost shack grew smaller and smaller, like debris spinning at the bottom of a sink, until it diminished and disappeared. Just like his life. Down the fucking drain.

⚔

The Russian leaned toward the cockpit and yelled into the pilot's ear. "We got ourselves a live one." He held up the evidence bags containing the two radios and four automatic rifles with Czech markings. "New equipment from Eastern Bloc. Coming through those tunnels. This guy will tell us where they are. Or wish he'd died like the rest of them."

⚔

A gust blew through the open gangway and buffeted the aircraft. Frankie's teeth chattered while he huddled behind the mound of death, the only shelter from the wind's blast.

Then the Russian passed him a hood. "Put this over your head and slide to the front."

Hebrew rants blared over the cockpit radio, while from behind came the sound of grunts and of things being dragged. Laughter, likely prompted by a lame joke, brought a terse retort from the sergeant. The engine's vibration found its way deep into his core and then the first rays of sunrise touched the back of his hands. With his legs buzzing like amputated stumps, he wiggled his toes to prod their circulation. Then the aircraft rolled into its descent, jostling him as they touched down. The engine died and agitated voices and boots ran toward them. The dead bodies scraped like cargo as they were pulled from the hold.

"Get on your feet." The Russian yanked the hood off his head and he squinted into the morning sunlight and out to the tarmac. The flag-draped body of the soldier lay next to the Palestinian corpses. With the helicopter's deck slick under his feet, he reached the doorway and stopped. Below him the bodies were being tagged. The Russian cuffed him from behind. "Get off."

"There's only four down there," Frankie said. He looked back into the bloodstained hold and then back at the row of bodies. "One's missing. Where's Asaf?"

"No questions."

"What do you mean...no questions? Where the fuck is he?"

The Russian slapped him hard across the head and pulled him back in- ide. With eyes like daggers, he twisted Frankie's sweater tight around his neck and breathed into his face. The rankness made Frankie jerk back.

"Look at me, you fucking traitor, and listen. There were only four attack- ers. You say anything different and I will point to you as the one who killed our man. You will hang or rot in jail for the rest of your life."

"But why? Why Asaf?" The Russian looked down at the traumatized gunner who watched his brother being zipped into a body bag.

"You saw how he mutilated that guy." The Russian wrapped his knuckles on his forehead. "He went crazy in here. I don't want him brought up on any charges. He's lost enough already."

A guard tugged Frankie down to the tarmac and the Russian jumped down beside him. "Remember what I said, Yankee. Not a fucking word."

A muzzle coaxed him toward a building with opaque windows. He looked back to the tarmac where it and the helicopter were being hosed down and scrubbed. He thought of Issa's last words and knew his life had changed forever. He would never forgive him for this.

CHAPTER 27

Gabor Erhmann set down the phone with the hint of a smile. He ran his finger down his list of names until he came to that of Dieter Groule and crossed it off. Groule had been an SS guard at Treblinka. He'd boasted of starving his dogs for days so they were rabid-like when a shipment of Jews arrived at the camp. Survivor statements described children eaten, 'limb by limb, organ by organ'.

Groule asserted that his dogs prevented the unruly behavior of new arrivals before they were sent to the showers. He bragged that his processing numbers doubled those of his counterparts. He disappeared just before the German surrender but when his name repeatedly surfaced on witness depositions, Dieter Groule earned a place on Erhmann's list.

The call had come from his old friend, Abba Brisker, who was dying of esophageal cancer on the kibbutz of Ein Hahoresh. A co-founder of, Nakam, Abba informed Erhmann that Groule had been tracked down on an island off the British Columbia coast. Disguising themselves as fishermen, the Nakam operatives invited Groule on their boat, where for two days they entertained him by using his fingers, toes and intestines as bait. Just before he expired, they dumped him into the Pacific with a cement block tied around his ankles.

At the end of their conversation, Abba asked Erhmann out to the kibbutz to discuss a matter that had just been brought to his attention by colleagues within the Israeli Defense Forces. "Please come soon," Abba said. "My time is almost up."

⋏

When Erhmann walked into Abba's room the next day, a virtual skeleton of his friend lay in the bed, a reminder of what he'd seen in Auschwitz.

"Shalom, old friend." Erhmann kissed Abba on both cheeks and sat beside him. Abba forced a weak smile and reached for a notepad and pencil from the bedside table. He scratched with a trembling hand. Easier this way, he wrote. Good news about Groule. I never thought we would find him.

"Yes, but I'm sorry to see that you're not doing better."

Abba shook his head and scribbled down three more sentences.

"I have no regrets. Life has been worthwhile. Do you remember a dentist named Mendelssohn?

Erhmann scanned the first two statements and then lifted his eyes when he read the third. He stared back at Abba and said: "Yes, I remember that name. I interviewed him years ago...after we discovered the dental files of Colonel Heinz Bauer."

Abba nodded.

"We were investigating Bauer's suicide around Munich."

Abba scratched another question across the pad before the pencil dropped from his hand. What happened to Mendelssohn?

"He moved to Los Angeles. He taught at a dental school there I think. He's probably retired by now." Erhmann could see his friend's concentration slipping.

"I can see you're tired, Abba," he said. "You must rest. We can talk about this another time."

Abba's hand clutched the pad once more and he printed the name, Komorov.

"General Alexi Komorov?"

Abba nodded and his eyelids fluttered until they closed.

"You want me to speak to him?"

The rasp in Abba's chest stilled. Erhmann rubbed the cold emaciated fingers until his eyes turned glassy and he pulled the sheet over Abba's head. He tore off the top page of the writing pad and walked down to the nursing station. "Please call Mister Brisker's family. He has gone to his reward."

Erhmann gave the eulogy at Brisker's funeral, and expressed his condolences to the family for a final time. He drove back to Jerusalem and arrived at Israeli Defense Headquarters for an appointment with General Alexi Komorov.

"Thank you for seeing me, General." The barrel-chested man in his sixties motioned him to an armchair and offered him coffee.

"Too bad about our old friend," Komorov said.

"Yes, we go a long way back. I will miss him."

"I visited with him last week and mentioned an incident where one of our outposts was ambushed. We lost one soldier but killed four of them and took a fifth prisoner. He's an American named, Mendelssohn. Abba thought you might know something about him."

"I hadn't heard anything about an ambush," Erhmann said.

"We're keeping it quiet for now. Mendelssohn gave us his name but that's it. He's demanding to see a lawyer. We're keeping him in solitary until we find out what the hell he was doing there."

"Here's what I know," Erhmann said. He pulled a sheet of notes from his pocket.

"I interviewed a dentist by that name back in 1949. He'd escaped from Austria under the name of Mueller. When he tried to cross our border from Syria, the British suspected he was a spy. A dentist serving in Palestine with the Canadian Army identified him as Mendelssohn. He'd been using the name of Mueller to hide his Jewish identity.

"Abba and I had worked together on a suicide investigation about three years before. The remains of an SS war criminal, Colonel Heinz Bauer, and five officers were discovered in the basement of a villa not far from Munich. Working under the guise of foresters they were compromised by someone.

Before they could be taken into custody, the officers poisoned themselves with cyanide. All except one who set a timer on an incendiary bomb and then shot himself in the head. Not much remained except charred bones, but the one who shot himself had some extensive dental work. Using SS dental records, a forensic team identified the skull as Bauer. Abba and I were always suspicious."

"For what reason?"

"There was a large exit wound in the left side of the skull but no bone fragments anywhere. Finding a copy of his dental chart in the file also struck me as unusual. That's why we interviewed Mendelssohn.

"I remember him being defensive at the time. He'd treated many Nazi officers with gold fillings but he didn't remember anything particular about Bauer other than his fear of needles. He said it wasn't unusual for military men to request a copy of their dental records. For forensic identification, if they were killed.

"Bauer has never surfaced but not a day has passed where the image of that beast's face has not crossed my mind. It may have been him in that villa but something inside me isn't willing to let go. It's like an ulcer eating into the pit of my stomach. If he's still out there, I owe it to my family. He'll beg to die if I ever find him."

Erhmann unclenched his hand and brought the cup to his lips. "He'd be into his seventies now, so time's running short. What can you tell me about this American?"

The general poured more coffee and stirred in lumps of sugar.

He opened a file with a mug shot of Frankie and a photograph of Friedrich wearing an academic gown. He slid them across to Erhmann.

"Father and son," he said. "He got stopped at the Rafah crossing for routine questioning. He was carrying two bags of dental tools and supplies. He told the guard that he'd come to volunteer at the refugee camp.

"The guard recognized another man on the bus. His name is Hassan Mashuur, a member of the Muslim Brotherhood. Also tied up with Hamas in Gaza. They said they didn't know each other but the guard suspected they might be together. He couldn't arrest either of them but to gain some time, he told Mendelssohn he needed to get official authorization from the US embassy back in Cairo.

"Because it was Mashuur, we called in the Egyptian police. They put a tail on them both. Instead of going back to Cairo on the bus as he'd been ordered, Mendelssohn got into a vehicle with Mashuur. The Egyptians followed them and discovered a tunnel, one of the first ones they found. They blew it up, but both Mendelssohn and Mashuur must have already got through. We lost track of them. We heard rumors of a cave-in but nothing confirmed. Then weeks later, Mendelssohn shows up as part of this Palestinian raiding party. He was the only survivor."

"What do you think this has to do with Bauer?"

"We've heard rumors about a German who might be smuggling arms into Gaza. Probably through those tunnels. The terrorists who attacked the outpost had new Czech weapons and short wave radios. It's the first time we've seen that."

"I still don't understand. Why Bauer?"

"Take a look at these." Komorov slid two more photographs across to Erhmann. "Not much to go on," he said. "These are old, taken just before the '48 war."

The first picture showed two Palestinian men waving their fists in the air. In the background, a man with a fair complexion and an unruly beard stood next to a sign with the acronym UNRWA. The man looked away from the camera as if he wasn't aware that he was being photographed. In a second close-up of the man, something that looked like an ink-spot near the rim of his upper lip caught Erhmann's eye.

"He doesn't look Arabic, does he?" Komorov said. "These were taken about forty-five years ago. He turned the close-up picture over and read what was written. "There was a suggestion that he might be an Argentinean with German roots called Sonnenberg. At the time, there were a lot of them serving with the UN mission. But he never popped up again so that was that. When I heard rumors about a German being involved with this latest round of arms smuggling, I remembered that picture so I dug it out. I showed it to Abba. If it was Bauer, he thought you might recognize him."

Erhmann contemplated the two pictures and rubbed his forehead to jog his memory. The block letters of the United Nations acronym seemed to jibe with the name. Then it came to him.

"I've heard that name, Sonnenberg, before," he said. "Years ago at a UN Relief Centre. It was a foundation that donated wheelchairs and other equipment for refugees. So maybe this was the German who ran it." He scrutinized the two pictures again. "He certainly doesn't look like Bauer but it's been a long time. When I last I saw him in Auschwitz he was clean shaven." He pointed to the spot near the man's lip. "This is what intrigues me though. It could be an ink mark but there's something I remember from the first time I saw him. Bauer had a gold-trimmed front tooth. I have another old photograph back at my office. From Auschwitz. I'll compare it to this one and to his dental records."

"It's a long shot but I know Abba shared your suspicions about Bauer's disappearance," Komorov said. "When I mentioned the ambush and the American's name, he remembered your interview. He saw the possibility of this connection. If this Doctor Mendelssohn senior has information he hasn't been sharing, his memory might be refreshed if he knows that his son's future is at stake."

"What are you saying?" Erhmann said.

"His son was the only survivor of that raiding party. He's facing murder charges and if convicted, he'll get a life sentence. We don't have enough evidence to charge this Sonnenberg with anything but if Mendelssohn senior identified him as Bauer, he'd be convicted as a war criminal. He could hang or get life. Either way, it would be the end of him. If he's behind this smuggling operation like we suspect, it's a double win. The tribunal could go easier on the son, if that were to happen. They could order his release and let the Americans deal with him."

"Would you put that in writing?"

"Don't push me, Erhmann."

"I only want to be clear. I'll see what I can do."

From his office in Jerusalem, Erhmann asked Aaron Weinstock, a Mossad agent recently transferred from Jerusalem to Los Angeles, to locate a current address and phone number for Doctor Friedrich Mendelssohn. Weinstock promised to call back as soon as he had anything.

Erhmann went to the musty basement of the office and rifled through stacks of boxes until he found the one labeled: SS Colonel Heinz Bauer. He took it upstairs and sat down to read.

In a file that had 'Case Closed' stamped across its front cover, he found a copy of the dental chart with treatments completed between January and November 1943. The technical abbreviations in the entries made no sense to him but an accompanying letter by a dentist with the American Occupation Forces confirmed that a skull discovered in the villa was that of Heinz Bauer. The dental work in the skull matched that described in the chart.

The facing page contained renderings of individual teeth, which were numbered. Each entry was prefaced by the tooth number to which it referred. Renderings were shaded in pencil to illustrate the shape of each gold filling.

The front teeth were unmarked except for the upper right central incisor, shaded about its perimeter and across one corner. Erhmann found the corresponding tooth number on the opposite page. A filling had been placed in January 1943. He read the German words, "incisal rand brusch" which he translated as "fracture of the edge of the tooth".

The image of Bauer on an Auschwitz guard tower was burned into Erhmann's memory. Particularly the sparkle beneath Bauer's upper lip as it reflected a flashbulb's explosion. He flipped through the file until he found the envelope containing the old photograph of the colonel on the tower. The sparkle under the lip remained clear. He compared the photograph with the clipping Komorov had given him of Sonnenberg. What looked like an ink stain in the newsprint, could be the glitter of gold. In exactly the same spot.

Erhmann's notes from his 1949 interview with Friedrich Mendelssohn confirmed that Mendelssohn had admitted treating Bauer but had denied knowledge of his suicide. Erhmann reviewed the rest---three exit visas to America, addresses, a position in the Faculty of Dentistry at the University of Southern California in Los Angeles.

His phone rang. Through the window darkness had fallen. Erhmann checked his watch. Still early afternoon in California.

"Hello Gabor," Weinstock said. "It took a bit of digging but I've got what you need. The taxman knows everything, right? Mendelssohn lives in a senior residence in Beverley Hills. Parkside Grove Retirement Lodge."

Erhmann wrote down the address and phone number. "Thanks for this Aaron. It's a case that's been closed for years but we just received some new information. I'll set up a meeting and let you know when I'm coming."

Chapter 28

Since Frankie's disappearance Friedrich had retreated into a cocoon that even his friend Miriam could not penetrate. For the first week he stayed locked in his room at the lodge, only opening his door for a care aide who brought his meals. When the grayness of the room closed around him, he returned to the garden to resume work on a sculpture of Eva's face as he remembered her on the morning before she died. The sense of loss he'd felt then had enveloped him once again. Now three weeks later, his emotions had turned darker and his anger more consuming. How could Frankie have done such a thing?

When Erhmann's shadow loomed across the table, Friedrich cocked his head back and looked up.

"Fine work," Erhmann said. "You have gifted hands."

Friedrich waited for a clue about why Erhmann had come. When he said nothing further, Friedrich shook his head and pointed to the folded card that had announced Erhmann with two words: *Your son.*

"What's this about?"

"I needed to get your attention. The staff at the front desk didn't want to let me see you."

"I understand," Friedrich said. "But unfortunately my hands work better than my memory these days. Should I know you?" He set the spatula down and as his hand settled onto his lap, it resumed its tremor.

"We met years ago," Erhmann said. "You may not remember. I'm from Israel."

"And you're obviously here about my ne'er-do-well, son."

"I'm afraid so." Erhmann took a seat across the table.

"He should have never married that shiksa," Friedrich said. "All his problems began when he tried to impress her parents. The debts, the drugs, all of that. He ruined his life. He shamed his profession and our family name. Especially the memory of his mother. I hope you put him in jail where he belongs."

Erhmann said nothing.

"The police told me he had flown to Cairo. They said they lost track of him but I'm not surprised that he went to Israel. He thinks he might learn something about his biological parents."

"I wasn't aware he was adopted," Erhmann said. "There's nothing in our records that show this."

"His parents were killed in the 1948 War." Friedrich picked up his spatula and ran it down the bridge of the sculpture's nose, and then set it aside again and hacked into a handkerchief to clear his throat. A recurring accumulation of mucous bothered him more and more.

"He was the son of my employees. Arabs. The father Sunni, his mother a Shia orphan. The father's family had shunned them for marrying. My wife, Eva, God bless her soul, insisted that we adopt Frankie. He would have ended up in a refugee camp if we hadn't protected him. We obtained a forged birth certificate and claimed him as our son."

"I see," Erhmann said. "When did he become aware of this?"

"About the adoption, as soon as he could understand. When he became a teenager, we told him he was Arabic. He was only a year old when they died. I'm so embarrassed by what he's done, I don't want to see anybody."

His hands trembled and he shook his head. "Not even my old friends." Wiping the glassiness from his eyes, he looked up at Erhmann. "I'm glad you caught up to him before he got into more trouble. The sooner he's extradited to stand trial, the better. I'll be there to help him, but he has to accept his punishment. It's the honorable thing to do."

"I'm afraid there's more to it than skipping bail," Erhmann said.

Friedrich sighed and rubbed his head. "Oy Vey. When will it end with him?"

"He's going to spend the rest of his life in prison."

Friedrich stared into Erhmann's eyes, locking his fingers in a vain attempt to still them, while Erhmann explained what he knew about the raid and the soldier's death.

"What you're saying can't be true," Friedrich said. "He's made some very serious errors, but he's not a killer. He planned to work with the disadvantaged in Vietnam. He'd been there with a USC Outreach and it had a tremendous affect on him. There must be a mistake. I'll get a lawyer and have him brought back here, where at least he'll receive a fair trial."

"There's no mistake. And the Israeli government will never allow his release. Politically it's impossible." His voice hit its lowest level and his eyes burned with the intensity of a blast furnace.

Friedrich blinked as the memory surfaced.

"You're the man who questioned me about a German SS officer many years ago."

"Colonel Heinz Bauer." Erhmann's facial expression hardened.

"This has something to do with him?"

"That's up to you."

"I don't understand."

"If you have any knowledge about Bauer that you didn't share with me before, you should do it now. It may make it easier for your son."

"What more is there to know? It's well documented. He committed suicide. I read that he was identified with forensic dental records. This is a fact."

"Is it? Funny how you didn't know about his suicide at our first meeting in Jerusalem. Maybe you do have more to tell me."

"Is this some kind of interrogation? That was over forty years ago. I'm a confused old man. I can't remember what I said."

Erhmann opened his briefcase and handed Friedrich the photograph of the Palestinian fighters with a lighter skinned man in the background that Komorov had given him. "We have reason to believe that this might be Bauer. Have you ever seen this?"

Friedrich adjusted his glasses and brought the image closer.

"Never." He had seen it on a bill-board somewhere years before, but the lie escaped his lips as if an automatic switch had been flipped on. He flushed and the tempo of his tremor heightened. The photograph slipped from his fingers and fluttered to the floor.

Erhmann picked it up and raised his voice. "This bearded man standing behind the others. Does he look familiar? He goes by the name of Herrmann Sonnenberg."

"How do you propose to help my son?"

"Tell me the truth and maybe we can talk."

As Friedrich searched Erhmann's eyes, he recognized the burden of sorrow within them, the same indelible scar etched into the expressions of all the survivors he had come to know over the years. He had tried to suppress his own knowledge of the Holocaust since they had sailed out of Tel Aviv to start a new life in America, but a rising swell of shame flooded up within him. He had considered himself a German first, and reluctantly, a Jew second. After the Nazi persecutions of 1933, he had chosen to bury his heritage and disassociate himself from the plight of his people. He wanted all of it to disappear, so he could pursue his beloved work. He wanted to be revered for his expertise and lead a normal secular life.

Instead he had sealed his fate by restoring the skull in 1943. Unless he denied complicity, he was a dead man. Even if Bauer himself couldn't take revenge, someone else in the SS network would.

He focused on the photograph again and took a deep breath. "I must confess that I have seen this picture before," he said. "But other than the lighter skin, that man does not resemble the Bauer I knew."

"If we could find this man and bring him in, could you determine whether or not he's Bauer?"

"You must understand. It was the hardest decision I ever had to make."

"Go on."

"Not until you give me something in writing."

"Your son is being held on murder charges. He will be tried by a military tribunal, not a civilian court. Mossad is involved. We may gain his release if we're able to convict Bauer with your testimony, but there's no guarantee.

It's possible that Sonnenberg is a weapons smuggler wanted by the army. We need to stop those weapons. If we can arrest the smuggler and bring a Nazi to justice, it's a win for both of us. In that case, the tribunal may be more inclined to free your son, but the American government will still extradite him. We have no power to prevent that."

"I understand," Friedrich said. "Prepare the documentation and contact me when you have this Sonnenberg in your custody."

Erhmann pulled a typewritten sheet from his briefcase. "If you agreed to cooperate, I expected you would want something in writing. All you need to do is sign."

Friedrich adjusted his glasses and brought the letter closer.

"I'd normally show this to a lawyer, but now is not the time." He followed the text with a wandering finger, his lips moving as he read through each sentence twice.

I, Doctor Friedrich Mendelssohn, guarantee my full cooperation in the criminal investigation of Colonel Heinz Bauer. This will include my examination of all forensic evidence and my sworn testimony at any trial that may occur in the future.

I understand that if my testimony leads to a conviction of Colonel Bauer for war crimes, my son, Doctor Frank Mendelssohn, currently incarcerated by Israeli military authorities, will be shown consideration for the charges against him and possibly be released into the custody of U.S. authorities.

"That's it? Friedrich said. "There's no authorizing signature. No stamp. This isn't worth the paper it's written on."

"It's the best I could do."

"What if this isn't your man? What happens to Frankie then?"

"I'll do everything I can to gain his release. But, I can't promise anything."

"You're saying this is his only chance?"

"Yes."

Friedrich met Erhmann's eyes, looking for any sign of doubt or accommodation. He saw nothing. He coughed more phlegm into his handkerchief and said, "Give me the pen."

Erhmann stabilized the sheet as Friedrich scrawled his signature at the bottom.

"Do you know where the forensic material on Bauer is located?" Friedrich said.

"With the Justice Department in Bonn."

"Can you obtain it?"

"Yes, but it could take a month or two before a formal request makes its way through channels. Why do you ask?"

"I was hiding under the name of Mueller when Bauer uncovered my Jewish identity. He threatened to turn me in to the Gestapo unless I accepted his offer. It's been a worm burrowing in the back of my mind ever since."

"What kind of offer?"

"He presented me with the skull of a man and claimed he had committed suicide at one of the work camps. The skull had a bullet hole on one side."

"And a large exit wound on the other," Erhmann said.

"Yes. The dentition was similar to Bauer's except for one missing lower molar. He asked me to create an identical set of fillings in the skull to those in his mouth. He vowed to die defending Berlin against the Russians, and he wanted it for forensic identification. When I questioned his motives, he was insulted that I doubted his integrity. He threatened to arrest me. I had very little time. The information about my ancestry was already in the Gestapo pipeline, and Bauer could only delay things for so long. I managed to bargain for my wife as well as myself, and he agreed to arrange our visas and flights out of Austria in exchange for the work."

"We can obtain the remains of the skull. But how will you know if it's him or not?"

"Bring me what you have. I need to examine it myself. I'll know if he used it as a decoy or if he did in fact kill himself. If I prove that he's dead, this investigation is over. Then you must seek Frankie's release immediately."

"I'll try. But that's the best I can promise."

Friedrich searched the deep-set eyes again and saw that he would get nothing more from Erhmann.

"Tell me how you'll know," Erhmann said. "It'll save a lot of time. We can have it examined by forensic experts in Germany."

Friedrich shook his head. "I've lost my trust in people, I don't know, Mister Erhmann. I must see the skull with my own eyes." He pushed the sheet of paper back toward Erhmann. "If there's no skull, you might as well tear this up."

As Erhmann left, relief swept through Friedrich. The guilt over facilitating the freedom of a mass-murderer lifted along with his fear of Bauer's revenge. Frankie mattered more.

From the privacy of his room, he called George Beesley. His old friend had known Frankie since he was a child and he was a man of integrity in whom Friedrich could always confide. He explained his predicament and asked George to recommend a criminal lawyer who could represent Frankie on the drug and fraud charges.

CHAPTER 29

Rattling foot shackles and the grunts of prisoners kept Frankie edgy and awake through the night. The glare from the ceiling bulb was impossible to escape and his head felt as if it were being squeezed in a vise.

Hearing the clang of keys in the cell door, he bolted to his feet.

The door swung open and a guard ushered in a man wearing an unpressed suit with a white shirt and a black tie. A security badge clipped to his pocket identified him as G. Erhmann. His flat expression made him look like a man fed up with his work. Like a fucking undertaker.

Erhmann spoke to the guard with an accent that Frankie couldn't place. "Lock it and wait outside."

The door closed behind him and he motioned Frankie to sit at the table. He brought a cigarette to his lips and offered one to Frankie, which he refused. Erhmann threw the pack on the table and struck a match. His exhalation of smoke drifted up through a ventilation screen in the ceiling. He walked around to the other side and sat down.

"What have you got to say for yourself?"

"Nothing," Frankie said. "Not until I speak to a lawyer."

"Do you realize where you are?"

"Enlighten me," Frankie said. "No one else has."

"This is a military interrogation centre. You've been charged as a terrorist. You have no recourse to a lawyer. Anything you say can be held against you by a tribunal. But the more cooperative you are, the easier it could be for you."

To Frankie's left was a mirrored window. Above it, he saw the blinking light of a camera.

"What about due process? I'm an American citizen for Christ sake. Surely that counts for something."

"Not in here. You'll be kept in solitary confinement until your trial. No contact with anyone. After the evidence of the murder of Private Abelman is presented, you'll be convicted and sent to a maximum-security institution. You'll serve a life sentence without parole."

Erhmann's final words, uttered without the flicker of an eye, turned Frankie's face white. He grabbed the pack of cigarettes and looked for a light. Erhmann struck a match and as Frankie's cheeks puckered he began to cough.

Erhmann twisted the cap off a bottle of water and set it in front of him.

"Is there anything you want to say or should I call the guard?"

"What happens if I tell you what I know?"

"That depends on what it's worth to us. Why don't you begin and we'll see where it goes." Erhmann reached into his breast pocket and pulled out a pen and pad.

Frankie recounted his problems back home up to the moment he'd flipped out and flown to Cairo---the messy divorce, the drugs, the booze, the bad business deal and Joey Kazlov's threats. He explained how he'd ended up dealing Percodan and Ritalin to keep Kazlov at bay.

"Did you ever speak to your father about this?"

"Yeah, but not about everything. You know my father?"

"Yes. He's distraught about the shame you've brought on your family. And your profession."

"That's the way he looks at everything. It's always about the goddamned profession and his fucking reputation. He probably mentioned the shiksa bitch he told me not to marry. Never stopped blaming me for that either."

"Kandi Edwards?"

"Yeah, my ex. Honey do this, honey do that. She drove me nuts."

"How did you get involved with the raid?"

"After the bust, I knew I was done. Jail time for sure." Frankie exhaled and crushed out the butt. "I was released on bail over the weekend, so I split before the news got out. It was a chicken-shit cop-out, but getting bum-fucked in jail freaked me out. Jesus..." He lit another cigarette and coughed into Erhmann's face. He grabbed for the water. "Sorry."

"How did you get into Gaza?"

Frankie took a good look at Erhmann. He'd swear his expression hadn't changed since they'd sat down. The man was a fucking stone.

"I got into Cairo with no problem and figured I'd be okay. I picked up some dental supplies and caught a bus to Rafah but the border guards told me to go back to the American Embassy in Cairo for authorization."

"And you didn't."

"I'd met a guy on the bus, Hassan. He worked in the refugee camp and said they could use my help. He said he could get me across."

"Through a tunnel?"

"Yeah. That scared the living shit out of me. I'm claustrophobic as hell."

"This was Hassan Mashuur?"

"Yeah."

"He and his brother are well known. Members of the Muslim Brotherhood. They're on a watch-list. Hassan hasn't been seen for awhile."

"He's dead. There was an explosion and the tunnel caved in. I was with him when it happened. His legs were crushed. He died of infection."

Erhmann brought a coal to the tip of his cigarette. "Tell me about the raid."

"After the tunnel was destroyed, Hassan's guys suspected me of being a spy. Some even wanted to slit my throat. I had to prove my loyalty by going. They wanted hostages for a prisoner exchange."

"What happened when you got there?"

"It was complete fuck-up," Frankie said. He recalled the details of the raid. "I was the only one who made it."

Erhmann extinguished his butt and pulled out the photograph he'd shown to Friedrich several days before. He pushed it across the table.

"Do you recognize any of these men?"

Frankie looked down at the fuzzy black and white photograph and pulled it closer for a better look. "No. Who are they?"

"It's an old picture. The faces may have changed somewhat over the years. You're sure?"

"I'm certain. Should I know them?"

Erhmann pointed to the person standing behind the two fighters. "We believe this man may have served in the Nazi SS. We've heard rumors about a German smuggling arms into Gaza. The weapons and radios recovered from the raid were manufactured in Czechoslovakia. We think there might be a connection."

"I've never seen that man but I did hear mumblings about a German."

"From who?"

"Khader. The guy who led the raid."

Erhmann closed his notepad. "Good. That's enough for now." He stood up to knock on the door of the cell. As keys jangled in the lock, he turned back to Frankie.

"In view of your cooperation we'll make your stay here a bit more comfortable. The guard will transfer you to a cell with a shower and a proper bed. There's even a television set and a kettle to make tea."

⚔

Erhmann stood before Komorov's desk at military headquarters in Jerusalem.

"Since we last spoke, General, I've flown to California where I met with Dr. Friedrich Mendelssohn, the father of the man captured in the raid. When he heard about his son, he provided more information about Heinz Bauer, which may prove useful. I just came from the remand compound where I interviewed the son, Frank. We had a productive conversation as well. I feel that we have enough circumstantial evidence to continue."

Without lifting his eyes, Komorov continued to shuffle through the stack of papers on his desk.

Erhmann sensed that he had only a few minutes before the general dismissed him.

"I won't keep you, General, but the son said something this morning that makes me think we're on the right track."

"What's that?" Komorov scribbled his signature at the bottom of a page.

"You mentioned a German the last time I saw you. Someone you suspected of smuggling weapons."

Komorov looked up and met Erhmann's eyes.

"He said one of the terrorists spoke of a German."

"And?"

"That's all he said."

Komorov looked across the desk with eyes that hadn't seen a full night's sleep in weeks. He drew on a pipe and exhaled before setting down his pen.

"Mossad agents in Cairo have their eye on Sonnenberg, but he doesn't look anything like the guy in the old photo I showed you before. This could be a different person. Here. See what you think."

Komorov pulled a surveillance photograph from a drawer and handed it to Erhmann. The image was of a man with thinning gray hair and a trimmed moustache and goatee. His neutral expression showed no evidence of his front teeth. He had some distortion across the bridge of the nose as if the cartilage had been altered and his left eyelid drooped.

"Not much similarity," Erhmann agreed. "What does he do in Cairo?"

"Import-export. He brings cars in from Europe and wholesales them to dealers in Cairo. Mercedes and BMW's. He buys carpets in Istanbul and ships them back. Always travels first class."

"Apparently Bauer liked his comforts too. Whom could I talk to about this?"

"I'll make some inquiries and be in touch."

⅄

Three days later, following a call from Komorov, Erhmann drove to Tel Aviv. He picked his way through residential streets overlooking the Mediterranean and stopped in front of a two-story house with a tile roof, similar to every other one on the block. An aide showed him into a room with drawn curtains where he sat on a couch and waited. Several minutes later, a man strode in and closed the door. His tie was loose and the sleeves of his shirt were rolled back. He introduced himself as Agent Asher Harel.

"General Komorov brought me up to speed on what you're doing," Harel said. "Sonnenberg's been on our radar for a while. He's been seen with individuals connected to Hamas. He also runs a foundation that supports orphanages and schools in Gaza. His organization has applied to start projects in some of our Arab communities but they haven't been approved. We suspect that he might be involved in arms smuggling but we've found nothing concrete. It's just a hunch."

He glanced at his watch. "Komorov also mentioned something about a Nazi war criminal, Heinz Bauer."

"Yes, and I know you're busy so I'll keep this short," Erhmann said. "Komorov is holding an American who was involved in a raid on one of our outposts near Gaza."

"I'm familiar with that," Harel said. "We lost a soldier. But what's this got to do with the Nazi?"

"The prisoner is the son of a former Israeli citizen, Dr. Friedrich Mendelssohn. He has now admitted that he used a skull to make a copy of Bauer's dental work near the end of the war. This blows the case against Bauer wide open again."

"So you're thinking that the skull they found back then was a decoy?" Harel said.

"Possibly. And maybe Sonnenberg and Bauer are the same man."

Harel turned on a television set and dimmed the lights. He flicked a switch and a video camera began to hum. Erhmann watched a series of numbers flash across the screen before three men could be seen sitting at an outdoor cafe.

"We took this earlier this year in the Marais district of Paris. The guy with the sunglasses is Herrmann Sonnenberg. The other two are Hamas fundraisers."

The men onscreen stood and shook hands. The lips of one of the men facing the camera moved and the others laughed.

Erhmann saw a flash under the edge of Sonnenberg's upper lip.

"Stop it right there," he said. "Right where he laughs."

Harel reversed the tape and then ran it forward in slow motion. He reached the frame and paused.

Erhmann went to the screen and pressed his finger on the spot. "Here. Can you see? It's a reflection. This could be a gold-trimmed tooth. We have two other photos that show a sparkle in the same place. It's described in his chart as well."

Heral walked forward for a closer look.

"Weren't those fillings common back then? I know I've seen them before."

"It could be a coincidence," Erhmann said. "Everything else in his mouth would have to correlate."

"This is all the footage we have. He's on our watch list but not a high priority. Those men also do business in carpets and autos, so that meeting could be legitimate. He has apartments in Cairo, Paris and Munich but we don't have the resources right now to keep track of him."

"If we knew his whereabouts, my team could abduct him and examine his mouth. If he's the wrong person, we'd just let him go."

"It's been over forty years since he was reported dead. He could have lost some teeth during that time or had fillings replaced. I know my dentist's work doesn't last forever. Something breaks or he finds another goddamned cavity."

"That's true," Erhmann said.

"And if this is Bauer, and he gets wind that someone's on his track, especially concerning his dental work, he'll react to the threat. The dentist in the States is the only one who could testify against him. The Nazi SS still have a wide network of connections throughout the world. His life could be put in danger."

"You're right," Erhmann said. "I've been too focused on getting my hands around the bastard's neck."

Herel switched off the set and turned the lights back up. "This won't be easy but I'll tell you what I can do." He pulled a slip of paper from his pocket. "This is Sonnenburg's address in Paris. He spends time there when the previous year's models are being sold off cheap. That's around now and it's your best chance for surveillance. He frequents cafes around his neighborhood in Marais, so you can observe him close up. See if your suspicions are confirmed. If they are, get back to me and I'll see what I can do."

Herel thrust out his right hand. "I have another meeting. Good luck, Mr. Erhmann."

⅄

Outside, Erhmann wrenched open the car door and groped in the glove compartment for a vial of nitroglycerine tablets. He slipped one under his tongue. The angina pains always hurt more when he got excited or agitated. The relief vas immediate as the drug diffused through his mucosa. He drove through the afternoon traffic cursing the choked streets until he reached the main highway back to Jerusalem.

That evening, he booked a late flight to Paris and made a reservation at the Hotel de la Sorbonne, a favorite for its subterranean jazz cellar where he loved to sip cognac and catch the last set. Located just across the Seine from the Marais district, it would be an easy twenty-five minute stroll to Sonnenberg's apartment on Rue de Rivioli.

Chapter 30

Erhmann stepped outside his hotel as a street cleaner rumbled past at the end of an overnight shift. He strolled along the empty sidewalks around the Sorbonne carrying a camera bag until shopkeepers opened for the day. He fortified himself with a double espresso and his first cigarette of the morning before crossing the bridge to the Marais. He followed a brick-paved alley flanked by antique shops until he reached the Rue de Rivioli. The street buzzed with traffic and pedestrians on their way to work.

He blended into the flow and perused addresses until he saw Sonnenberg's apartment block on the opposite side of the street. At a newspaper kiosk, he leafed through a copy of the International Herald Tribune and scouted for signs of activity. The building's ground floor housed a bookstore with religious titles in the window. Next to it, the mannequins in a tailor's shop displayed the proprietor's creations. He crossed at the light and walked up to the filigreed entrance gate where an intercom button for the building custodian was mounted alongside. Beyond, a walkway edged by boxwood led to the front door and a list of apartment numbers and names.

When the front door opened, Erhmann backed away from the gate and stood next to a transit sign as if waiting for a bus. Through the grating he could see a man who had tattooed arms and the physique of a weight lifter. Keys jingled from his belt while he swept up the leaves scattered about the front door and threw them in a trash bin. Without acknowledging Erhmann's presence, he came out to the street and turned toward the intersection. Erhmann stuck his foot inside the gate just before it re-latched. While the custodian waited for the traffic light at the end of the block, he slipped inside and ran his eye down the list of tenants. When he didn't see the name Sonnenberg, he looked up at the apartment windows but all the curtains remained drawn. The gate creaked and he heard the rattle of keys behind him.

"Looking for someone?"

Erhmann turned and smiled. "I'm trying to locate an old friend. It's his sixty-fifth birthday but I can't see his name on the board. I guess I'm at the wrong place. Sorry."

He received a blank stare in return. "This is a private residence. You're not to enter without pressing the buzzer out there. You're trespassing." He pointed toward the gate. "Leave now or I'll call the police."

"I wanted to surprise him and I didn't want to disturb anyone. My apology." He bowed his head in deference and stepped back out to the street. Half a block down, he crossed at the traffic light and doubled back to a patisserie across from the building. He asked the waiter for an outside table and ordered cappuccino and a buttered croissant. He smothered the croissant with strawberry preserves and allowed himself a moment to luxuriate in its flavors.

As he sipped his cappuccino, the movement of lace curtains in a third floor window of the apartment building drew his attention. He dropped his gaze to the front page of his newspaper. Fifteen minutes later, he dabbed a napkin across his lips and removed the camera from its bag. Holding it up, he asked a man at the next table to take his picture.

"Merci, monsieur. Ma premiere fois a Paris." Continuing with his tourist disguise, he stood and snapped photos of the ornate architecture on the street. As the apartment building came into the frame, he took a wide-angle shot before zooming in on the curtained window he had noticed on the third floor. He sensed a shadow standing behind the curtain and put the camera away. He glanced at his watch. Just past nine o'clock. He ordered a second cappuccino, lit a cigarette and resumed reading his paper.

When the filigreed gate next swung open, a well-dressed couple stepped out to the street. They paused next to the curb while the woman's lappoodle relieved itself in the gutter. The dog finished and she accepted the gentleman's arm and sashayed down the sidewalk, admiring her reflection in shop windows.

The man beside her walked with the bearing of an aging athlete, but he used a cane to support an obvious weakness on his left side. He wore dark sunglasses and sported a goatee and moustache that matched the gray fabric of his suit. They stopped for a moment to chat with the tailor and then continued to the corner where they crossed over to the patisserie. Erhmann discerned from their lively chatter that they knew the proprietor. He recognized their German accents as they spoke French. The man resembled Sonnenberg and could be Bauer.

A suffocating squeeze from his cardiac arteries took his breath away. His cup and saucer clattered as he dug into his camera bag for the pills and jostled the table. The waiter hurried over and asked if he needed anything.

He slid a tablet under his tongue and said, "Une tasse de leau, s'il vous plait."

"Suremont, monsieur."

The couple came outside and walked past him to a table down the row. Pretending to read while listening to them order, their pronunciation confirmed his first impression. Definitely German.

The woman leafed through a leather-bound binder. When she spoke, Erhmann strained to hear what she was saying over the hum of traffic.

"You have a busy day ahead of you," she said, looking at the binder. "Your first meeting is with the Foundation Board at eleven o'clock to discuss starting a project in Beirut. The board wants your approval before they proceed to the next stage."

The man nodded and exhaled smoke from a small cigar while the woman wrote notes with a pen. As she looked across the table in Erhmann's direction and spoke again, he raised his paper and turned the page to avoid her eyes.

"At lunch you will meet with Monsieur Gronet from the Mercedes head office. They have a new promotion to discuss. After that you will have time for a nap before your dental appointment."

Erhmann folded his newspaper and left enough cash under the saucer to cover his bill. With his back to the couple, he lifted his camera bag off the chair and walked away. Meetings with a foundation board and an auto executive coincided with Heral's intelligence. He might not be on a wild goose chase, after all.

He walked to the far end of the block and then crossed at a light and doubled back on the other side. Approaching the patisserie from across the street, he slipped his camera from its bag and waited for a group of pedestrians to pass until he could get a clear view of the couple. He took two quick close-up shots and then stowed the camera and walked behind another sidewalk vendor, where he browsed magazines and kept an eye on them.

A Mercedes Benz sedan rounded the corner and double-parked in front of the patisserie. Erhmann pulled out his camera again. When the driver stepped out and opened the back door for the couple and their dog, he recognized the custodian's physique and the tattoos on his forearms. Hidden behind the rack of magazines, he shot three more pictures and scribbled down the licence plate number with the time, date and location. Satisfied that he had enough, he waited until the car pulled away and then walked back toward a camera shop near his hotel to have the film processed.

⋏

Herrmann Sonnenberg tore off his sunglasses and spat out a volley of German epithets. The woman closed her eyes and waited until he had finished.

"Did you recognize him?" The driver glanced back in his rear-view mirror. "He's tall and thin. Hard to miss."

"I saw him from my window sitting in front of Pierre's," Sonnenberg said. "He was gawking about with a camera, taking pictures. I thought he was a tourist."

"We went down for a closer look after I got dressed," the woman said. "Neither of us have ever seen him before."

"He's not German. From the east. Hungarian, maybe. I got suspicious when I saw him sneak through the gate after I went for coffee. That's why I called you, Frau Drechsler."

"Only Germans live in the building," she said. "It seems odd."

"Mutterficker Juden!" Sonnenberg slapped his hand on the leather arm rest. "After all these years. You'd think they'd get over it."

The woman patted the top of his clenched hand. "Enough, Herrmann," she said, her tone quiet but commanding.

Sonnenberg fell silent, acknowledging her glare with an acquiescent blink of his right eye. His left iris drifted in a dull glaze, the only feature his surgeons could not alter without removing the eyeball completely.

"This is what we know so far," she said. "Our contacts in Bonn informed us of an Israeli request for all the forensic evidence gathered after the Munich suicides. There have been no such requests since the proceedings concluded in 1946. That's why I asked Bernhardt to keep me aware of anything out of the ordinary. We're also watching the apartments in Cairo and Munich but there have been no reports of anything."

Sonnenberg brushed her hand away and flexed his knuckles. "I told you, Petra, that dentist, Mendelssohn, is the only one who could know. He must have provided information to one of their investigation teams."

"But why?" Petra said. "He hasn't divulged anything before. He knows it would put him and his family in jeopardy."

"It doesn't matter why," Sonnenberg said. "He's the only one who could testify. The lives of too many orphaned children depend on my foundation. I cannot allow this Jewish fool to compromise their future. We must see to that."

"What do you suggest?"

"He's an old man. A Zurich bank employee, who is loyal to our cause, notified me when Mendelssohn had the contents of a safety deposit box transferred to Los Angeles about forty years ago. You must locate him and make an accident."

Petra frowned. "You're sure you want to do this?"

Sonnenberg met her eyes and nodded.

"Very well." She tapped on the back of the seat and caught the driver's eye in the rear-view mirror. "Bernhardt. You will take care of this. Prepare to leave on short notice."

"Ja, Frau Drechsler."

⅄

Erhmann picked up the processed photographs and caught a taxi to the Israeli Embassy where Asher Harel met him. They took an elevator to a second floor office that overlooked a treed garden at the back of the building. Two Mossad agents stood when they walked into the room. Harel introduced the men and poured coffee. "Let's see what you have," he said, looking at Erhmann.

Erhmann spread the photographs out on the table. "It's Sonnenberg. I took these of him and a woman yesterday at a patisserie across from the address you gave me. I couldn't see his name on the apartment directory."

"He's stayed there before," Heral said. "That woman might be his secretary."

Erhmann pointed to the photo with the Mercedes. "The guy in the tee-shirt is the driver who came to pick them up. He's also the custodian of the building who caught me snooping around." Erhmann took a slip of paper from his pocket. "Here's the licence number."

Heral handed it to one of the men who stood up and left the room.

"Sonnenberg and the woman may have been checking me out because they took a table down from where I was sitting in the pattiserie. When I recognized the custodian picking them up a half hour later, I put two and two together. I'm sure he called them after he caught me inside the gate."

"That's Petra Dreschler," said the other agent. "That's her married name but she's divorced. Her father was Heinz Bauer's younger brother. He was killed in North Africa. She's long been associated with the National Democratic Party in Germany. She attends functions with the far right Front National here in France. No criminal background, but she's definitely on the inside."

"Do you think she could be involved in helping SS fugitives?"

"I wouldn't be surprised."

They looked up as the other agent hustled back into the room and closed the door. "The car's registered to Petra Drechsler. Apartment 302, 16 rue de Rivioli."

"Bingo," said Herel. "Sonnenberg is staying with her while he's in town doing business." He raised his coffee cup in a mock toast to the others. "What do we know about this other guy, the driver?"

"We've seen him before with Dreschsler," said the agent. "His name is Bernhardt Stangler. He's her handyman-bodyguard. He chauffeurs her every-where and does maintenance around the building. He lives in a small room in the basement and spends a lot of time at a gym on the next block. He's worked as a bouncer and has been charged with assault a couple of times."

Harel addressed the two agents. "Okay, the connection to Bauer is pretty clear. Put surveillance on Sonnenberg and keep track of his whereabouts." He turned to Erhmann. "What about Mendelssohn? How do you plan to handle him?"

"He wants to examine the skull. As soon as we obtain it, I'll take it over there. If it's positive, we can proceed."

Harel stood up and looked at his watch. "We'll meet in two weeks to see what we've got. Shalom."

⋏

In the late afternoon Drechsler poured tea for Sonnenberg and Stangler. She opened her binder on the coffee table of her apartment and looked across at the two men.

"We've located Mendelssohn in California. And we received some other material that sheds light on why the Israelis have requested information."

Sonnenberg's brow furrowed.

"What's that?"

"Did you know that he has a son?"

"Spare me, Petra. I haven't seen him in over forty years. Just tell me what you've got."

"The son's a dentist as well, but apparently not cut from the same cloth as his father. This is a copy taken from the Los Angeles Times. He was recently charged with possession of prescription drugs for the purpose of traffick-ing. He jumped bail and was tracked to Cairo. But he hasn't been seen since. There's been no mention in the Israeli media and of course the police and military have no comment on the matter."

"What are you saying?" Sonnenberg asked.

"It's hard to say." Drechsler stirred sugar into her tea. "Maybe he slipped into Israel undetected but that's doubtful. He's vanished."

"What about the old man?" Sonnenberg said.

"He lives in a senior home in the Beverley Hills area of Los Angeles. We have an address and a picture. She laid out another copy showing Doctor Friedrich Mendelssohn displaying several pieces of sculpture. This is from a magazine article about the residence. Apparently he's one of their stars. He has a tremor condition but he still keeps active."

She looked at Stangler. "He keeps a strict schedule and goes out by himself each morning at ten, to a park next door where he walks through the trails. He returns an hour later. I'll leave the details up to you. You're booked to leave this evening."

"He may have some other information," Sonnenberg said. "There was a letter with a Swiss bank describing what he'd done in exchange for his passage out of the country. It was his insurance against a double-cross. This was what he'd transferred to the bank in Los Angeles, I suppose."

"We must assume it's still in existence," Drechsler said. "In any case it would be inaccessible to us. I've inquired about intercepting the skull but it's been released to the Israeli embassy. We were too late on that, unfortunately." She closed her binder and met Sonnenberg's eye.

"Mendelssohn must be eliminated. Without his testimony there's no case. If a letter surfaces, we can argue that it's a fake. Our best strategy now is for you to go about your business as usual, Onkel. Bernhardt will take care of things in Los Angeles. He'll contact us as soon as he's finished."

"Very well," Sonnenberg said. "I'm not leaving for Munich until the end of the week." He looked at Stangler. "You should be done by then."

CHAPTER 31

Erhmann flew all night to Los Angeles and was met by agent Aaron Weinstock. In Erhmann's hotel room, Weinstock pointed to an aluminum case with combination locks.

"Everything we received from Bonn is in there," he said. "Harel wants this matter given highest priority. Two of us are staying next door, in room 405. We've got cameras in both the hallway and your room. We'll listen in on any phone calls and keep an eye on who comes and goes. I'll drive you to Mendelssohn's residence in the morning."

"Fine. I'll contact him to set up a time and let you know." Erhmann rubbed his eyes and yawned. "I'm getting way too old for these red-eyes. I'm going to call room service for something to eat and turn in."

✦

Using a German passport identifying him as Bernhardt Schroeder, Stangler cleared customs in the early afternoon and caught a cab to a hotel on Santa Monica Boulevard. On the front seat of a rental car in the hotel garage, he found directions to the Parkside Grove Retirement Lodge. He drove up into the hills and parked at the front entrance of the nature preserve that bordered the lodge.

A creek ran diagonally from one side of the ten-acre compound to the other. A gravel path skirted the creek's southern edge until it veered north over a footbridge. Underneath, a modest flow gurgled down through the rocks to a glassy pool where ducks swam.

Stangler followed the path until he arrived at the footbridge. He crossed to the north side and hurried down the path toward a grove of willows. With the echo of tumbling water masking any noise from the street, he pried apart the willow stems and looked down a steep grade to the streambed. Looking around to ensure he was alone, he let the stems swish back together and continued along the path until it emerged from the trees. A short sidewalk led to the residence.

Returning to his hotel, he ordered a cheeseburger and a beer and then booked a wake-up call for seven the next morning.

⅄

Erhmann closed the door to his room and called Parkside Grove.

"Doctor Friedrich Mendelssohn, please. It's Mr. Erhmann calling."

"I just saw him go outside," the receptionist said. "Hang on and I'll have someone fetch him."

While he waited on the line, he paged through the documents of forensic evidence found in the basement of the villa. When he came to the copy of Bauer's chart, another spasm gripped his chest. He slipped a tablet under his tongue and caught his breath.

A croaky voice came over the phone.

"Hello."

"Yes, Doctor Mendelssohn. Gabor Erhmann. I'm back in town and have the material that we spoke about. I'd like to meet you tomorrow morning. Around ten o'clock, if that's convenient"

"That will be fine," Friedrich said. "I usually go for my walk around that time but I'll go at nine instead. When you arrive, come right to my room where we can meet in private."

⅄

The following morning, everything was quiet as Stangler stepped out of his car with a newspaper. He strolled around the perimeter of the preserve until he reached the main entrance he had used the day before. Two people with dogs on leash stood and chatted. He sat on a bench and opened his newspaper to the photograph that Drechsler had provided, of Friedrich exhibiting his sculptures.

As the sun rose over the trees, a stooped man with hiking poles came toward him. Friedrich walked by and entered the grove. Stangler folded the newspaper into his cargo-pants and stood to follow. Glancing over his shoulder, he saw the dog owners returning to their cars.

⋏

Erhmann woke refreshed after sleeping a solid eight hours. At 7:45 a.m. he spoke to Weinstock on the phone. "I know what the traffic's like, so let's drive over there now. Mendelssohn planned to go for a walk around nine. I'd like to join him."

At 8:55 the navy-blue Chevrolet Impala with consulate plates pulled up to the front of the residence. Erhmann went inside for a moment then hurried back out.

"Wait in the lobby with the case," he said. "Mendelssohn left a few minutes ago. I'll catch up with him. We should be back around ten."

"No problem," Weinstock said. "I've got some calls to make."

Erhmann walked down the sidewalk at a measured pace until he found the main street entrance. Two dogs barked as their owners coaxed them into the back of their cars. The air carried the fragrance of blossoming foliage. He dug in his pocket and rattled his vial of pills, just in case. Entering the woods, he heard the trickle of water.

As was his habit, Friedrich paused on Eva's bridge to sprinkle breadcrumbs for the ducks. He put the empty sandwich bag into his pocket and continued over to the other side, where he braced his poles into the gravel and started down toward the willow patch.

Stangler waited behind a bush and then stepped back on the trail and crept forward to close the gap.

⋏

Erhmann caught his first sight of the waterfall that he'd been hearing through the trees. On the footbridge he paused and looked down at the reflection of sunbeams cascading through the leaves. He inhaled the crispness rising off the water. And then, the serenity of the moment shattered with Friedrich's cry.

"Leave me alone! I have no money. What are you doing? No, no!"

Erhmann rushed toward the sounds of distress. The same muscular, tattooed arms he'd seen in Paris pushed Friedrich backward into the thicket of willows. "Back off," Erhmann shouted.

Friedrich fought to free himself from Stangler's grip but Stangler threw him down hard near the base of the stems. Then he wheeled around to face Erhmann's charge.

"Get to the residence, Doctor. Call the police," Erhmann yelled.

Stangler snickered at the towering figure bearing down on him. "Well, look who's here. The Jew who doesn't know how to mind his own business." He crouched and circled Erhmann, closing the distance with his knees bent, fists clenched, preparing to pounce.

Erhmann snapped a branch off a fallen tree and swung down on the shorter man. Stangler pirouetted and ripped the club from Erhmann's grasp, driving its splintered point deep into his gut. Erhmann pitched forward and was knocked flat by a vicious chop to his head.

Blinking up into an umbrella of leaves, Erhmann's caught Stangler's boot as it grazed across his face. Birds scattered at the sharp crack that reverberated through the woods. Stangler hit the ground writhing, his ankle skewed ninety degrees to his shin. With the force of an anaconda, Erhmann locked onto Stangler's throat and squeezed. The German gagged and choked until his eyes rolled back and Erhmann suddenly released his grip.

Stangler gasped for air and watched the giant fall to the side clutching his chest. He looked to the willows where he'd thrown Friedrich, but the old man was gone. "Fuck!" Screaming with pain, he grabbed the branch next to Erhmann's hand, and used it as a crutch. "Mutterficker Jude." As sirens wailed in the distance, he dragged himself to his car, wedged in behind the wheel and drove away.

In the shady grove, mouth agape and eyes ajar, Gabor Erhmann lay sprawled and motionless.

⋏

From the lobby of the lodge, where he had been flirting with the receptionist, Aaron Weinstock heard a commotion coming from the side entrance. He jumped to his feet and helped Friedrich to a chair.

"What the hell's going on?"

"Dr. Mendelssohn was mugged in the park," said one of the attendants.

"Where's Gabor?" Weinstock asked.

Friedrich wheezed to catch his breath, his voice barely a whisper. "He rescued me. Mr. Erhmann."

The receptionist called from behind her desk. "The police and an ambulance are on their way."

Weinstock crouched down beside Friedrich. "Doctor Mendelssohn, listen to me. My name is Aaron Weinstock. I came here with Mister Erhmann. Where is he?"

"On the path below the bridge. He might be hurt. You must hurry."

Weinstock reached across the counter and handed the case to the receptionist. "Don't let this out of your sight."

He ran after the attendants, following them down to the park until they came upon the unconscious hulk next to the trail. Weinstock put his ear next to Erhmann's mouth and pressed his finger against the carotid artery at the side of his neck. "Still breathing, but hardly a pulse. Go back and bring the medics. Tell them it's a heart attack. Hurry."

At the sight of Erhmann's frozen gaze, Weinstock's special ops training went into overdrive. He jammed his fingers into Erhmann's mouth and retrieved a dislodged partial denture. He wrenched back Erhmann's neck and sealed his mouth over the flaccid lips. When he had completed three rounds of inflations and compressions, two paramedics crouched down beside him.

"Good job, buddy. We'll take it from here."

⋏

From his office at the consulate, Weinstock placed an encrypted phone call to Harel at Mossad headquarters. He paced back and forth for fifteen minutes before Harel came on the line.

"What is it?"

Weinstock knew his former special ops commander as a jovial man, but from the tone of his voice, he dispensed with pleasantries and got to the point.

"There's been an assault on Mendelssohn. Erhmann drove off the attacker but suffered a heart attack. He's touch and go, right now."

"Mendelssohn?"

"In shock and under sedation."

"Does it have anything to do with the Sonnenberg thing?"

"Can't say. If Erhmann pulls through, he might know something. When I found him, he was unconscious. The attacker was gone and there were no weapons around. We had just arrived to have Mendelssohn examine the evidence."

"We're up to our fucking balls over here," Heral said. "They snuck a bomber onto a school bus this morning. Killed thirty kids and the driver. Burnt them alive."

"Fucking butchers."

"It's just beginning," Heral said. "Don't call me back unless you've got something. I can't talk now."

The line went dead and Weinstock set down the phone. He paged through his Rolodex and called Parkside Grove. The receptionist recognized his voice.

"Sorry to hear what happened," she said. "I hope your partner's okay."

"It's not good," Weinstock said. "He might not pull through. How's Mendelssohn doing?"

"He's resting. His friend Miriam is keeping an eye on him."

"Connect me with the director. We're putting in a security detail. It's on the way."

⅄

Stangler cursed as he hobbled into his hotel room on crutches, a cast binding his left ankle. He made a call to Paris. Dreschler answered. When she heard his voice, she handed the receiver to Sonnenberg.

"Is everything taken care of?"

"Your suspicion was confirmed," Stangler said.

"What do you mean?"

"That man I caught snooping inside the apartment gate. I was about to push Mendelssohn down a cliff like an accident when the brute attacked me. The sonovabitch broke my ankle. I'm on fucking crutches and can hardly move. I know he recognized me, but then he collapsed. It looked like he had a heart attack. I don't know if he's dead or alive."

"What about Mendelssohn?"

"Maybe a little roughed up, but that's all. What do you want me to do now?"

"Surely it's no coincidence. This must have something to do with the request for information in Bonn. They're using Mendelssohn to identify the remains. Somehow they have connected it to me."

"Do you want me to try again?"

"They've probably set up a security perimeter. They may also know that you're injured and they'll be watching the airport. Wait in your room. I'll discuss this with our people in Los Angeles. Someone will be in touch. He will introduce himself as Adolph. He'll tell you what to do."

⚔

Three days later, waking with stents in his cardiac arteries, Erhmann learned from the hospital staff that Aaron Weinstock had saved his life. He recuperated for the rest of the week until he felt ready to move. Then he and Weinstock met with the director of Parkside Grove, Rosalia Gonzales. She escorted them to Friedrich's room. The security guard unlocked the latch and Friedrich's sallow face appeared from behind the door. He motioned for them to enter and shuffled back to his kitchen table.

"It's a relief to see you again," he said, looking at Erhmann. "I can't thank you enough for rescuing me. A moment later and I would have been over that cliff."

"We're both very fortunate. Thanks to Aaron here."

Weinstock smiled and set the aluminum case on the table.

"From now on you'll have to be more careful when you go out," Erhmann said.

"Meaning I won't be able to walk in my own neighborhood?"

"Only if you're accompanied by someone. This wasn't your average mugging, doctor. We believe it's related to the Bauer investigation. I must apologize. We didn't see it coming." He groaned and lowered himself on a chair.

"Have they found the culprit yet?"

Erhmann shook his head as Friedrich poured coffee.

"Had you ever seen him before?" Erhmann said.

"No and he never said a word. He just grabbed me and started pushing me off the path."

"I came across him in Paris about three weeks ago," Erhmann said. "He works as a bodyguard for Herrmann Sonnenberg." He handed Friedrich the picture of Stangler stepping out of the Mercedes.

"That's him, alright. I remember those crude tattoos."

Erhmann sifted through a stack of photos until he found the recent close-up of Sonnenberg. "Does this man look familiar?"

Friedrich concentrated on the image of a fit-looking man in his late sixties. "Are you thinking that this is Bauer?" A furrow creased his brow.

"It's possible," Erhmann said. "Israeli intelligence suspects him of smugglings guns into Gaza. He moves between Cairo, Munich and Paris. His legitimate business is import/export. Cars and carpets. Do you see any similarities?"

"The Bauer I knew had a full head of hair and was clean-shaven. And with those sunglasses, it's hard to tell." He held the photograph closer and dwelled on the face. "Maybe a trace of facial scarring here," he said, pointing to the left side of Sonnenberg's face. "Does he walk with a limp?"

"Yes and he uses a cane."

Friedrich brought the photograph closer once more and then shook his head and set it down.

"I agree that it's hard to tell," Erhmann said. "I only saw him twice in Auschwitz. If it's him, it's a good disguise."

"Let me see the skull," Friedrich said.

Weinstock twirled the combinations and opened the case. He stripped back the wrapping and handed the skull to Friedrich.

The bone was more charred than Friedrich remembered. With five lower front teeth broken off and wires splinting the lower jaw together, the specimen looked so unlike what he had visualized. Both men watched as he rotated the skull to expose the entry wound on the right side. "About the diameter of a pencil," he said. "That's how I remember it."

He turned the skull to the left where a larger section of the cranial shell was missing.

"The exit wound," Erhmann said.

Friedrich traced his finger along the ragged perimeter.

"He set bombs to go off after he shot himself," Erhmann said. "According to the examiner's description, the lower jaw was broken."

"Yes, it was intact before," Friedrich said. "They've bound it back together with this wire."

"We never located any debris from that exit wound," Erhmann said. "That made us suspicious. On the other hand, there were two explosions and soldiers were tromping around before the site was secured."

Friedrich opened the lower jaw. Some of the gold fillings had been distorted by heat. He rubbed his index finger over the tarnished surfaces. "Do you have a copy of the chart?"

"Yes sir," Weinstock said, sorting through the case. "There's also a document signed by the examining forensic dentist. It confirms his opinion that all the fillings in the skull follow the configurations described in the chart."

"Is that your handwriting?" Erhmann said.

Friedrich recognized the disciplined flow on the page, another skill that had abandoned him in the last few years. "Yes, it's mine," he said. His eyes moved between the chart and the skull. His notes accurately defined what he saw on each tooth. Almost thirty minutes later, he raised his eyes to Erhmann and Weinstock.

"Everything in the skull matches the record," he said.

"Can you tell if it's him or a fake?" Erhmann said.

"I can tell you that. But first I need your promise that I will be able to see my son. You're holding him in solitary confinement. I want him to know that I'm standing behind him, no matter what he's done."

"That wasn't part of the deal."

"It is now." Friedrich laid his glasses next to the skull and folded his hands.

Erhmann rolled his eyes and looked at Weinstock who shook his head and said, "Military won't allow it."

"I know my son," Friedrich said. "He's made some bad decisions but he's not a bad person. Right now he'll be blaming himself. He's ashamed and embarrassed and he won't want to face me. I'm worried that he'll do something stupid and I fear the worst. I must speak to him in person. He must understand there's still hope; that I'm here to support him."

"I'll see what I can do but it may take awhile," Erhmann said.

"Take all this with you, then," Friedrich said. "I've had enough for today."

After they left the room Friedrich poured himself an ounce of cognac, a small luxury he allowed himself now that Eva was gone, and waited for the liquor to do its job. The work in the skull was his. With the examination of only two more areas, he would know whether the skull was indeed a relic of Heinz Bauer or the decoy that he had created.

Chapter 32

Bernhardt Stangler hobbled out of the hotel on crutches, a searing spike shooting up from his ankle. An hour earlier he had jolted awake to the ring of the telephone. Adolph. He would arrive in a white Suburban with Nevada plates. The vehicle pulled to a stop in front of him. He hoisted himself into the backseat and closed the door. Adolph glanced at him through wraparound sunglasses and drove away.

"You've spoken to Herr Sonnenberg, jah?"

"He said you'd contact me with instructions."

"Correct. The guy who broke your ankle is Gabor Erhmann. He's part of an organization called Nakam. They're all about torture and they have a long reach. That abduction of Groule in Canada was theirs."

"I heard about that," Stangler said. "Ruthless motherfuckers."

"Erhmann had a heart attack but he's a tough nut. He survived and we've followed him since he was released from the hospital. He and a Mossad agent were at the residence yesterday. They spent two hours inside, probably meeting with the dentist, Mendelssohn. The agent carried a case that the German government uses to transport archival material. We believe that Mendelssohn is providing information to implicate Herr Sonnenberg in war crimes. Our orders are to stop this from going any further. Whatever is necessary."

"What's the plan?" Stangler popped back two more codeines and carefully elevated his ankle onto the seat.

"We can't get to Mendelssohn unless he leaves the residence, and he hasn't been out since the altercation. He has round-the-clock security. Erhmann's also being watched by Mossad at his hotel. Our only opportunity may be to intercept him when he arrives or leaves Mendelssohn's residence. If we can get rid of him and the evidence, it will go a long way to solving this problem. We'll deal with Mendelssohn when things cool off. Fucking double-crossing Jew."

The Suburban took the exit off the freeway and wound up through the canyons leading to Parkside Grove. Adolph slowed for a construction crew doing repair work to a guard railing on a tight corner. Beyond blocks of granite piled to one side, the road fell in a sheer drop-off. Adolph glanced in the rear-view mirror. He met Stangler's gaze and grinned.

"You're a quick study, Bernhardt."

"Ideal place for an accident." Stangler grimaced as the car thumped across uneven breaks in the pavement.

Adolph drove past the residence and made a U-turn. He pulled up to the curb, behind a blue mini-van, a vantage point that allowed a clear view of the parking lot. The decal on the rear door of the van read; *Advance Cable TV Network*. He picked up his phone.

"Any sign of them?"

After a pause, he said, "Okay. It's early yet. They weren't here until after lunch yesterday. Once they go inside, pull up beside their car and go to work. We'll follow you on the way down." He turned back to Stangler. "Get some rest. I'll wake you when its time."

⅄

Erhmann read the message from Harel and phoned Friedrich.

"We've just received approval for one hour visitations as soon as you can be transported to Jerusalem," he said. "In the meantime, we're monitoring him twenty-four hours a day."

"That's a relief," Friedrich said.

"You'll need to identify the skull first."

"Fine. Come over after lunch. Around two."

"I'll make the flight arrangements," Erhmann said. "Pack a bag. We'll be taking you back to the consulate tonight. It's more secure there. We'll probably leave tomorrow sometime."

⅄

As the Impala with consulate plates turned into the parking lot, Adolph crushed his cigarette into the ashtray. Through binoculars, he watched Erhmann exit the car carrying a camera bag. Weinstock unlocked the trunk and lifted out the hard-shelled aluminum case. When they entered the building Adolph spoke into his phone.

The mini-van started its engine and rolled down the street to park next to the Impala. The driver wearing white coveralls, stepped out and then bent down between the two vehicles, as if he'd dropped something. When he stood, he continued to the rear of the van and withdrew a tool box and a coil of coaxial cable.

His partner, in a matching uniform, unhooked a ladder from the roof rack and lifted it to his shoulder. As they walked together toward the cable boxes on the outside of the building, the driver glanced back at the Suburban and raised the coil high over his head.

⅄

"Set up the camera," Erhmann said.

Weinstock extended the legs of a tripod and attached a video camera to the mounting bracket. He switched it on and focused on the table where Friedrich and Erhmann sat next to each other.

"We'll record your examination of the skull," Erhmann said. "These matters can take a long time to move through the system. If anything happens to prevent you from testifying, this recorded evidence will stand up in court. Weinstock pressed the record button and delivered a verbal introduction. Friedrich and Erhmann each nodded toward the camera as he spoke their names. He read out Bauer's archival case number, the date, the location and the time at which the recording was occurring.

Erhmann reached into the camera bag and withdrew an envelope. "I have more pictures of Sonnenberg taken over the last few weeks. See what you think." He handed the photos to Friedrich who flipped through them one by one.

"Pretty much the same as what you showed me before," Friedrich said. "He could be one of a million Germans out there with a war injury."

"It's never easy," Erhmann said, with a sigh. He snapped open the locks. "You can begin with the specimen."

Friedrich took the skull from the case and held it up with the eye sockets facing him. The upper front teeth were all intact except for one; the right central incisor. A solitary gold filling replaced the inside corner edge.

"Bauer told me that he fractured this tooth on the hatch door when he jumped from his tank. Did any of those recent shots show his lips apart? I didn't notice. My eyes are getting bad."

"I think there is one where he's grinning," Erhmann said, sifting through the photographs. "Yes, here it is. It was taken off a video."

Friedrich moved a magnifying lens back and forth until he locked on a clear image. "There we go. The upper right central incisor. Can you see that glint?"

"It's one of the few where he smiles," Erhmann said.

"Pretty serious fellow."

"Maybe he's worried."

"We'll know in a minute." Friedrich lifted the skull and detached two clips that held the lower jaw in place. "These must have been inserted by the forensic team to hold everything together." He set the lower jaw on the table and turned the skull upside down, exposing the teeth in the upper arch. He pointed to the fillings in the two molars on the right side.

"I have to remove these two." He took a Swiss Army Knife from his pocket and flipped open the blade. "This is how we'll find out if it's a fake or the real thing."

Weinstock jumped to his feet. "No, no, no. That's tampering with evidence, Doctor. I'm not sure I can allow it. I don't want to be held responsible."

"It makes no difference," Erhmann said. "The case has been closed for years. Go ahead Doctor. Be as careful as you can."

Friedrich cradled the cranium in his lap and inspected the tarnished gold in the two molars. The edges that he'd burnished to perfection had curled from the intensity of the inferno. He pried his blade into the gaps that had been created and both fillings fell into the palm of his hand. He handed the skull to Erhmann and picked away the shards of cement clinging to the undersides of the fillings. He blew away the loose chips and examined each filling under magnification. "This is not Heinz Bauer's skull. It's the copy I made."

"How can you be sure?"

"I gave him the restored duplicate on the same day that I seated these last two fillings." He held up the chart. "You can see it here, at his final appointment. After that, I extracted his molar to match what you see here in the lower jaw." He ran his finger through the gap created by the missing tooth. "My wife Eva distrusted Bauer the most. She despised Nazis and especially him. That's why I engraved swastikas into the underside of his last two fillings before cementing them. These two are unmarked, as you can see. This proves that it's the decoy."

"You're absolutely positive?" Erhmann rubbed his finger across the unblemished surfaces.

"Did you not hear me?" Friedrich removed his glasses and his voice shook the room. "My son's life is on the line. I mean what I say." He took a deep breath to calm himself. He had a long way to go yet.

Erhmann checked with Weinstock. "Do you have it all recorded?"

"Every last word," Weinstock said.

"Good. I don't doubt for a moment what you have told us, Doctor. We'll get you to your son as soon as possible. The El Al flight leaves at nine tomorrow morning. I have business class tickets for both of us. Once we arrive, we'll go directly to the detention centre." He looked over at Weinstock.

"Put those two unmarked fillings in an envelope and have Doctor Mendelssohn write his signature across the sealed flap. We'll need them for the trial. When you get back to the consulate, call Asher Heral and let him know what we've discovered. Tell him that we have enough evidence to bring Sonnenberg in for questioning."

To Friedrich, he said, "Are you prepared to perform the dental examination on him?"

"If Frankie can assist. I'll need him to record and corroborate the evidence."

"We can arrange that."

Weinstock set the wrapped skull back into the case and placed blocks of foam around it. He licked the inside flap of the envelope and handed it to Friedrich. "Please sign this for me."

"It's getting late, Aaron," Erhmann said. "Take the car and the specimen back to the consulate. Try to contact Heral before he's gone for the day. I'll stay here and help Doctor Mendelssohn pack his things. We'll take a cab over later." He turned to Friedrich. "You'll be comfortable in the consulate guest suite tonight. We'll be escorted to the airport tomorrow and taken to a private lounge until the plane leaves. El Al is well versed in these types of operations. After what's just happened, we can't be too careful."

"I understand," Friedrich said. "I'll get ready."

"I'll see Aaron to the car and confirm everything for tomorrow. I'll come to your room in about an hour."

When they had left and Friedrich heard the click of the guard locking the deadbolt, he slumped into his armchair. From the sidetable, he picked up a framed photograph of Eva and him on Frankie's graduation day. How he wished she were with him now. His face crinkled at the thought and then stiffened as he contemplated what lay ahead. He closed his eyes and whispered, "I promise you, my darling, that I will bring our son home. And Heinz Bauer will be punished for what he did."

He exhaled and felt the burden that he'd carried for so many years beginning to lift. For the moment at least, the trembling in his hands had almost stopped.

But in the bedroom as he folded each garment into his suitcase, a deep sense of apprehension swept through him. He pushed it aside. Through the confrontations to come, he would not let the bastard intimidate him.

All the same, he wouldn't forget the gunmetal coldness in Bauer's eyes. As if yesterday, he remembered the blanched knuckles, the sweaty imprints on the hand-rests. And the sounds, clear and sharp at the moment of deliverance. The snapping fibers and cracking of bone as he wrestled the three-rooted molar from the Colonel's jaw---all done without a whimper or a drop of anesthetic. The man was a goddamn automaton.

If Sonnenberg was indeed Heinz Bauer, he would not submit easily. Detail obsessed, Bauer would have considered every scenario with a contingency plan for each. And while Friedrich didn't doubt the durability of his work, it had been over forty years. The roots of Bauer's teeth and the bone that supported them may have not withstood the grinding and clenching that necessitated the treatment in the first place. What if Bauer had more teeth missing now? What if some his work had been replaced with other fillings of a different design or material?

λ

Erhmann and Weinstock spoke to the security guards outside the room and then turned down the hallway toward the director's office. Erhmann informed Rosalia Gonzalez that Doctor Mendelssohn would be travelling to visit relatives in Israel.

"I'll be accompanying him there," he said. "We have an early flight tomorrow morning so we'll be staying out near the airport tonight. Are there any precautions, food allergies, medications, that I need to be aware of?"

"I'll give you a list of the meds he takes," Gonzalez said. "Even with his tremor condition he keeps surprisingly fit. We see him doing push ups every day as well as all that walking. How long will he be gone?"

"We're taking him back to see his son," Erhmann said. "It's an open ended ticket. His rent will be paid as usual. We'll be in touch when he decides to return home."

"I'm glad you're looking so well," Gonzalez said. "That was quite a scare."

"Tough to keep the old guy down." Weinstock patted Erhmann on the back and laughed before they turned and walked out to the car. Erhmann sat in the passenger seat while Weinstock stowed the case in the trunk and then got in behind the wheel.

"Leave the case with the duty officer and I'll pick it up when we get there," Erhmann said. "I'll keep the camera with me and review the video while he's getting ready. I think we've got everything but I want to be sure there are no loose ends."

Erhmann glanced to his right and nodded to the driver of the cable van who backed out of the parking spot beside them.

As soon as the van turned down the street, the driver spoke into his phone.

"Looks like they're about to leave."

"Take your position," Adolph said.

Weinstock backed out of the parking space and stopped on the other side of the lot, where a hedge blocked the view of his car from the Suburban. Erhmann stepped out with the camera. "I'll call you tomorrow before we leave."

"Alright. Talk to you then."

As Erhmann returned to the residence, Weinstock wheeled the Impala out of the exit and slowed to a crawl for the van stopped in the middle of the street about a hundred feet away. One of the workmen stood on the back bumper securing the ladder with a strap. He jumped down, waved an apology to Weinstock and slid back in the vehicle. Weinstock nodded and followed the van toward the freeway. The white Suburban drifted away from the curb and trailed behind. Erhmann seated himself in the lobby and pressed the rewind button on the video camera.

Weinstock checked his watch. Close to five o'clock. He dialed his wife on his mobile phone and left a message. "Hi hon. You must be picking up the kids from soccer. We got tied up with an interview this afternoon. I'll be late for supper. Keep it warm and I'll be there as soon as I can. I love you guys."

He lit a cigarette and exhaled out the open window as he approached the bend in the road. Sunshine flashed off the chrome grill of the Suburban following behind. He switched on the radio and tuned to the traffic station. The orange signs came into view and the radio announcer recommended alternate routes due to a rash of accidents. Gridlock all the fucking way, he thought. Sucking on his cigarette, he rounded the blind corner and then slammed on his brakes, almost colliding with the rear of the van. Behind him, the Suburban's engine roared. His eyes darted to his rear-view mirror.

Before he could say, "What the fuck?" his head whip-sawed backward and the cigarette flew from his lips. Jamming down the brake pedal, he fought the steering wheel with braced arms as the car skidded toward the edge of the road. His front wheels jumped the embankment and the underbelly snagged.

Spewing gravel and rocks, the Suburban reversed gears and made another charge. Weinstock grappled to open his door as reflections off the grill blinded him. The Suburban slammed into his rear end and launched the Impala over the cliff.

Adolph pulled back from the rim and pressed the button on a remote detonator. The Suburban shuddered from the shockwave. Adolph spun his tires and followed the van down the hill.

⅄

The explosion rattled the front windows of the lobby as if something huge had collided with the building. Gonzalez came running from her office.

"What the hell was that?" Erhamnn said.

"It felt like an earthquake," she said. The chandelier wavered from side to side and they both ran for the door.

As soon as he stepped outside, Erhmann sniffed and it hit him.

"It was a fucking bomb." His words came out clipped and dry, their anger unmistakable. "Call 911." He grabbed a fire extinguisher and started toward the tower of black smoke.

⅄

Erhmann's heart pounded as he rounded the curve and saw the scattered orange signs. His lungs burned but he felt no pain in his chest. An agonized wail carried over the roar of fire. He scrambled to the edge and then backed away from heat that singed his eyebrows. Weinstock's blazing silhouette sat trapped behind the wheel.

Images from the darkest regions of his mind surfaced; open death pits where spirits screamed out for Weinstock's release. His knees buckled and he dug his fingers into the bark of a tree until death reached out its hand to Weinstock and silenced him. The rear half the car had been vaporized. Everything was gone.

Fire-crew jumped down from their truck and unravelled a length of hose. "What the hell happened?"

"A bomb," Erhmann said.

The commander barked out an order. "Get down there before this gets away on us. It's dry as hell around here." Six fire fighters pulled down their masks and skidded toward the burning vehicle.

"Treat it as a crime scene," Erhmann yelled.

His words were cut short by a policeman.

"It's okay, sir. They'll just douse the flames. A detective from homicide is on his way." He pointed at two officers stringing yellow ribbons across the road. "Won't anybody be going down there until we get this sorted out."

An unmarked car skidded up to the perimeter. A paunchy man wearing a sweat suit stepped out. "That's Detective Mitchell," said the policeman. "He'll take over from here."

Erhmann rubbed at the blisters on his forehead and followed the policeman over to the car.

When Mitchell had been brought up to speed, he motioned Erhmann into the back seat.

"Were there any witnesses? Any other traffic that you noticed?"

Erhmann gazed through the windshield at the dissipating column of smoke and answered with as much accuracy as his mind would summon.

"A cable TV crew left the parking lot a few minutes before. But I've lost track of time. They could have been gone when Weinstock reached this point."

"What company?"

Erhmann squeezed his eyes to recall. "I had other things on my mind and wasn't paying attention. I remember seeing two guys carrying a ladder and some cable. Advance Cable Company, I think. The director, Mrs. Gonzalez, might know."

"We've got people up there right now. Let's have a look where he went over." They approached the spot where the car had been pushed off the road. A team of fireman cut away the tangled frame and an ambulance crew unzipped a body bag.

"These skid marks look like he was standing on the brakes." Mitchell's eyes followed the ruts back until he pointed to another set that looked wider and deeper.

"Those were made by a heavier vehicle, four wheel drive. Looks like they had a collision." He pointed to chunks of white plastic in the ruts.

"What color was it?" He nodded down the slope.

"Dark blue. Chevrolet Impala," Erhmann said.

Mitchell called over to one of the investigators. "Pick up all this white molding," he said, pointing to the debris. "Could be a hit and run."

"I don't remember any white vehicle," Erhmann said. "Maybe it was coming up the hill."

"Doesn't look like it," Mitchell said. "Unless it made a U-turn. What can you tell me about the driver?" He glanced below, to where the paramedics were zipping up the body bag.

"Aaron Weinstock. He was a security agent attached to the Israeli consulate. He was carrying sensitive material."

"About what?"

"Nazi war crimes."

"Christ, you guys never let go, do you?" Mitchell's snicker was snuffed by the threat from Erhmann's eyes. "Sorry, meant no offense." He focused on his notes.

"If you're finished for now, I have to check with someone back at the residence." Erhmann handed the detective a card. "If you have any more questions, call the consulate. I'll be leaving the country in the morning but they'll know how to contact me." He ducked under the tape and trudged up the road. Friedrich and one of his guards stood outside with the crowd on the front parking lot.

"What's going on?" Friedrich asked. "They won't tell us anything."

"Weinstock's dead. His car blew up at the bottom of the ravine."

"I recognize the smell," Friedrich said. "From the war."

"You're right," Erhmann said. "Someone planted it."

"You think Bauer had something..."

"I have no doubt," Erhmann said. "If we don't pick up Sonnenberg right away, he'll disappear. I need to make some phone calls. Get your luggage and wait in the lobby. I'll meet you there in a few minutes."

⚔

Erhmann called the consulate for an escorted pick up and then hurried back down to the crash site. He slid down the bank and confirmed that the aluminum case and its contents were gone. Only a few shards of metal remained embedded in the surrounding trees. Detective Mitchell joined him.

"We're certain it was a bomb," he said. "We'll know more when we get the analysis done. The car was definitely shoved over the edge." He pointed to the wider tread marks being imprinted by an investigator. "Any idea who'd want to do this?"

"Aaron and I were interviewing Doctor Friedrich Mendelssohn. His son ɟ being held in an Israeli military prison. I'll be escorting him back to Israel tomorrow. That's all I can tell you."

"How does that relate to the Nazi matter?" Mitchell looked away as the flare in Erhmann's eyes locked on him again.

"It's complicated. Mendelssohn was identifying some forensic material that no longer exists." He squinted down at the carnage.

"Sounds like an FBI matter," Mitchell said.

"You know how to get hold of me."

✦

Friedrich opened the cedar chest containing Eva's ashes and the old photographs of their departure from Tel Aviv. Inside he also saw the vial with Bauer's extracted molar. It could be a useful comparison to whatever was in Sonnenberg's mouth. He tucked the chest among his clothes and buckled his suitcase. Unlatching the door, he asked one of the guards to bring his luggage and accompany him to the memorial garden in the courtyard. At Eva's gravestone, he ran his fingers over the polished granite and gazed at the stars overhead. "I promise you darling. I will bring him back."

"What the hell are you doing out here in the dark?" Erhmann said. "I thought you were in your room."

"I wanted to spend a moment here before we go. Israel meant the world to her. I'm bringing an urn of her ashes and a few other mementos to leave there."

As he followed Erhmann and the guard to the car, a warm sensation swept through him and he sensed Eva's strength. She would be there to support him on the long journey to come.

CHAPTER 33

The El Al jumbo jet touched down into Tel Aviv shortly after sundown. As Erhmann and Friedrich stepped onto the tarmac, they loosened their ties and shed their jackets to get relief from the heat radiating off the asphalt. Agents, who had already collected their luggage, escorted them to a car with its air conditioning on high. They were driven to the house where Asher Heral awaited them.

Heral's eyes were bloodshot and his clothes looked as if he'd slept in them for a week. His odor suggested that he hadn't had time for a shower either.

"I'd forgotten how hot it can get here," Friedrich said. He shook Heral's hand and lowered himself into a chair. "When will I see my son?"

"I've arranged a meeting tomorrow morning at ten. I thought you'd appreciate a chance to rest."

"That makes sense," Friedrich said. Though with the anxiety he felt over meeting Frankie, sleep wouldn't come easily.

"We'll give you some time together first. Then we'll have your son and a physician do the examinations. We'll keep you hidden behind an observation window."

Friedrich looked at Erhmann. "I thought you wanted me to do the examination."

"We thought it best to keep you out of view," Erhmann said. "We want to see how he reacts. We'll bring you in after those two fillings are removed. That will be the final determination."

"He's being held on suspicion of smuggling but there's a limit on how long we can detain him," Heral said. "There's a shipment of automobiles scheduled to arrive next week. As soon as the ship docks, the containers will be quarantined for inspection. But if they're clean, we'll have to let him go."

"Unless we make a positive identification," Erhmann said. "That proves he's Bauer."

"Yes. Let's hope we're on the right track." Heral turned toward Friedrich. "Your son is facing very serious charges."

"That's why I'm here," Friedrich said. "Any father would do the same." He'd always done what he thought was best for Frankie. He had no doubt that he'd made mistakes. But being here now was not one of them. He would do whatever was necessary to gain his son's freedom, regardless of the peril to himself.

"How did you apprehend him?" Erhmann said.

"We tracked him to Cairo and had him picked up by the Egyptian secret service. They owed us one. He's been taken to the same facility where Doctor Mendelssohn's son is being held."

"Bauer's evidence was destroyed by the bomb that killed Aaron but fortunately we have a video showing Doctor Mendelssohn examining the skull."

"The skull I examined was not Colonel Bauer's," Friedrich said. "If he's hiding under the guise of Herrmann Sonnenberg, I'll know."

"He's been under arrest for twelve hours now," Heral said. "We're subjecting him to continuous interrogation with little time for sleep. By tomorrow, he'll be less defensive. If you confirm his identity as Bauer, we won't have to release him. Then we can take our time inspecting the shipment and his auto compounds in Cairo and Munich. Of course, he's denied all of the allegations."

An attendant knocked on the door and entered with a tray of hot food.

"Okay, that's enough for now," Heral said. "When you're finished eating, he'll show you to your rooms. I'll pick you up tomorrow at nine. Shalom and good night, gentlemen."

ᛉ

Frankie roused from a fitful sleep with the blankets off the side of the bed.

"Time to get up." A guard flicked on the lights and raised the blind.

Frankie pulled on his clothes and followed the guard into a room where he received clean underwear, a set of medical scrubs and a pair of white sneakers. When he had showered, the guard handed him a towel and pointed to a sink, upon which lay a razor, toothbrush and comb.

Frankie groomed himself and dressed. Then he said, "Can I ask what's going on?"

The guard pointed to a tray of cold cuts, bread and coffee. "Help yourself. Your father's arrived. When you're finished here, I'll take you to meet him."

Frankie took a sip of the coffee and felt it burn all the way down. His stomach churned at the thought of confronting Friedrich.

For as long as he could remember, he'd felt the same way whenever he'd not measured up. But this had been his biggest fuck-up ever. As a Mendelssohn, so much more was expected of him.

With a cold sweat soaking the back of his scrubs, he finished a glass of water and looked up at the guard. "I can't eat. Let's go."

✦

The ankle cuffs made him hobble with short chopped steps while another chain connecting his feet to his wrists had him bent over like an old man. "You've got to be kidding with all this bullshit."

"Routine procedure," said the guard. "Same as everyone else. I'll take them off before you see him."

"Can't wait," Frankie mumbled.

His guts swooned as the elevator dropped to a basement where white fluorescent tubes buzzed from the ceiling.

The guard pulled keys from his belt and removed the cuffs. "He's in there."

Frankie entered the unmarked door and met Friedrich's sad wounded eyes. He felt his body shrink. As Friedrich gripped the arm of the chair to stand Frankie stepped forward to help him up.

"I'm okay," Friedrich said, waving him away. "You're the one who needs help."

The words cut like a slash. "You want me to get down on my knees and tell you how sorry I am? I know I fucked up...okay?"

"I didn't mean it that way."

"Yeah, right." When he sat, his whole body shook. Friedrich reached over to touch him but he jerked away. "Why are you here?"

"Because I'm all you've got right now. No matter what's happened, I'll do everything I can to get you out."

"You have no idea how bad this is."

"I do. But there's more you need to know."

"Spare me," Frankie said. "I'm already stressed out." He stood and paced the room. "I need a smoke."

"Sit the fuck down." Frankie had never heard Friedrich utter the f-word before... even during his worst indiscretions. He stopped and pulled up a chair. "Okay, I'm sorry. I'm listening."

Friedrich pulled out a handkerchief, cleared his nose and took a sip of water. Then he began to speak.

For the next ten or fifteen minutes, Frankie listened and barely took a breath. Friedrich's voice rose and fell like an echo and his gaze drifted off into space. He related the accident that led to the death of his friend Mueller. He spoke of moving to America under a new identity and of his romance with Katrina. His voice descended as he moved on to his rescue of Eva and of SS Colonel Heinz Bauer's ultimatum. "It was his way or the gas chamber for Eva and me." The mention of her name made his voice break.

He described what he had done to the teeth in the skull and spoke of the misgivings Eva and he felt when Bauer's identity was confirmed by experts investigating the multiple suicides. "We were the only two people who knew it could be a fake. But to divulge anything would have put our lives at risk... yours included."

"What happened to him?" Frankie said.

"That's the question. Nobody knows but as you're aware, it's impossible to commit the perfect crime."

Frankie's eyes hardened across the table.

"Sorry," Friedrich said. "Slip of the tongue."

Frankie rolled his eyes. "You're killing me, pops."

"Have you ever heard of Nazi hunters?"

"Of course."

"Gabor Erhmann has devoted his life to this."

"I'm not surprised," Frankie said. "He questioned me before you got here. Something about him put me on edge like he had a hidden agenda."

"He holds Bauer responsible for the murder of his family. He helped investigate the suicide. There were inconsistencies that made him suspicious but he couldn't prove anything. He interrogated me back in 1949 when he found records connecting me to Bauer. I lied about having any knowledge."

"Why?"

"Like I said. There would have been reprisals."

Frankie stood up again and paced, a cigarette locked between his fingers. I can't believe you never told me this."

"Only Eva and I knew. We hadn't seen or heard of him since the night we left Vienna. Nobody else ever needed to know. Not even you."

"Then why now?"

"Erhmann thinks he's on Bauer's trail."

"Seriously?"

"Yes. The Israelis have detained a man named Herrmann Sonnenberg. He's a German businessman. Erhmann thinks he could be Bauer hiding under a disguise."

"I remember that name from the clinic in Gaza. I was told it's a foundation run by a German businessman who supports orphanages. I also overheard some Muslim Brotherhood guys mention a German. You think we're talking about the same guy?"

"Possibly. They also think he could be involved with arms smuggling."

"Jesus, this is getting weird. A benevolent Nazi arms smuggler?"

"Under different circumstances, it would be the perfect disguise," Friedrich said. "In a few minutes, you and a physician will be introduced to Sonnenberg as military personnel doing routine examinations. There'll be a copy of Bauer's chart behind the chair. You'll recognize my writing. If he has a mouthful of gold fillings that correspond to what's in the chart, there's a possibility he may be Bauer. In that case, you'll numb him up and remove the two fillings in the upper right molars. If they're engraved underneath, we'll know it's him."

"What if he objects?"

"Bauer had a phobia of needles. If Sonnenberg resists an injection, it'll be a clue. Nevertheless the fillings will have to come out, even if we have to put him out with a general anesthetic."

"What if there isn't any similarity to the fillings in the chart?"

It was the question Friedrich had been dreading and one he hadn't allowed himself to consider. A dental match was his only ace in the hole, Frankie's only chance. But there could be no more lies. "We'll have to think of something else then," he said. "Right now he's our best bet."

"Or I'm toast? Is that what you're saying?"

"I'm cashing in the Bauer chip. It's dangerous but it's your only hope."

"Meaning?"

"Erhmann contacted me after you got yourself into this mess." Frankie's teeth ground together and Friedrich raised a hand in retreat.

"Sorry. Let me put it another way. After he told me what had happened to you, he offered me a reason to change my mind. I have an understanding with him that you could be released into my custody...if the evidence and my testimony lead to Bauer's conviction. This is where you come in. Bauer doesn't know who you are and there's no reason he would recognize you.

"Those two fillings are the key. I examined the skull just before we flew over here. The two on the upper right were unmarked, confirming it was the duplicate skull. It was destroyed later the same day in an explosion that also took the life of a Mossad agent. They set off a bomb with a remote device."

"You've got to be kidding," Frankie said. "This is unreal."

"Do not underestimate this man, Frankie. He's a ruthless killer. These Nazis will do anything to preserve their secrets."

A sharp knock sounded on the door and the lights in the room blinked off and on.

"They're ready for you now," Friedrich said. "We'll be observing every-thing through a one way mirror and there are microphones and cameras in the ceiling. If what you see corresponds to the chart, we'll remove those fill-ings right away. If he turns out to be Bauer, he'll be arrested and charged. He won't be going anywhere."

⚔

Frankie stepped off the elevator into a sunlit hallway where an arrow pointed to the clinic. A man about Frankie's age greeted him.

"Doctor Mendelssohn. I'm Avi Broskovitch, Army Medical Corps. I'll be doing the physical on this detainee. What do you know about him?"

"I've never seen him before. I was told to do a dental assessment."

They entered an examination room where Sonnenberg waited in a chair. Broskovitch closed the door behind them and Frankie glanced at the one-way mirror on the wall. Sonnenberg stared, stone-faced and grim. Frankie returned his glare with the best game face he could muster. Looking a mass-murderer in the eye spiked his adrenalin like a hit of cocaine.

"What's this all about? I've done nothing wrong." The words carried a thick German accent.

Frankie noticed the promising reflection of gold beneath the rim of his upper lip.

"Routine medical and dental assessment," Broskovitch said. "Take off your shirt and trousers and we'll get started."

Sonnenberg grunted and stood to undress. A long scar ran down the side of his left thigh, the skin distorted and pale. The entire leg looked shrunken compared to its counterpart. When he removed his shirt, the sheen of skin grafts covered his left torso and arm. A separate graft on his neck terminated just above the angle of his jaw. His left eye looked dead.

But when he stood on a scale for the physician to measure his height and weight, his body looked hard and lean.

Broskovitch wrapped a blood pressure tourniquet around Sonnenberg's arm and took a reading. "120 over 85. How old are you, sir?"

"Sixty-nine,"

"That's excellent," Broskovitich said. "Exercise much?"

"I walk about ten kilometers each day along with two hundred push-ups. It's been my routine for years."

"Wish I could say the same. Are you currently taking any medications?"

"Nothing."

Broskovitich ran his fingers along the scar on the left thigh. He eyes followed the track of the skin grafts until he met Sonnenberg's gaze.

As Frankie watched, he understood that with all the physical pain Sonnenberg had endured, frightening the man would not be easy.

"From the war," Sonnenberg said. "I'm lucky to have survived."

"Any other surgeries besides these? After the war, I mean."

"A few cosmetic procedures. I deal in luxury automobiles and I need to look my best. He ran his finger along his left eyelid and across the bridge of his nose."

"That's all we need," Broskovitch said. "You can get dressed, sir." He scribbled in his chart and looked over at Frankie. "He's all yours."

Frankie lifted the cover from a tray that held a mouth mirror, a sharp explorer, a gum probe and a pair of latex gloves. Sonnenberg lowered himself into the dental chair, a grin creasing the taut skin of his face.

"What's so funny?"

"This is a waste of time."

"So let's get it over with," Frankie said, while he focused the surgical lamp on Sonnenberg's mouth. "Open wide."

"I'll save you the trouble."

With a pop of released suction, Sonnenberg dislodged a complete upper denture and a lower partial denture with silver clasps. Sporting the wizened grin of a toothless old man, he chuckled and handed both to Frankie. The tip of his tongue flicked back and forth like a lizard's.

Frankie stared at him wide-eyed and set the two dentures on the tray.

"How long have you worn these?" His voice cracked and he glanced toward the one-way mirror.

"After the war, I got abscesses in the gums. They did some surgeries but they kept coming back. I finally got fed up and had most of them pulled out.

Except for these few on the bottom. They were joined together to make them last longer."

Frankie stretched Sonnenberg's cheeks aside to examine the interior of his mouth. The palate and toothless ridge where the upper teeth had once been embedded looked pink and healthy, a testament to the denture's snug fit. The six remaining lower front teeth were joined together with porcelain-metallic caps. Frankie had used the same technique to stabilize teeth where bone around the roots had been eroded by periodontal disease.

He pulled down Sonnenberg's lower lip and looked at the splinted caps. Tobacco stained tartar clung like black coral and the gums were angry red. Sonnenberg pressed his index finger against the teeth. Rivulets of blood and pus leached out.

"You need a deep scaling down there," Frankie said.

"They're coming out," Sonnenberg said. "I have an appointment next month."

Frankie noticed the gold filling in the right central incisor of the upper denture. He pointed to the tooth and his eyes queried Sonnenberg for an explanation.

"I had an excellent dentist in Munich during the war. He was an artist. His specialty was restoring teeth with gold, but he could do nothing about the abscesses. He had placed a gold filling like that into my natural front tooth. I remember how hard he worked to do a perfect job, carving the wax in my mouth, making several castings in gold before he was satisfied with the fit. I always felt it made me look youthful. Sadly he was killed in the bombing near the end."

Sonnenberg slipped the upper denture back into his mouth and smiled. "Makes me look distinguished, don't you think?" He laughed while he inserted the lower denture and clamped his teeth together. "The abscesses were poisoning my system. After suffering with toothaches and infections, I said, enough. With all my business travel, it was too inconvenient."

"Who made the dentures?" Frankie said.

"Oh, I forget his name. He was an older man from Berlin. He's probably dead by now. I requested that he remove the front filling from my own tooth and put it in the denture. I must admit that even as an old man, I'm still guilty of vanity." He grinned to show the tooth and winked. "The ladies find that little flash of gold very attractive."

Frankie scribbled down a final entry in the chart. Sonnenberg had obviously never been to California. The hottest ladies and the coolest dudes only wanted white, white or whiter. But Sonnenberg was on a roll and wouldn't shut up.

"My old dentist in Munich often spoke of his respected colleague from Vienna. I believe the name was Mueller. He published many articles on gold dentistry. Perhaps you've heard of him?"

"Never," Frankie said. His face flushed as he turned to Broskovitch who stood on the other side of the chair.

"I'm done," he said, handing the chart to Broskovitch.

Sonnenberg reached out and grabbed Frankie's arm.

"I'm sorry. I didn't get your name, Herr Doctor."

"This isn't a social call," Frankie said. The quiver of Sonnenberg's opaque eye sent a jolt up his spine.

"As you wish," Sonnenberg said. "But I would appreciate the common courtesy of rinsing my mouth. The taste of those gloves is disgusting."

Frankie grabbed two paper cups off the counter and filled one with water. "Rinse with one and spit into the other," he said.

When Sonnenberg finished, he wiped his mouth with an embroidered handkerchief and said to Frankie, "You should look up the articles written by Doctor Mueller. He was a world authority in those years. You'd find them interesting. You might even learn something." Then he turned to Broskovitch. "Are you both finished?"

"All done. The guard will take you back to your cell."

Pulling free of an unsolicited handshake, Frankie watched Sonnenberg turn on his heel and march out the door. The bastard knew more than he was letting on. He looked at the mirror.

Friedrich's voice sounded through the speaker.

"We'll be right there."

"He's in pretty good shape for his age," Broskovitch said. "Was something going on between you two, or was I just imagining things?"

"The guy's off his rocker," Frankie said, as the other three men tromped into the room.

Erhmann steamed as he slammed the door. "The sonovabitch was baiting you," he hissed. "He was mocking us."

"I couldn't believe my eyes when he popped those goddamn dentures out," Frankie said.

"I'm sure that's him," Erhmann said. "The bastard was pissing all over us. He knows he's off the hook. Why was I so naive to think that he wouldn't get rid of any incriminating evidence? Even the video is useless now. I should have dealt with him in Paris when I had the chance."

Friedrich went to the counter and held up the paper cup containing a bubbled mix of water, saliva and streaks of blood. To Broskovitch, he said, "Do you have a sterile container for this?"

As Broskovitch rummaged through the cupboards, Friedrich turned to Heral. "How much longer can you keep him here?"

"Another week at the most," Heral said.

Erhmann looked ready to explode. "Is that why you want that jar of gob? It's a complete joke. What the hell will you do with it?"

"If he's Bauer, he's done a hell of a job disguising himself," Friedrich said. "I would have never recognized him. He looks like any other wounded veteran to me. But I agree with you, Gabor, he seems to know something's going on. The way he looked at Frankie, it was as if he recognized him. And the mention of Mueller. That wasn't coincidental. It was reckless bravado. He knows the skull's been destroyed and he's confident that with most of his teeth missing, there's no way to do a comparative identification. We need to find another way."

He spoke to Heral. "I'd like to make a phone call back to the States. I was reading about some new DNA technologies. I'm not sure if they have an application here but I have colleagues back at USC who might know."

"It's hopeless," Erhmann said. "Let the sonovabitch go, Heral. We'll get rid of him."

"Don't even think about trying to hijack this, Gabor," Friedrich said. "We have an agreement. Frankie's life's on the line."

"That was then, this is now," Erhmann said. "Everything's changed."

"I told you my position before we started," Heral said, to Friedrich. "It looks like you may have hit a dead end here. We'll keep Sonnenberg locked up until we've had a chance to inspect his latest shipment of cars. If we come up empty, I have to set him free. This arrangement for your son will be null and void, I'm afraid."

Frankie felt himself turn the shade of the dying as he listened. This wasn't going to end well.

A guard carrying handcuffs and a chain opened the door and nodded in his direction. "Time to go."

Friedrich hugged Frankie and patted him on the shoulder. "Don't give up hope," he said. "I might be able to do more." His eyes met Heral's as Frankie left the room. "You said we have about seven days?"

"No more than that," Heral said.

"Just give me your word that you won't hand him over to Mister Erhmann before then. There may still be a way to bring Bauer to justice...and to secure Frankie's release. I just need a bit more time."

"One week and that's it," Erhmann said. "Then he's mine."

"I'll be the one who makes that decision," Heral said.

CHAPTER 34

H eral took Friedrich and Erhmann to an office one floor above the clinic. He pointed to the phone on the table. "It's a secure line, Doctor. Dial the number and they'll connect you."

"Thank you," Friedrich said. "If you have a moment sir, there's one more thing I must discuss before I make this call."

"Sure," he said, placing files into a briefcase. "But please be brief."

Any leverage Friedrich had with Heral was fleeting. The time to take advantage of his position was now. "There was a massacre of Palestinian civilians in late 1947, on the eve of the war. The Israeli military covered it up. My son's biological parents were killed. If the evidence I provide convicts Sonnenberg for war crimes, it could also benefit the State of Israel by putting a smuggling operation out of business. If so, I want your assistance in recovering the bodies and having them buried with the respect they deserve. I know you can't guarantee anything. I just want your word that you'll try."

"This is news to me," Heral said. He snapped his case closed. "Where did this occur?"

"On the main road between Jerusalem and the Jordanian border. They were being transported to a refugee camp. I know the approximate location. I saw the Israelis burying the bodies. It's branded in my mind."

"Why the hell are you bringing this up now?" Erhmann said. "The IDF won't touch this. They've got enough on their hands without digging up something that's going to fuel the fire."

Friedrich ignored the outburst and focused on Heral. "It could actually serve as an olive branch with the Palestinians, sir."

Heral glanced at his watch and grabbed the briefcase. "I've got another meeting. When I'm done, I'll talk to Komorov." He moved to the door. "Revelations about a cover-up will be inconvenient. But it's a small price to pay and the decent thing to do. It could save lives. We'll see what the general says."

"Thank you sir," Friedrich said. "My evidence may bring Bauer to justice, but there's no doubt that identifying those remains...will...bring my son back to me. Also, seeing that we're tight for time, is there a forensic pathologist here in Israel who I might speak to?"

"This is a goddamn travesty. He's reaching for straws." Erhmann flung the door open and stomped out.

"I know the head pathologist at the Abu Kabir Forensic Institute in Tel Aviv," Heral said. "I believe they've been doing some research with DNA. I'll call him."

Erhmann's muttering could be heard out in the hallway. "Don't let him bother you," Heral said, with a grin. "He's always been an incorrigible old bastard."

Friedrich shook Heral's hand. "Thank you, Asher. Abu Kabir will be a good place to start."

⋏

The white sign at the gate announced the Abu Kabir Institute the following afternoon. The two-story stucco building took its name from the Palestinian village that existed on the site before it was depopulated in 1948. Friedrich had an appointment to see the chief pathologist, Abraham Hiss. As he walked down the hallway past technicians at lab benches, the organic smell of tooth structure reminded him of happier days, when he'd had his students section extracted teeth to study their internal anatomy. He stopped at the open doorway of a small office next to the laboratory. A man wearing a white lab coat looked up from his desk and smiled.

"Doctor Mendelssohn. I've been expecting you." Hiss took off his glasses and shook Friedrich's hand. "How can I help you, sir? Asher didn't have time to fill me in with all the details."

"Thank you for seeing me. I know you're a busy man so I'll get right to the point. This concerns a criminal investigation. Mr. Heral thought you may be able to provide some advice. We're trying to identify a German businessman whom we have reason to suspect may be a war criminal, named Heinz Bauer. We have Bauer's dental records but during an oral examination the other day, we discovered that most of the businessman's teeth had been extracted. It made any comparison impossible. My son's future is on the line."

"Asher did say something about that. Very unfortunate. He mentioned that you had an idea?"

"After the examination, the man requested water to rinse his mouth. I kept what he spit out and I have it here in this container, a sample of his saliva."

"And what do you propose we do with that?"

Friedrich reached into his pocket and pulled out the vile containing the molar. He held it up for Hiss to see. "I extracted this lower first molar from Bauer's mouth back in 1943. I brought it along in case it could be used for comparative purposes."

"You're sure it's the same tooth?"

"I'm positive. It's never been out of my possession. I used it as a teaching aid for many years. I've been reading about the latest advances in DNA identification. I'm wondering if we could use it as a comparison to his saliva?"

Hiss raised the vial to the light coming through the window. "What's it stored in?" he said.

"Sterile water with drop of buffered Formalin."

"That's good. It's remarkable that you still have it after all these years."

"Yes. I never wanted to lose it so I kept it in my study at home. I have magnified slides of it that I used in all my lectures. I had my students carve replicas to its exact dimensions. Over the years they referred to it as, Mendelssohn's Masterpiece. I never imagined I'd need it for something like this."

"Well you've come to the right place," Hiss said. "We're one of the few research labs in the world that have been working on this. You can hear that tapping sound out in the lab. Those technicians are pulverizing teeth to analyze."

"That's what I smelled when I came in."

"Yes, it gets a little stinky."

"You think it's worth a try then?"

"Definitely."

"My problem is time," Friedrich said. "Heral can only hold this man for another week. If this evidence serves to identify and convict him, it may also put an end to a smuggling operation. If so, there's a chance that my son could be released."

"Asher saved my life during the '67 war," Hiss said. "This is the least I can do. We'll get started on it right away. As soon as I've got something, I'll call you. Three or four days at most."

⋏

Arriving at Camp Anatot Detention Centre, Friedrich passed through security and was shown to the room where Frankie was held. Inside, the air stank of tobacco. Frankie stood by the window, a cigarette smoldering in his fingers.

"Looks like you've been up all night," Friedrich said.

"I've haven't slept worth a damn since all this shit started." Frankie smothered the cigarette in the ashtray and coughed out the final drag.

"All that coffee and nicotine won't help."

"Enough with the lectures, Dad. What difference will it make anyway?"

"Alright, alright," Friedrich said, with a sigh. "Let's sit down. We have a lot to discuss."

Frankie grabbed a pot of coffee and poured them both a cup. He pulled another cigarette from his pack and looked at Friedrich with the eyes of a hopeless man. "Okay," he said. "Shoot."

"I'll start at the beginning," Friedrich said. "I brought an urn of Eva's ashes, which I want to bury here in Israel. In the same location where your parents, Adlyia and Jamal, were buried."

"What the hell are you talking about?"

Friedrich sipped from his cup and considered how much to divulge. The last thing he wanted to do was create false hopes. He needed to go easy, step by step.

"I told you before that Adlyia and Jamal were killed but I never gave you all the details. They lost their lives with about forty to fifty others and were buried in a mass grave. I saw it with my own eyes and I made a mental note of the location."

Frankie's gaze lifted from the floor and met Friedrich's.

"The whole thing was covered up and it's never been divulged. I have Mr. Harel's word that if we can identify Sonnenberg as Bauer and get him convicted they may reopen an investigation as to what happened. My hope is that the bodies will be exhumed and given a proper burial. Regardless of what happens, I want to lay Eva's ashes with them. She loved them as her own."

"That would mean a lot to me."

"For me as well," Friedrich said.

Frankie stood up to pace. "But coming up with a match on Sonnenberg when he has hardly any teeth left! That's pretty far-fetched, isn't it? What have you got to go on?"

"They're working with that saliva sample. Maybe something will come of it, who knows. They're also going to inspect the next shipment of cars coming in for Sonnenberg's company. If they find he's smuggling arms, he might come clean. We've got to keep our hopes up, Frankie."

"I can't see that happening, Dad. You might as well face it. I'm fucked."

"Is there any evidence that you have to share? Things that could assist the Israelis?"

"Like what?"

"Anything you might be able to tell them about the terrorists who put you up to this."

"I know the name of the main guy. Issa Mashurr. It was his younger brother, Hassan, who made the first contact with me."

"Have you told them this?"

"Yeah, I told Erhmann about him and how things went down during the raid. But what I need is a good lawyer to sort this out."

"That won't help," Friedrich said. "You're being held on terrorist charges. It's not like a regular court."

"There's one other thing," Frankie said. He switched on the radio and turned up the volume. He motioned for Friedrich to stand next to him and whispered.

"When I was brought back here by helicopter, there were six bodies in the hold. Five Palestinians and the one Israeli soldier. They blindfolded me during the trip. When they uncovered my eyes, I saw there were only four Palestinians next to the Israeli. They threw the other body overboard during the flight because it had been so badly mutilated by bullets. I knew him. He was a nice young guy who worked with me in the Rafah clinic. The gunner responsible for his death was the brother of the soldier who had been killed. He would have faced charges. He went wacko and unloaded his machine gun on the kid after he'd surrendered."

"You could use that as a bargaining chip," Friedrich said. "They could go easier on you if they're worried it might leak out."

"I've been warned already," Frankie said. "The sergeant in the helicopter told me that if I said anything about a missing body, he'd testify that I shot the Israeli soldier. If he did, they'd hang me for sure."

"I see."

"And that's not the only problem. The kid was Issa Mashurr's son. When he finds out, he'll be coming for revenge. He runs the Muslim Brotherhood in Gaza. They're nasty buggers who hate Jews. They've got all kinds of explosives to make bombs. And people who will detonate themselves for the cause."

They heard a loud wrap on the door. "Visiting time's over," said the guard.

"Try to rest," Friedrich said. "I'll see you tomorrow. Hopefully, I'll have more news."

⅄

Friedrich sat in the back seat of the taxi and gazed out at the parched land-scape. His ears perked with the sound of agitated Hebrew voices coming over the radio. He tapped the driver on the shoulder and raised his eyebrows.

"Another suicide bomb," said the man. "Not far from your hotel."

The driver took a detour to the back entrance as sirens echoed through the neighborhood. Friedrich stepped out into the heat and was met with the sickening smell of spent explosives. The memory of it filled him with angst and made him nauseous. He took the elevator to his room, where the light on his phone was blinking. Abraham Hiss had left a voice message.

"Call me when you get in."

He dialed the operator and got connected to Hiss's private phone at the Institute.

"Hello, Doctor Mendelssohn. You got my message."

"Yes. Are you having any luck?"

"We retrieved ample material from your tooth to work with. When we do this procedure we're careful not to introduce contamination. Our techni-cians isolate the samples in plastic sacks to protect them from airborne DNA carried in sneezes and such. We use a mortar and pestle method to grind the samples into powder for analysis.

"I also spent a whole day at the detention centre this week. Unbeknownst to Sonnenberg, I collected extra samples of his DNA from the dishes and cutlery he used at his meals. We also got samples from the cigarette butts in his ashtray.

"We compared the sequences in the tooth material to the saliva sample that you provided and with the samples that I obtained. We also compared the tooth material to DNA I took from two other men. One works here at the lab and the other is a different inmate at the prison. To rule out observer bias, all comparisons were done by scientists I know and respect. They had no idea what or whom they were matching. In each case they came up with the same answers. This could be your man."

"You mean we're in the clear?"

"Not yet. It's mandatory that we obtain external validation of our results," Hiss said. "I've already sent samples to the FBI laboratory in Washington and to another university research laboratory in Grenada, Spain. I have spoken to the directors and they will give this highest priority. If their results confirm ours, the evidence will be indisputable in any court of law."

"That's fantastic news," Friedrich said. It was the best he'd felt in months. Bauer would pay for his crimes and Frankie wouldn't spend the rest of his life in an Israeli dungeon. Eva would finally rest in peace. "You have no idea what this means to me."

"I do know what it means to lose a son," Hiss said. "My eldest was killed last year in Gaza. A couple of kids with a pipe bomb. Any way I can help end this madness, I'm pleased to do so."

Chapter 35

Shortly after calls to prayer echoed from a mosque across the canal in Port Faud, Erhmann and Harel stood next to an Egyptian police car in a compound surrounded by a chain link fence. They watched as three containers addressed to Sonnenberg Autocar in Cairo were set down next to each other. From the back seat of the police car, a dog whined.

When opened, each container held four vehicles in accordance with the shipping manifest; a mix of luxury sedans, half-ton trucks and sports cars.

"They'll bring them out with that forklift," Heral said, as a diesel engine coughed and sputtered in the chilled morning air. He looked over at the Egyptian officers. "We'll let them take the lead. Don't want to get pushy in their backyard."

Each vehicle was jam-packed with Sony television sets, electronic recording devices and cartons of denim jeans from Levi and Calvin Klein. Boxes printed with corporate logos held medical equipment and pharmaceuticals from Siemens and Bayer.

After all the vehicles had been cleared, the dog handler went to work and several officers sorted through the boxes. Heral pointed to four reinforced crates off to the side, sent from the Sonnenberg Foundation in Munich and addressed to the Cairo warehouse. They still hadn't been opened. The dog sniffed around each one and wagged its tail.

"Let's check those out," Harel said, to the officer in command. As soon as the wooden slats were pried apart, he read the stamped tags detailing the equipment specifications. "X-ray machines, by the looks of it."

The dog jumped up with his front paws and sniffed inside.

"Looks like he's found something else," Erhmann said.

The officers removed the plastic wrappings and set each machine on the ground. As they inspected each one, the dog jumped back up to the crate's rim and barked.

Harel pulled out a knife, reached inside and sank his blade into the base. He smiled at Erhmann. "False bottoms."

The policemen ripped away thick layers of cardboard to reveal curved ammunition magazines bundled together with duct-tape. In the other three crates they found two-way radios, gun-barrels, firing assemblies and stocks made from plywood. The smell of gun grease wafted through the air.

"That's the scent he picked up," Harel said. He lifted different parts from each crate and inside of three minutes, he'd assembled a fully operational assault rifle.

"Like riding a bike, eh?" Erhmann chuckled.

"I could do it in my sleep," Heral said. "It's an AK-47. They're so reliable that we tweaked a knock-off called the Galil. They don't jam or overheat. They'll still shoot even if they're covered in mud or full of sand. A kid can use the goddamned things. Unfortunately that's what happening."

"Ah, Kalash." The Egyptian officer used the Russian slang for the weapon, as he called his men over to look.

"Probably from Czechoslovakia," Heral said. "It looks like they're in decent shape. My guess is about twenty to a crate plus the ammo. Some radios too."

"What happens now?"

"We'll leave that up to Komorov," Heral said. "This will be tough to prove. Sonnenberg will deny that he knew anything about it. But at least he won't be going anywhere for a little longer."

"A little longer?" Erhmann said. "I thought this was all we needed."

"He's breaking Egyptian law and they'll want us to hand him over."

"That's ridiculous," Erhmann said. "With their screwed up system, he'll pay them off to let him go."

"Leave it with me," Heral said. "I know the officer in charge. We'll work something out. You should be pleased. This'll give Mendelssohn more time to work on the forensics."

"I'm not holding my breath on that bullshit," Erhmann said. "It's a goddamn pipedream. I'd just like to get my hands on that Nazi pig and cross him off my list."

⅄

Three weeks later at nine-thirty in the morning, General Komorov and two senior IDF officers sat down at the front of a briefing room and called the tribunal to order.

Heral had worked his magic again. With the discovery of the smuggled weapons and the possible DNA match from Hiss, he had met with Herrmann Sonnenberg and his team of lawyers, flown in from Munich. Heral listened to the lawyers' demands that their client be tried in a civilian court or be released and then he presented Sonnenberg with two options: face an IDF military tribunal on both smuggling and war criminal charges with access to legal counsel or be released into the custody of the Egyptian army.

As the lawyers huddled to consider their response, Heral made his final point. "To be clear before you decide, gentlemen," he said, "if you choose the latter, not only will your client face arms smuggling charges without right of due process, but he will also spend years rotting in an Egyptian hole before the matter is ever brought to trial."

Sonnenberg chose to stake his fate with the Israelis. Harel tied up the loose ends with the Egyptians by putting hard-to-obtain American tank parts and a dollop of baksheesh into the right hands.

⅄

Herrmann Sonnenberg listened while the charges of war crimes against Colonel Heinz Bauer were presented. His right eye burned like a hot coal as he watched the first witness take the stand.

The female prosecutor spoke in the confident manner of a sabra. "Please introduce yourself." She wore no makeup on her emotionless features and was dressed in a fitted military uniform, with oxfords polished to a glass finish.

"Doctor Friedrich Mendelssohn." Friedrich's voice rang strong as he looked directly at Sonnenberg.

In response to the prosecutor's questions, he revealed the arrangement he had made with Bauer under the threat of being turned over to the Gestapo. As he expounded on each question, he made no effort to avoid Sonnenberg's gaze.

The prosecutor, born into a prominent Israeli legal family, reviewed the chronology of events from November 1943 to the present, and then prefaced her final question with a statement.

"Dr. Mendelssohn, please correct me if I'm wrong. You're telling us that rather than stand up to this man, SS Colonel Heinz Bauer, and refuse his offer, you chose to help him avoid the consequences of his murderous actions against the Jewish people."

Caught off guard by the accusation, Friedrich held back and took deep breaths, hardly able to believe what he'd just heard. He canvassed the hard expressions in the court and searched for words that would explain the truth. Stilling his fingers on the edge of the stand, he cleared his throat and raised his voice so everyone in the room was certain to hear.

"Who are you to judge, lieutenant? You were born and raised in a country founded and defended by people like myself who managed to survive the holocaust by whatever means we could. You are a product of one of these immigrant families from Europe and yet you have the nerve to be so pompous and ignorant. What use could my wife and I have been to this country if our lives had been snuffed out in the gas chambers of Auschwitz? Would it have ensured that Colonel Heinz Bauer was captured and prosecuted? Not likely, without the testimony that I am now providing...because I'm alive. Your question is an insult and you should be ashamed."

Komorov rapped his gavel on the table. He addressed Friedrich's scarlet face and said, "My apology, Doctor. The lieutenant is out of order and will see me in my office when this is over." He turned his intensity on the young woman who shuffled the pages in front of her. "Does the prosecutor have any more questions or are we finished?"

"I'm sorry for my insensitive remark, General," she said. "We who were born here, have been taught to fight against those who would harm us rather than acquiesce. But I see the doctor's point and I offer my sincere apology. One more question."

"Get on with it," Komorov said.

"If the skull you refer to, Dr. Mendelssohn, has been destroyed and if the accused has had most of his natural teeth removed, how can you be certain that this man, Herrman Sonnenberg, is indeed the war criminal, Colonel Heinz Bauer?"

"With technology that did not exist until a year ago."

"And what is that?"

"DNA profiling."

"Please elaborate."

Friedrich looked to the front row and pointed to where Abraham Hiss at. "I'm not an expert in these matters. Doctor Hiss will be much better able to explain the technique."

"Thank you, Doctor. I have no further questions. We ask Doctor Abraham Hiss to come forward."

Friedrich felt the fire of Sonnenberg's glare as he stepped down.

With a fierce look of determination in his eyes, Abraham Hiss declared to tell the truth and introduced himself as chief pathologist of the Abu Kabir Forensic Institute.

"Would you please elaborate on Dr. Mendelssohn's remarks regarding DNA profiling, sir."

"Yes thank you. I believe that defense counsel has our written report in this matter and has had ample time to review it. We were able to obtain untainted DNA samples from a tooth that Dr. Mendelssohn extracted from Colonel Bauer in 1943. We matched DNA from the tooth with multiple salivary samples obtained from that man, Mr. Sonnenberg. Our results have been corroborated by two other independent research laboratories in America and Europe. They are conclusive."

Komorov turned to the Munich lawyers and said: "Any rebuttal?"

The lead lawyer, distinguished by his silver hair and ramrod posture, rose to speak.

"We take issue with the reliability of the tooth sample used in the analysis, sir. The specimen is almost 45 years old and has been stored in a Formalin solution for all that time. We have documentation to show that the DNA material could have become destabilized and is therefore not valid for comparison."

Komorov looked at Hiss. "You may answer."

"I have seen the documentation that the gentleman speaks of but we're certain the dentin in the body of the tooth remained uncompromised. The results are accurate."

"That is only his opinion," said the lawyer. "We have several experts who will testify otherwise."

Sonnenberg smirked as Friedrich raised his hand to speak. Komorov looked over and acknowledged him. "I must remind you Doctor, you're still under oath."

Friedrich cleared the mucous from his throat. "We do have another tooth sample but accessing it will be difficult. Nevertheless, we will obtain it if necessary," he said. "To do a second test."

"This was not brought to our attention," said the lawyer. "We were told that there was only one tooth sample."

Komorov nodded toward Friedrich again.

"After the visual examination of Mister Sonnenberg was completed, we requested a panoramic x-ray of his jaws and discovered an impacted lower third molar. This tooth has never been exposed to the environment. It would provide an unadulterated specimen to compare with the tooth material we used. Any difference between the DNA of the two teeth would confirm the destabilization of our sample and would invalidate it. But since our results show a direct match between the extracted tooth and Mister Sonnenberg's saliva, we're confident this is not the case. However, we're willing to take this extra step...if it's necessary."

"What did you mean by...difficult to access?" Komorov asked.

"If I may, sir. I brought this along in case the discussion arose." Friedrich stood and went to the prosecutor's table where an assistant brought forward his briefcase and a portable x-ray viewer. Friedrich clipped the film against the screen and switched on the light. He pointed to the lower jaw where the embedded molar lay prone.

"This tooth is described as being horizontally impacted. This shadow you see below is the canal containing the main nerve in the lower jaw. It runs to all the teeth on this side as well as to the chin and lower lip." Friedrich glanced at Sonnenberg, whose forehead had become moist and shiny.

He cleared his throat again so that everyone would hear the details, related as vividly as he could manage. "The removal is complicated by the tooth's proximity to this nerve and another one nearby which runs to the tongue. Exposing the molar will first require chiselling away a thick capsule of bone to create an access window. The tooth will then be cut and split with drills so it can be retrieved in pieces through this window. Even with the most precise surgical technique, the operation will cause damage to both nerves."

Komorov frowned. "And what is the result of that?"

"Permanent numbness of the tongue, chin and lip on that side. It's possible there will be disturbances with chewing and the sense of taste. Some people dribble."

The last comment sent Sonnenberg over the edge. The smirk gone, his face had blanched white. He gagged and spat vomit into his hands.

Yes, Friedrich thought. Good job.

"We'll adjourn for lunch," Komorov said, glancing at the floor. "There's a restroom outside in the hall." He addressed the guard at the back of the room. "Call someone to clean up this mess."

As Sonnenberg was led from the room, the silver-haired barrister spoke to Komorov. "We request a recess to consult with our client...before proceeding further."

λ

When the court reconvened, Asher Harel provided testimony on the weapons that police had discovered in the cargo containers. The defense countered that their client had no knowledge of the guns and ammunition. They argued that the cartons had been tampered with after the x-ray machines left the Sonnenberg offices in Munich.

Komorov scanned his notes.

"Explain the role of the Sonnenberg Foundation in this and how it relates to the auto business."

Sonnenberg nudged his lawyer and whispered in his ear. The lead barrister stood and addressed the tribunal. "Mister Sonnenberg requests that he provide this information in his own words. But as his representatives, we ask that all subsequent questions be addressed to us."

As Sonnenberg stood and walked to the front, Friedrich looked for any sign of the limp he remembered with Bauer. Sonnenberg used a cane and Friedrich could see he favored his left side but clearly the man remained strong and fit.

He raised his right hand and took an oath to tell the truth. Then he began.

"The last war in Europe was a tragedy for everyone but especially for the children left as orphans. Petra Dreschler was one of them. Her father died a hero in battle and her mother was killed by Allied bombs near the end of the war. After my discharge from the army, I returned to Munich and started an automobile business that became successful. All around me I witnessed the terrible suffering of children left alone. With funds donated from my company I formed the Sonnenberg Foundation which opened its first orphanage in Munich. When we expanded our business to the Middle East, I saw an even greater need and we changed our focus. We now operate three orphanages with schools and clinics in Gaza. We have several hundred children under our care. Petra Dreschler is our executive director."

He stepped down and returned to his seat while the court remained hushed. Komorov scribbled on a yellow pad before raising his eyes to the barrister. "Is there anything more?"

"We ask the court's indulgence to question Doctor Frank Mendelssohn."

"In what regard?" Komorov said.

"To corroborate the testimony given by Mister Sonnenberg. Doctor Mendelssohn served as a dentist at one of the orphanages in Gaza."

"He also was part of a terrorist operation that killed an Israeli soldier," Komorov said. "His testimony will carry no weight in this court."

"We only wish to add it to the record, sir."

"Very well," said Komorov. He spoke to the guard in the back of the room. "Bring him up."

Frankie was led to the front. He looked at Friedrich and then over at Erhmann who scowled from the back of the room.

The lead barrister began the exchange. "You heard the testimony given by Mister Sonnenberg in regards to the orphanages supported by his foundation. Do you have anything that you wish to add?"

"After arriving in Rafah, I volunteered at an orphanage operated by the Muslim Brotherhood."

"Who was your contact?" Komorov said.

"Issa Mashuur."

A bellowing voice from the back rocked the courtroom. "Mashuur is a terrorist with Jewish blood on his hands. He's as bad as the Nazis."

Komorov glared toward the rear of the room where Erhmann stood shaking his fist, pointing at Frankie. "That man's admitting that he associated with a terrorist! How can we believe anything he says?"

"Sit down," shouted Komorov.

Frankie looked over at Sonnenberg and his lawyers. "Everything that Mister Sonnenberg said about his company and the foundation he operates is news to me. I knew nothing about that relationship although I'd heard rumors about an anonymous German donor. Most of the equipment we used was manufactured by Siemens, a German company that sells medical and dental equipment. I assumed that was the source of the donations. What I do know is that the equipment and supplies we received allowed us to provide top-notch care to the children. They were all well fed and clothed. They seemed happy for the most part."

"Were you aware of any anti-Israeli manifestations on the part of the Brotherhood staff?"

"I never heard or saw anything like that although there is palpable animosity toward Jews throughout Gaza. It wasn't hard to see that, especially during the uprisings. I kept my head down and did the work I was trained to do."

"Why were you involved in the attack on our outpost?" Komorov said.

"Members of the Brotherhood suspected me of being a spy. They insisted I prove my loyalty by taking part."

"You could have refused and left," Komorov said.

"I was brought into Gaza through an illegal tunnel. Before we went underground I tried to turn back. Issa's brother, Hassan, made it clear that wasn't going to happen. I knew too much."

"You're saying that the Brotherhood didn't incite hatred in the children."

"From what I could see, a corporate donor from Europe provided resources and the Brotherhood was grateful for the assistance. They weren't about to risk their funding. The welfare of the children was their only priority.

"But what the kids see and hear on the street is another matter. The Brotherhood has a big influence on their lives as they grow older. It's a right-of-passage to be on the front lines throwing stones. Lots of peer group pressure to hate Jews and be a part of the Intifada."

Komorov looked at the Sonnenberg's lawyer. "Anything more?"

Sonnenberg nudged his lead barrister and said, "Yes, go ahead."

"After consultation, Mister Sonnenberg requests that we open a negotiation."

"For what?" Komorov said.

"His life."

Another roar came from the back of the room. Erhmann knocked over his chair and stood up waving his fist. "There can be no negotiation with a mass murderer. He knows we have him. Hang him like the dog he is."

"Sit down and shut up, Erhmann!" Komorov said. "Or I'll have you removed." He spoke to the lawyer.

"Deliver a signed proposal to my office tomorrow morning at nine and we'll consider it." He looked at the guards at the back of the room. "Return the accused and Doctor Mendelssohn to their cells."

CHAPTER 36

Three days later, Friedrich stood speechless as Frankie walked through the gate of the military prison. If he never lived another day, he would be satisfied with what he had accomplished. Eva would be proud. His knees wobbled under the strain as Frankie draped his arms around him.

"I'm so sorry about this, Dad." Frankie's body shook and his tears wet the side of Friedrich's neck. "I'm the luckiest man in the world to have you as my father."

"We've both been through a lot," Friedrich said. "It's over now."

"The worst part is that I involved you."

Friedrich stepped back so he could look into Frankie's eyes.

"You would have done the same for me. I haven't been an innocent bystander in this either. If I hadn't always been so negative, maybe you would have confided in me more."

Frankie wiped his sleeve across his eyes and his voice broke. "When nobody else gave a damn about me, I had the audacity to blame you for my problems. What a complete fucking asshole!" He stuck a cigarette between his lips and his hands trembled to light it.

"I don't know what I thought I would find over here," he said, exhaling a cloud of smoke. "Some kind of nirvana? What a joke. You don't realize what you've got until you piss it all away. I let you down big-time, Dad. It won't happen again. I promise."

"Sometimes a crisis like this is what we need, to see what's real and what's not," Friedrich said. He motioned toward Erhmann, who waited at a distance with a bitter expression, his arms crossed. "We better go talk to him. He's not happy with how they handled Bauer."

"All made up now?" Erhmann said, as they approached. "Pretty dramatic. Like a scene from a Hollywood movie."

"Cut it out, Gabor," Friedrich said. "What would a vengeful bastard like you know about love and family?"

Erhmann winced from the sting of his insult and Friedrich recognized the pain that flooded his eyes. He reached up to touch Erhmann's shoulder.

"I'm sorry, Gabor. That wasn't fair. We're both saying things we don't mean. Let's try and be civil."

Erhmann nodded and waited for him to continue.

"I know you're unhappy with the decision, but think about it for a minute. Bauer will spend the rest of his life in prison, alone and forgotten. He's allowed only limited visits from Dreschler and those will be monitored. He'll never see another sunrise or another sunset or have people around to praise him for what he did. For a psychopathic narcissist, it's the ultimate torture. The isolation will drive him mad."

"It's not close to what he deserves," Erhmann said. "I should have taken care of him back in Paris. It's unconscionable, letting a mass murderer live. Whose stupid fucking idea was this?"

Frankie moved closer to Erhmann. "Mine," he said. "Sonnenberg made the proposal but he wanted a hell of a lot more. Like maintaining control of his company with his niece, Dreschler, in complete charge of operations. And with only a portion of the profits going to the orphanages. When Komorov consulted with me in private, he was on the fence. I pushed for leniency in return for what we got. It's a great deal. It's transparent and everything goes to the kids."

"Yeah and the bastard gets to live in a private cell with television and all the rest. How sweet is that?"

"That was the trade-off. Incarceration in a maximum-security prison with a few comforts. In return, he agreed to turn his company and the foundation into a trust. A board appointed by your government will manage it. Nothing will go for weapons that will contribute to more death on both sides. Can't get much better than that.

"I spent six weeks working in those orphanages before they forced me to take part in that raid. I got to know a lot of the kids, especially the younger ones. They have dreams like children everywhere, but they need to feel that they have a chance at a better life. It's the board's responsibility to provide a framework that will make that happen. The Brotherhood won't be making any decisions."

"You're dreaming, Mendelssohn." Erhmann glared and stepped closer. "You're not from here. You don't know how these animals think. Revenge and death are all they know."

"That's all the more reason, Gabor," Friedrich said. "This could help break the cycle." He thrust his arms between Frankie and Erhmann who stood face-to-face, a Palestinian and a Jew ready to tear each other apart. What else was new? He pressed his hands against their chests until they dropped their fists and backed away. "That's enough, both of you."

"What about the gun smuggling?" Erhmann said. "They never got him on that. All Bauer wants to do is kill Jews. To finish what he couldn't complete."

"There was no way to legally connect him with that," Friedrich said. "Anybody could have tampered with the crates between the time they were picked up at Sonnenberg's warehouse and delivered to the shipping company the following day. The success is that the operation's been shut down. That's the bonus the army wanted."

"Bauer's not stupid. He'll find another way. He's got a network of fanatics like the ones who attacked us and killed Weinstock. He may even send someone after you or Frankie-boy here for exposing him."

"That's the risk I took from the start," Friedrich said.

"Bauer only made the deal when he had no other choice," Erhmann said. "He'll still have a say in how his business is run."

"He doesn't have a vote on the board and neither does Dreschler," Frankie said. "And what if it had gone the other way? Komorov's a courageous man.

He made an enlightened decision. The three officers were in that room for over thirty-six hours. It was a close vote. You're not the only one who wanted to see Bauer swing from a rope. If vengeance had prevailed, this deal would have never happened."

"Who's to say that those Arab kids won't be the ones trying to annihilate us ten or fifteen years from now?"

"Come on now, Gabor," Friedrich said. "You're being too pessimistic. Your thirst for revenge is killing you. You think that heart attack was a fluke? Spend your energy working with the foundation to make sure that it doesn't happen. You could play a big part in this."

Friedrich pointed toward the car. "I've booked rooms for us all in the King David Hotel. We'll go back there now, have a rest and get cleaned up. This evening we're joining Harel and Komorov for dinner."

As Erhmann walked off in front of them, Friedrich said to Frankie. "We'll speak to the General tonight about accessing the site where Jamal and Adlyia are buried. I've already spoken to Doctor Hiss. He said he would do everything he could to help us identify the remains."

✠

In the car, Frankie drew hard on another cigarette. Friedrich had managed his release but his many other problems would take years to sort out, with jail time still only a heartbeat away. He turned to his father. "When are they taking me back to the States?"

"Good news on that. I wanted to wait until you were out before I told you. The drug charges have been dropped, so the extradition order's been lifted."

"You've got to be kidding. How...?"

"The guy who bought the drugs...,"

"Lenny Goldstein."

"He'd been picked up the week before in an undercover operation involving the Russian mafia. He was associated with the real estate guy."

"Kazlov," Frankie said. "That figures."

"They were running cocaine and guns up to British Columbia and bringing back marijuana. The police already had Goldstein for dealing pills but they wanted his supplier. He set you up that night to save his own bacon. I called my old friend George Beesley for advice and he referred me to some hotshot lawyers. They're expensive, but good. The police didn't have a proper search warrant to look in your car, so the charges were dropped over technicalities like that. You might still have problems with your licence and the insurance matters but we'll deal with that when you're back. I think the IRS wants to talk to you too."

Frankie pulled out another cigarette and lit it. "What about the practice?"

"I hired another associate to take your place and she's fitting in well. The practice is generating a modest profit and every penny's going to pay off the bank loans and legal bills. It will take a few years, but once we're in the clear, the associates will have an opportunity to buy in. At your discretion of course, after you're back."

"You're a genius, Dad. How can I ever repay you for this?"

"Come back into my life, Frankie. That's all I ask."

CHAPTER 37

The next morning Frankie woke to a cacophony of horns and the smell of diesel exhaust. He yanked back the drapes to see pilgrims crowded against the pitted granite of the Wailing Wall. The light made his temples throb. He remembered having a great dinner with expensive wine. Then he made the mistake of going back to the bar for a nightcap. After that he had no recollection of when or how he got to his room. His mouth had the foul taste of cigars and cognac. He squinted at the shrill ring of the phone and stumbled to the bedside table to answer.

"Good morning," Friedrich said. "Sleep well?"

"Yeah," Frankie said, his voice so low it could have been coming from the back of a cave. "Just woke up."

"They're coming for us in an hour. I'll meet you in the lobby."

⅄

Frankie washed down two ibuprofen tablets and took the elevator to the lobby. Friedrich, Erhmann and Komorov stood in a group with three other men he didn't recognize.

"Welcome to the land of the living," Friedrich said. He chuckled as he recognized the sheepish grin that always crossed Frankie's face whenever he was out of bounds. "I don't blame you one bit," he said. "It was a night deserving of celebration. At my age, I just had to get to bed."

As Friedrich clapped him on the back, Frankie winced and coughed to clear the tar in his throat.

"I want you to meet these people from Abu Kabir," Friedrich said. "They'll be doing the investigation at the site."

⋏

Departing the city in a camouflaged truck, Frankie sweated between Friedrich and Komorov while Erhmann rode in the front. Hiss and his men followed behind in a second vehicle. The streets of East Jerusalem were choked with machinery and building cranes. Pristine stucco apartment dwellings stretched up terraced hillsides on either side of the road.

"My God," Friedrich said, surveying his old neighborhood. "This wasn't even part of Israel when Eva and I left. The amount of construction! I had no idea."

"Spoils of war. Right, General?" Erhmann grinned and glanced to the backseat.

"It's coming back to haunt us," Komorov said. "The orthodox factions push for this new development and the politicians sit back and let it happen. Many young men and women die for their stupidity."

For another hour they drove in silence, stopping and starting through the construction zone until the driver wheeled the vehicle onto a roadway of broken pavement that led east toward Jericho and the Jordanian border. Up ahead, Friedrich recognized the rugged mountains bordering a valley. Memories of what had happened there many years before left him lightheaded and nauseous. As the steep inclines of the canyon walls came into clearer view, he tapped the driver on the shoulder and motioned to pull over. He wrenched open the door and heaved up his breakfast. Then, he rinsed his mouth with bottled water and slid back inside. "Sorry about that," he said.

The trucks crawled into the most tortuous part of the road, where cliffs cast elongated shadows. Friedrich imagined how dark and frightening it must have been in the middle of the night, perfect for an ambush. As the driver manoeuvred out of the box canyon onto a straighter road with less severe slopes, sunlight appeared again. Friedrich grunted and pointed to a side-road where a sign read: *Authorized Vehicles Only*. They drove up a cindered grade, past a quarry where dump trucks were being loaded. Driving blind through dust they climbed higher to the top of a ridge, where the air cleared and the road ended. Below them stretched the Judean desert.

Frankie, Erhmann and Komorov got out while Friedrich swished his mouth again with what remained of the water. When he finished he joined the others who looked east toward the Jordan River.

Like a curtain being drawn back, the images of carnage flooded into Friedrich's mind with terrible clarity, as if the scene he'd witnessed years before had been hidden by the thinnest of veils. With tears smearing his vision, he looked down at boulders scattered alongside the road and remembered the oily plumes that rose from the destroyed transports. A breeze from below brushed his face and with it came the scent of turned earth. The whine of the front-end loader replayed in his mind like tinnitus. Komorov and Hiss huddled over a map.

"This is where I saw it happen," Friedrich said. "The army had blocked the highway, but I was familiar with some trails that led up this way." He addressed Frankie. "I was on Jamal's motorcycle."

He pointed to a rocky pinnacle off to his right where a cluster of white-washed apartments shimmered in the sun. "I used that outcrop of rock up there as a landmark. But I don't recall those buildings."

"It's a new orthodox settlement," Komorov said.

Near the desert floor was another larger settlement that was surrounded by a metal fence topped with barbed-wire. The entrance stood about two hundred yards off the highway.

"And that?" Friedrich asked.

"The place up top has a more religious bent," Komorov said. "Down there, it's all business, established about five years ago. They manufacture electronic equipment."

To his left, Friedrich recognized the domed summit he had used as a second landmark. He stretched out his arms between the two points and looked straight down to where a paved lane ran from the highway to the front gate of the lower compound. He shivered even as the sun burned through his cotton shirt.

"That's where they dug the pit," he said, pointing to the turn-off. "Right where that lane joins the highway. At the time, I did a quick triangulation between those two elevations. The grave is down there. Under those boulders. It might be partially covered by that lane."

"Are you sure?" Komorov said.

"I'll never forget that crag on the right or that smooth dome on the left."

"Let's go down and take a look," Komorov said.

A cloak of dust shrouded both vehicles as they lurched back down the hill. The general's demeanor had become more serious since they'd left the city and Friedrich wondered how much he already knew about the incident. He glanced sideways at Frankie's sallow face. The shirt Frankie had put on fresh that morning was stained with sweat. Friedrich tapped Erhmann on the shoulder for another bottle of water and handed it to Frankie.

"Are you okay with all this?" he asked.

Frankie swished his mouth and swallowed. He looked at Friedrich with hollow eyes and took a deep breath.

"What will we find down there?"

"We'll leave that up to Hiss," Friedrich said. "I'm sure they'll do some preliminary probing first."

Komorov turned toward them as he overheard their conversation. "I know the man in charge at the plant. We'll speak to him first, but I'm sure we'll need authorization from IDF headquarters before we do anything."

They drove to the entrance gate where Komorov showed his identification and spoke to the two guards. Both wore denim coveralls and carried AK-47 knockoffs slung over their shoulders. Through the gate, they followed a road until they came to the front of the industrial building they had seen from above. Vared Yericho Administration Centre.

"I'll be a few minutes," Komorov said.

Frankie, Erhmann and Friedrich walked to the edge of the parking lot and watched field workers tending gardens and orchards. Several men hovered over beehives. Farther off, children chased each other around a playground in stark contrast to the scrub desert and bedraggled Arab villages they had passed on the highway.

"This sure doesn't look like Gaza," Frankie said. "It's a different world." He turned to Erhmann. "What kind of electronics business do they run here?"

"All for the military." He looked at the administration building. "There's even a helicopter pad on the roof."

They turned at a sound from behind.

Komorov and another man shared a laugh like old friends as they trotted down the front steps. The man's leathered features were a testament to the hot winds already kicking up pirouettes of sand. An unruly beard brushed the bib of his coveralls.

"Boris Pekarsky, chief administrator," Komorov said.

"I was telling Alexi that we've only been here since 1987," Pekarsky said. "This incident that concerns you happened when?"

"The night of October 22, 1947," Friedrich said.

"So what exactly happened...forty years ago?"

"A convoy was transporting emergency supplies to a kibbutz along the border during the early fighting of the war. In the middle of the convoy one transport truck carried about fifty Palestinians...men, women and children. They'd been forced from their homes in an East Jerusalem neighborhood by Irgun militia. I think they were being taken to a refugee camp inside Jordan, in retaliation for an attack on an Israeli platoon the night before."

"They would have been taking them to Agabat Jaber or Ein Sultan. Two larger camps on the other side of Jericho." Pekarsky pointed east and said, "Thatta way."

"Sounds like you're from the States," Friedrich said.

"Haven't been back for years," Pekarsky said. "I came here about the same time as my old Ruskie friend, Alexi."

"Boris and I served in the army together," Komorov said. "We go a long way back."

"You were saying?" Pekarsky turned his attention back to Friedrich.

"They were ambushed. The truck carrying the Palestinians got hit. When I saw it the next morning it was a smoldering piece of junk. The army had closed the road but I was able to sneak through on some of those back trails. From that ridge up there I saw them filling a pit with bodies." He looked at Frankie. "Two of them were my adopted son's parents."

"I've never heard of this," Pekarsky said.

"The Israelis didn't want anyone to know about the civilian deaths, especially the British or the Americans. This was just before the declaration. It was a massacre. None of the people from that neighborhood were ever seen or heard from again."

"Are you sure you're in the right place?"

"As sure as I can be," Friedrich said. "We have professionals here from the Abu Kabir Forensic Institute. They would like to carry out a preliminary investigation where I believe the bodies may be buried. Your cooperation would be appreciated."

"We're having a lot of trouble right now with the locals," Pekarsky said. "Not as bad as Gaza but the same idea. It's hard to understand. The Arabs under our control are better off than they are in any of the surrounding countries. Doesn't make any goddamn sense. I'd hate to start something and make things worse. It could bring back old memories. Like stirring up a hornet's nest."

The way the man pronounced hornet without the *r*, hit Friedrich. "You're not from Brooklyn, are you sir? The accent, I mean."

"Yes sir," Pekarsky said. "Been a Dodger fan forever." He laughed. "It's in my blood."

Friedrich looked closer at Pekarsky, but his memory of the young officer's face on that awful night escaped him. It had occurred so quickly, so long ago. It couldn't be.

Abraham Hiss stepped forward and introduced himself. "We'll be very discreet, sir. A small excavation is all we need to confirm the location. If we come upon any human remains, we'll have to contact the Palestinian authorities as well. If this is indeed the site of a mass grave, we'll try to identify the bodies and have them returned to the surviving families. It's the only humane thing to do."

"I'll have to speak with the council," Pekarsky said. "Things are difficult around here right now. We're surrounded by fanatics."

The answer didn't take long. Friedrich, Frankie and Erhmann had returned to the hotel and were relaxing in the shaded garden next to the pool. A uniformed attendant approached and handed Erhmann a piece of paper.

"It's Komorov," he said. He pried himself up and followed the attendant to a hotel phone near the bar. As he listened and then spoke, his body language did not bode well. He hung up the receiver, barked an order to the bartender and walked back to them.

"It's not going to happen," he said, to Frankie. "Welcome to the Israeli-Palestinian conundrum."

"Why the hell not?" Frankie blurted. "How can they stop us? It's our right." After what he had put Friedrich through and the successful prosecution of Bauer, he wasn't about to follow arbitrary rules about what he could and couldn't do. "If it wasn't for us you wouldn't have a goddamn country."

"Your American naivety amazes me," Erhmann said. "Hand over some money, walk in and start giving orders. Expect everyone to jump and do it your way. That area is part of the West Bank. It's been under our occupation since we won the '67 war. My guess is that you don't even know what that means."

Frankie glared. "I know all about the six day war."

"Well you should know this too, Einstein. There's not a damned thing you can do in that zone if it's not sanctioned by the army or the government. If there were Jewish corpses down there, you might have had a chance. But with all this Intifada bullshit, we're not doing any favors for fucking Arabs."

"Careful what you say, Gabor," Friedrich said, tapping his hand on the table. "This is Frankie's family we're talking about here."

"If Frankie hadn't talked the tribunal into giving a more lenient sentence to the butcher who murdered my family, I might be more empathetic."

"For Christ's sake, Erhmann. Let it go." Frankie's outburst raised eyes around the pool. He leaned toward Erhmann and lowered his voice. "You Israelis are the ones who have no idea what's happening. You're sitting on a time bomb. The Palestinians are fed up with being treated like third class citizens."

"They aren't doing too badly," Erhmann said. "Most of them wouldn't be able to put food on the table if it wasn't for our economy. You saw all that construction the other day."

"Yeah, you're right. Building houses for Jewish families on Palestinian land. I wouldn't have gone broke if we'd had a business model like that back in Santa Barbara. Free land with an unlimited supply of cheap labor. Sweet deal, I'd say." He thought of all the men and women who'd served his drinks and cleaned his room since he'd been in the hotel. "Reminds me of how we treat the Mexicans, back home."

"They had a choice back in '48 and they never took it. They got greedy and wanted it all. In '67 they tried to steal it back again. You can't turn your back on them or they'll slit your throat. It's the rule of the jungle...right out here in the desert."

Friedrich dragged his chair closer and spoke, his voice weak but his tone firm.

"Are you sure there's nothing more you can do, Gabor? I did help you find Bauer and put him away."

"It doesn't make any difference what I think. This order came straight from military headquarters. It's a no go, period."

"I must speak to General Komorov once more," Friedrich said. "He's got a sensible head on his shoulders. Surely there's another way around this."

"That's not going to happen either," Erhmann said. "His hands are tied by the politicians." He looked back at Frankie. "But you're right about one thing, Franko. The shit is starting to overflow and we're going to have to flush the toilet again."

Chapter 38

The waiter set down two beers, two double shots of single malt and a tall orange juice and soda for Friedrich. The music from the speakers became fainter and then stopped. A moment of static preceded an introduction on Voice of Israel Radio announcing that Prime Minister, Yitzhak Rabin, was about to address the nation.

In a somber tone, Rabin reiterated how the patience of Israeli citizens had been stretched to the breaking point in the face of Palestinian intransigence and deceit. He spoke of a cowardly attack where a fifteen-year-old girl had been stabbed in the neck while on her way to school. A subsequent riot had left a seventeen-year-old Palestinian boy shot to death by an Israeli soldier. Unrest had now spread to the Balata and Kalandia refugee camps in the West Bank. Rabin expressed his government's sympathy to the families of the brave Israeli troops who had been killed and injured.

His voice then rose with a flourish as he declared that he had the support of all parties in the Knesset in putting a stop to the so-called Intifada. The army had been given orders to take up positions in Gaza and the West Bank. Terrorists would be brought to justice so that Israeli citizens would not feel threatened in their own country.

Frankie coughed up a mouthful of beer that backed into his sinuses. After what he'd seen in Rafah, this meant nothing but more bloodshed ahead. He thought of the dead Israeli soldier and his psychotic brother at the outpost.

The sight of a gagging Palestinian teenager with an airway stuck through his trachea and the sickening image of Asaf's riddled body raced through his mind. He threw back half his whiskey and followed it with a swig of beer. He got it. The place was a revolving death zone. Someone needed to step up with a different solution.

"Tribe against tribe," Erhmann said. "It's a land feud that'll never end. We should just level those camps. They breed like rabbits. There'll be no end to them."

"Not unless you give them a fair share of the pie," Frankie said.

"It'll never happen. They're not like us."

"Can you not hear what you're saying, Gabor?" Friedrich said. "It's the same tune the Nazis sang back in '33." In the back of his mind, he remembered a similar comment he had made when Eva demanded that they adopt Fadi. Would it ever be possible to put these ancient feelings to rest?

Erhmann cupped his ear to hear the rest of the broadcast.

Rabin called on reservists to set down their tools, leave their families and report to their units to protect Jewish soil. The only sounds around the pool were the chirps of starlings among the branches. As Rabin signed off, a disk jockey's lame joke about shaking up the souk segued into a guitar riff that jarred the speakers back to life with the opening bars of "Rock the Casbah".

Behind his aviator sunglasses, Frankie fixed his gaze on two blonds in bikinis who bounced to the beat. "It's the Clash," he said. "I love these guys." He drummed his fingers on the tabletop, finished his scotch and chased it back with another mouthful of cleansing lager. Another of the band's hits that he'd often played at USC fundraisers with his alumni band came to mind. "Should I Stay or Should I Go?"

⚔

Friedrich's tremors had become more pronounced since his arrival eight weeks before. His fingers, arms and even his face were in a state of perpetual motion. Erhmann had suggested a clinic which prescribed a new medication but Frankie didn't see any change. Bauer's trial and the tedious negotiations that followed had left their mark.

When Frankie checked on him, he had fallen asleep. The television, on low volume, displayed young reservists saying goodbye to their families, followed by images of an Arab mob screaming, "Itbach al-yahud"--- "Murder the Jews". The next item made him cringe as he looked at the smoldering mini-van where eight Israeli soldiers had been incinerated by a roadside bomb. He switched off the set, closed the bedroom door and dialed Erhmann's number. He held the receiver to his ear and waited for the thick Hungarian accent.

"What is it?" Erhmann was gruff.

"Something the matter?"

"I've got a tooth that's giving me trouble. It's the one that holds my lower denture in place. I'm seeing the dentist tomorrow."

"Sorry about that. I won't keep you then. I'm taking Dad back home. He's not doing well and there's nothing more for him here."

"When are you going?"

"Whenever I can get a flight. Once he's settled in, I'm thinking about coming back."

"What the hell for?"

"I want to make sure this new arrangement with the foundation gets on the right track. I'm going to contact Issa Mashuur. He pretty much runs things in Gaza. We'll need him on-side if it's to work."

"Now I know you're fucking crazy." Erhmann's bellow made Frankie pull the receiver from his ear. "Mashuur is a murderer. He'll do all he can to turn those orphanages into incubators of hate. He can't have anything to do with them. If Komorov heard about this he'd send you back to prison. Mashuur's responsible for most of these suicide attacks. He's on our most-wanted list and there's a price on his head. We don't need you here, Mendelssohn. Get out of our country and don't come back. You caused enough goddamned trouble."

Frankie hung up the phone and rummaged through his wallet for a crumpled slip of paper with a phone number. He dialed and waited until Issa's voice came on the other end of the line.

"Hello Issa. Frankie Mendelssohn."

"What do you want? I thought you were in prison."

"They released me after my father and I gave testimony that led to the conviction of a Nazi war criminal, Heinz Bauer. He went under the alias Herrmann Sonnenberg. It's his foundation that supports your orphanages in Gaza."

The buzz on the phone line was punctuated by the tortured contractions of emphysema. Frankie listened and waited.

"You being the only survivor of the raid convinced many that you are a spy," Issa said. "Being released on a pretense like this will only confirm it. It will be difficult for people to think otherwise. I have some doubts myself."

"I understand," Frankie said. "It's untrue but that's not why I called. I want to talk to you about, Asaf."

"Don't mention his name. He was a coward. He ran and they shot him. We found his body. They dropped him like a bag of shit from a helicopter."

"I knew that's what you'd think but it's not what happened. He saved my life. He stood up in front of the Israeli gunner who was about to kill me. He could have easily slipped away but instead he drew the gunner's attention. The soldier shot him and not me. Asaf was a brave young man."

Frankie waited for his words to register.

After a moment of silence, Issa's voice came back on the line. "Thank you for telling me this. It brings some peace to my heart but it's still not enough. You're on a death list and I cannot help you."

"I discovered the mass grave where my Arabic parents are buried," Frankie said. "It's close to an Israeli settlement called Vared Yericho. We're trying to get authorization to have the bodies exhumed and returned to their families."

"I know where it is. There used to be an Arab village there where I lost many friends. The Irgun destroyed it during the '48 war. We won't allow the bodies to be disturbed. It'll turn into another Israeli propaganda trick they'll use against us."

"It doesn't have to be hijacked like that," Frankie said. "It could be used to start a dialogue."

"You're suffering from delusions, Mendelssohn. When a thief steals part of your home there's only one thing to do. Cut off his hand."

Explosions and shouting sounded in the background. "There's something happening outside," Issa said, his voice urgent. "I must go."

The line went dead. He'd been a fool to ever think that he had a role to play in this land, where lies and discrimination were the only rule of law. It was time to go. He turned on the television where live images of another skirmish flickered across the screen. Friedrich opened his bedroom door and came into the salon. He sat down on the sofa beside Frankie and watched the latest news bulletin from Gaza.

"More trouble," Frankie said. "They're really going at each other."

"When I arrived here two months ago, I hoped that things might have changed since we left," Friedrich said. He nodded toward the image of a fireball that consumed the screen. "But it's worse than ever."

Frankie pulled on a cigarette and turned up the volume, filling the room with cracks of gunfire as Israeli troops fired rubber bullets into a crowd. Palestinian boys flung rocks and advanced through clouds of teargas.

"I'm afraid to think where this is going," Friedrich said. "It's beyond anyone's control."

Frankie crushed the butt into an ashtray and flicked off the set. "What will happen when we get home?"

"I'm relieved you've decided to come back with me. I sensed that you were thinking of staying but it's just not worth it. With me it's pretty simple. I miss Miriam and my other friends at the lodge. And I need to get back into my exercise routine. I'm getting weaker."

Frankie looked out the window on the old city. "Not much more for either of us here, is there?"

"We've done all we can," Friedrich said. "What will you do about work?"

"I'm not sure. I know that making beautiful people more beautiful doesn't do it for me anymore. I'm thinking about setting up something like the Sonnenberg Foundation. There're lots of kids in the LA area who could benefit from that."

"That's a good idea but getting your licence reinstated may take awhile. In the meantime I can help you raise money. I still have lots of contacts. After you're relicensed, you could operate your foundation and even practice part-time. Pick and choose the dentistry you want to do."

"Right," Frankie said. "Take it step-by-step."

He cradled Friedrich in his arms and pulled him close. For all they'd been through, for all their differences and harsh words, there was no one like Dad. His love wasn't the kind that came tied with ribbons and bows but it was always there, clear-eyed, on point and with no bullshit. His father was the best friend he'd ever had.

He let Friedrich go and pointed to more images of smoke and flame on the screen.

"Those kids don't stand a chance. They're throwing stones because they can't see a future for themselves."

Next up, was news that seven hundred thousand Palestinians with Israeli citizenship, were demonstrating in sympathy with their brethren in the West Bank and Gaza. They called it, Peace Day, a gross misnomer, as the camera continued to show crowds in the streets waving tricolor flags and chanting "In baladna, yahud kalabna"---"This is our country and the Jews are our dogs."

The phone rang. "It must be Erhmann." Frankie picked up the receiver and nearly choked when he heard the voice on the other end. "Issa?"

"I'm coming to your room."

⅄

When the knock came, Frankie looked through the peep hole and saw a clean shaven man wearing a tailored suit and tie. "Who is it?"

"It's me, Issa."

Frankie recognized the rasp and unlatched the door. The heavy-set Palestinian standing in front of him represented everything that Jews loathed. In so many ways, the two ethnic groups were the same. Both wanted nothing more than respect and hope for a secure future. The chasm separating them would not be an easy one to cross.

"What the hell are you doing here?" Frankie spoke in a whisper. He pulled Issa into the room and looked both ways down the hallway before he latched the door. "I didn't recognize you." The Italian cut suit reminded him of the stuff Lenny Goldstein used to sell.

"We came across last night, to support the demonstrations on the West Bank. I can't stay long, but I wanted to speak with you face-to-face."

Friedrich looked up from the sofa.

"Issa, this is my father, Friedrich." The two men shook hands and Issa sat.

"Knowing that Asaf died a martyr rather than a coward restores my family's honor. I know a man who took part in the battle that killed your parents. He lives with his daughter in the Rafah camp. After I spoke to you, I called him. He told me what he remembered of that night."

Frankie leaned in closer while Friedrich's eyes stayed fixed in time.

"When the truck exploded, the people tried to save themselves by jumping out. The Israelis assumed they were joining the battle against them. Our men thought they were Israeli reinforcements. Both sides started shooting. They were all killed in the crossfire."

"So they just dumped them in a ditch?" Frankie said.

"The Israelis were worried about the political ramifications. The vote on statehood was coming up at the UN. A civilian massacre would have put it in jeopardy."

"We're going to see that those victims are recovered," Friedrich said.

"The Israelis will do nothing to help us," Issa said. "And until we throw off their yoke, we'll let the bodies rest. We'll do it when...we are ready. This will not be their final resting place."

Frankie looked at Issa. "I appreciate you coming to tell me this, but you've put yourself in danger. There're agents all over this place."

"That's why the fancy disguise. We know that many of us will die, but we will not rest until we take back our land and establish an Islamic state. You cannot come back to Gaza. Leave and take your father with you. Before it's too late." He shook hands with both of them and moved into the hallway. "Until we meet again...when this is over. God willing."

✦

Issa stepped into the elevator and pressed the button for the lobby. Just before the doors slid closed, a hand reached in and pried them apart. A tall man with brooding eyes stepped in and looked straight ahead while Issa pressed the button again. Gabor Erhmann's fingers brushed against the Glock in his jacket pocket. It was all he could do to restrain himself from emptying the chamber into the person beside him. In tight silence the two men watched the floor indicator descend until the bell rang and the doors parted to the lobby. Erhmann exited first and walked outside. A moment later Issa came through the front doors and Erhmann nodded to a workman standing next to a utility truck. Issa stepped over to a waiting car and as it melded into the traffic, the workman climbed into his truck with a crew of agents. Erhmann watched them pull away and follow.

Chapter 39

At the bar where he regularly spent his lonely evenings, thirty-five-year old Tobias Abraham, a high security prison guard, couldn't believe his luck. Beatrix, a long-legged brunette who shared his taste for Schnapps, had been listening to his tales of woe for several hours. No one else had cared that his ex-wife's lawyers were hounding him for alimony. But Beatrix, she was an exception.

"I'm sorry to hear about this, my friend," she said. "If they were to inform your employer you could lose your job. Then there would be no money. That would be the worst thing, especially for Sarah and Jacob. Your ex-wife is a mean spiteful woman but your children certainly don't deserve this. Let me help."

"What the hell can you do?"

"I can see it in your eyes that you're a good, strong man, Tobias. This is not all your fault. You're going through a rough time right now because of the break-up of your family. I'm not a rich woman, but I can lend you some money to help pay your obligations. So your job isn't put in jeopardy. I'm willing to give you a hand. All I ask is that you do me one little favor."

"What's that?"

"Do you know an inmate named Herrmann Sonnenberg?"

"He's in solitary under twenty-four-hour surveillance. Some shifts, I watch him on a monitor and take him his food."

Beatrix lifted her Schnapps and took a sip. "He's my former boss. A very generous man. But now he's paying for serious mistakes he made in his past. I'm sure you're aware."

"He's a goddamned war criminal," Tobias said. "They should have hung him."

"I only knew him after the war. It's a tragedy."

"Why do you mention him?"

"He was very good to my family in Munich after we lost everything. When my father was killed, my mother had four of us children to support. I'm the oldest. Herrmann hired my mother as his first employee. He paid for all our education and then provided us with jobs. I was shocked to learn that he'd been found guilty of war crimes."

"What is your...little favor?"

"He loved his Schnapps, just like we do." She looked at the bartender and ordered another round. "If I lend you the money would you deliver him a bottle, so that at least he can have a little comfort in the evenings?"

⚔

Petra Dreschler closed her journal and raised her eyes to the four distinguished looking men sitting with her in the boardroom of a Munich business tower.

"Thank you for coming today, gentlemen. I want to conclude by bringing you up to date on the progress of our operations since the imprisonment of Colonel Bauer. As you can imagine, this whole nasty business has been very stressful for him. Not only for his future, but especially his concern about those loyal members of Odessa, who are dependent on the foundation's secret grants that provide their housing, food and nursing care. Many of these men are dear friends and former comrades of Onkle.

"Due to the sensitive nature of these monetary transfers, all records have been destroyed and nothing will ever be divulged. We are working through other channels to secure alternative sources of funding for these men. The Israeli government takes control of the foundation's finances at the end of the month. The Colonel is vehement that this outrageous theft should not go unanswered and that the perpetrators should be made to pay.

"One of our undercover agents, Beatrix Metzner, contacted me today. She has made arrangements with the prison guard that we chose. Tonight, he will receive his money and the bottle of Schnapps at his home. Tomorrow, he'll deliver it at the beginning of his evening shift.

"Beatrix has also been in close communication with our Hamas brethren on the ground. She's been assured that they're monitoring the other targets and will carry out Onkle's orders when the opportunities present themselves.

"I want to thank you for your assistance in this undertaking. Onkle extends his appreciation and his warmest regards to each of you."

"Will you be speaking to him after the operations are concluded?"

"No."

"As it should be," said the man sitting closest to her.

"Yes and we will never meet here again," Dreshler said. "All correspondence between us will be burned. Nevertheless, our message will be clear and the mission of Odessa will continue under new code name, Resurrection. You will be contacted when our military campaign of eradication is set to resume." She gathered her belongings and stood to leave the room.

The four men rose as one, clicked their heels and raised their right arms. "Heil Hitler."

⅄

Gabor Erhmann brewed another double espresso to give himself an extra jolt as the throbbing in his tooth had kept him awake all night. The clock showed he had an hour before his appointment. He stirred in two extra lumps of sugar and sat down with a newspaper. The headline caught his eye. **Brotherhood Leader, Issa Mashuur, Killed.**

When he finished reading through the article, he called Asher Heral. "Well done, my friend. That didn't take long."

"I didn't expect it to happen so soon, either," Heral said. "We followed him from the hotel to a house on the West Bank. We intercepted a phone conversation and heard him ordering another bomber onto a school bus. We followed the guy and took him out just before he got on. This was Mashurr's payback. He'd already returned to Gaza. A rocket obliterated him and two of his deputies after they left the orphanage where Mendelssohn worked. It was a clean kill. No kids hurt."

"Good to hear," Erhamnn said. "Mashurr was the last one on my list."

"Meaning?"

"With both him and Bauer gone, I'm leaving the killing up to you now, Asher. I'm finished."

"Finally going to retire, eh."

"Not a chance. I want you to get me on the board of the foundation. So I can see that all the money gets to the kids and isn't pissed away on administrative bullshit."

"I'm sure Komorov will appreciate your input. I'll get back to you."

"All right. Now, I'm off to the goddamned dentist."

"Lucky you."

⅄

Erhmann lowered himself into the back seat of a Mercedes taxi and rubbed the side of his jaw. He gave the driver directions and then closed his eyes to doze. He rocked back and forth with the stop and go motion of the traffic until the car jerked to a stop. He stiffened when both back doors were wrenched open and two burly Palestinian men jammed themselves in beside him. Before he could protest, one man pressed a pistol against his temple and a sharp pain pierced his right shoulder. His eyelids flickered and then he coughed and slumped forward.

The driver squealed out of his lane and made the first right turn into a maze of side streets. Rounding a corner to the back of a building, he stopped for a moment while the two men dragged Erhmann from the back seat and stuffed him into the trunk of another large sedan. The men jumped into the second vehicle and both cars drove off in separate directions.

⅄

Frankie retrieved a message on the phone and scribbled down the information. He hung up the receiver and said to Friedrich, "Reservations confirmed. We leave for LA tomorrow night."

"What about Eva's ashes?" Friedrich said.

"Erhmann spoke to Komorov on our behalf. He got the okay from Pekarsky out at Vared Yericho. Spreading the ashes won't be a problem. The concierge has arranged a driver to take us to the site. I've changed my mind about searching for the remains. It'll just turn into a political circus. I've found the closure I need. With Mom's ashes near Adlyia and Jamal, I'll be ready to go home." He held Friedrich in a long embrace and then stepped back. "Let's get ready. It's a two-hour drive and we need to get back before dark. It's still dangerous out there."

⋏

With the sun dropping in a mottled sky, Frankie and Friedrich stepped from the car and walked toward the scattered boulders at the side of the road. When they reached a spot in the middle, Frankie opened the urn and poured half the ashes into Friedrich's hands. As Friedrich watched the specks of gray drift down, he said, "I should be saying kaddish, but I can't remember any of the words. I never was much of a praying type."

"They're reunited, Dad, and that's what counts."

"There is one short prayer I remember my mother saying when I was a child," Friedrich said. "As long as we live, they too will live: for they are now a part of us: as we remember them." He squeezed Frankie's arm as the sun slipped below the horizon. Eva's spirit had brought them together again.

"Let's get back to the car," Frankie said. "Looks like weather coming. I don't need you stumbling on something."

As they walked back, a stiff breeze tossed up zephyrs of sand that swirled amongst the boulders. "I almost feel that she's here with us," Friedrich said, rubbing his eyes.

"Come on, Dad," Frankie said. "It's just getting windy. Get in the damn car."

A violent gust almost pulled the back door from his hand as he opened it. Then a rifle shot cracked through the air. The car window shattered and glass fragments flew into Friedrich's face.

Frankie pushed him to the ground.

"Stay down, Dad. Somebody's shooting at us from up there." Frankie pointed toward the ledge from where they had surveyed the site of the massacre. But before he could crouch for cover, a muzzle flashed and a sudden heaviness rocked his chest. His knees folded and he collapsed next to Friedrich.

A wet patch of crimson expanded on the front of Frankie's shirt and sirens wailed inside the compound. A barrage from a fifty-calibre machine gun on the roof of the administration building raked the pinnacle.

Friedrich's ears buzzed, his face numbed by pin-pricks of glass. "Oh my God, no." He scrambled on all fours to the open back door of the car and yelled at the driver who cowered on the floor beneath the dashboard.

"Drive to the gate and bring an ambulance. Hurry! Hurry! My son's bleeding to death."

Frankie's color matched that of the purple sky, his chest soaked with blood.

Friedrich tore off Frankie's shirt and found a wound the size of a poker chip. "Stay with me, son."

Frankie's diaphragm heaved to inflate his collapsing lung. This was the same sucking chest wound Mueller had suffered in 1933. The shrapnel had also severed Mueller's spinal cord. God forbid. Friedrich smothered the hole with his American Express Card. The card sealed as the lung filled and lifted when Frankie exhaled.

After several minutes, each of them feeling like hours, three men charged through the gate and ran toward him with emergency gear. The machine gun had fallen quiet.

"He's been struck in the chest and maybe the spine," Friedrich said. "Be careful when you move him."

"Let me in here." One of the men dropped to his knees and cinched an oxygen mask over Frankie's nose. "There's a military chopper on the way right now."

"He's a fighter," Friedrich said. "Keep him alive."

The medic slapped the inside of Frankie's arm to find a vein and snapped at Friedrich. "Give us some room."

Friedrich stepped back and squinted up at the pinnacle, where the shrubbery had been shorn clean by bullets. Bauer's gaze had chilled him to the core when he'd given his testimony. But he'd been too complacent. He should have known the bastard would retaliate.

The helicopter made a thundering descent to the roof of the administration building as the medics strapped a board under Frankie. They stabilized his neck and spine and then lifted him up. With an oxygen canister by his side and a plasma line dangling from his arm they carried him to the ambulance.

A firm hand touched Friedrich's shoulder and he looked up to see Boris Pekarsky.

"This is what I was afraid of," Pekarsky said. "We've sent a team up there but whoever fired those shots probably had an escape vehicle. Most likely homegrown terrorists. They slip back into the villages around here and it's impossible to track them down. This is the third time this month."

Pekarsky opened the door and helped him into the front seat of the ambulance. "There's an elevator that will take us to the roof. You can fly back to the hospital with your son." He handed Friedrich his bloodstained credit card. "This is what saved him. He's still got a chance."

The chopper lifted off and the pilot gained altitude fast to avoid gunshots from the Arab villages below. Friedrich felt himself squeezed against the side of the cabin, but never took his eyes off Frankie's chest, which rose and fell with the hiss of pressurized oxygen. Pekarsky's remarks about local terrorists, combined with Issa's warnings to Frankie about being on a death list, left Friedrich cold. Bauer wasn't the only one who wanted them dead. Even Erhmann crossed his mind.

⅄

After midnight, a surgeon shook Friedrich awake in his chair. Still half dazed, Friedrich's eyes begged the doctor for good news.

"The bullet tore through the pulmonary artery but we repaired it. Part of the slug lodged in his back and we've left it there. His spinal cord wasn't involved. He's resting now. It'll be a several weeks before he can travel, but we expect a full recovery. Keeping him breathing with that card was a nifty idea. The medics told me. Not many people would think of it."

"I saw a wound like that many years ago and remembered how they sealed it. I'm so forgetful these days, it's a wonder I thought of it. I'm just thankful that he'll be okay. I'm sure the shots were meant for me. He saved my life. When the first bullet hit the car window he pushed me down and he got hit by the second one."

"You were both lucky. Around here snipers don't miss. Was it windy?"

Friedrich did a double take. "Come to think of it there was a huge gust right then. I got sand in my eyes. I'd been feeling the strong presence of my deceased wife because we'd just spread her ashes. Maybe that's why the bullet hit the window. It was blown off course."

The doctor picked up the chart and Friedrich didn't say more. What did it matter? Nobody, including Frankie, would ever believe that Eva had saved his life. It was only for him to know.

"When can I see him?"

"We'll have someone take you back to your hotel now. Call later this afternoon and we'll let you know."

⅄

Erhmann's eyes jarred apart into utter blackness. Gas fumes from a chainsaw stung his nostrils as it chewed through something outside the car. The whirrs of power drills and saws carried the scent of cut wood. Men's laughter and Arab voices echoed nearby. He twisted about to bring his hands to the front of his face but could see nothing in the darkness. The lid of the trunk felt only inches away. Trapped, he turned from one side to the other searching for his phone, but both it and his wallet were gone. He pried himself away from the floor and tore away the felt lining until he found the lid of the spare tire compartment. He slid his hand underneath and pulled out the handle of the tire jack. Rolling on his back, he clutched the steel rod in both hands and waited.

The crunch of footsteps and cackle of voices approached, and he tensed to strike. When the key turned the lock, his body followed the upward trajectory of the lid and he lashed out. The first two men who leaned in, met instant death. A second wave of four struggled to pin him down, while a fifth pried the jack-handle from his hands. A sledge hammer to his forehead knocked him senseless and the stab of another needle left him unconscious.

A drug used to sedate horses kept Erhmann comatose until the first spike tore through the flesh of his right wrist. His body went rigid as if he had been struck by a thunderbolt and his eyes bulged like domes against the moonlight. Slivers of rugged timber pierced deep under his skin and his brain screamed but the duct tape sealing his lips left him mute. A light on the cab of a truck illuminated the grizzled face of a man who knelt beside him. The man pressed the button of a power drill and sunk holes into both his kneecaps.

Erhmann strained to free himself, but from his neck to his feet, his naked body was roped to the scaffold of a cross. The joint between the shaft and the crossbeam groaned as another railroad spike savaged through his left wrist. With blood spurting from both arms and knees, they folded his feet one over the other, and hammered the final spike into place. Scrawled in blood above his head, the Hebrew word: *Nakam*.

A steel cable attached to the arm of a front-end loader lifted the crucifix into an upright position and then dropped it hard into the base of a narrow hole. They cut the rope binding him, and he dangled from the spikes. The flesh and tendons of his limbs tore from their moorings. He had never felt such exquisite pain, a hundred times more intense than anything he had experienced at Auschwitz. As hurled rocks pelted his body, his eyes glazed and his blood pressure skyrocketed.

Sledge hammers echoed into the night as they drove wedges alongside the stock so it stood tall and prominent over the maximum security prison on the outskirts of Jerusalem. A torch carried by a young boy sent flames leaping up the creosoted structure, a symbol of death visible for miles.

Amid raised fists and blood-curdling shouts of "Itbach al-yahud", the carpenters and their sons grabbed the tools, jumped into vehicles and roared off into the night. Within the prison walls, a fire engine's siren blared and spotlights from guard towers lit the hillside. Two trucks raced through the gate toward the inferno that crowned the summit.

A swath of sheet lightning cast a purple glow over the distant hills of Judea and Samaria with a rolling barrage of thunder following in its wake. Erhmann's eyes flickered at the brightness that illuminated his agony and the birthright of his people. The calls of Apa, Apa, rang clear in his mind and the merciful hands of death drew him to her bosom. His panting grew shallower until his damaged heart relented. His eyes fell shut and his head dropped to the side.

⚔

Heinz Bauer smiled as he heard the faint sound of sirens within the prison grounds. He came out of the bathroom wearing his robe, turned on the late evening news and opened the bottle of Schnapps that Tobias Abraham had delivered at the beginning of his shift. With his back turned to the monitoring camera, Bauer reached inside the opaque bottle with his little finger and fished out a tiny sack of powder. He poured two glasses of schnapps. When he had sifted the powder into one glass, he turned to face the monitor. He held up the bottle and smiled, certain Tobias was watching. He pointed at the two glasses and said, "A small nightcap perhaps."

He sat and watched as the last item on the newscast described a sniper attack on two American dentists near the Jewish settlement of Vared Yericho. No further details were available. Taking a sip from his glass, he muttered, "Doppelkreuzungs Juden. I hope they're both dead." He listened for the sequence of buttons being pushed on the automatic lock. Then the door clicked open and Tobias stood in the doorway, cold sweat spotting his brow.

"I want to express my appreciation, Private Abraham. This was a courageous thing to do. I know you can't stay." He stepped to the counter and handed Tobias the other glass. "Here, drink it up and get back to your station. No one ever needs to know."

Tobias reached out a shaky hand. He raised the glass and threw the ice cold spirit back in one gulp. In an instant, his eyes bugged out and he reached for his throat. Bauer dragged him into the room and slammed the door. He pulled the pistol from the Tobias's holster and a well placed bullet shattered the overhead monitor.

He ripped off Tobias's shirt and belt and used the horn of the buckle to carve a swastika deep into the guard's heaving belly. He looped the belt around Tobias's neck like a collar and tugged it tight while laughing and smearing his own chest in the Jew's blood with the words, 'Juden dog'. He gripped the pistol in his right hand and let his robe fall to the floor.

The re-entry timer on the door clicked down thirty seconds and triggered the alarm. The location of the breach flashed throughout the section. Heinz Bauer stood naked and waited, emptying his bladder into the gaping mouth of Tobias Abraham who lay sprawled on the floor, wide-eyed and still. Guards smashing through the door were greeted by the crack of a single gunshot.

Bauer dropped to the floor, a hole through his right temple. Brains, blood and jagged fragments of bone splattered the nearest wall.

⚔

Four weeks after the sniper attack, a stern looking Asher Harel pushed Frankie's wheelchair up the ramp of an EL Al 747 bound for Los Angeles. When Frankie had lowered himself into a seat by the window, Friedrich sat beside him.

"I'm not doing this to be polite," Heral said. "I wanted to make damn sure you're both on this plane. You talked us into letting that bastard live and he thanked us by killing two more Jews, one who was my very good friend."

"We're as sorry about all that as you are, Asher," Friedrich said. "It's horrific what they did to Gabor and what Bauer did to the guard. These awful things just keep repeating themselves around here. Nothing's changed and we should have known. The sniper attack had to be connected. Somehow we were spared."

"We found no evidence left behind but I wouldn't be surprised it was the SS network. On the other hand, Mashuur could have ordered it before he left or maybe it was locals. We'll never know but somebody wanted to get you guys. And maybe they still do."

"Will we have to worry when we get home?" Friedrich said. "Surely, whoever did it, knows we both survived."

"Dreschler won't want to attract attention now that Bauer's dead. Hamas and the Brotherhood will stick to their neighbourhood. You should be okay as long as you stay where you fucking belong. Not over here."

"You won't be seeing my face around here again," Friedrich said. "I'm exhausted but at least I've made peace with my wife and I have my son back. I've done what I came to do."

"We're going to need some guidance with that dental clinic," Heral said, looking at Frankie. "Can I call upon you for that?"

"No problem," Frankie said. "I'm setting up a similar organization for kids in LA. There will be plenty we can do together. Call me anytime."

"I'm thankful that I could be of some service to the State of Israel," Friedrich said. "I've always had my doubts about this notion of a Jewish homeland. Too elitist for me. If it hadn't been for the Nuremberg Laws and Bauer's ultimatum, I would've been content to live life as an assimilated German Jew. Instead the Nazis stamped me like a steel plate. They woke me up to who I am and I couldn't thank them more. The people of Israel can always count on me, Heral. Shalom and good luck."

Friedrich wiped a tear from his eye as Heral left the cabin. He thought of Erhmann, the brooding giant who had suffered the most and who ultimately lost his life bringing men like Bauer to justice. Silently, he prayed for him. "God bless you, Gabor."

A flight attendant approached with a tray of champagne. "Just what the doctors ordered," he said, and passed a flute to each of them.

Frankie laughed and wrapped his arm around Friedrich's shoulders to propose a toast. "To team, Mendelssohn."

"I'll drink to that," Friedrich said. "No matter what Heral says, we're leaving things a little better than when we found them."

"Damn right," Frankie said. "I didn't want to say anything to piss him off but I am coming back."

Friedrich's eyes widened and his tremor quickened, almost spilling the champagne over his lap.

"Why would you want to do that after all that's happened? It's far too dangerous."

Frankie raised his glass for a refill. He took a deep breath and looked at Friedrich. "When you were walking back to the car, I knelt down to pick up a bit of the earth where Adlyia and Jamal were buried. I got this unbelievable rush. It's been on my mind ever since and now I realize what it meant."

Friedrich leaned closer to hear over the whine of the engines.

"After I get my feet wet with the operation back home, I'm going to raise money for orphanages in the Arab and Mizrahim communities," Frankie said.

"Mizrahim. You mean Jewish immigrants from Muslim countries."

"I saw a program on TV when I was in the hospital. Those places are like goddamn third world. You'd never know they're a part of Israel. That's where I would've ended up, if not for you and Mom. It's my destiny, Dad. That's why I'm here. To help kids who aren't as lucky as I was. Maybe I can keep them from throwing rocks and getting killed in the streets. Steer them in the right direction."

"Dream on," Friedrich said. "Eva and I tried to do that with our office in Jerusalem. We hired staff and accepted patients from both communities. We hoped that when people got to know each other they'd realize they're not so different. But it didn't work then and it won't now. This place has always been a toxic soup but now it's coming to boil."

"I know it'll be tough," Frankie said. "Divisions here run deep but I have to engage. It's my turn to pick up where you and Mom left off. I want to drive that third option of optimism and reconciliation. Otherwise what?"

"I used to think that, but after all the mayhem I've seen, I'm throwing in the towel. I've had it."

"I was running away from everything when I came here," Frankie said. "But now I realize I had no choice. I was running toward something."

Friedrich looked Frankie hard in the eye for a moment and then he nodded. "I think you're right. You may have found yourself a new vocation, Doctor."

Frankie raised his glass and smiled. "You bet. Like father, like son. L'Chaim."

"Inshallah," Friedrich said.

"Right on, Dad. Cover all the bases."

64901321R00202

Made in the USA
Charleston, SC
16 December 2016